Shadows Against the Dark

Collected Tales of Horror

The DOUBLE BOOKED® Collection

Desiderio
The Veil and the Shade

The Turn of the Screw
Shadows Against the Dark: Collected Tales of Horror

Cane
The Conjure Woman: Uncle Julius and His Stories

Marie and the Nutcracker
A Christmas Carol

Man Cub: The Complete Mowgli Stories
Rikki-Tikki-Tavi and Other Tales from The Jungle Book

Peter Pan
The Never Boy

Alice's Adventures in Wonderland
Through the Looking Glass

Shadows Against the Dark

Collected Tales of Horror

edited and with an introduction by

C. S. R. Calloway

This is a work of fiction. All names, characters, businesses, places, events, and incidents portrayed in this novel are either fictitious or used fictitiously.

The Turn of the Screw & Shadows Against the Dark: Collected Tales of Horror

Published by CSRC Storytelling
Los Angeles, CA 99503

ISBN: 978-1-7358967-8-6 (Paperback)
ISBN: 978-1-7358967-9-3 (Ebook)

Jacket illustrations by Mateus Roberts
Jacket designed by Ahmed Khalid
First Edition: June 2021

Contents

Introduction

I've only had one repeat nightmare in my life. Its first occurrence came when I was five years old, the summer before I started the first grade. My family had just moved from Sacramento to Atlanta and we had settled into an apartment complex nearly hidden in the hills amidst the Eastern hophornbeams with their fireworks of branches and the stilt-trunked loblolly pines. The nightmare took this location—my home, but still unfamiliar—and transplanted it directly into the narrative. I recall it explicitly:

My sister and I are across the street at a neighbors' apartment. We're planning to stay for the night, and I realize I've forgotten to bring a change of socks for the next morning. It's already dark outside, so my sister—a year and a half older than I—accompanies me in order to quickly go back to our residence and retrieve my socks. Making it exactly halfway across the street, we freeze in place when all of the lights on the side of the apartment complex in front of us shutter into darkness. The white and blue architecture blinks to black leaving the stars above as the only proof I hadn't lost complete sight. Instinctively, my sister and I turn back in time to see the other half of the complex join this depressive eclipse. Tiny and alone except for each other and the suddenly present wind, we turn to our right towards the end of the cul-de-sac, where a line of towering, bulbous trees shoot up from an island of turf amid the circling concrete. An ominous rustling brings my attention to the highest branches of these trees, which are slowly pulled apart as if by giant inky hands or invisible paws. Deep laughter booms down the street in our direction as the trees are bent further away from each other, but I don't see the source of the movement or the laughter, only more darkness—cavernous and imperceptible.

Six or seven years later, living in a completely different home in a completely different city, I had the nightmare once more. Exactly the same—again the Atlanta apartments, again the socks, again the lights, and again the darkness growing between the branches. I have never been able to dissect or digest any meaning from the dream. It remains an unsettling skip in the playing of my mental record. Only years later would I realize what frightened me so about the dream.

The horror was not just the darkness, but the darkness juxtaposed with more darkness. It's the same source of my jumpy, unsettled feelings while driving on the highway at night and seeing the indistinct silhouette of mountains in the distance. The looming shadows against the dark horizon suggest a danger greater than the open road. It's akin to the fluctuating shape in the corner of a darkened room that never quite takes hold of an identity. Or mammoth clouds through a plane's window on a red eye flight, or worse, those same clouds lurking low after sundown, pregnant with rain. Or, perhaps one of my greatest agitators, transmission towers rising above a twilight city, conversely static in movement and sound, suggesting the kind of active, sinister existence that only manifests when one is not looking.

They're provocations of the mind, really, these shadows against the dark. There's a familiar level of blackness that we become accustomed to—a limitation of perception—and the juxtaposition of shade versus gloom, of dread versus despair, takes something familiar and even comforting and sets it off by one clock tick. If darkness is the absence of light, then darkness upon darkness implies that there is something there embodying or imitating a greater absence—a presence of something worse. Is that really a mountain, or some giant beast lying in wait? Is this truly absolute evil or is there a greater evil that I've been heretofore ignorant of? It's the disquieting concept that normalcy is situational, and the petrifying realization that true darkness is inestimable.

The following pages contain English language classics from white male writers who depict similar themes of unknowable darkness within an assortment of narratives, from the upsetting to the macabre, of escalating horrors, unknowable terrors, and danger lurking in the guise of something once familiar. In the opening story, Washington Irving's "The Legend of Sleepy Hollow," a journey home for schoolmaster Ichabod Crane is no longer mundane, but fraught with terror from the specter of a headless local legend. In the following story, "The Voice in the Dark," William Hope Hodgson presents the theme quite literally, when a stranger in a rowboat approaches a schooner to beg for food in the blackness of night. W. W. Jacobs penned the third story, "The Monkey's Paw," in which a husband and wife take possession of a wish-granting object that induces tragic volatility in their once-simple lives. "The Fall of the House of Usher," written by the morbid maestro Edgar Allan Poe, details the sickness and tragedy that befall a brother and sister, seen through the eyes of a friend and houseguest. "The Willows" follows—a creeping and claustrophobic world created by Algernon Blackwood where the typical hostilities of nature begin to hint at something more severe and far less natural. In the concluding tale "The Bottle Imp," Robert Louis Stevenson presents the journey of a poor Hawaiian who purchases a cursed bottle, leading to a life filled with crushing, intensifying dread.

Introduction

Each of these collected stories dance on the edge of the abyss. Ichabod Crane's flight from the Headless Horseman puts me in mind of those two innocent dream children facing their own impending horroscape. Each knock on the door in Jacob's fiction, each wish cast by the Hawaiian on the bottle, each sound echoing through the Usher house, and each new mystery told by the rowboat narrator or discovered in Blackwood's willows: they repurpose the familiar into darker and darker hues of fright and danger. It illustrates a truth I've grown to learn since my repeating nightmare—a truth as beneficial as it is alarming:

The greatest terrors are not seen; they are suggested.

C.S.R. Calloway

Notes on the text:

To make these stories more accessible to contemporary readers, minor changes have been made with spelling, punctuation, capitalization, and spacing. British spellings ("colour" instead of "color") have been altered throughout. Obvious typographical errors in the original texts have been corrected.

The Legend of Sleepy Hollow

Washington Irving

(FOUND AMONG THE PAPERS OF THE LATE DIEDRICH KNICKERBOCKER.)

A pleasing land of drowsy-head it was,
Of dreams that wave before the half-shut eye,
And of gay castles in the clouds that pays,
For ever flushing round a summer sky.
CASTLE OF INDOLENCE

In the bosom of one of those spacious coves which indent the eastern shore of the Hudson, at that broad expansion of the river denominated by the ancient Dutch navigators the Tappan Zee, and where they always prudently shortened sail and implored the protection of St. Nicholas when they crossed, there lies a small market-town or rural port which by some is called Greensburg, but which is more generally and properly known by the name of Tarry Town. This name was given, we are told, in former days by the good housewives of the adjacent country from the inveterate propensity of their husbands to linger about the village tavern on market days. Be that as it may, I do not vouch for the fact, but merely advert to it for the sake of being precise and authentic. Not far from this village, perhaps about two miles, there is a little valley, or rather lap of land, among high hills, which is one of the quietest places in the whole world. A small brook glides through it, with just murmur enough to lull one to repose, and the occasional whistle of a quail or tapping of a woodpecker is almost the only sound that ever breaks in upon the uniform tranquillity.

I recollect that when a stripling my first exploit in squirrel-shooting was in a grove of tall walnut trees that shades one side of the valley. I had wandered into it at noontime, when all Nature is peculiarly quiet, and was startled by the roar of my own gun as it broke the Sabbath stillness around and was prolonged and reverberated by the angry echoes. If ever I should wish for a retreat whither I might steal from the world and its distractions and dream quietly away the remnant of a troubled life, I know of none more promising than this little valley.

From the listless repose of the place and the peculiar character of its inhabitants, who are descendants from the original Dutch settlers, this sequestered glen has long been known by the name of SLEEPY HOLLOW, and its rustic lads are called the Sleepy Hollow Boys throughout all the neighboring country. A drowsy, dreamy influence seems to hang over the land and to pervade the very atmosphere. Some say that the place was bewitched by a High German doctor during the early days of the settlement; others, that an old Indian chief, the prophet or wizard of his tribe, held his powwows there before the country was discovered by Master Hendrick Hudson. Certain it is, the place still continues under the sway of some witching power that holds a spell over the minds of the good people, causing them to walk in a continual reverie. They are given to all kinds of marvelous beliefs, are subject to trances and visions, and frequently see strange sights and hear music and voices in the air. The whole neighborhood abounds with local tales, haunted spots, and twilight superstitions; stars shoot and meteors glare oftener across the valley than in any other part of the country, and the nightmare, with her whole ninefold, seems to make it the favorite scene of her gambols.

The dominant spirit, however, that haunts this enchanted region, and seems to be commander-in-chief of all the powers of the air, is the apparition of a figure on horseback without a head. It is said by some to be the ghost of a Hessian trooper whose head had been carried away by a cannonball in some nameless battle during the Revolutionary War, and who is ever and anon seen by the country-folk hurrying along in the gloom of night as if on the wings of the wind. His haunts are not confined to the valley, but extend at times to the adjacent roads, and especially to the vicinity of a church at no great distance. Indeed, certain of the most authentic historians of those parts, who have been careful in collecting and collating the floating facts concerning this spectre, allege that the body of the trooper, having been buried in the churchyard, the ghost rides forth to the scene of battle in nightly quest of his head, and that the rushing speed with which he sometimes passes along the Hollow, like a midnight blast, is owing to his being belated and in a hurry to get back to the churchyard before daybreak.

Such is the general purport of this legendary superstition, which has furnished materials for many a wild story in that region of shadows; and the spectre is known at all the country firesides by the name of the Headless Horseman of Sleepy Hollow.

It is remarkable that the visionary propensity I have mentioned is not confined to the native inhabitants of the valley, but is unconsciously imbibed by every one who resides there for a time. However wide awake they may have been before they entered that sleepy region, they are sure in a little time to inhale the witching influence of the air and begin to grow imaginative—to dream dreams and see apparitions.

I mention this peaceful spot with all possible laud, for it is in such little retired Dutch valleys, found here and there embosomed in the great State of New York, that population, manners, and customs remain fixed, while the great torrent of migration and improvement, which is making such incessant changes in other parts of this restless country, sweeps by them unobserved. They are like those little nooks of still water which border a rapid stream where we may see the straw and bubble riding quietly at anchor or slowly revolving in their mimic harbor, undisturbed by the rush of the passing current. Though many years have elapsed since I trod the drowsy shades of Sleepy Hollow, yet I question whether I should not still find the same trees and the same families vegetating in its sheltered bosom.

In this by-place of Nature there abode, in a remote period of American history—that is to say, some thirty years since—a worthy wight of the name of Ichabod Crane, who sojourned, or, as he expressed it, "tarried," in Sleepy Hollow for the purpose of instructing the children of the vicinity. He was a native of Connecticut, a State which supplies the Union with pioneers for the mind as well as for the forest, and sends forth yearly its legions of frontier woodmen and country schoolmasters. The cognomen of Crane was not inapplicable to his person. He was tall, but exceedingly lank, with narrow shoulders, long arms and legs, hands that dangled a mile out of his sleeves, feet that might have served for shovels, and his whole frame most loosely hung together. His head was small, and flat at top, with huge ears, large green glassy eyes, and a long snip nose, so that it looked like a weathercock perched upon his spindle neck to tell which way the wind blew. To see him striding along the profile of a hill on a windy day, with his clothes bagging and fluttering about him, one might have mistaken him for the genius of Famine descending upon the earth or some scarecrow eloped from a cornfield.

His school-house was a low building of one large room, rudely constructed of logs, the windows partly glazed and partly patched with leaves of old copybooks. It was most ingeniously secured at vacant hours by a withe twisted in the handle of the door and stakes set against the window-shutters, so that, though a thief might get in with perfect ease, he would find some embarrassment in getting out—-an idea most probably borrowed by the architect, Yost Van Houten, from the mystery of an eel-pot. The school-house stood in a rather lonely but pleasant situation, just at the foot of a woody hill, with a brook running close by and a formidable birch tree growing at one end of it. From hence the low murmur of his pupils' voices, conning over their lessons, might be heard in a drowsy summer's day like the hum of a bee-hive, interrupted now and then by the authoritative voice of the master in the tone of menace or command, or, peradventure, by the appalling sound of the birch as he urged some tardy loiterer along the flowery path of knowledge. Truth to say, he was a conscientious man, and ever bore in mind the golden maxim, "Spare the rod and spoil the child." Ichabod Crane's scholars certainly were not spoiled.

I would not have it imagined, however, that he was one of those cruel potentates of the school who joy in the smart of their subjects; on the contrary, he administered justice with discrimination rather than severity, taking the burden off the backs of the weak and laying it on those of the strong. Your mere puny stripling, that winced at the least flourish of the rod, was passed by with indulgence; but the claims of justice were satisfied by inflicting a double portion on some little tough, wrong-headed, broad-skirted Dutch urchin, who sulked and swelled and grew dogged and sullen beneath the birch. All this he called "doing his duty by their parents;" and he never inflicted a chastisement without following it by the assurance, so consolatory to the smarting urchin, that "he would remember it and thank him for it the longest day he had to live."

When school-hours were over he was even the companion and playmate of the larger boys, and on holiday afternoons would convoy some of the smaller ones home who happened to have pretty sisters or good housewives for mothers noted for the comforts of the cupboard. Indeed it behooved him to keep on good terms with his pupils. The revenue arising from his school was small, and would have been scarcely sufficient to furnish him with daily bread, for he was a huge feeder, and, though lank, had the dilating powers of an anaconda; but to help out his maintenance he was, according to country custom in those parts, boarded and lodged at the houses of the farmers whose children he instructed. With these he lived successively a week at a time, thus going the rounds of the neighborhood with all his worldly effects tied up in a cotton handkerchief.

That all this might not be too onerous on the purses of his rustic patrons, who are apt to consider the costs of schooling a grievous burden and schoolmasters as mere drones, he had various ways of rendering himself both useful and agreeable. He assisted the farmers occasionally in the lighter labors of their farms, helped to make hay, mended the fences, took the horses to water, drove the cows from pasture, and cut wood for the winter fire. He laid aside, too, all the dominant dignity and absolute sway with which he lorded it in his little empire, the school, and became wonderfully gentle and ingratiating. He found favor in the eyes of the mothers by petting the children, particularly the youngest; and like the lion bold, which whilom so magnanimously the lamb did hold, he would sit with a child on one knee and rock a cradle with his foot for whole hours together.

In addition to his other vocations, he was the singing-master of the neighborhood and picked up many bright shillings by instructing the young folks in psalmody. It was a matter of no little vanity to him on Sundays to take his station in front of the church-gallery with a band of chosen singers, where, in his own mind, he completely carried away the palm from the parson. Certain it is, his voice resounded far above all the rest of the congregation, and there are peculiar quavers still to be heard in that church, and which may even be heard half a mile off, quite to the opposite side of the mill-pond on a still Sunday morning, which are said to be legitimately descended from the nose of Ichabod Crane. Thus, by divers little makeshifts in that ingenious way which is commonly denominated "by hook and by crook," the worthy pedagogue got on tolerably enough, and was thought, by all who understood nothing of the labor of headwork, to have a wonderfully easy life of it.

The schoolmaster is generally a man of some importance in the female circle of a rural neighborhood, being considered a kind of idle, gentleman-like personage of vastly superior taste and accomplishments to the rough country swains, and, indeed, inferior in learning only to the parson. His appearance, therefore, is apt to occasion some little stir at the tea-table of a farmhouse and the addition of a supernumerary dish of cakes or sweetmeats, or, peradventure, the parade of a silver tea-pot. Our man of letters, therefore, was peculiarly happy in the smiles of all the country damsels. How he would figure among them in the churchyard between services on Sundays, gathering grapes for them from the wild vines that overrun the surrounding trees; reciting for their amusement all the epitaphs on the tombstones; or sauntering, with a whole bevy of them, along the banks of the adjacent mill-pond, while the more bashful country bumpkins hung sheepishly back, envying his superior elegance and address.

From his half-itinerant life, also, he was a kind of traveling gazette, carrying the whole budget of local gossip from house to house, so that his appearance was always greeted with satisfaction. He was, moreover, esteemed by the women as a man of great erudition, for he had read several books quite through, and was a perfect master of Cotton Mather's History of New England Witchcraft, in which, by the way, he most firmly and potently believed.

He was, in fact, an odd mixture of small shrewdness and simple credulity. His appetite for the marvelous and his powers of digesting it were equally extraordinary, and both had been increased by his residence in this spellbound region. No tale was too gross or monstrous for his capacious swallow. It was often his delight, after his school was dismissed in the afternoon, to stretch himself on the rich bed of clover bordering the little brook that whimpered by his school-house, and there con over old Mather's direful tales until the gathering dusk of the evening made the printed page a mere mist before his eyes. Then, as he wended his way by swamp and stream and awful woodland to the farmhouse where he happened to be quartered, every sound of Nature at that witching hour fluttered his excited imagination—the nocturnal moan of the whip-poor-will from the hillside; the boding cry of the tree-toad, that harbinger of storm; the dreary hooting of the screech-owl, or the sudden rustling in the thicket of birds frightened from their roost. The fire-flies, too, which sparkled most vividly in the darkest places, now and then startled him as one of uncommon brightness would stream across his path; and if, by chance, a huge blockhead of a beetle came winging his blundering flight against him, the poor varlet was ready to give up the ghost, with the idea that he was struck with a witch's token. His only resource on such occasions, either to drown thought or drive away evil spirits, was to sing psalm tunes; and the good people of Sleepy Hollow, as they sat by their doors of an evening, were often filled with awe at hearing his nasal melody, "in linked sweetness long drawn out," floating from the distant hill or along the dusky road.

Another of his sources of fearful pleasure was to pass long winter evenings with the old Dutch wives as they sat spinning by the fire, with a row of apples roasting and spluttering along the hearth, and listen to their marvelous tales of ghosts and goblins, and haunted fields, and haunted brooks, and haunted bridges, and haunted houses, and particularly of the headless horseman, or Galloping Hessian of the Hollow, as they sometimes called him. He would delight them equally by his anecdotes of witchcraft and of the direful omens and portentous sights and sounds in the air which prevailed in the earlier times of Connecticut, and would frighten them woefully with speculations upon comets and shooting stars, and with the alarming fact that the world did absolutely turn round and that they were half the time topsy-turvy.

But if there was a pleasure in all this while snugly cuddling in the chimney-corner of a chamber that was all of a ruddy glow from the crackling wood-fire, and where, of course, no spectre dared to show its face, it was dearly purchased by the terrors of his subsequent walk homewards. What fearful shapes and shadows beset his path amidst the dim and ghastly glare of a snowy night! With what wistful look did be eye every trembling ray of light streaming across the waste fields from some distant window! How often was he appalled by some shrub covered with snow, which, like a sheeted spectre, beset his very path! How often did he shrink with curdling awe at the sound of his own steps on the frosty crust beneath his feet, and dread to look over his shoulder, lest he should behold some uncouth being tramping close behind him! And how often was he thrown into complete dismay by some rushing blast howling among the trees, in the idea that it was the Galloping Hessian on one of his nightly scourings!

All these, however, were mere terrors of the night, phantoms of the mind that walk in darkness; and though he had seen many spectres in his time, and been more than once beset by Satan in divers shapes in his lonely perambulations, yet daylight put an end to all these evils; and he would have passed a pleasant life of it, in despite of the devil and all his works, if his path had not been crossed by a being that causes more perplexity to mortal man than ghosts, goblins, and the whole race of witches put together, and that was—a woman.

Among the musical disciples who assembled one evening in each week to receive his instructions in psalmody was Katrina Van Tassel, the daughter and only child of a substantial Dutch farmer. She was a blooming lass of fresh eighteen, plump as a partridge, ripe and melting and rosy-cheeked as one of her father's peaches, and universally famed, not merely for her beauty, but her vast expectations. She was withal a little of a coquette, as might be perceived even in her dress, which was a mixture of ancient and modern fashions, as most suited to set off her charms. She wore the ornaments of pure yellow gold which her great-great-grandmother had brought over from Saardam, the tempting stomacher of the olden time, and withal a provokingly short petticoat to display the prettiest foot and ankle in the country round.

Ichabod Crane had a soft and foolish heart towards the sex, and it is not to be wondered at that so tempting a morsel soon found favor in his eyes, more especially after he had visited her in her paternal mansion. Old Baltus Van Tassel was a perfect picture of a thriving, contented, liberal-hearted farmer. He seldom, it is true, sent either his eyes or his thoughts beyond the boundaries of his own farm, but within those everything was snug, happy, and well-conditioned. He was satisfied with his wealth but not proud of it, and piqued himself upon the hearty abundance, rather than the style, in which he lived. His stronghold was situated on the banks of the Hudson, in one of those green, sheltered, fertile nooks in which the Dutch farmers are so fond of nestling. A great elm tree spread its broad branches over it, at the foot of which bubbled up a spring of the softest and sweetest water in a little well formed of a barrel, and then stole sparkling away through the grass to a neighboring brook that bubbled along among alders and dwarf willows. Hard by the farmhouse was a vast barn, that might have served for a church, every window and crevice of which seemed bursting forth with the treasures of the farm; the flail was busily resounding within it from morning to night; swallows and martins skimmed twittering about the eaves; and rows of pigeons, some with one eye turned up, as if watching the weather, some with their heads under their wings or buried in their bosoms, and others, swelling, and cooing, and bowing about their dames, were enjoying the sunshine on the roof. Sleek, unwieldy porkers were grunting in the repose and abundance of their pens, whence sallied forth, now and then, troops of sucking pigs as if to snuff the air. A stately squadron of snowy geese were riding in an adjoining pond, convoying whole fleets of ducks; regiments of turkeys were gobbling through the farmyard, and guinea-fowls fretting about it, like ill-tempered housewives, with their peevish, discontented cry. Before the barn-door strutted the gallant cock, that pattern of a husband, a warrior, and a fine gentleman, clapping his burnished wings and crowing in the pride and gladness of his heart—sometimes tearing up the earth with his feet, and then generously calling his ever-hungry family of wives and children to enjoy the rich morsel which he had discovered.

The pedagogue's mouth watered as he looked upon this sumptuous promise of luxurious winter fare. In his devouring mind's eye he pictured to himself every roasting-pig running about with a pudding in his belly and an apple in his mouth; the pigeons were snugly put to bed in a comfortable pie and tucked in with a coverlet of crust; the geese were swimming in their own gravy; and the ducks pairing cosily in dishes, like snug married couples, with a decent competency of onion sauce. In the porkers he saw carved out the future sleek side of bacon and juicy relishing ham; not a turkey but he beheld daintily trussed up, with its gizzard under its wing, and, peradventure, a necklace of savory sausages; and even bright Chanticleer himself lay sprawling on his back in a side-dish, with uplifted claws, as if craving that quarter which his chivalrous spirit disdained to ask while living.

As the enraptured Ichabod fancied all this, and as he rolled his great green eyes over the fat meadow-lands, the rich fields of wheat, of rye, of buckwheat, and Indian corn, and the orchards burdened with ruddy fruit, which surrounded the warm tenement of Van Tassel, his heart yearned after the damsel who was to inherit these domains, and his imagination expanded with the idea how they might be readily turned into cash and the money invested in immense tracts of wild land and shingle palaces in the wilderness. Nay, his busy fancy already realized his hopes, and presented to him the blooming Katrina, with a whole family of children, mounted on the top of a wagon loaded with household trumpery, with pots and kettles dangling beneath, and he beheld himself bestriding a pacing mare, with a colt at her heels, setting out for Kentucky, Tennessee, or the Lord knows where.

When he entered the house the conquest of his heart was complete. It was one of those spacious farmhouses with high-ridged but lowly-sloping roofs, built in the style handed down from the first Dutch settlers, the low projecting eaves forming a piazza along the front capable of being closed up in bad weather. Under this were hung flails, harness, various utensils of husbandry, and nets for fishing in the neighboring river. Benches were built along the sides for summer use, and a great spinning-wheel at one end and a churn at the other showed the various uses to which this important porch might be devoted. From this piazza the wondering Ichabod entered the hall, which formed the centre of the mansion and the place of usual residence. Here rows of resplendent pewter, ranged on a long dresser, dazzled his eyes. In one corner stood a huge bag of wool ready to be spun; in another a quantity of linsey-woolsey just from the loom; ears of Indian corn and strings of dried apples and peaches hung in gay festoons along the walls, mingled with the gaud of red peppers; and a door left ajar gave him a peep into the best parlor, where the claw-footed chairs and dark mahogany tables shone like mirrors; andirons, with their accompanying shovel and tongs, glistened from their covert of asparagus tops; mock-oranges and conch-shells decorated the mantelpiece; strings of various-colored birds' eggs were suspended above it; a great ostrich egg was hung from the centre of the room, and a corner cupboard, knowingly left open, displayed immense treasures of old silver and well-mended china.

From the moment Ichabod laid his eyes upon these regions of delight the peace of his mind was at an end, and his only study was how to gain the affections of the peerless daughter of Van Tassel. In this enterprise, however, he had more real difficulties than generally fell to the lot of a knight-errant of yore, who seldom had anything but giants, enchanters, fiery dragons, and such-like easily-conquered adversaries to contend with, and had to make his way merely through gates of iron and brass and walls of adamant to the castle keep, where the lady of his heart was confined; all which he achieved as easily as a man would carve his way to the centre of a Christmas pie, and then the lady gave him her hand as a matter of course. Ichabod, on the contrary, had to win his way to the heart of a country coquette beset with a labyrinth of whims and caprices, which were forever presenting new difficulties and impediments, and he had to encounter a host of fearful adversaries of real flesh and blood, the numerous rustic admirers who beset every portal to her heart, keeping a watchful and angry eye upon each other, but ready to fly out in the common cause against any new competitor.

Among these the most formidable was a burly, roaring, roistering blade of the name of Abraham—or, according to the Dutch abbreviation, Brom—Van Brunt, the hero of the country round, which rang with his feats of strength and hardihood. He was broad-shouldered and double-jointed, with short curly black hair and a bluff but not unpleasant countenance, having a mingled air of fun and arrogance. From his Herculean frame and great powers of limb, he had received the nickname of BROM BONES, by which he was universally known. He was famed for great knowledge and skill in horsemanship, being as dexterous on horseback as a Tartar. He was foremost at all races and cockfights, and, with the ascendancy which bodily strength acquires in rustic life, was the umpire in all disputes, setting his hat on one side and giving his decisions with an air and tone admitting of no gainsay or appeal. He was always ready for either a fight or a frolic, but had more mischief than ill-will in his composition; and with all his overbearing roughness there was a strong dash of waggish good-humor at bottom. He had three or four boon companions who regarded him as their model, and at the head of whom he scoured the country, attending every scene of feud or merriment for miles around. In cold weather he was distinguished by a fur cap surmounted with a flaunting fox's tail; and when the folks at a country gathering descried this well-known crest at a distance, whisking about among a squad of hard riders, they always stood by for a squall. Sometimes his crew would be heard dashing along past the farm-houses at midnight with whoop and halloo, like a troop of Don Cossacks, and the old dames, startled out of their sleep, would listen for a moment till the hurry-scurry had clattered by, and then exclaim, "Ay, there goes Brom Bones and his gang!" The neighbors looked upon him with a mixture of awe, admiration, and good-will, and when any madcap prank or rustic brawl occurred in the vicinity always shook their heads and warranted Brom Bones was at the bottom of it.

This rantipole hero had for some time singled out the blooming Katrina for the object of his uncouth gallantries, and, though his amorous toyings were something like the gentle caresses and endearments of a bear, yet it was whispered that she did not altogether discourage his hopes. Certain it is, his advances were signals for rival candidates to retire who felt no inclination to cross a line in his amours; insomuch, that when his horse was seen tied to Van Tassel's paling on a Sunday night, a sure sign that his master was courting—or, as it is termed, "sparking"—within, all other suitors passed by in despair and carried the war into other quarters.

Such was the formidable rival with whom Ichabod Crane had to contend, and, considering all things, a stouter man than he would have shrunk from the competition and a wiser man would have despaired. He had, however, a happy mixture of pliability and perseverance in his nature; he was in form and spirit like a supple jack—yielding, but although; though he bent, he never broke and though he bowed beneath the slightest pressure, yet the moment it was away, jerk! he was as erect and carried his head as high as ever.

To have taken the field openly against his rival would have been madness for he was not man to be thwarted in his amours, any more than that stormy lover, Achilles. Ichabod, therefore, made his advances in a quiet and gently-insinuating manner. Under cover of his character of singing-master, he made frequent visits at the farm-house; not that he had anything to apprehend from the meddlesome interference of parents, which is so often a stumbling-block in the path of lovers. Balt Van Tassel was an easy, indulgent soul; he loved his daughter better even than his pipe, and, like a reasonable man and an excellent father, let her have her way in everything. His notable little wife, too, had enough to do to attend to her housekeeping and manage her poultry for, as she sagely observed, ducks and geese are foolish things and must be looked after, but girls can take care of themselves. Thus while the busy dame bustled about the house or plied her spinning-wheel at one end of the piazza, honest Balt would sit smoking his evening pipe at the other, watching the achievements of a little wooden warrior who, armed with a sword in each hand, was most valiantly fighting the wind on the pinnacle of the barn. In the meantime, Ichabod would carry on his suit with the daughter by the side of the spring under the great elm, or sauntering along in the twilight, that hour so favorable to the lover's eloquence.

I profess not to know how women's hearts are wooed and won. To me they have always been matters of riddle and admiration. Some seem to have but one vulnerable point, or door of access, while others have a thousand avenues and may be captured in a thousand different ways. It is a great triumph of skill to gain the former, but still greater proof of generalship to maintain possession of the latter, for the man must battle for his fortress at every door and window. He who wins a thousand common hearts is therefore entitled to some renown, but he who keeps undisputed sway over the heart of a coquette is indeed a hero. Certain it is, this was not the case with the redoubtable Brom Bones; and from the moment Ichabod Crane made his advances, the interests of the former evidently declined; his horse was no longer seen tied at the palings on Sunday nights, and a deadly feud gradually arose between him and the preceptor of Sleepy Hollow.

Brom, who had a degree of rough chivalry in his nature, would fain have carried matters to open warfare, and have settled their pretensions to the lady according to the mode of those most concise and simple reasoners, the knights-errant of yore—by single combat; but Ichabod was too conscious of the superior might of his adversary to enter the lists against him: he had overheard a boast of Bones, that he would "double the schoolmaster up and lay him on a shelf of his own school-house;" and he was too wary to give him an opportunity. There was something extremely provoking in this obstinately pacific system; it left Brom no alternative but to draw upon the funds of rustic waggery in his disposition and to play off boorish practical jokes upon his rival. Ichabod became the object of whimsical persecution to Bones and his gang of rough riders. They harried his hitherto peaceful domains; smoked out his singing school by stopping up the chimney; broke into the schoolhouse at night in spite of its formidable fastenings of withe and window stakes, and turned everything topsy-turvy; so that the poor schoolmaster began to think all the witches in the country held their meetings there. But, what was still more annoying, Brom took all opportunities of turning him into ridicule in presence of his mistress, and had a scoundrel dog whom he taught to whine in the most ludicrous manner, and introduced as a rival of Ichabod's, to instruct her in psalmody.

In this way, matters went on for some time without producing any material effect on the relative situation of the contending powers. On a fine autumnal afternoon Ichabod, in pensive mood, sat enthroned on the lofty stool whence he usually watched all the concerns of his little literary realm. In his hand he swayed a ferule, that sceptre of despotic power; the birch of justice reposed on three nails behind the throne, a constant terror to evildoers; while on the desk before him might be seen sundry contraband articles and prohibited weapons detected upon the persons of idle urchins, such as half-munched apples, popguns, whirligigs, fly-cages, and whole legions of rampant little paper gamecocks. Apparently there had been some appalling act of justice recently inflicted, for his scholars were all busily intent upon their books or slyly whispering behind them with one eye kept upon the master, and a kind of buzzing stillness reigned throughout the school-room. It was suddenly interrupted by the appearance of a negro in tow-cloth jacket and trousers, a round-crowned fragment of a hat like the cap of Mercury, and mounted on the back of a ragged, wild, half-broken colt, which he managed with a rope by way of halter. He came clattering up to the school door with an invitation to Ichabod to attend a merry-making or "quilting frolic" to be held that evening at Mynheer Van Tassel's; and, having delivered his message with that air of importance and effort at fine language which a negro is apt to display on petty embassies of the kind, he dashed over the brook, and was seen scampering away up the hollow, full of the importance and hurry of his mission.

All was now bustle and hubbub in the late quiet school-room. The scholars were hurried through their lessons without stopping at trifles; those who were nimble skipped over half with impunity, and those who were tardy had a smart application now and then in the rear to quicken their speed or help them over a tall word. Books were flung aside without being put away on the shelves, inkstands were overturned, benches thrown down, and the whole school was turned loose an hour before the usual time, bursting forth like a legion of young imps, yelping and racketing about the green in joy at their early emancipation.

The gallant Ichabod now spent at least an extra half hour at his toilet, brushing and furbishing up his best, and indeed only, suit of rusty black, and arranging his locks by a bit of broken looking-glass that hung up in the school-house. That he might make his appearance before his mistress in the true style of a cavalier, he borrowed a horse from the farmer with whom he was domiciliated, a choleric old Dutchman of the name of Hans Van Ripper, and, thus gallantly mounted, issued forth like a knight-errant in quest of adventures. But it is meet I should, in the true spirit of romantic story, give some account of the looks and equipments of my hero and his steed. The animal he bestrode was a broken-down plough-horse that had outlived almost everything but his viciousness. He was gaunt and shagged, with a ewe neck and a head like a hammer; his rusty mane and tail were tangled and knotted with burrs; one eye had lost its pupil and was glaring and spectral, but the other had the gleam of a genuine devil in it. Still, he must have had fire and mettle in his day, if we may judge from the name he bore of Gunpowder. He had, in fact, been a favorite steed of his master's, the choleric Van Ripper, who was a furious rider, and had infused, very probably, some of his own spirit into the animal; for, old and broken down as he looked, there was more of the lurking devil in him than in any young filly in the country.

Ichabod was a suitable figure for such a steed. He rode with short stirrups, which brought his knees nearly up to the pommel of the saddle; his sharp elbows stuck out like grasshoppers'; he carried his whip perpendicularly in his hand like a sceptre; and as his horse jogged on the motion of his arms was not unlike the flapping of a pair of wings. A small wool hat rested on the top of his nose, for so his scanty strip of forehead might be called, and the skirts of his black coat fluttered out almost to his horse's tail. Such was the appearance of Ichabod and his steed as they shambled out of the gate of Hans Van Ripper, and it was altogether such an apparition as is seldom to be met with in broad daylight.

It was, as I have said, a fine autumnal day, the sky was clear and serene, and Nature wore that rich and golden livery which we always associate with the idea of abundance. The forests had put on their sober brown and yellow, while some trees of the tenderer kind had been nipped by the frosts into brilliant dyes of orange, purple, and scarlet. Streaming files of wild-ducks began to make their appearance high in the air; the bark of the squirrel might be heard from the groves of beech and hickory nuts, and the pensive whistle of the quail at intervals from the neighboring stubble-field.

The small birds were taking their farewell banquets. In the fulness of their revelry they fluttered, chirping and frolicking, from bush to bush and tree to tree, capricious from the very profusion and variety around them. There was the honest cock robin, the favorite game of stripling sportsmen, with its loud querulous note; and the twittering blackbirds, flying in sable clouds; and the golden-winged woodpecker, with his crimson crest, his broad black gorget, and splendid plumage; and the cedar-bird, with its red-tipt wings and yellow-tipt tail and its little monteiro cap of feathers; and the blue jay, that noisy coxcomb, in his gay light-blue coat and white under-clothes, screaming and chattering, bobbing and nodding and bowing, and pretending to be on good terms with every songster of the grove.

As Ichabod jogged slowly on his way his eye, ever open to every symptom of culinary abundance, ranged with delight over the treasures of jolly Autumn. On all sides he beheld vast store of apples—some hanging in oppressive opulence on the trees, some gathered into baskets and barrels for the market, others heaped up in rich piles for the cider-press. Farther on he beheld great fields of Indian corn, with its golden ears peeping from their leafy coverts and holding out the promise of cakes and hasty pudding; and the yellow pumpkins lying beneath them, turning up their fair round bellies to the sun, and giving ample prospects of the most luxurious of pies; and anon he passed the fragrant buckwheat-fields, breathing the odor of the beehive, and as he beheld them soft anticipations stole over his mind of dainty slapjacks, well buttered and garnished with honey or treacle by the delicate little dimpled hand of Katrina Van Tassel.

Thus feeding his mind with many sweet thoughts and "sugared suppositions," he journeyed along the sides of a range of hills which look out upon some of the goodliest scenes of the mighty Hudson. The sun gradually wheeled his broad disk down into the west. The wide bosom of the Tappan Zee lay motionless and glassy, excepting that here and there a gentle undulation waved and prolonged the blue shadow of the distant mountain. A few amber clouds floated in the sky, without a breath of air to move them. The horizon was of a fine golden tint, changing gradually into a pure apple green, and from that into the deep blue of the mid-heaven. A slanting ray lingered on the woody crests of the precipices that overhung some parts of the river, giving greater depth to the dark-gray and purple of their rocky sides. A sloop was loitering in the distance, dropping slowly down with the tide, her sail hanging uselessly against the mast, and as the reflection of the sky gleamed along the still water it seemed as if the vessel was suspended in the air.

It was toward evening that Ichabod arrived at the castle of the Heer Van Tassel, which he found thronged with the pride and flower of the adjacent country—old farmers, a spare leathern-faced race, in homespun coats and breeches, blue stockings, huge shoes, and magnificent pewter buckles; their brisk withered little dames, in close crimped caps, long-waisted shortgowns, homespun petticoats, with scissors and pincushions and gay calico pockets hanging on the outside; buxom lasses, almost as antiquated as their mothers, excepting where a straw hat, a fine ribbon, or perhaps a white frock, gave symptoms of city innovation; the sons, in short square-skirted coats with rows of stupendous brass buttons, and their hair generally queued in the fashion of the times, especially if they could procure an eel-skin for the purpose, it being esteemed throughout the country as a potent nourisher and strengthener of the hair.

Brom Bones, however, was the hero of the scene, having come to the gathering on his favorite steed Daredevil—a creature, like himself full of metal and mischief, and which no one but himself could manage. He was, in fact, noted for preferring vicious animals, given to all kinds of tricks, which kept the rider in constant risk of his neck, for he held a tractable, well-broken horse as unworthy of a lad of spirit.

Fain would I pause to dwell upon the world of charms that burst upon the enraptured gaze of my hero as he entered the state parlor of Van Tassel's mansion. Not those of the bevy of buxom lasses with their luxurious display of red and white, but the ample charms of a genuine Dutch country tea-table in the sumptuous time of autumn. Such heaped-up platters of cakes of various and almost indescribable kinds, known only to experienced Dutch housewives! There was the doughty doughnut, the tenderer oily koek, and the crisp and crumbling cruller; sweet cakes and short cakes, ginger cakes and honey cakes, and the whole family of cakes. And then there were apple pies and peach pies and pumpkin pies; besides slices of ham and smoked beef; and moreover delectable dishes of preserved plums and peaches and pears and quinces; not to mention broiled shad and roasted chickens; together with bowls of milk and cream,—all mingled higgledy-piggledy, pretty much as I have enumerated them, with the motherly teapot sending up its clouds of vapor from the midst. Heaven bless the mark! I want breath and time to discuss this banquet as it deserves, and am too eager to get on with my story. Happily, Ichabod Crane was not in so great a hurry as his historian, but did ample justice to every dainty.

He was a kind and thankful creature, whose heart dilated in proportion as his skin was filled with good cheer, and whose spirits rose with eating as some men's do with drink. He could not help, too, rolling his large eyes round him as he ate, and chuckling with the possibility that he might one day be lord of all this scene of almost unimaginable luxury and splendor. Then, he thought, how soon he'd turn his back upon the old school-house, snap his fingers in the face of Hans Van Ripper and every other niggardly patron, and kick any itinerant pedagogue out of doors that should dare to call him comrade!

Old Baltus Van Tassel moved about among his guests with a face dilated with content and good-humor, round and jolly as the harvest moon. His hospitable attentions were brief, but expressive, being confined to a shake of the hand, a slap on the shoulder, a loud laugh, and a pressing invitation to "fall to and help themselves."

And now the sound of the music from the common room, or hall, summoned to the dance. The musician was an old gray-headed negro who had been the itinerant orchestra of the neighborhood for more than half a century. His instrument was as old and battered as himself. The greater part of the time he scraped on two or three strings, accompanying every movement of the bow with a motion of the head, bowing almost to the ground and stamping with his foot whenever a fresh couple were to start.

Ichabod prided himself upon his dancing as much as upon his vocal powers. Not a limb, not a fibre about him was idle; and to have seen his loosely hung frame in full motion and clattering about the room you would have thought Saint Vitus himself, that blessed patron of the dance, was figuring before you in person. He was the admiration of all the negroes, who, having gathered, of all ages and sizes, from the farm and the neighborhood, stood forming a pyramid of shining black faces at every door and window, gazing with delight at the scene, rolling their white eyeballs, and showing grinning rows of ivory from ear to ear. How could the flogger of urchins be otherwise than animated and joyous? The lady of his heart was his partner in the dance, and smiling graciously in reply to all his amorous oglings, while Brom Bones, sorely smitten with love and jealousy, sat brooding by himself in one corner.

When the dance was at an end Ichabod was attracted to a knot of the sager folks, who, with old Van Tassel, sat smoking at one end of the piazza gossiping over former times and drawing out long stories about the war.

This neighborhood, at the time of which I am speaking, was one of those highly favored places which abound with chronicle and great men. The British and American line had run near it during the war; it had therefore been the scene of marauding and infested with refugees, cow-boys, and all kinds of border chivalry. Just sufficient time had elapsed to enable each storyteller to dress up his tale with a little becoming fiction, and in the indistinctness of his recollection to make himself the hero of every exploit.

There was the story of Doffue Martling, a large blue-bearded Dutchman, who had nearly taken a British frigate with an old iron nine-pounder from a mud breastwork, only that his gun burst at the sixth discharge. And there was an old gentleman who shall be nameless, being too rich a mynheer to be lightly mentioned, who, in the battle of Whiteplains, being an excellent master of defense, parried a musket-ball with a small sword, insomuch that he absolutely felt it whiz round the blade and glance off at the hilt: in proof of which he was ready at any time to show the sword, with the hilt a little bent. There were several more that had been equally great in the field, not one of whom but was persuaded that he had a considerable hand in bringing the war to a happy termination.

But all these were nothing to the tales of ghosts and apparitions that succeeded. The neighborhood is rich in legendary treasures of the kind. Local tales and superstitions thrive best in these sheltered, long-settled retreats but are trampled under foot by the shifting throng that forms the population of most of our country places. Besides, there is no encouragement for ghosts in most of our villages, for they have scarcely had time to finish their first nap and turn themselves in their graves before their surviving friends have travelled away from the neighborhood; so that when they turn out at night to walk their rounds they have no acquaintance left to call upon. This is perhaps the reason why we so seldom hear of ghosts except in our long-established Dutch communities.

The immediate causes however, of the prevalence of supernatural stories in these parts, was doubtless owing to the vicinity of Sleepy Hollow. There was a contagion in the very air that blew from that haunted region; it breathed forth an atmosphere of dreams and fancies infecting all the land. Several of the Sleepy Hollow people were present at Van Tassel's, and, as usual, were doling out their wild and wonderful legends. Many dismal tales were told about funeral trains and mourning cries and wailings heard and seen about the great tree where the unfortunate Major Andre was taken, and which stood in the neighborhood. Some mention was made also of the woman in white that haunted the dark glen at Raven Rock, and was often heard to shriek on winter nights before a storm, having perished there in the snow. The chief part of the stories, however, turned upon the favorite spectre of Sleepy Hollow, the headless horseman, who had been heard several times of late patrolling the country, and, it was said, tethered his horse nightly among the graves in the churchyard.

The sequestered situation of this church seems always to have made it a favorite haunt of troubled spirits. It stands on a knoll surrounded by locust trees and lofty elms, from among which its decent whitewashed walls shine modestly forth, like Christian purity beaming through the shades of retirement. A gentle slope descends from it to a silver sheet of water bordered by high trees, between which peeps may be caught at the blue hills of the Hudson. To look upon its grass-grown yard, where the sunbeams seem to sleep so quietly, one would think that there at least the dead might rest in peace. On one side of the church extends a wide woody dell, along, which raves a large brook among broken rocks and trunks of fallen trees. Over a deep black part of the stream, not far from the church, was formerly thrown a wooden bridge; the road that led to it and the bridge itself were thickly shaded by overhanging trees, which cast a gloom about it even in the daytime, but occasioned a fearful darkness at night. Such was one of the favorite haunts of the headless horseman, and the place where he was most frequently encountered. The tale was told of old Brouwer, a most heretical disbeliever in ghosts, how he met the horseman returning from his foray into

Sleepy Hollow, and was obliged to get up behind him; how they galloped over bush and brake, over hill and swamp, until they reached the bridge, when the horseman suddenly turned into a skeleton, threw old Brouwer into the brook, and sprang away over the tree-tops with a clap of thunder.

This story was immediately matched by a thrice-marvelous adventure of Brom Bones, who made light of the galloping Hessian as an arrant jockey. He affirmed that on returning one night from the neighboring village of Sing-Sing he had been over taken by this midnight trooper; that he had offered to race with him for a bowl of punch, and should have won it too, for Daredevil beat the goblin horse all hollow, but just as they came to the church bridge the Hessian bolted and vanished in a flash of fire.

All these tales, told in that drowsy undertone with which men talk in the dark, the countenances of the listeners only now and then receiving a casual gleam from the glare of a pipe, sank deep in the mind of Ichabod. He repaid them in kind with large extracts from his invaluable author, Cotton Mather, and added many marvelous events that had taken place in his native state of Connecticut and fearful sights which he had seen in his nightly walks about Sleepy Hollow.

The revel now gradually broke up. The old farmers gathered together their families in their wagons, and were heard for some time rattling along the hollow roads and over the distant hills. Some of the damsels mounted on pillions behind their favorite swains, and their light-hearted laughter, mingling with the clatter of hoofs, echoed along the silent woodlands, sounding fainter and fainter until they gradually died away, and the late scene of noise and frolic was all silent and deserted. Ichabod only lingered behind, according to the custom of country lovers, to have a tete-a-tete with the heiress, fully convinced that he was now on the high road to success. What passed at this interview I will not pretend to say, for in fact I do not know. Something, however, I fear me, must have gone wrong, for he certainly sallied forth, after no very great interval, with an air quite desolate and chop-fallen. Oh these women! these women! Could that girl have been playing off any of her coquettish tricks? Was her encouragement of the poor pedagogue all a mere sham to secure her conquest of his rival? Heaven only knows, not I! Let it suffice to say, Ichabod stole forth with the air of one who had been sacking a hen-roost, rather than a fair lady's heart. Without looking to the right or left to notice the scene of rural wealth on which he had so often gloated, he went straight to the stable, and with several hearty cuffs and kicks roused his steed most uncourteously from the comfortable quarters in which he was soundly sleeping, dreaming of mountains of corn and oats and whole valleys of timothy and clover.

It was the very witching time of night that Ichabod, heavy-hearted and crestfallen, pursued his travel homewards along the sides of the lofty hills which rise above Tarry Town, and which he had traversed so cheerily in the afternoon. The hour was as dismal as himself. Far below him the Tappan Zee spread its dusky and indistinct waste of waters, with here and there the tall mast of a sloop riding quietly at anchor under the land. In the dead hush of midnight he could even hear the barking of the watch-dog from the opposite shore of the Hudson; but it was so vague and faint as only to give an idea of his distance from this faithful companion of man. Now and then, too, the long-drawn crowing of a cock, accidentally awakened, would sound far, far off, from some farm-house away among the hills; but it was like a dreaming sound in his ear. No signs of life occurred near him, but occasionally the melancholy chirp of a cricket, or perhaps the guttural twang of a bull-frog from a neighboring marsh, as if sleeping uncomfortably and turning suddenly in his bed.

All the stories of ghosts and goblins that he had heard in the afternoon now came crowding upon his recollection. The night grew darker and darker; the stars seemed to sink deeper in the sky, and driving clouds occasionally had them from his sight. He had never felt so lonely and dismal. He was, moreover, approaching the very place where many of the scenes of the ghost-stories had been laid. In the centre of the road stood an enormous tulip tree which towered like a giant above all the other trees of the neighborhood and formed a kind of landmark. Its limbs were gnarled and fantastic, large enough to form trunks for ordinary trees, twisting down almost to the earth and rising again into the air. It was connected with the tragical story of the unfortunate Andre, who had been taken prisoner hard by, and was universally known by the name of Major Andre's tree. The common people regarded it with a mixture of respect and superstition, partly out of sympathy for the fate of its ill-starred namesake, and partly from the tales of strange sights and doleful lamentations told concerning it.

As Ichabod approached this fearful tree he began to whistle: he thought his whistle was answered; it was but a blast sweeping sharply through the dry branches. As he approached a little nearer he thought he saw something white hanging in the midst of the tree: he paused and ceased whistling, but on looking more narrowly perceived that it was a place where the tree had been scathed by lightning and the white wood laid bare. Suddenly he heard a groan: his teeth chattered and his knees smote against the saddle; it was but the rubbing of one huge bough upon another as they were swayed about by the breeze. He passed the tree in safety, but new perils lay before him.

About two hundred yards from the tree a small brook crossed the road and ran into a marshy and thickly-wooded glen known by the name of Wiley's Swamp. A few rough logs, laid side by side, served for a bridge over this stream. On that side of the road where the brook entered the wood a group of oaks and chestnuts, matted thick with wild grape-vines, threw a cavernous gloom over it. To pass this bridge was the severest trial. It was at this identical spot that the unfortunate Andre was captured, and under the covert of those chestnuts and vines were the sturdy yeomen concealed who surprised him. This has ever since been considered a haunted stream, and fearful are the feelings of the schoolboy who has to pass it alone after dark.

As he approached the stream his heart began to thump; he summoned up, however, all his resolution, gave his horse half a score of kicks in the ribs, and attempted to dash briskly across the bridge; but instead of starting forward, the perverse old animal made a lateral movement and ran broadside against the fence. Ichabod, whose fears increased with the delay, jerked the reins on the other side and kicked lustily with the contrary foot: it was all in vain; his steed started, it is true, but it was only to plunge to the opposite side of the road into a thicket of brambles and alder bushes. The schoolmaster now bestowed both whip and heel upon the starveling ribs of old Gunpowder, who dashed forward, snuffing and snorting, but came to a stand just by the bridge with a suddenness that had nearly sent his rider sprawling over his head. Just at this moment a plashy tramp by the side of the bridge caught the sensitive ear of Ichabod. In the dark shadow of the grove on the margin of the brook he beheld something huge, misshapen, black, and towering. It stirred not, but seemed gathered up in the gloom, like some gigantic monster ready to spring upon the traveller.

The hair of the affrighted pedagogue rose upon his head with terror. What was to be done? To turn and fly was now too late; and besides, what chance was there of escaping ghost or goblin, if such it was, which could ride upon the wings of the wind? Summoning up, therefore, a show of courage, he demanded in stammering accents, "Who are you?" He received no reply. He repeated his demand in a still more agitated voice. Still there was no answer. Once more he cudgeled the sides of the inflexible Gunpowder, and, shutting his eyes, broke forth with involuntary fervor into a psalm tune. Just then the shadowy object of alarm put itself in motion, and with a scramble and a bound stood at once in the middle of the road. Though the night was dark and dismal, yet the form of the unknown might now in some degree be ascertained. He appeared to be a horseman of large dimensions and mounted on a black horse of powerful frame. He made no offer of molestation or sociability, but kept aloof on one side of the road, jogging along on the blind side of old Gunpowder, who had now got over his fright and waywardness.

Ichabod, who had no relish for this strange midnight companion, and bethought himself of the adventure of Brom Bones with the Galloping Hessian, now quickened his steed in hopes of leaving him behind. The stranger, however, quickened his horse to an equal pace. Ichabod pulled up, and fell into a walk, thinking to lag behind; the other did the same. His heart began to sink within him; he endeavored to resume his psalm tune, but his parched tongue clove to the roof of his mouth and he could not utter a stave. There was something in the moody and dogged silence of this pertinacious companion that was mysterious and appalling. It was soon fearfully accounted for. On mounting a rising ground, which brought the figure of his fellow-traveller in relief against the sky, gigantic in height and muffled in a cloak, Ichabod was horror-struck on perceiving that he was headless! but his horror was still more increased on observing that the head, which should have rested on his shoulders, was carried before him on the pommel of the saddle. His terror rose to desperation, he rained a shower of kicks and blows upon Gunpowder, hoping by a sudden movement to give his companion the slip; but the spectre started full jump with him. Away, then, they dashed through thick and thin, stones flying and sparks flashing at every bound. Ichabod's flimsy garments fluttered in the air as he stretched his long lank body away over his horse's head in the eagerness of his flight.

They had now reached the road which turns off to Sleepy Hollow; but Gunpowder, who seemed possessed with a demon, instead of keeping up it, made an opposite turn and plunged headlong down hill to the left. This road leads through a sandy hollow shaded by trees for about a quarter of a mile, where it crosses the bridge famous in goblin story, and just beyond swells the green knoll on which stands the whitewashed church.

As yet the panic of the steed had given his unskillful rider an apparent advantage in the chase; but just as he had got halfway through the hollow the girths of the saddle gave away and he felt it slipping from under him. He seized it by the pommel and endeavored to hold it firm, but in vain, and had just time to save himself by clasping old Gunpowder round the neck, when the saddle fell to the earth, and he heard it trampled under foot by his pursuer. For a moment the terror of Hans Van Ripper's wrath passed across his mind, for it was his Sunday saddle; but this was no time for petty fears; the goblin was hard on his haunches, and (unskilled rider that he was) he had much ado to maintain his seat, sometimes slipping on one side, sometimes on another, and sometimes jolted on the high ridge of his horse's back-bone with a violence that he verily feared would cleave him asunder.

An opening in the trees now cheered him with the hopes that the church bridge was at hand. The wavering reflection of a silver star in the bosom of the brook told him that he was not mistaken. He saw the walls of the church dimly glaring under the trees beyond. He recollected the place where Brom Bones' ghostly competitor had disappeared. "If I can but reach that bridge," thought Ichabod, "I am safe." Just then he heard the black steed panting and blowing close behind him; he even fancied that he felt his hot breath. Another convulsive kick in the ribs, and old Gunpowder sprang upon the bridge; he thundered over the resounding planks; he gained the opposite side; and now Ichabod cast a look behind to see if his pursuer should vanish, according to rule, in a flash of fire and brimstone. Just then he saw the goblin rising in his stirrups, and in the very act of hurling his head at him. Ichabod endeavored to dodge the horrible missile, but too late. It encountered his cranium with a tremendous crash; he was tumbled headlong into the dust, and Gunpowder, the black steed, and the goblin rider passed by like a whirlwind.

The next morning the old horse was found, without his saddle and with the bridle under his feet, soberly cropping the grass at his master's gate. Ichabod did not make his appearance at breakfast; dinner-hour came, but no Ichabod. The boys assembled at the school-house and strolled idly about the banks of the brook but no schoolmaster. Hans Van Ripper now began to feel some uneasiness about the fate of poor Ichabod and his saddle. An inquiry was set on foot, and after diligent investigation they came upon his traces. In one part of the road leading to the church was found the saddle trampled in the dirt; the tracks of horses' hoofs, deeply dented in the road and evidently at furious speed, were traced to the bridge, beyond which, on the bank of a broad part of the brook, where the water ran deep and black, was found the hat of the unfortunate Ichabod, and close beside it a spattered pumpkin.

The brook was searched, but the body of the schoolmaster was not to be discovered. Hans Van Ripper, as executor of his estate, examined the bundle which contained all his worldly effects. They consisted of two shirts and a half, two stocks for the neck, a pair or two of worsted stockings, an old pair of corduroy small-clothes, a rusty razor, a book of psalm tunes full of dog's ears, and a broken pitch-pipe. As to the books and furniture of the school-house, they belonged to the community, excepting Cotton Mather's History of Witchcraft, a New England Almanac, and a book of dreams and fortune-telling; in which last was a sheet of foolscap much scribbled and blotted in several fruitless attempts to make a copy of verses in honor of the heiress of Van Tassel. These magic books and the poetic scrawl were forthwith consigned to the flames by Hans Van Ripper, who from that time forward determined to send his children no more to school, observing that he never knew any good come of this same reading and writing. Whatever money the schoolmaster possessed—and he had received his quarter's pay but a day or two before—he must have had about his person at the time of his disappearance.

The mysterious event caused much speculation at the church on the following Sunday. Knots of gazers and gossips were collected in the churchyard, at the bridge, and at the spot where the hat and pumpkin had been found. The stories of Brouwer, of Bones, and a whole budget of others were called to mind, and when they had diligently considered them all, and compared them with the symptoms of the present case, they shook their heads and came to the conclusion that Ichabod had been carried off by the galloping Hessian. As he was a bachelor and in nobody's debt, nobody troubled his head any more about him, the school was removed to a different quarter of the hollow and another pedagogue reigned in his stead.

It is true an old farmer, who had been down to New York on a visit several years after, and from whom this account of the ghostly adventure was received, brought home the intelligence that Ichabod Crane was still alive; that he had left the neighborhood, partly through fear of the goblin and Hans Van Ripper, and partly in mortification at having been suddenly dismissed by the heiress; that he had changed his quarters to a distant part of the country, had kept school and studied law at the same time, had been admitted to the bar, turned politician, electioneered, written for the newspapers, and finally had been made a justice of the Ten Pound Court. Brom Bones too, who shortly after his rival's disappearance conducted the blooming Katrina in triumph to the altar, was observed to look exceedingly knowing whenever the story of Ichabod was related, and always burst into a hearty laugh at the mention of the pumpkin; which led some to suspect that he knew more about the matter than he chose to tell.

The old country wives, however, who are the best judges of these matters, maintain to this day that Ichabod was spirited away by supernatural means; and it is a favorite story often told about the neighborhood round the intervening fire. The bridge became more than ever an object of superstitious awe, and that may be the reason why the road has been altered of late years, so as to approach the church by the border of the mill-pond. The schoolhouse, being deserted, soon fell to decay, and was reported to be haunted by the ghost of the unfortunate pedagogue; and the plough-boy, loitering homeward of a still summer evening, has often fancied his voice at a distance chanting a melancholy psalm tune among the tranquil solitudes of Sleepy Hollow.

POSTSCRIPT FOUND IN THE HANDWRITING OF THE LATE MR. KNICKERBOCKER.

The preceding tale is given almost in the precise words in which I heard it related at a Corporation meeting of the ancient city of Manhattoes, at which were present many of its sagest and most illustrious burghers. The narrator was a pleasant, shabby, gentlemanly old fellow in pepper-and-salt clothes, with a sadly humorous face, and one whom I strongly suspected of being poor, he made such efforts to be entertaining. When his story was concluded there was much laughter and approbation, particularly from two or three deputy aldermen who had been asleep the greater part of the time. There was, however, one tall, dry-looking old gentleman, with beetling eyebrows, who maintained a grave and rather severe face throughout, now and then folding his arms, inclining his head, and looking down upon the floor, as if turning a doubt over in his mind. He was one of your wary men, who never laugh but upon good grounds—when they have reason and the law on their side. When the mirth of the rest of the company had subsided and silence was restored, he leaned one arm on the elbow of his chair, and sticking the other akimbo, demanded, with a slight but exceedingly sage motion of the head and contraction of the brow, what was the moral of the story and what it went to prove.

The story-teller, who was just putting a glass of wine to his lips as a refreshment after his toils, paused for a moment, looked at his inquirer with an air of infinite deference, and, lowering the glass slowly to the table, observed that the story was intended most logically to prove—

"That there is no situation in life but has its advantages and pleasures—provided we will but take a joke as we find it;

"That, therefore, he that runs races with goblin troopers is likely to have rough riding of it.

"Ergo, for a country schoolmaster to be refused the hand of a Dutch heiress is a certain step to high preferment in the state."

The cautious old gentleman knit his brows tenfold closer after this explanation, being sorely puzzled by the ratiocination of the syllogism, while methought the one in pepper-and-salt eyed him with something of a triumphant leer. At length he observed that all this was very well, but still he thought the story a little on the extravagant—there were one or two points on which he had his doubts.

"Faith, sir," replied the story-teller, "as to that matter, I don't believe one-half of it myself."

D. K.

The Voice in the Night

William Hope Hodgson

It was a dark, starless night. We were becalmed in the northern Pacific. Our exact position I do not know; for the sun had been hidden during the course of a weary, breathless week by a thin haze which had seemed to float above us, about the height of our mastheads, at whiles descending and shrouding the surrounding sea.

With there being no wind, we had steadied the tiller, and I was the only man on deck. The crew, consisting of two men and a boy, were sleeping forward in their den, while Will—my friend, and the master of our little craft—was aft in his bunk on the port side of the little cabin.

Suddenly, from out of the surrounding darkness, there came a hail:

"Schooner, ahoy!"

The cry was so unexpected that I gave no immediate answer, because of my surprise.

It came again—a voice curiously throaty and inhuman, calling from somewhere upon the dark sea away on our port broadside:

"Schooner, ahoy!"

"Hullo!" I sang out, having gathered my wits somewhat. "What are you? What do you want?"

"You need not be afraid," answered the queer voice, having probably noticed some trace of confusion in my tone. "I am only an old—man."

The pause sounded odd, but it was only afterward that it came back to me with any significance.

"Why don't you come alongside, then?" I queried somewhat snappishly, for I liked not his hinting at my having been a trifle shaken.

"I—I—can't. It wouldn't be safe. I—" The voice broke off, and there was silence.

"What do you mean?" I asked, growing more and more astonished. "What's not safe? Where are you?"

I listened for a moment, but there came no answer. And then, a sudden indefinite suspicion, of I knew not what, coming to me, I stepped swiftly to the binnacle and took out the lighted lamp. At the same time, I knocked on the deck with my heel to waken Will. Then I was back at the side, throwing the yellow funnel of light out into the silent immensity beyond our rail. As I did so, I heard a slight muffled cry, and then the sound of a splash, as though someone had dipped oars abruptly. Yet I cannot say with certainty that I saw anything; save, it seemed to me, that with the first flash of the light there had been something upon the waters, where now there was nothing.

"Hullo, there!" I called. "What foolery is this?"

But there came only the indistinct sounds of a boat being pulled away into the night.

Then I heard Will's voice from the direction of the after scuttle:

"What's up, George?"

"Come here, Will!" I said.

"What is it?" he asked, coming across the deck.

I told him the queer thing that had happened. He put several questions; then, after a moment's silence, he raised his hands to his lips and hailed:

"Boat, ahoy!"

From a long distance away there came back to us a faint reply, and my companion repeated his call. Presently, after a short period of silence, there grew on our hearing the muffled sound of oars, at which Will hailed again.

This time there was a reply: "Put away the light."

"I'm damned if I will," I muttered; but Will told me to do as the voice bade, and I shoved it down under the bulwarks.

"Come nearer," he said, and the oar strokes continued. Then, when apparently some half dozen fathoms distant, they again ceased.

"Come alongside!" exclaimed Will. "There's nothing to be frightened of aboard here."

"Promise that you will not show the light?"

"What's to do with you," I burst out, "that you're so infernally afraid of the light?"

"Because—" began the voice, and stopped short.

"Because what?" I asked quickly.

Will put his hand on my shoulder. "Shut up a minute, old man," he said in a low voice. "Let me tackle him."

He leaned more over the rail. "See here, mister," he said, "this is a pretty queer business, you coming upon us like this, right out in the middle of the blessed Pacific. How are we to know what sort of a hanky-panky trick you're up to? You say there's only one of you. How are we to know, unless we get a squint at you—eh? What's your objection to the light, anyway?"

As he finished, I heard the noise of the oars again, and then the voice came; but now from a greater distance, and sounding extremely hopeless and pathetic.

"I am sorry—sorry! I would not have troubled you, only I am hungry, and—so is she."

The voice died away, and the sound of the oars, dipping irregularly, was borne to us.

"Stop!" sang out Will. "I don't want to drive you away. Come back! We'll keep the light hidden if you don't like it."

He turned to me. "It's a damned queer rig, this; but I think there's nothing to be afraid of?"

There was a question in his tone, and I replied, "No, I think the poor devil's been wrecked around here, and gone crazy."

The sound of the oars drew nearer.

"Shove that lamp back in the binnacle," said Will; then he leaned over the rail and listened. I replaced the lamp and came back to his side. The dipping of the oars ceased some dozen yards distant.

"Won't you come alongside now?" asked Will in an even voice. "I have had the lamp put back in the binnacle."

"I—I cannot," replied the voice. "I dare not come nearer. I dare not even pay you for the—the provisions."

"That's all right," said Will, and hesitated. "You're welcome to as much grub as you can take—" Again he hesitated.

"You are very good!" exclaimed the voice. "May God, who understands everything, reward you—" It broke off huskily.

"The—the lady?" said Will abruptly. "Is she—"

"I have left her behind upon the island," came the voice.

"What island?" I cut in.

"I know not its name," returned the voice. "I would to God—" it began, and checked itself as suddenly.

"Could we not send a boat for her?" asked Will at this point.

"No!" said the voice, with extraordinary emphasis. "My God! No!" There was a moment's pause; then it added, in a tone which seemed a merited reproach, "It was because of our want I ventured—because her agony tortured me."

"I am a forgetful brute!" exclaimed Will. "Just wait a minute, whoever you are, and I will bring you up something at once."

In a couple of minutes he was back again, and his arms were full of various edibles. He paused at the rail.

"Can't you come alongside for them?" he asked.

"No—I dare not," replied the voice, and it seemed to me that in its tones I detected a note of stifled craving, as though the owner hushed a mortal desire. It came to me then in a flash that the poor old creature out there in the darkness was suffering for actual need for that which Will held in his arms; and yet, because of some unintelligible dread, refraining from dashing to the side of our schooner and receiving it. And with the lightninglike conviction there came the knowledge that the Invisible was not mad, but sanely facing some intolerable horror.

"Damn it, Will!" I said, full of many feelings, over which predominated a vast sympathy. "Get a box. We must float off the stuff to him in it."

This we did, propelling it away from the vessel, out into the darkness, by means of a boat hook.

In a minute a slight cry from the Invisible came to us, and we knew that he had secured the box.

A little later he called out a farewell to us, and so heartful a blessing that I am sure we were the better for it. Then, without more ado, we heard the ply of oars across the darkness.

"Pretty soon off," remarked Will, with perhaps just a little sense of injury.

"Wait," I replied. "I think somehow he'll come back. He must have been badly needing that food."

"And the lady," said Will. For a moment he was silent; then he continued, "It's the queerest thing ever I've tumbled across since I've been fishing."

"Yes," I said, and fell to pondering.

And so the time slipped away—an hour, another, and still Will stayed with me; for the queer adventure had knocked all desire for sleep out of him.

The third hour was three parts through when we heard again the sound of oars across the silent ocean.

"Listen!" said Will, a low note of excitement in his voice.

"He's coming, just as I thought," I muttered.

The dipping of the oars grew nearer, and I noted that the strokes were firmer and longer. The food had been needed.

They came to a stop a little distance off the broadside, and the queer voice came again to us through the darkness:

"Schooner, ahoy!"

"That you?" asked Will.

"Yes," replied the voice. "I left you suddenly, but—but there was great need."

"The lady?" questioned Will.

"The—lady is grateful now on earth. She will be more grateful soon in—in heaven."

Will began to make some reply, in a puzzled voice, but became confused and broke off. I said nothing. I was wondering at the curious pauses, and apart from my wonder, I was full of a great sympathy.

The voice continued, "We—she and I, have talked, as we shared the result of God's tenderness and yours—"

Will interposed, but without coherence

"I beg of you not to—to belittle your deed of Christian charity this night," said the voice. "Be sure that it has not escaped His notice."

It stopped, and there was a full minute's silence. Then it came again. "We have spoken together upon that which—which has befallen us. We had thought to go out, without telling anyone of the terror which has come into our—lives. She is with me in believing that tonight's happenings are under a special ruling, and that it is God's wish that we should tell to you all that we have suffered since —since—"

"Yes?" said Will softly.

"Since the sinking of the Albatross."

"Ah!" I exclaimed involuntarily. "She left Newcastle for 'Frisco some six months ago, and hasn't been heard of since."

"Yes" answered the voice. "But some few degrees to the north of the line, she was caught in a terrible storm and dismasted. When the calm came, it was found that she was leaking badly, and presently, it falling to a calm, the sailors took to the boats, leaving—leaving a young lady—my fiancée—and myself upon the wreck.

"We were below, gathering together a few of our belongings, when they left. They were entirely callous, through fear, and when we came up upon the decks, we saw them only as small shapes afar off upon the horizon. Yet we did not despair, but set to work and constructed a small raft. Upon this we put such few matters as it would hold, including a quantity of water and some ship's biscuit. Then, the vessel being very deep in the water, we got ourselves onto the raft and pushed off.

"It was later that I observed we seemed to be in the way of some tide or current, which bore us from the ship at an angle, so that in the course of three hours, by my watch, her hull became invisible to our sight, her broken masts remaining in view for a somewhat longer period. Then, toward evening, it grew misty, and so through the night. The next day we were still encompassed by the mist, the weather remaining quiet.

"For four days we drifted through this strange haze, until, on the evening of the fourth day, there grew upon our ears the murmur of breakers at a distance. Gradually it became plainer, and somewhat after midnight, it appeared to sound upon either hand at no very great space. The raft was raised upon a swell several times, and then we were in smooth water, and the noise of the breakers was behind.

"When the morning came, we found that we were in a sort of great lagoon, but of this we noticed little at the time; for close before us, through the enshrouding mist, loomed the hull of a large sailing vessel. With one accord we fell upon our knees and thanked God, for we thought that here was an end to our perils. We had much to learn.

"The raft drew near to the ship, and we shouted on them to take us aboard; but none answered. Presently the raft touched against the side of the vessel, and seeing a rope hanging downward, I seized it and began to climb. Yet I had much ado to make my way up, because of a kind of gray, lichenous fungus that had seized upon the rope and blotched the side of the ship lividly.

"I reached the rail and clambered over it, onto the deck. Here I saw that the decks were covered in great patches with the gray masses, some of them rising into nodules several feet in height; but at the time I thought less of this matter than of the possibility of there being people aboard the ship. I shouted, but none answered. Then I went to the door below the poop deck. I opened it and peered in. There was a great smell of staleness, so that I knew in a moment that nothing living was within, and with the knowledge, I shut the door quickly, for I felt suddenly lonely.

"I went back to the side where I had scrambled up. My—my sweetheart was still sitting quietly upon the raft. Seeing me look down, she called up to know whether there were any aboard the ship. I replied that the vessel had the appearance of having been long deserted, but that if she would wait a little, I would see whether there was anything in the shape of a ladder by which she could ascend to the deck. Then we would make a search through the vessel together. A little later, on the opposite side of the decks, I found a rope side ladder. This I carried across, and a minute afterward she was beside me.

"Together we explored the cabins and apartments in the afterpart of the ship, but nowhere was there any sign of life. Here and there, within the cabins themselves, we came across odd patches of that queer fungus; but this, as my sweetheart said, could be cleansed away.

"In the end, having assured ourselves that the after portion of the vessel was empty, we picked our ways to the bows, between the ugly gray nodules of that strange growth; and here we made a further search, which told us that there was indeed none aboard but ourselves. "This being now beyond any doubt, we returned to the stern of the ship and proceeded to make ourselves as comfortable as possible. Together we cleared out and cleaned two of the cabins, and after that I made examination whether there was anything eatable in the ship. This I soon found was so, and thanked God for His goodness. In addition to this I discovered a fresh-water pump, and having fixed it, I found the water drinkable, though somewhat unpleasant to the taste.

"For several days we stayed aboard the ship without attempting to get to the shore. We were busily engaged in making the place habitable. Yet even thus early we became aware that our lot was even less to be desired than might have been imagined; for though, as a first step, we scraped away the odd patches of growth that studded the floors and walls of the cabins and saloon, yet they returned almost to their original size within the space of twenty-four hours, which not only discouraged us but gave us a feeling of vague unease.

"Still we would nor admit ourselves beaten, so set to work afresh, and not only scraped away the fungus but soaked the places where it had been with carbolic, a canful of which I had found in the pantry. Yet by the end of the week the growth had returned in full strength, and in addition it had spread to other places, as though our touching it had allowed germs from it to travel elsewhere.

"On the seventh morning, my sweetheart woke to find a small patch of it growing on her pillow, close to her face. At that, she came to me, as soon as she could get her garments upon her. I was in the galley at the time, lighting the fire for breakfast."

'Come here, John,' she said, and led me aft. When I saw the thing upon her pillow I shuddered, and then and there we agreed to go right out of the ship and see whether we could not fare to make ourselves more comfortable ashore.

"Hurriedly we gathered together our few belongings, and even among these I found that the fungus had been at work, for one of her shawls had a little lump of it growing near one edge. I threw the whole thing over the side without saying anything to her.

"The raft was still alongside, but it was too clumsy to guide, and I lowered down a small boat that hung across the stern, and in this we made our way to the shore. Yet as we drew near to it, I became gradually aware that here the vile fungus, which had driven us from the ship, was growing riot. In places it rose into horrible, fantastic mounds, which seemed almost to quiver, as with a quiet life, when the wind blew across them. Here and there it took on the forms of vast fingers, and in others it just spread out flat and smooth and treacherous.

Odd places, it appeared as grotesque stunted trees, extraordinarily kinked and gnarled—the whole quaking vilely at times.

"At first it seemed to us that there was no single portion of the surrounding shore which was not hidden beneath the masses of the hideous lichen; yet in this I found we were mistaken, for somewhat later, coasting along the shore at a little distance, we descried a smooth white patch of what appeared to be fine sand, and there we landed. It was not sand. What it was I do not know.

All that I have observed is that upon it the fungus will not grow; while everywhere else, save where the sandlike earth wanders oddly, pathwise, amid the gray desolation of the lichen, there is nothing but that loathsome grayness.

"It is difficult to make you understand how cheered we were to find one place that was absolutely free from the growth, and here we deposited our belongings. Then we went back to the ship for such things as it seemed to us we should need. Among other matters, I managed to bring ashore with me one of the ship's sails. With it I constructed two small tents, which, though exceedingly rough-shaped, served the purposes for which they were intended. In these we lived and stored our various necessities, and thus for a matter of some four weeks all went smoothly and without particular unhappiness. Indeed, I may say with much happiness—for—we were together.

"It was on the thumb of her right hand that the growth first showed. It was only a small circular spot, much like a little gray mole My God! How the fear leaped to my heart when she showed me the place. We cleansed it, between us, washing it with carbolic and water. In the morning of the following day she showed her hand to me again. The gray warty thing had returned. For a little while we looked at one another in silence. Then, still wordless, we started again to remove it. In the midst of the operation she spoke suddenly."

'What's that on the side of your face, dear?' Her voice was sharp with anxiety. I put my hand up to feel."

'There! Under the hair by your ear. A little to the front a bit.' My finger rested upon the place, and then I knew."

'Let us get your thumb done first,' I said. And she submitted, only because she was afraid to touch me until it was cleansed. I finished washing and disinfecting her thumb, and then she turned to my face. After it was finished we sat together and talked awhile of many things; for there had come into our lives sudden, very terrible thoughts. We were, all at once, afraid of something worse than death. We spoke of loading the boat with provisions and water and making our way out onto the sea; yet we were helpless, for many causes, and—and the growth had attacked us already. We decided to stay. God would do with us what was His will. We would wait.

"A month, two months, three months passed and the places grew somewhat, and there had come others. Yet we fought so strenuously with the fear that its headway was but slow, comparatively speaking.

"Occasionally we ventured off to the ship for such stores as we needed. There we found that the fungus grew persistently. One of the nodules on the main deck soon became as high as my head.

"We had now given up all thought or hope of leaving the island. We had realized that it would be unallowable to go among healthy humans with the thing from which we were suffering.

"With this determination and knowledge in our minds we knew that we should have to husband our food and water; for we did not know, at that time, but that we should possibly live for many years.

"This reminds me that I have told you that I am an old man. Judged by years this is not so. But—but—"

He broke off, then continued somewhat abruptly, "As I was saying, we knew that we should have to use care in the matter of food. But we had no idea then how little food there was left of which to take care. It n was a week later that I made the discovery that all the other bread tanks—which I had supposed full—were empty, and that (beyond odd tins of vegetables and meat, and some other matters) we had nothing on which to depend but the bread in the tank which I had already opened.

"After learning this I bestirred myself to do what I could, and set to work at fishing in the lagoon; but with no success. At this I was somewhat inclined to feel desperate, until the thought came to me to try outside the lagoon, in the open sea.

"Here, at times, I caught odd fish, but so infrequently that they proved of but little help in keeping us from the hunger which threatened. It seemed to me that our deaths were likely to come by hunger, and not by the growth of the thing which had seized upon our bodies. "We were in this state of mind when the fourth month wore out. Then I made a very horrible discovery. One morning, a little before midday, I came off from the ship with a portion of the biscuits which were left. In the mouth of her tent I saw my sweetheart sitting, eating something." 'What is it, my dear?' I called out as I leaped ashore. Yet, on hearing my voice, she seemed confused, and turning, slyly threw something toward the edge of the little clearing. It fell short, and a vague suspicion having arisen within me, I walked across and picked it up. It was a piece of the gray fungus.

"As I went to her with it in my hand, she turned deadly pale; then a rose red.

"I felt strangely dazed and frightened.

" 'My dear! My dear!' I said, and could say no more. Yet at my words she broke down and cried bitterly. Gradually, as she calmed, I got from her the news that she had tried it the preceding day, and—and liked it. I got her to promise on her knees not to touch it again, however great our hunger. After she had promised, she told me that the desire for it had come suddenly, and that until the moment of desire, she had experienced nothing toward it but the most extreme repulsion.

"Later in the day, feeling strangely restless and much shaken with the thing which I had discovered, I made my way along one of the twisted paths—formed by the white, sandlike substance—which led among the fungoid growth. I had, once before, ventured along there, but not to any great distance. This time, being involved in perplexing thought, I went much farther than hitherto.

"Suddenly I was called to myself by a queer hoarse sound on my left. Turning quickly, I saw that there was movement among an extraordinarily shaped mass of fungus close to my elbow. It was swaying uneasily, as though it possessed life of its own. Abruptly, as I stared, the thought came to me that the thing had a grotesque resemblance to the figure of a distorted human creature. Even as the fancy flashed into my brain, there was a slight, sickening noise of tearing, and I saw that one of the branchlike arms was detaching itself from the surrounding masses, and coming toward me. The head of the thing, a shapeless gray ball, inclined in my direction. I stood stupidly, and the vile arm brushed across my face. I gave out a frightened cry and ran back a few paces. There was a sweetish taste upon my lips where the thing had touched me. I licked them, and was immediately filled with an inhuman desire. I turned and seized a mass of the fungus.

Then more, and—more. I was insatiable. In the midst of devouring, the remembrance of the morning's discovery swept into my amazed brain. It was sent by God. I dashed the fragment I held to the ground. Then, utterly wretched and feeling a dreadful guiltiness, I made my way back to the encampment.

"I think she knew, by some marvelous intuition which love must have given, so soon as she set eyes on me. Her quiet sympathy made it easier for me, and I told her of my sudden weakness, yet omitted to mention the extraordinary thing which had gone before. I desired to spare her all unnecessary terror.

"But for myself I had added an intolerable knowledge, to breed an incessant terror in my brain; for I doubted not that I had seen the end of one of these men who had come to the island in the ship in the lagoon; and in that monstrous ending I had seen our own.

"Thereafter we kept from the abominable food, though the desire for it had entered into our blood. Yet our dreary punishment was upon us; for day by day, with monstrous rapidity, the fungoid growth took hold of our poor bodies. Nothing we could do would check it materially, and so—and so—we who had been human became—Well, it matters less each day. Only—only we had been man and maid!

"And day by day the fight is more dreadful to withstand the hunger-lust for the terrible lichen.

"A week ago we ate the last of the biscuit, and since that time I have caught three fish. I was out here fishing tonight when your schooner drifted upon me out of the mist. I hailed you. You know the rest, and may God, out of His great heart, bless you for your goodness to a—a couple of poor outcast souls."

There was the dip of an oar—another. Then the voice came again, and for the last time, sounding through the slight surrounding mist, ghostly and mournful.

"God bless you! Good-by!"

"Good-by," we shouted together hoarsely, our hearts full of many emotions I glanced about me. I became aware that the dawn was upon us.

The sun flung a stray beam across the hidden sea, pierced the mist dully, and lit up the receding boat with a gloomy fire. Indistinctly I saw something nodding between the oars. I thought of a sponge—a great, gray nodding sponge. The oars continued to ply. They were gray—as was the boat—and my eyes searched a moment vainly for the conjunction of hand and oar. My gaze flashed back to the —head. It nodded forward as the oars went backward for the stroke. Then the oars were dipped, the boat shot out of the patch of light, and the—the thing went nodding into the mist.

The Monkey's Paw

W. W. Jacobs

I

Without, the night was cold and wet, but in the small parlor of Laburnam Villa the blinds were drawn and the fire burned brightly. Father and son were at chess, the former, who possessed ideas about the game involving radical changes, putting his king into such sharp and unnecessary perils that it even provoked comment from the white-haired old lady knitting placidly by the fire.

"Hark at the wind," said Mr. White, who, having seen a fatal mistake after it was too late, was amiably desirous of preventing his son from seeing it.

"I'm listening," said the latter, grimly surveying the board as he stretched out his hand. "Check."

"I should hardly think that he'd come to-night," said his father, with his hand poised over the board.

"Mate," replied the son.

"That's the worst of living so far out," bawled Mr. White, with sudden and unlooked-for violence; "of all the beastly, slushy, out-of-the-way places to live in, this is the worst. Pathway's a bog, and the road's a torrent. I don't know what people are thinking about. I suppose because only two houses in the road are let, they think it doesn't matter."

"Never mind, dear," said his wife, soothingly; "perhaps you'll win the next one."

Mr. White looked up sharply, just in time to intercept a knowing glance between mother and son. The words died away on his lips, and he hid a guilty grin in his thin grey beard.

"There he is," said Herbert White, as the gate banged to loudly and heavy footsteps came toward the door.

The old man rose with hospitable haste, and opening the door, was heard condoling with the new arrival. The new arrival also condoled with himself, so that Mrs. White said, "Tut, tut!" and coughed gently as her husband entered the room, followed by a tall, burly man, beady of eye and rubicund of visage.

"Sergeant-Major Morris," he said, introducing him.

The sergeant-major shook hands, and taking the proffered seat by the fire, watched contentedly while his host got out whiskey and tumblers and stood a small copper kettle on the fire.

At the third glass his eyes got brighter, and he began to talk, the little family circle regarding with eager interest this visitor from distant parts, as he squared his broad shoulders in the chair and spoke of wild scenes and doughty deeds; of wars and plagues and strange peoples.

"Twenty-one years of it," said Mr. White, nodding at his wife and son. "When he went away he was a slip of a youth in the warehouse. Now look at him."

"He don't look to have taken much harm," said Mrs. White, politely.

"I'd like to go to India myself," said the old man, "just to look round a bit, you know."

"Better where you are," said the sergeant-major, shaking his head. He put down the empty glass, and sighing softly, shook it again.

"I should like to see those old temples and fakirs and jugglers," said the old man. "What was that you started telling me the other day about a monkey's paw or something, Morris?"

"Nothing," said the soldier, hastily. "Leastways nothing worth hearing."

"Monkey's paw?" said Mrs. White, curiously.

"Well, it's just a bit of what you might call magic, perhaps," said the sergeant-major, offhandedly.

His three listeners leaned forward eagerly. The visitor absent-mindedly put his empty glass to his lips and then set it down again. His host filled it for him.

"To look at," said the sergeant-major, fumbling in his pocket, "it's just an ordinary little paw, dried to a mummy."

He took something out of his pocket and proffered it. Mrs. White drew back with a grimace, but her son, taking it, examined it curiously.

"And what is there special about it?" inquired Mr. White as he took it from his son, and having examined it, placed it upon the table.

"It had a spell put on it by an old fakir," said the sergeant-major, "a very holy man. He wanted to show that fate ruled people's lives, and that those who interfered with it did so to their sorrow. He put a spell on it so that three separate men could each have three wishes from it."

His manner was so impressive that his hearers were conscious that their light laughter jarred somewhat.

"Well, why don't you have three, sir?" said Herbert White, cleverly.

The soldier regarded him in the way that middle age is wont to regard presumptuous youth. "I have," he said, quietly, and his blotchy face whitened.

"And did you really have the three wishes granted?" asked Mrs. White.

"I did," said the sergeant-major, and his glass tapped against his strong teeth.

"And has anybody else wished?" persisted the old lady.

"The first man had his three wishes. Yes," was the reply; "I don't know what the first two were, but the third was for death. That's how I got the paw."

His tones were so grave that a hush fell upon the group.

"If you've had your three wishes, it's no good to you now, then, Morris," said the old man at last. "What do you keep it for?"

The soldier shook his head. "Fancy, I suppose," he said, slowly. "I did have some idea of selling it, but I don't think I will. It has caused enough mischief already. Besides, people won't buy. They think it's a fairy tale; some of them, and those who do think anything of it want to try it first and pay me afterward."

"If you could have another three wishes," said the old man, eyeing him keenly, "would you have them?"

"I don't know," said the other. "I don't know."

He took the paw, and dangling it between his forefinger and thumb, suddenly threw it upon the fire. White, with a slight cry, stooped down and snatched it off.

"Better let it burn," said the soldier, solemnly.

"If you don't want it, Morris," said the other, "give it to me."

"I won't," said his friend, doggedly. "I threw it on the fire. If you keep it, don't blame me for what happens. Pitch it on the fire again like a sensible man."

The other shook his head and examined his new possession closely. "How do you do it?" he inquired.

"Hold it up in your right hand and wish aloud," said the sergeant-major, "but I warn you of the consequences."

"Sounds like the Arabian Nights," said Mrs. White, as she rose and began to set the supper. "Don't you think you might wish for four pairs of hands for me?"

Her husband drew the talisman from pocket, and then all three burst into laughter as the sergeant-major, with a look of alarm on his face, caught him by the arm.

"If you must wish," he said, gruffly, "wish for something sensible."

Mr. White dropped it back in his pocket, and placing chairs, motioned his friend to the table. In the business of supper the talisman was partly forgotten, and afterward the three sat listening in an enthralled fashion to a second installment of the soldier's adventures in India.

"If the tale about the monkey's paw is not more truthful than those he has been telling us," said Herbert, as the door closed behind their guest, just in time for him to catch the last train, "we sha'nt make much out of it."

"Did you give him anything for it, father?" inquired Mrs. White, regarding her husband closely.

"A trifle," said he, coloring slightly. "He didn't want it, but I made him take it. And he pressed me again to throw it away."

"Likely," said Herbert, with pretended horror. "Why, we're going to be rich, and famous and happy. Wish to be an emperor, father, to begin with; then you can't be henpecked."

He darted round the table, pursued by the maligned Mrs. White armed with an antimacassar.

Mr. White took the paw from his pocket and eyed it dubiously. "I don't know what to wish for, and that's a fact," he said, slowly. "It seems to me I've got all I want."

"If you only cleared the house, you'd be quite happy, wouldn't you?" said Herbert, with his hand on his shoulder. "Well, wish for two hundred pounds, then; that 'll just do it."

His father, smiling shamefacedly at his own credulity, held up the talisman, as his son, with a solemn face, somewhat marred by a wink at his mother, sat down at the piano and struck a few impressive chords.

"I wish for two hundred pounds," said the old man distinctly.

A fine crash from the piano greeted the words, interrupted by a shuddering cry from the old man. His wife and son ran toward him.

"It moved," he cried, with a glance of disgust at the object as it lay on the floor.

"As I wished, it twisted in my hand like a snake."

"Well, I don't see the money," said his son as he picked it up and placed it on the table, "and I bet I never shall."

"It must have been your fancy, father," said his wife, regarding him anxiously.

He shook his head. "Never mind, though; there's no harm done, but it gave me a shock all the same."

They sat down by the fire again while the two men finished their pipes. Outside, the wind was higher than ever, and the old man started nervously at the sound of a door banging upstairs. A silence unusual and depressing settled upon all three, which lasted until the old couple rose to retire for the night.

"I expect you'll find the cash tied up in a big bag in the middle of your bed," said Herbert, as he bade them good-night, "and something horrible squatting up on top of the wardrobe watching you as you pocket your ill-gotten gains."

He sat alone in the darkness, gazing at the dying fire, and seeing faces in it. The last face was so horrible and so simian that he gazed at it in amazement. It got so vivid that, with a little uneasy laugh, he felt on the table for a glass containing a little water to throw over it. His hand grasped the monkey's paw, and with a little shiver he wiped his hand on his coat and went up to bed.

II.

In the brightness of the wintry sun next morning as it streamed over the breakfast table he laughed at his fears. There was an air of prosaic wholesomeness about the room which it had lacked on the previous night, and the dirty, shriveled little paw was pitched on the sideboard with a carelessness which betokened no great belief in its virtues.

"I suppose all old soldiers are the same," said Mrs. White. "The idea of our listening to such nonsense! How could wishes be granted in these days? And if they could, how could two hundred pounds hurt you, father?"

"Might drop on his head from the sky," said the frivolous Herbert.

"Morris said the things happened so naturally," said his father, "that you might if you so wished attribute it to coincidence."

"Well, don't break into the money before I come back," said Herbert as he rose from the table. "I'm afraid it'll turn you into a mean, avaricious man, and we shall have to disown you."

His mother laughed, and following him to the door, watched him down the road; and returning to the breakfast table, was very happy at the expense of her husband's credulity. All of which did not prevent her from scurrying to the door at the postman's knock, nor prevent her from referring somewhat shortly to retired sergeant-majors of bibulous habits when she found that the post brought a tailor's bill.

"Herbert will have some more of his funny remarks, I expect, when he comes home," she said, as they sat at dinner.

"I dare say," said Mr. White, pouring himself out some beer; "but for all that, the thing moved in my hand; that I'll swear to."

"You thought it did," said the old lady soothingly.

"I say it did," replied the other. "There was no thought about it; I had just—What's the matter?"

His wife made no reply. She was watching the mysterious movements of a man outside, who, peering in an undecided fashion at the house, appeared to be trying to make up his mind to enter. In mental connection with the two hundred pounds, she noticed that the stranger was well dressed, and wore a silk hat of glossy newness. Three times he paused at the gate, and then walked on again. The fourth time he stood with his hand upon it, and then with sudden resolution flung it open and walked up the path. Mrs. White at the same moment placed her hands behind her, and hurriedly unfastening the strings of her apron, put that useful article of apparel beneath the cushion of her chair.

She brought the stranger, who seemed ill at ease, into the room. He gazed at her furtively, and listened in a preoccupied fashion as the old lady apologized for the appearance of the room, and her husband's coat, a garment which he usually reserved for the garden. She then waited as patiently as her sex would permit, for him to broach his business, but he was at first strangely silent.

"I—was asked to call," he said at last, and stooped and picked a piece of cotton from his trousers. "I come from 'Maw and Meggins.'"

The old lady started. "Is anything the matter?" she asked, breathlessly. "Has anything happened to Herbert? What is it? What is it?"

Her husband interposed. "There, there, mother," he said, hastily. "Sit down, and don't jump to conclusions. You've not brought bad news, I'm sure, sir;" and he eyed the other wistfully.

"I'm sorry—" began the visitor.

"Is he hurt?" demanded the mother, wildly.

The visitor bowed in assent. "Badly hurt," he said, quietly, "but he is not in any pain."

"Oh, thank God!" said the old woman, clasping her hands. "Thank God for that! Thank—"

She broke off suddenly as the sinister meaning of the assurance dawned upon her and she saw the awful confirmation of her fears in the other's averted face. She caught her breath, and turning to her slower-witted husband, laid her trembling old hand upon his. There was a long silence.

"He was caught in the machinery," said the visitor at length in a low voice.

"Caught in the machinery," repeated Mr. White, in a dazed fashion, "yes."

He sat staring blankly out at the window, and taking his wife's hand between his own, pressed it as he had been wont to do in their old courting-days nearly forty years before.

"He was the only one left to us," he said, turning gently to the visitor. "It is hard."

The other coughed, and rising, walked slowly to the window. "The firm wished me to convey their sincere sympathy with you in your great loss," he said, without looking round. "I beg that you will understand I am only their servant and merely obeying orders."

There was no reply; the old woman's face was white, her eyes staring, and her breath inaudible; on the husband's face was a look such as his friend the sergeant might have carried into his first action.

"I was to say that 'Maw and Meggins' disclaim all responsibility," continued the other. "They admit no liability at all, but in consideration of your son's services, they wish to present you with a certain sum as compensation."

Mr. White dropped his wife's hand, and rising to his feet, gazed with a look of horror at his visitor. His dry lips shaped the words, "How much?"

"Two hundred pounds," was the answer.

Unconscious of his wife's shriek, the old man smiled faintly, put out his hands like a sightless man, and dropped, a senseless heap, to the floor.

III.

In the huge new cemetery, some two miles distant, the old people buried their dead, and came back to a house steeped in shadow and silence. It was all over so quickly that at first they could hardly realize it, and remained in a state of expectation as though of something else to happen—something else which was to lighten this load, too heavy for old hearts to bear.

But the days passed, and expectation gave place to resignation—the hopeless resignation of the old, sometimes miscalled, apathy. Sometimes they hardly exchanged a word, for now they had nothing to talk about, and their days were long to weariness.

It was about a week after that the old man, waking suddenly in the night, stretched out his hand and found himself alone. The room was in darkness, and the sound of subdued weeping came from the window. He raised himself in bed and listened.

"Come back," he said, tenderly. "You will be cold."

"It is colder for my son," said the old woman, and wept afresh.

The sound of her sobs died away on his ears. The bed was warm, and his eyes heavy with sleep. He dozed fitfully, and then slept until a sudden wild cry from his wife awoke him with a start.

"The paw!" she cried wildly. "The monkey's paw!"

He started up in alarm. "Where? Where is it? What's the matter?"

She came stumbling across the room toward him. "I want it," she said, quietly. "You've not destroyed it?"

"It's in the parlor, on the bracket," he replied, marveling. "Why?"

She cried and laughed together, and bending over, kissed his cheek.

"I only just thought of it," she said, hysterically. "Why didn't I think of it before? Why didn't you think of it?"

"Think of what?" he questioned.

"The other two wishes," she replied, rapidly. "We've only had one."

"Was not that enough?" he demanded, fiercely.

"No," she cried, triumphantly; "we'll have one more. Go down and get it quickly, and wish our boy alive again."

The man sat up in bed and flung the bedclothes from his quaking limbs. "Good God, you are mad!" he cried, aghast.

"Get it," she panted; "get it quickly, and wish—Oh, my boy, my boy!"

Her husband struck a match and lit the candle. "Get back to bed," he said, unsteadily. "You don't know what you are saying."

"We had the first wish granted," said the old woman, feverishly; "why not the second?"

"A coincidence," stammered the old man.

"Go and get it and wish," cried his wife, quivering with excitement.

The old man turned and regarded her, and his voice shook. "He has been dead ten days, and besides he—I would not tell you else, but—I could only recognize him by his clothing. If he was too terrible for you to see then, how now?"

"Bring him back," cried the old woman, and dragged him toward the door. "Do you think I fear the child I have nursed?"

He went down in the darkness, and felt his way to the parlor, and then to the mantelpiece. The talisman was in its place, and a horrible fear that the unspoken wish might bring his mutilated son before him ere he could escape from the room seized upon him, and he caught his breath as he found that he had lost the direction of the door. His brow cold with sweat, he felt his way round the table, and groped along the wall until he found himself in the small passage with the unwholesome thing in his hand.

Even his wife's face seemed changed as he entered the room. It was white and expectant, and to his fears seemed to have an unnatural look upon it. He was afraid of her.

"Wish!" she cried, in a strong voice.

"It is foolish and wicked," he faltered.

"Wish!" repeated his wife.

He raised his hand. "I wish my son alive again."

The talisman fell to the floor, and he regarded it fearfully. Then he sank trembling into a chair as the old woman, with burning eyes, walked to the window and raised the blind.

He sat until he was chilled with the cold, glancing occasionally at the figure of the old woman peering through the window. The candle-end, which had burned below the rim of the china candlestick, was throwing pulsating shadows on the ceiling and walls, until, with a flicker larger than the rest, it expired. The old man, with an unspeakable sense of relief at the failure of the talisman, crept back to his bed, and a minute or two afterward the old woman came silently and apathetically beside him.

Neither spoke, but lay silently listening to the ticking of the clock. A stair creaked, and a squeaky mouse scurried noisily through the wall. The darkness was oppressive, and after lying for some time screwing up his courage, he took the box of matches, and striking one, went downstairs for a candle.

At the foot of the stairs the match went out, and he paused to strike another; and at the same moment a knock, so quiet and stealthy as to be scarcely audible, sounded on the front door.

The matches fell from his hand and spilled in the passage. He stood motionless, his breath suspended until the knock was repeated. Then he turned and fled swiftly back to his room, and closed the door behind him. A third knock sounded through the house.

"What's that?" cried the old woman, starting up.

"A rat," said the old man in shaking tones—"a rat. It passed me on the stairs."

His wife sat up in bed listening. A loud knock resounded through the house.

"It's Herbert!" she screamed. "It's Herbert!"

She ran to the door, but her husband was before her, and catching her by the arm, held her tightly.

"What are you going to do?" he whispered hoarsely.

"It's my boy; it's Herbert!" she cried, struggling mechanically. "I forgot it was two miles away. What are you holding me for? Let go. I must open the door."

"For God's sake don't let it in," cried the old man, trembling.

"You're afraid of your own son," she cried, struggling. "Let me go. I'm coming, Herbert; I'm coming."

There was another knock, and another. The old woman with a sudden wrench broke free and ran from the room. Her husband followed to the landing, and called after her appealingly as she hurried downstairs. He heard the chain rattle back and the bottom bolt drawn slowly and stiffly from the socket. Then the old woman's voice, strained and panting.

"The bolt," she cried, loudly. "Come down. I can't reach it."

But her husband was on his hands and knees groping wildly on the floor in search of the paw. If he could only find it before the thing outside got in. A perfect fusillade of knocks reverberated through the house, and he heard the scraping of a chair as his wife put it down in the passage against the door. He heard the creaking of the bolt as it came slowly back, and at the same moment he found the monkey's paw, and frantically breathed his third and last wish.

The knocking ceased suddenly, although the echoes of it were still in the house. He heard the chair drawn back, and the door opened. A cold wind rushed up the staircase, and a long loud wail of disappointment and misery from his wife gave him courage to run down to her side, and then to the gate beyond. The street lamp flickering opposite shone on a quiet and deserted road.

The Fall of the House of Usher

Edgar Allan Poe

Son coeur est un luth suspendu;
Sitôt qu'on le touche il rèsonne.
De Béranger.

During the whole of a dull, dark, and soundless day in the autumn of the year, when the clouds hung oppressively low in the heavens, I had been passing alone, on horseback, through a singularly dreary tract of country; and at length found myself, as the shades of the evening drew on, within view of the melancholy House of Usher. I know not how it was—but, with the first glimpse of the building, a sense of insufferable gloom pervaded my spirit. I say insufferable; for the feeling was unrelieved by any of that half-pleasurable, because poetic, sentiment, with which the mind usually receives even the sternest natural images of the desolate or terrible. I looked upon the scene before me—upon the mere house, and the simple landscape features of the domain—upon the bleak walls—upon the vacant eye-like windows—upon a few rank sedges—and upon a few white trunks of decayed trees—with an utter depression of soul which I can compare to no earthly sensation more properly than to the after-dream of the reveler upon opium—the bitter lapse into everyday life—the hideous dropping off of the veil. There was an iciness, a sinking, a sickening of the heart—an unredeemed dreariness of thought which no goading of the imagination could torture into aught of the sublime. What was it—I paused to think—what was it that so unnerved me in the contemplation of the House of Usher? It was a mystery all insoluble; nor could I grapple with the shadowy fancies that crowded upon me as I pondered. I was forced to fall back upon the unsatisfactory conclusion, that while, beyond doubt, there *are* combinations of very simple natural objects which have the power of thus affecting us, still the analysis of this power lies among considerations beyond our depth. It was possible, I reflected, that a mere different arrangement of the particulars of the scene, of the details of the picture, would be sufficient to modify, or perhaps to annihilate its capacity for sorrowful impression; and, acting upon this idea, I reined my horse to the precipitous brink of a black and lurid tarn that lay in unruffled luster by the dwelling, and gazed down—but with a shudder even more thrilling than before—upon the remodeled and inverted images of the gray sedge, and the ghastly tree-stems, and the vacant and eye-like windows.

Nevertheless, in this mansion of gloom I now proposed to myself a sojourn of some weeks. Its proprietor, Roderick Usher, had been one of my boon companions in boyhood; but many years had elapsed since our last meeting. A letter, however, had lately reached me in a distant part of the country—a letter from him—which, in its wildly importunate nature, had admitted of no other than a personal reply. The MS. gave evidence of nervous agitation. The writer spoke of acute bodily illness—of a mental disorder which oppressed him—and of an earnest desire to see me, as his best, and indeed his only personal friend, with a view of attempting, by the cheerfulness of my society, some alleviation of his malady. It was the manner in which all this, and much more, was said—it was the apparent *heart* that went with his request—which allowed me no room for hesitation; and I accordingly obeyed forthwith what I still considered a very singular summons.

Although, as boys, we had been even intimate associates, yet I really knew little of my friend. His reserve had been always excessive and habitual. I was aware, however, that his very ancient family had been noted, time out of mind, for a peculiar sensibility of temperament, displaying itself, through long ages, in many works of exalted art, and manifested, of late, in repeated deeds of munificent yet unobtrusive charity, as well as in a passionate devotion to the intricacies, perhaps even more than to the orthodox and easily recognizable beauties, of musical science. I had learned, too, the very remarkable fact, that the stem of the Usher race, all time-honored as it was, had put forth, at no period, any enduring branch; in other words, that the entire family lay in the direct line of descent, and had always, with very trifling and very temporary variation, so lain. It was this deficiency, I considered, while running over in thought the perfect keeping of the character of the premises with the accredited character of the people, and while speculating upon the possible influence which the one, in the long lapse of centuries, might have exercised upon the other—it was this deficiency, perhaps, of collateral issue, and the consequent undeviating transmission, from sire to son, of the patrimony with the name, which had, at length, so identified the two as to merge the original title of the estate in the quaint and equivocal appellation of the "House of Usher"—an appellation which seemed to include, in the minds of the peasantry who used it, both the family and the family mansion.

I have said that the sole effect of my somewhat childish experiment—that of looking down within the tarn—had been to deepen the first singular impression. There can be no doubt that the consciousness of the rapid increase of my superstition—for why should I not so term it?—served mainly to accelerate the increase itself. Such, I have long known, is the paradoxical law of all sentiments having terror as a basis. And it might have been for this reason only, that, when I again uplifted my eyes to the house itself, from its image in the pool, there grew in my mind a strange fancy—a fancy so ridiculous, indeed, that I but mention it to show the vivid force of the sensations which oppressed me. I had so worked upon my imagination as really to believe that about the whole mansion and domain there hung an atmosphere peculiar to themselves and their immediate vicinity—an atmosphere which had no affinity with the air of heaven, but which had reeked up from the decayed trees, and the gray wall, and the silent tarn—a pestilent and mystic vapor, dull, sluggish, faintly discernible, and leaden-hued.

Shaking off from my spirit what *must* have been a dream, I scanned more narrowly the real aspect of the building. Its principal feature seemed to be that of an excessive antiquity. The discoloration of ages had been great. Minute fungi overspread the whole exterior, hanging in a fine tangled web-work from the eaves. Yet all this was apart from any extraordinary dilapidation. No portion of the masonry had fallen; and there appeared to be a wild inconsistency between its still perfect adaptation of parts, and the crumbling condition of the individual stones. In this there was much that reminded me of the specious totality of old wood-work which has rotted for long years in some neglected vault, with no disturbance from the breath of the external air. Beyond this indication of extensive decay, however, the fabric gave little token of instability. Perhaps the eye of a scrutinizing observer might have discovered a barely perceptible fissure, which, extending from the roof of the building in front, made its way down the wall in a zigzag direction, until it became lost in the sullen waters of the tarn.

Noticing these things, I rode over a short causeway to the house. A servant in waiting took my horse, and I entered the Gothic archway of the hall. A valet, of stealthy step, thence conducted me, in silence, through many dark and intricate passages in my progress to the *studio* of his master. Much that I encountered on the way contributed, I know not how, to heighten the vague sentiments of which I have already spoken. While the objects around me—while the carvings of the ceilings, the sombre tapestries of the walls, the ebon blackness of the floors, and the phantasmagoric armorial trophies which rattled as I strode, were but matters to which, or to such as which, I had been accustomed from my infancy—while I hesitated not to acknowledge how familiar was all this—I still wondered to find how unfamiliar were the fancies which ordinary images were stirring up. On one of the staircases, I met the physician of the family. His countenance, I thought, wore a mingled expression of low cunning and perplexity. He accosted me with trepidation and passed on. The valet now threw open a door and ushered me into the presence of his master.

The room in which I found myself was very large and lofty. The windows were long, narrow, and pointed, and at so vast a distance from the black oaken floor as to be altogether inaccessible from within. Feeble gleams of encrimsoned light made their way through the trellised panes, and served to render sufficiently distinct the more prominent objects around; the eye, however, struggled in vain to reach the remoter angles of the chamber, or the recesses of the vaulted and fretted ceiling. Dark draperies hung upon the walls. The general furniture was profuse, comfortless, antique, and tattered. Many books and musical instruments lay scattered about, but failed to give any vitality to the scene. I felt that I breathed an atmosphere of sorrow. An air of stern, deep, and irredeemable gloom hung over and pervaded all.

Upon my entrance, Usher arose from a sofa on which he had been lying at full length, and greeted me with a vivacious warmth which had much in it, I at first thought, of an overdone cordiality—of the constrained effort of the *ennuyé* man of the world. A glance, however, at his countenance, convinced me of his perfect sincerity. We sat down; and for some moments, while he spoke not, I gazed upon him with a feeling half of pity, half of awe. Surely, man had never before so terribly altered, in so brief a period, as had Roderick Usher! It was with difficulty that I could bring myself to admit the identity of the wan being before me with the companion of my early boyhood. Yet the character of his face had been at all times remarkable. A cadaverousness of complexion; an eye large, liquid, and luminous beyond comparison; lips somewhat thin and very pallid, but of a surpassingly beautiful curve; a nose of a delicate Hebrew model, but with a breadth of nostril unusual in similar formations; a finely moulded chin, speaking, in its want of prominence, of a want of moral energy; hair of a more than web-like softness and tenuity; these features, with an inordinate expansion above the regions of the temple, made up altogether a countenance not easily to be forgotten. And now in the mere exaggeration of the prevailing character of these features, and of the expression they were wont to convey, lay so much of change that I doubted to whom I spoke. The now ghastly pallor of the skin, and the now miraculous luster of the eye, above all things startled and even awed me. The silken hair, too, had been suffered to grow all unheeded, and as, in its wild gossamer texture, it floated rather than fell about the face, I could not, even with effort, connect its Arabesque expression with any idea of simple humanity.

In the manner of my friend I was at once struck with an incoherence—an inconsistency; and I soon found this to arise from a series of feeble and futile struggles to overcome an habitual trepidancy—an excessive nervous agitation. For something of this nature I had indeed been prepared, no less by his letter, than by reminiscences of certain boyish traits, and by conclusions deduced from his peculiar physical conformation and temperament. His action was alternately vivacious and sullen. His voice varied rapidly from a tremulous indecision (when the animal spirits seemed utterly in abeyance) to that species of energetic concision—that abrupt, weighty, unhurried, and hollow-sounding enunciation—that leaden, self-balanced and perfectly modulated guttural utterance, which may be observed in the lost drunkard, or the irreclaimable eater of opium, during the periods of his most intense excitement.

It was thus that he spoke of the object of my visit, of his earnest desire to see me, and of the solace he expected me to afford him. He entered, at some length, into what he conceived to be the nature of his malady. It was, he said, a constitutional and a family evil, and one for which he despaired to find a remedy—a mere nervous affection, he immediately added, which would undoubtedly soon pass off. It displayed itself in a host of unnatural sensations. Some of these, as he detailed them, interested and bewildered me; although, perhaps, the terms, and the general manner of the narration had their weight. He suffered much from a morbid acuteness of the senses; the most insipid food was alone endurable; he could wear only garments of certain texture; the odors of all flowers were oppressive; his eyes were tortured by even a faint light; and there were but peculiar sounds, and these from stringed instruments, which did not inspire him with horror.

To an anomalous species of terror I found him a bounden slave. "I shall perish," said he, "I must perish in this deplorable folly. Thus, thus, and not otherwise, shall I be lost. I dread the events of the future, not in themselves, but in their results. I shudder at the thought of any, even the most trivial, incident, which may operate upon this intolerable agitation of soul. I have, indeed, no abhorrence of danger, except in its absolute effect—in terror. In this unnerved—in this pitiable condition—I feel that the period will sooner or later arrive when I must abandon life and reason together, in some struggle with the grim phantasm, FEAR."

I learned, moreover, at intervals, and through broken and equivocal hints, another singular feature of his mental condition. He was enchained by certain superstitious impressions in regard to the dwelling which he tenanted, and whence, for many years, he had never ventured forth—in regard to an influence whose supposititious force was conveyed in terms too shadowy here to be re-stated—an influence which some peculiarities in the mere form and substance of his family mansion, had, by dint of long sufferance, he said, obtained over his spirit—an effect which the *physique* of the gray walls and turrets, and of the dim tarn into which they all looked down, had, at length, brought about upon the *morale* of his existence.

He admitted, however, although with hesitation, that much of the peculiar gloom which thus afflicted him could be traced to a more natural and far more palpable origin—to the severe and long-continued illness—indeed to the evidently approaching dissolution—of a tenderly beloved sister—his sole companion for long years—his last and only relative on earth. "Her decease," he said, with a bitterness which I can never forget, "would leave him (him the hopeless and the frail) the last of the ancient race of the Ushers." While he spoke, the lady Madeline (for so was she called) passed slowly through a remote portion of the apartment, and, without having noticed my presence, disappeared. I regarded her with an utter astonishment not unmingled with dread—and yet I found it impossible to account for such feelings. A sensation of stupor oppressed me, as my eyes followed her retreating steps. When a door, at length, closed upon her, my glance sought instinctively and eagerly the countenance of the brother—but he had buried his face in his hands, and I could only perceive that a far more than ordinary wanness had overspread the emaciated fingers through which trickled many passionate tears.

The disease of the lady Madeline had long baffled the skill of her physicians. A settled apathy, a gradual wasting away of the person, and frequent although transient affections of a partially cataleptical character, were the unusual diagnosis. Hitherto she had steadily borne up against the pressure of her malady, and had not betaken herself finally to bed; but, on the closing in of the evening of my arrival at the house, she succumbed (as her brother told me at night with inexpressible agitation) to the prostrating power of the destroyer; and I learned that the glimpse I had obtained of her person would thus probably be the last I should obtain—that the lady, at least while living, would be seen by me no more.

For several days ensuing, her name was unmentioned by either Usher or myself: and during this period I was busied in earnest endeavors to alleviate the melancholy of my friend. We painted and read together; or I listened, as if in a dream, to the wild improvisations of his speaking guitar. And thus, as a closer and still closer intimacy admitted me more unreservedly into the recesses of his spirit, the more bitterly did I perceive the futility of all attempt at cheering a mind from which darkness, as if an inherent positive quality, poured forth upon all objects of the moral and physical universe, in one unceasing radiation of gloom.

I shall ever bear about me a memory of the many solemn hours I thus spent alone with the master of the House of Usher. Yet I should fail in any attempt to convey an idea of the exact character of the studies, or of the occupations, in which he involved me, or led me the way. An excited and highly distempered ideality threw a sulphureous lustre over all. His long improvised dirges will ring forever in my ears. Among other things, I hold painfully in mind a certain singular perversion and amplification of the wild air of the last waltz of Von Weber. From the paintings over which his elaborate fancy brooded, and which grew, touch by touch, into vaguenesses at which I shuddered the more thrillingly, because I shuddered knowing not why;—from these paintings (vivid as their images now are before me) I would in vain endeavor to educe more than a small portion which should lie within the compass of merely written words. By the utter simplicity, by the nakedness of his designs, he arrested and overawed attention. If ever mortal painted an idea, that mortal was Roderick Usher. For me at least—in the circumstances then surrounding me—there arose out of the pure abstractions which the hypochondriac contrived to throw upon his canvass, an intensity of intolerable awe, no shadow of which felt I ever yet in the contemplation of the certainly glowing yet too concrete reveries of Fuseli.

One of the phantasmagoric conceptions of my friend, partaking not so rigidly of the spirit of abstraction, may be shadowed forth, although feebly, in words. A small picture presented the interior of an immensely long and rectangular vault or tunnel, with low walls, smooth, white, and without interruption or device. Certain accessory points of the design served well to convey the idea that this excavation lay at an exceeding depth below the surface of the earth. No outlet was observed in any portion of its vast extent, and no torch, or other artificial source of light was discernible; yet a flood of intense rays rolled throughout, and bathed the whole in a ghastly and inappropriate splendor.

I have just spoken of that morbid condition of the auditory nerve which rendered all music intolerable to the sufferer, with the exception of certain effects of stringed instruments. It was, perhaps, the narrow limits to which he thus confined himself upon the guitar, which gave birth, in great measure, to the fantastic character of his performances. But the fervid *facility* of his *impromptus* could not be so accounted for. They must have been, and were, in the notes, as well as in the words of his wild fantasias (for he not unfrequently accompanied himself with rhymed verbal improvisations), the result of that intense mental collectedness and concentration to which I have previously alluded as observable only in particular moments of the highest artificial excitement. The words of one of these rhapsodies I have easily remembered. I was, perhaps, the more forcibly impressed with it, as he gave it, because, in the under or mystic current of its meaning, I fancied that I perceived, and for the first time, a full consciousness on the part of Usher, of the tottering of his lofty reason upon her throne. The verses, which were entitled "The Haunted Palace," ran very nearly, if not accurately, thus:

I.

In the greenest of our valleys,
By good angels tenanted,
Once a fair and stately palace—
Radiant palace—reared its head.
In the monarch Thought's dominion—
It stood there!
Never seraph spread a pinion
Over fabric half so fair.

II.

Banners yellow, glorious, golden,
On its roof did float and flow;
(This—all this—was in the olden
Time long ago)
And every gentle air that dallied,
In that sweet day,
Along the ramparts plumed and pallid,
A winged odor went away.

III.

Wanderers in that happy valley
Through two luminous windows saw
Spirits moving musically
To a lute's well-tunéd law,
Round about a throne, where sitting
(Porphyrogene!)
In state his glory well befitting,
The ruler of the realm was seen.

IV.

And all with pearl and ruby glowing

Was the fair palace door,
Through which came flowing, flowing, flowing,
And sparkling evermore,
A troop of Echoes whose sweet duty
Was but to sing,
In voices of surpassing beauty,
The wit and wisdom of their king.

V.

But evil things, in robes of sorrow,
Assailed the monarch's high estate;
(Ah, let us mourn, for never morrow
Shall dawn upon him, desolate!)
And, round about his home, the glory
That blushed and bloomed
Is but a dim-remembered story
Of the old time entombed.

VI.

And travellers now within that valley,
Through the red-litten windows, see
Vast forms that move fantastically
To a discordant melody;
While, like a rapid ghastly river,
Through the pale door,
A hideous throng rush out forever,
And laugh—but smile no more.

I well remember that suggestions arising from this ballad, led us into a train of thought wherein there became manifest an opinion of Usher's which I mention not so much on account of its novelty, (for other men—Watson, Dr. Percival, Spallanzani, and especially the Bishop of Llandaff—have thought thus,) as on account of the pertinacity with which he maintained it. This opinion, in its general form, was that of the sentience of all vegetable things. But, in his disordered fancy, the idea had assumed a more daring character, and trespassed, under certain conditions, upon the kingdom of inorganization. I lack words to express the full extent, or the earnest *abandon* of his persuasion. The belief, however, was connected (as I have previously hinted) with the gray stones of the home of his forefathers. The conditions of the sentience had been here, he imagined, fulfilled in the method of collocation of these stones—in the order of their arrangement, as well as in that of the many *fungi* which overspread them, and of the decayed trees which stood around—above all, in the long undisturbed endurance of this arrangement, and in its reduplication in the still waters of the tarn. Its evidence—the evidence of the sentience—was to be seen, he said, (and I here started as he spoke,) in the gradual yet certain condensation of an atmosphere of their own about the waters and the walls. The result was discoverable, he added, in that silent, yet importunate and terrible influence which for centuries had moulded the destinies of his family, and which made *him* what I now saw him—what he was. Such opinions need no comment, and I will make none.

Our books—the books which, for years, had formed no small portion of the mental existence of the invalid—were, as might be supposed, in strict keeping with this character of phantasm. We pored together over such works as the Ververt et Chartreuse of Gresset; the Belphegor of Machiavelli; the Heaven and Hell of Swedenborg; the Subterranean Voyage of Nicholas Klimm by Holberg; the Chiromancy of Robert Flud, of Jean D'Indaginé, and of De la Chambre; the Journey into the Blue Distance of Tieck; and the City of the Sun of Campanella. One favorite volume was a small octavo edition of the *Directorium Inquisitorium*, by the Dominican Eymeric de Gironne; and there were passages in Pomponius Mela, about the old African Satyrs and OEgipans, over which Usher would sit dreaming for hours. His chief delight, however, was found in the perusal of an exceedingly rare and curious book in quarto Gothic—the manual of a forgotten church—the *Vigiliae Mortuorum secundum Chorum Ecclesiae Maguntinae*.

I could not help thinking of the wild ritual of this work, and of its probable influence upon the hypochondriac, when, one evening, having informed me abruptly that the lady Madeline was no more, he stated his intention of preserving her corpse for a fortnight, (previously to its final interment,) in one of the numerous vaults within the main walls of the building. The worldly reason, however, assigned for this singular proceeding, was one which I did not feel at liberty to dispute. The brother had been led to his resolution (so he told me) by consideration of the unusual character of the malady of the deceased, of certain obtrusive and eager inquiries on the part of her medical men, and of the remote and exposed situation of the burial-ground of the family. I will not deny that when I called to mind the sinister countenance of the person whom I met upon the staircase, on the day of my arrival at the house, I had no desire to oppose what I regarded as at best but a harmless, and by no means an unnatural, precaution.

At the request of Usher, I personally aided him in the arrangements for the temporary entombment. The body having been encoffined, we two alone bore it to its rest. The vault in which we placed it (and which had been so long unopened that our torches, half smothered in its oppressive atmosphere, gave us little opportunity for investigation) was small, damp, and entirely without means of admission for light; lying, at great depth, immediately beneath that portion of the building in which was my own sleeping apartment. It had been used, apparently, in remote feudal times, for the worst purposes of a donjon-keep, and, in later days, as a place of deposit for powder, or some other highly combustible substance, as a portion of its floor, and the whole interior of a long archway through which we reached it, were carefully sheathed with copper. The door, of massive iron, had been, also, similarly protected. Its immense weight caused an unusually sharp grating sound, as it moved upon its hinges.

Having deposited our mournful burden upon tressels within this region of horror, we partially turned aside the yet unscrewed lid of the coffin, and looked upon the face of the tenant. A striking similitude between the brother and sister now first arrested my attention; and Usher, divining, perhaps, my thoughts, murmured out some few words from which I learned that the deceased and himself had been twins, and that sympathies of a scarcely intelligible nature had always existed between them. Our glances, however, rested not long upon the dead—for we could not regard her unawed. The disease which had thus entombed the lady in the maturity of youth, had left, as usual in all maladies of a strictly cataleptical character, the mockery of a faint blush upon the bosom and the face, and that suspiciously lingering smile upon the lip which is so terrible in death. We replaced and screwed down the lid, and, having secured the door of iron, made our way, with toil, into the scarcely less gloomy apartments of the upper portion of the house.

And now, some days of bitter grief having elapsed, an observable change came over the features of the mental disorder of my friend. His ordinary manner had vanished. His ordinary occupations were neglected or forgotten. He roamed from chamber to chamber with hurried, unequal, and objectless step. The pallor of his countenance had assumed, if possible, a more ghastly hue—but the luminousness of his eye had utterly gone out. The once occasional huskiness of his tone was heard no more; and a tremulous quaver, as if of extreme terror, habitually characterized his utterance. There were times, indeed, when I thought his unceasingly agitated mind was laboring with some oppressive secret, to divulge which he struggled for the necessary courage. At times, again, I was obliged to resolve all into the mere inexplicable vagaries of madness, for I beheld him gazing upon vacancy for long hours, in an attitude of the profoundest attention, as if listening to some imaginary sound. It was no wonder that his condition terrified—that it infected me. I felt creeping upon me, by slow yet certain degrees, the wild influences of his own fantastic yet impressive superstitions.

It was, especially, upon retiring to bed late in the night of the seventh or eighth day after the placing of the lady Madeline within the donjon, that I experienced the full power of such feelings. Sleep came not near my couch—while the hours waned and waned away. I struggled to reason off the nervousness which had dominion over me. I endeavored to believe that much, if not all of what I felt, was due to the bewildering influence of the gloomy furniture of the room—of the dark and tattered draperies, which, tortured into motion by the breath of a rising tempest, swayed fitfully to and fro upon the walls, and rustled uneasily about the decorations of the bed. But my efforts were fruitless. An irrepressible tremor gradually pervaded my frame; and, at length, there sat upon my very heart an incubus of utterly causeless alarm. Shaking this off with a gasp and a struggle, I uplifted myself upon the pillows, and, peering earnestly within the intense darkness of the chamber, harkened—I know not why, except that an instinctive spirit prompted me—to certain low and indefinite sounds which came, through the pauses of the storm, at long intervals, I knew not whence. Overpowered by an intense sentiment of horror, unaccountable yet unendurable, I threw on my clothes with haste (for I felt that I should sleep no more during the night), and endeavored to arouse myself from the pitiable condition into which I had fallen, by pacing rapidly to and fro through the apartment.

I had taken but few turns in this manner, when a light step on an adjoining staircase arrested my attention. I presently recognized it as that of Usher. In an instant afterward he rapped, with a gentle touch, at my door, and entered, bearing a lamp. His countenance was, as usual, cadaverously wan—but, moreover, there was a species of mad hilarity in his eyes—an evidently restrained *hysteria* in his whole demeanor. His air appalled me—but anything was preferable to the solitude which I had so long endured, and I even welcomed his presence as a relief.

"And you have not seen it?" he said abruptly, after having stared about him for some moments in silence—"you have not then seen it?—but, stay! you shall." Thus speaking, and having carefully shaded his lamp, he hurried to one of the casements, and threw it freely open to the storm.

The impetuous fury of the entering gust nearly lifted us from our feet. It was, indeed, a tempestuous yet sternly beautiful night, and one wildly singular in its terror and its beauty. A whirlwind had apparently collected its force in our vicinity; for there were frequent and violent alterations in the direction of the wind; and the exceeding density of the clouds (which hung so low as to press upon the turrets of the house) did not prevent our perceiving the life-like velocity with which they flew careering from all points against each other, without passing away into the distance. I say that even their exceeding density did not prevent our perceiving this—yet we had no glimpse of the moon or stars—nor was there any flashing forth of the lightning. But the under surfaces of the huge masses of agitated vapor, as well as all terrestrial objects immediately around us, were glowing in the unnatural light of a faintly luminous and distinctly visible gaseous exhalation which hung about and enshrouded the mansion.

"You must not—you shall not behold this!" said I, shudderingly, to Usher, as I led him, with a gentle violence, from the window to a seat. "These appearances, which bewilder you, are merely electrical phenomena not uncommon—or it may be that they have their ghastly origin in the rank miasma of the tarn. Let us close this casement;—the air is chilling and dangerous to your frame. Here is one of your favorite romances. I will read, and you shall listen;—and so we will pass away this terrible night together."

The antique volume which I had taken up was the "Mad Trist" of Sir Launcelot Canning; but I had called it a favorite of Usher's more in sad jest than in earnest; for, in truth, there is little in its uncouth and unimaginative prolixity which could have had interest for the lofty and spiritual ideality of my friend. It was, however, the only book immediately at hand; and I indulged a vague hope that the excitement which now agitated the hypochondriac, might find relief (for the history of mental disorder is full of similar anomalies) even in the extremeness of the folly which I should read. Could I have judged, indeed, by the wild overstrained air of vivacity with which he harkened, or apparently harkened, to the words of the tale, I might well have congratulated myself upon the success of my design.

I had arrived at that well-known portion of the story where Ethelred, the hero of the Trist, having sought in vain for peaceable admission into the dwelling of the hermit, proceeds to make good an entrance by force. Here, it will be remembered, the words of the narrative run thus:

"And Ethelred, who was by nature of a doughty heart, and who was now mighty withal, on account of the powerfulness of the wine which he had drunken, waited no longer to hold parley with the hermit, who, in sooth, was of an obstinate and maliceful turn, but, feeling the rain upon his shoulders, and fearing the rising of the tempest, uplifted his mace outright, and, with blows, made quickly room in the plankings of the door for his gauntleted hand; and now pulling therewith sturdily, he so cracked, and ripped, and tore all asunder, that the noise of the dry and hollow-sounding wood alarummed and reverberated throughout the forest."

At the termination of this sentence I started, and for a moment, paused; for it appeared to me (although I at once concluded that my excited fancy had deceived me)—it appeared to me that, from some very remote portion of the mansion, there came, indistinctly, to my ears, what might have been, in its exact similarity of character, the echo (but a stifled and dull one certainly) of the very cracking and ripping sound which Sir Launcelot had so particularly described. It was, beyond doubt, the coincidence alone which had arrested my attention; for, amid the rattling of the sashes of the casements, and the ordinary commingled noises of the still increasing storm, the sound, in itself, had nothing, surely, which should have interested or disturbed me. I continued the story:

"But the good champion Ethelred, now entering within the door, was sore enraged and amazed to perceive no signal of the maliceful hermit; but, in the stead thereof, a dragon of a scaly and prodigious demeanor, and of a fiery tongue, which sate in guard before a palace of gold, with a floor of silver; and upon the wall there hung a shield of shining brass with this legend enwritten—

Who entereth herein, a conqueror hath bin;
Who slayeth the dragon, the shield he shall win;

And Ethelred uplifted his mace, and struck upon the head of the dragon, which fell before him, and gave up his pesty breath, with a shriek so horrid and harsh, and withal so piercing, that Ethelred had fain to close his ears with his hands against the dreadful noise of it, the like whereof was never before heard."

Here again I paused abruptly, and now with a feeling of wild amazement—for there could be no doubt whatever that, in this instance, I did actually hear (although from what direction it proceeded I found it impossible to say) a low and apparently distant, but harsh, protracted, and most unusual screaming or grating sound—the exact counterpart of what my fancy had already conjured up for the dragon's unnatural shriek as described by the romancer.

Oppressed, as I certainly was, upon the occurrence of this second and most extraordinary coincidence, by a thousand conflicting sensations, in which wonder and extreme terror were predominant, I still retained sufficient presence of mind to avoid exciting, by any observation, the sensitive nervousness of my companion. I was by no means certain that he had noticed the sounds in question; although, assuredly, a strange alteration had, during the last few minutes, taken place in his demeanor. From a position fronting my own, he had gradually brought round his chair, so as to sit with his face to the door of the chamber; and thus I could but partially perceive his features, although I saw that his lips trembled as if he were murmuring inaudibly. His head had dropped upon his breast—yet I knew that he was not asleep, from the wide and rigid opening of the eye as I caught a glance of it in profile. The motion of his body, too, was at variance with this idea—for he rocked from side to side with a gentle yet constant and uniform sway. Having rapidly taken notice of all this, I resumed the narrative of Sir Launcelot, which thus proceeded:

"And now, the champion, having escaped from the terrible fury of the dragon, bethinking himself of the brazen shield, and of the breaking up of the enchantment which was upon it, removed the carcass from out of the way before him, and approached valorously over the silver pavement of the castle to where the shield was upon the wall; which in sooth tarried not for his full coming, but feel down at his feet upon the silver floor, with a mighty great and terrible ringing sound."

No sooner had these syllables passed my lips, than—as if a shield of brass had indeed, at the moment, fallen heavily upon a floor of silver—I became aware of a distinct, hollow, metallic, and clangorous, yet apparently muffled reverberation. Completely unnerved, I leaped to my feet; but the measured rocking movement of Usher was undisturbed. I rushed to the chair in which he sat. His eyes were bent fixedly before him, and throughout his whole countenance there reigned a stony rigidity. But, as I placed my hand upon his shoulder, there came a strong shudder over his whole person; a sickly smile quivered about his lips; and I saw that he spoke in a low, hurried, and gibbering murmur, as if unconscious of my presence. Bending closely over him, I at length drank in the hideous import of his words.

"Not hear it?—yes, I hear it, and *have* heard it. Long—long—long—many minutes, many hours, many days, have I heard it—yet I dared not—oh, pity me, miserable wretch that I am!—I dared not—I *dared* not speak! *We have put her living in the tomb!* Said I not that my senses were acute? I *now* tell you that I heard her first feeble movements in the hollow coffin. I heard them—many, many days ago—yet I dared not—*I dared not speak!* And now—to-night—

Ethelred—ha! ha!—the breaking of the hermit's door, and the death-cry of the dragon, and the clangor of the shield!—say, rather, the rending of her coffin, and the grating of the iron hinges of her prison, and her struggles within the coppered archway of the vault! Oh whither shall I fly? Will she not be here anon? Is she not hurrying to upbraid me for my haste? Have I not heard her footstep on the stair? Do I not distinguish that heavy and horrible beating of her heart? Madman!"—here he sprang furiously to his feet, and shrieked out his syllables, as if in the effort he were giving up his soul—"*Madman! I tell you that she now stands without the door!*"

As if in the superhuman energy of his utterance there had been found the potency of a spell—the huge antique panels to which the speaker pointed, threw slowly back, upon the instant, their ponderous and ebony jaws. It was the work of the rushing gust—but then without those doors there *did* stand the lofty and enshrouded figure of the lady Madeline of Usher. There was blood upon her white robes, and the evidence of some bitter struggle upon every portion of her emaciated frame. For a moment she remained trembling and reeling to and fro upon the threshold—then, with a low moaning cry, fell heavily inward upon the person of her brother, and in her violent and now final death-agonies, bore him to the floor a corpse, and a victim to the terrors he had anticipated.

From that chamber, and from that mansion, I fled aghast. The storm was still abroad in all its wrath as I found myself crossing the old causeway. Suddenly there shot along the path a wild light, and I turned to see whence a gleam so unusual could have issued; for the vast house and its shadows were alone behind me. The radiance was that of the full, setting, and blood-red moon, which now shone vividly through that once barely-discernible fissure, of which I have before spoken as extending from the roof of the building, in a zigzag direction, to the base. While I gazed, this fissure rapidly widened—there came a fierce breath of the whirlwind—the entire orb of the satellite burst at once upon my sight—my brain reeled as I saw the mighty walls rushing asunder—there was a long tumultuous shouting sound like the voice of a thousand waters—and the deep and dank tarn at my feet closed sullenly and silently over the fragments of the "*House of Usher*."

The Willows

Algernon Blackwood

I

After leaving Vienna, and long before you come to Budapest, the Danube enters a region of singular loneliness and desolation, where its waters spread away on all sides regardless of a main channel, and the country becomes a swamp for miles upon miles, covered by a vast sea of low willow-bushes. On the big maps this deserted area is painted in a fluffy blue, growing fainter in color as it leaves the banks, and across it may be seen in large straggling letters the word Sumpfe, meaning marshes.

In high flood this great acreage of sand, shingle-beds, and willow-grown islands is almost topped by the water, but in normal seasons the bushes bend and rustle in the free winds, showing their silver leaves to the sunshine in an ever-moving plain of bewildering beauty. These willows never attain to the dignity of trees; they have no rigid trunks; they remain humble bushes, with rounded tops and soft outline, swaying on slender stems that answer to the least pressure of the wind; supple as grasses, and so continually shifting that they somehow give the impression that the entire plain is moving and alive. For the wind sends waves rising and falling over the whole surface, waves of leaves instead of waves of water, green swells like the sea, too, until the branches turn and lift, and then silvery white as their underside turns to the sun.

Happy to slip beyond the control of the stern banks, the Danube here wanders about at will among the intricate network of channels intersecting the islands everywhere with broad avenues down which the waters pour with a shouting sound; making whirlpools, eddies, and foaming rapids; tearing at the sandy banks; carrying away masses of shore and willow-clumps; and forming new islands innumerably which shift daily in size and shape and possess at best an impermanent life, since the flood-time obliterates their very existence.

Properly speaking, this fascinating part of the river's life begins soon after leaving Pressburg, and we, in our Canadian canoe, with gipsy tent and frying-pan on board, reached it on the crest of a rising flood about mid-July. That very same morning, when the sky was reddening before sunrise, we had slipped swiftly through still-sleeping Vienna, leaving it a couple of hours later a mere patch of smoke against the blue hills of the Wienerwald on the horizon; we had breakfasted below Fischeramend under a grove of birch trees roaring in the wind; and had then swept on the tearing current past Orth, Hainburg, Petronell (the old Roman Carnuntum of Marcus Aurelius), and so under the frowning heights of Thelsen on a spur of the Carpathians, where the March steals in quietly from the left and the frontier is crossed between Austria and Hungary.

Racing along at twelve kilometers an hour soon took us well into Hungary, and the muddy waters—sure sign of flood—sent us aground on many a shingle-bed, and twisted us like a cork in many a sudden belching whirlpool before the towers of Pressburg (Hungarian, Poszony) showed against the sky; and then the canoe, leaping like a spirited horse, flew at top speed under the grey walls, negotiated safely the sunken chain of the Fliegende Brucke ferry, turned the corner sharply to the left, and plunged on yellow foam into the wilderness of islands, sandbanks, and swamp-land beyond—the land of the willows.

The change came suddenly, as when a series of bioscope pictures snaps down on the streets of a town and shifts without warning into the scenery of lake and forest. We entered the land of desolation on wings, and in less than half an hour there was neither boat nor fishing-hut nor red roof, nor any single sign of human habitation and civilization within sight. The sense of remoteness from the world of humankind, the utter isolation, the fascination of this singular world of willows, winds, and waters, instantly laid its spell upon us both, so that we allowed laughingly to one another that we ought by rights to have held some special kind of passport to admit us, and that we had, somewhat audaciously, come without asking leave into a separate little kingdom of wonder and magic—a kingdom that was reserved for the use of others who had a right to it, with everywhere unwritten warnings to trespassers for those who had the imagination to discover them.

Though still early in the afternoon, the ceaseless buffetings of a most tempestuous wind made us feel weary, and we at once began casting about for a suitable camping-ground for the night. But the bewildering character of the islands made landing difficult; the swirling flood carried us in shore and then swept us out again; the willow branches tore our hands as we seized them to stop the canoe, and we pulled many a yard of sandy bank into the water before at length we shot with a great sideways blow from the wind into a backwater and managed to beach the bows in a cloud of spray. Then we lay panting and laughing after our exertions on the hot yellow sand, sheltered from the wind, and in the full blaze of a scorching sun, a cloudless blue sky above, and an immense army of dancing, shouting willow bushes, closing in from all sides, shining with spray and clapping their thousand little hands as though to applaud the success of our efforts.

"What a river!" I said to my companion, thinking of all the way we had traveled from the source in the Black Forest, and how he had often been obliged to wade and push in the upper shallows at the beginning of June.

"Won't stand much nonsense now, will it?" he said, pulling the canoe a little farther into safety up the sand, and then composing himself for a nap.

I lay by his side, happy and peaceful in the bath of the elements—water, wind, sand, and the great fire of the sun—thinking of the long journey that lay behind us, and of the great stretch before us to the Black Sea, and how lucky I was to have such a delightful and charming traveling companion as my friend, the Swede.

We had made many similar journeys together, but the Danube, more than any other river I knew, impressed us from the very beginning with its aliveness. From its tiny bubbling entry into the world among the pinewood gardens of Donaueschingen, until this moment when it began to play the great river-game of losing itself among the deserted swamps, unobserved, unrestrained, it had seemed to us like following the grown of some living creature. Sleepy at first, but later developing violent desires as it became conscious of its deep soul, it rolled, like some huge fluid being, through all the countries we had passed, holding our little craft on its mighty shoulders, playing roughly with us sometimes, yet always friendly and well-meaning, till at length we had come inevitably to regard it as a Great Personage.

How, indeed, could it be otherwise, since it told us so much of its secret life? At night we heard it singing to the moon as we lay in our tent, uttering that odd sibilant note peculiar to itself and said to be caused by the rapid tearing of the pebbles along its bed, so great is its hurrying speed. We knew, too, the voice of its gurgling whirlpools, suddenly bubbling up on a surface previously quite calm; the roar of its shallows and swift rapids; its constant steady thundering below all mere surface sounds; and that ceaseless tearing of its icy waters at the banks. How it stood up and shouted when the rains fell flat upon its face! And how its laughter roared out when the wind blew up-stream and tried to stop its growing speed! We knew all its sounds and voices, its tumblings and foamings, its unnecessary splashing against the bridges; that self-conscious chatter when there were hills to look on; the affected dignity of its speech when it passed through the little towns, far too important to laugh; and all these faint, sweet whisperings when the sun caught it fairly in some slow curve and poured down upon it till the steam rose.

It was full of tricks, too, in its early life before the great world knew it. There were places in the upper reaches among the Swabian forests, when yet the first whispers of its destiny had not reached it, where it elected to disappear through holes in the ground, to appear again on the other side of the porous limestone hills and start a new river with another name; leaving, too, so little water in its own bed that we had to climb out and wade and push the canoe through miles of shallows.

And a chief pleasure, in those early days of its irresponsible youth, was to lie low, like Brer Fox, just before the little turbulent tributaries came to join it from the Alps, and to refuse to acknowledge them when in, but to run for miles side by side, the dividing line well marked, the very levels different, the Danube utterly declining to recognize the newcomer. Below Passau, however, it gave up this particular trick, for there the Inn comes in with a thundering power impossible to ignore, and so pushes and incommodes the parent river that there is hardly room for them in the long twisting gorge that follows, and the Danube is shoved this way and that against the cliffs, and forced to hurry itself with great waves and much dashing to and fro in order to get through in time. And during the fight our canoe slipped down from its shoulder to its breast, and had the time of its life among the struggling waves. But the Inn taught the old river a lesson, and after Passau it no longer pretended to ignore new arrivals.

This was many days back, of course, and since then we had come to know other aspects of the great creature, and across the Bavarian wheat plain of Straubing she wandered so slowly under the blazing June sun that we could well imagine only the surface inches were water, while below there moved, concealed as by a silken mantle, a whole army of Undines, passing silently and unseen down to the sea, and very leisurely too, lest they be discovered.

Much, too, we forgave her because of her friendliness to the birds and animals that haunted the shores. Cormorants lined the banks in lonely places in rows like short black palings; grey crows crowded the shingle-beds; storks stood fishing in the vistas of shallower water that opened up between the islands, and hawks, swans, and marsh birds of all sorts filled the air with glinting wings and singing, petulant cries. It was impossible to feel annoyed with the river's vagaries after seeing a deer leap with a splash into the water at sunrise and swim past the bows of the canoe; and often we saw fawns peering at us from the underbrush, or looked straight into the brown eyes of a stag as we charged full tilt round a corner and entered another reach of the river. Foxes, too, everywhere haunted the banks, tripping daintily among the driftwood and disappearing so suddenly that it was impossible to see how they managed it.

But now, after leaving Pressburg, everything changed a little, and the Danube became more serious. It ceased trifling. It was half-way to the Black Sea, within seeming distance almost of other, stranger countries where no tricks would be permitted or understood. It became suddenly grown-up, and claimed our respect and even our awe. It broke out into three arms, for one thing, that only met again a hundred kilometers farther down, and for a canoe there were no indications which one was intended to be followed.

"If you take a side channel," said the Hungarian officer we met in the Pressburg shop while buying provisions, "you may find yourselves, when the flood subsides, forty miles from anywhere, high and dry, and you may easily starve. There are no people, no farms, no fishermen. I warn you not to continue. The river, too, is still rising, and this wind will increase."

The rising river did not alarm us in the least, but the matter of being left high and dry by a sudden subsidence of the waters might be serious, and we had consequently laid in an extra stock of provisions. For the rest, the officer's prophecy held true, and the wind, blowing down a perfectly clear sky, increased steadily till it reached the dignity of a westerly gale.

It was earlier than usual when we camped, for the sun was a good hour or two from the horizon, and leaving my friend still asleep on the hot sand, I wandered about in desultory examination of our hotel. The island, I found, was less than an acre in extent, a mere sandy bank standing some two or three feet above the level of the river. The far end, pointing into the sunset, was covered with flying spray which the tremendous wind drove off the crests of the broken waves. It was triangular in shape, with the apex up stream.

I stood there for several minutes, watching the impetuous crimson flood bearing down with a shouting roar, dashing in waves against the bank as though to sweep it bodily away, and then swirling by in two foaming streams on either side. The ground seemed to shake with the shock and rush, while the furious movement of the willow bushes as the wind poured over them increased the curious illusion that the island itself actually moved. Above, for a mile or two, I could see the great river descending upon me; it was like looking up the slope of a sliding hill, white with foam, and leaping up everywhere to show itself to the sun.

The rest of the island was too thickly grown with willows to make walking pleasant, but I made the tour, nevertheless. From the lower end the light, of course, changed, and the river looked dark and angry. Only the backs of the flying waves were visible, streaked with foam, and pushed forcibly by the great puffs of wind that fell upon them from behind. For a short mile it was visible, pouring in and out among the islands, and then disappearing with a huge sweep into the willows, which closed about it like a herd of monstrous antediluvian creatures crowding down to drink. They made me think of gigantic sponge-like growths that sucked the river up into themselves. They caused it to vanish from sight. They herded there together in such overpowering numbers.

Altogether it was an impressive scene, with its utter loneliness, its bizarre suggestion; and as I gazed, long and curiously, a singular emotion began to stir somewhere in the depths of me. Midway in my delight of the wild beauty, there crept, unbidden and unexplained, a curious feeling of disquietude, almost of alarm.

A rising river, perhaps, always suggests something of the ominous; many of the little islands I saw before me would probably have been swept away by the morning; this resistless, thundering flood of water touched the sense of awe. Yet I was aware that my uneasiness lay deeper far than the emotions of awe and wonder. It was not that I felt. Nor had it directly to do with the power of the driving wind—this shouting hurricane that might almost carry up a few acres of willows into the air and scatter them like so much chaff over the landscape. The wind was simply enjoying itself, for nothing rose out of the flat landscape to stop it, and I was conscious of sharing its great game with a kind of pleasurable excitement. Yet this novel emotion had nothing to do with the wind. Indeed, so vague was the sense of distress I experienced, that it was impossible to trace it to its source and deal with it accordingly, though I was aware somehow that it had to do with my realization of our utter insignificance before this unrestrained power of the elements about me. The huge-grown river had something to do with it too—a vague, unpleasant idea that we had somehow trifled with these great elemental forces in whose power we lay helpless every hour of the day and night. For here, indeed, they were gigantically at play together, and the sight appealed to the imagination.

But my emotion, so far as I could understand it, seemed to attach itself more particularly to the willow bushes, to these acres and acres of willows, crowding, so thickly growing there, swarming everywhere the eye could reach, pressing upon the river as though to suffocate it, standing in dense array mile after mile beneath the sky, watching, waiting, listening. And, apart quite from the elements, the willows connected themselves subtly with my malaise, attacking the mind insidiously somehow by reason of their vast numbers, and contriving in some way or other to represent to the imagination a new and mighty power, a power, moreover, not altogether friendly to us.

Great revelations of nature, of course, never fail to impress in one way or another, and I was no stranger to moods of the kind. Mountains overawe and oceans terrify, while the mystery of great forests exercises a spell peculiarly its own. But all these, at one point or another, somewhere link on intimately with human life and human experience. They stir comprehensible, even if alarming, emotions. They tend on the whole to exalt.

With this multitude of willows, however, it was something far different, I felt. Some essence emanated from them that besieged the heart. A sénse of awe awakened, true, but of awe touched somewhere by a vague terror. Their serried ranks, growing everywhere darker about me as the shadows deepened, moving furiously yet softly in the wind, woke in me the curious and unwelcome suggestion that we had trespassed here upon the borders of an alien world, a world where we were intruders, a world where we were not wanted or invited to remain—where we ran grave risks perhaps!

The feeling, however, though it refused to yield its meaning entirely to analysis, did not at the time trouble me by passing into menace. Yet it never left me quite, even during the very practical business of putting up the tent in a hurricane of wind and building a fire for the stew-pot. It remained, just enough to bother and perplex, and to rob a most delightful camping-ground of a good portion of its charm. To my companion, however, I said nothing, for he was a man I considered devoid of imagination. In the first place, I could never have explained to him what I meant, and in the second, he would have laughed stupidly at me if I had.

There was a slight depression in the center of the island, and here we pitched the tent. The surrounding willows broke the wind a bit.

"A poor camp," observed the imperturbable Swede when at last the tent stood upright, "no stones and precious little firewood. I'm for moving on early tomorrow—eh? This sand won't hold anything."

But the experience of a collapsing tent at midnight had taught us many devices, and we made the cozy gipsy house as safe as possible, and then set about collecting a store of wood to last till bed-time. Willow bushes drop no branches, and driftwood was our only source of supply. We hunted the shores pretty thoroughly. Everywhere the banks were crumbling as the rising flood tore at them and carried away great portions with a splash and a gurgle.

"The island's much smaller than when we landed," said the accurate Swede. "It won't last long at this rate. We'd better drag the canoe close to the tent, and be ready to start at a moment's notice. I shall sleep in my clothes."

He was a little distance off, climbing along the bank, and I heard his rather jolly laugh as he spoke.

"By Jove!" I heard him call, a moment later, and turned to see what had caused his exclamation. But for the moment he was hidden by the willows, and I could not find him.

"What in the world's this?" I heard him cry again, and this time his voice had become serious.

I ran up quickly and joined him on the bank. He was looking over the river, pointing at something in the water.

"Good heavens, it's a man's body!" he cried excitedly. "Look!"

A black thing, turning over and over in the foaming waves, swept rapidly past. It kept disappearing and coming up to the surface again. It was about twenty feet from the shore, and just as it was opposite to where we stood it lurched round and looked straight at us. We saw its eyes reflecting the sunset, and gleaming an odd yellow as the body turned over. Then it gave a swift, gulping plunge, and dived out of sight in a flash.

"An otter, by gad!" we exclaimed in the same breath, laughing.

It was an otter, alive, and out on the hunt; yet it had looked exactly like the body of a drowned man turning helplessly in the current. Far below it came to the surface once again, and we saw its black skin, wet and shining in the sunlight.

Then, too, just as we turned back, our arms full of driftwood, another thing happened to recall us to the river bank. This time it really was a man, and what was more, a man in a boat. Now a small boat on the Danube was an unusual sight at any time, but here in this deserted region, and at flood time, it was so unexpected as to constitute a real event. We stood and stared.

Whether it was due to the slanting sunlight, or the refraction from the wonderfully illumined water, I cannot say, but, whatever the cause, I found it difficult to focus my sight properly upon the flying apparition. It seemed, however, to be a man standing upright in a sort of flat-bottomed boat, steering with a long oar, and being carried down the opposite shore at a tremendous pace. He apparently was looking across in our direction, but the distance was too great and the light too uncertain for us to make out very plainly what he was about. It seemed to me that he was gesticulating and making signs at us. His voice came across the water to us shouting something furiously, but the wind drowned it so that no single word was audible. There was something curious about the whole appearance—man, boat, signs, voice—that made an impression on me out of all proportion to its cause.

"He's crossing himself!" I cried. "Look, he's making the sign of the Cross!"

"I believe you're right," the Swede said, shading his eyes with his hand and watching the man out of sight. He seemed to be gone in a moment, melting away down there into the sea of willows where the sun caught them in the bend of the river and turned them into a great crimson wall of beauty. Mist, too, had begun to ruse, so that the air was hazy.

"But what in the world is he doing at nightfall on this flooded river?" I said, half to myself. "Where is he going at such a time, and what did he mean by his signs and shouting? D'you think he wished to warn us about something?"

"He saw our smoke, and thought we were spirits probably," laughed my companion. "These Hungarians believe in all sorts of rubbish; you remember the shopwoman at Pressburg warning us that no one ever landed here because it belonged to some sort of beings outside man's world! I suppose they believe in fairies and elementals, possibly demons, too. That peasant in the boat saw people on the islands for the first time in his life," he added, after a slight pause, "and it scared him, that's all."

The Swede's tone of voice was not convincing, and his manner lacked something that was usually there. I noted the change instantly while he talked, though without being able to label it precisely.

"If they had enough imagination," I laughed loudly—I remember trying to make as much noise as I could—"they might well people a place like this with the old gods of antiquity. The Romans must have haunted all this region more or less with their shrines and sacred groves and elemental deities."

The subject dropped and we returned to our stew-pot, for my friend was not given to imaginative conversation as a rule. Moreover, just then I remember feeling distinctly glad that he was not imaginative; his stolid, practical nature suddenly seemed to me welcome and comforting. It was an admirable temperament, I felt; he could steer down rapids like a red Indian, shoot dangerous bridges and whirlpools better than any white man I ever saw in a canoe. He was a grand fellow for an adventurous trip, a tower of strength when untoward things happened. I looked at his strong face and light curly hair as he staggered along under his pile of driftwood (twice the size of mine!), and I experienced a feeling of relief. Yes, I was distinctly glad just then that the Swede was—what he was, and that he never made remarks that suggested more than they said.

"The river's still rising, though," he added, as if following out some thoughts of his own, and dropping his load with a gasp. "This island will be under water in two days if it goes on."

"I wish the wind would go down," I said. "I don't care a fig for the river."

The flood, indeed, had no terrors for us; we could get off at ten minutes' notice, and the more water the better we liked it. It meant an increasing current and the obliteration of the treacherous shingle-beds that so often threatened to tear the bottom out of our canoe.

Contrary to our expectations, the wind did not go down with the sun. It seemed to increase with the darkness, howling overhead and shaking the willows round us like straws. Curious sounds accompanied it sometimes, like the explosion of heavy guns, and it fell upon the water and the island in great flat blows of immense power. It made me think of the sounds a planet must make, could we only hear it, driving along through space.

But the sky kept wholly clear of clouds, and soon after supper the full moon rose up in the east and covered the river and the plain of shouting willows with a light like the day.

We lay on the sandy patch beside the fire, smoking, listening to the noises of the night round us, and talking happily of the journey we had already made, and of our plans ahead. The map lay spread in the door of the tent, but the high wind made it hard to study, and presently we lowered the curtain and extinguished the lantern. The firelight was enough to smoke and see each other's faces by, and the sparks flew about overhead like fireworks. A few yards beyond, the river gurgled and hissed, and from time to time a heavy splash announced the falling away of further portions of the bank.

Our talk, I noticed, had to do with the faraway scenes and incidents of our first camps in the Black Forest, or of other subjects altogether remote from the present setting, for neither of us spoke of the actual moment more than was necessary—almost as though we had agreed tacitly to avoid discussion of the camp and its incidents. Neither the otter nor the boatman, for instance, received the honor of a single mention, though ordinarily these would have furnished discussion for the greater part of the evening. They were, of course, distinct events in such a place.

The scarcity of wood made it a business to keep the fire going, for the wind, that drove the smoke in our faces wherever we sat, helped at the same time to make a forced draught. We took it in turn to make some foraging expeditions into the darkness, and the quantity the Swede brought back always made me feel that he took an absurdly long time finding it; for the fact was I did not care much about being left alone, and yet it always seemed to be my turn to grub about among the bushes or scramble along the slippery banks in the moonlight. The long day's battle with wind and water—such wind and such water!—had tired us both, and an early bed was the obvious program. Yet neither of us made the move for the tent. We lay there, tending the fire, talking in desultory fashion, peering about us into the dense willow bushes, and listening to the thunder of wind and river. The loneliness of the place had entered our very bones, and silence seemed natural, for after a bit the sound of our voices became a trifle unreal and forced; whispering would have been the fitting mode of communication, I felt, and the human voice, always rather absurd amid the roar of the elements, now carried with it something almost illegitimate. It was like talking out loud in church, or in some place where it was not lawful, perhaps not quite safe, to be overheard.

The eeriness of this lonely island, set among a million willows, swept by a hurricane, and surrounded by hurrying deep waters, touched us both, I fancy. Untrodden by man, almost unknown to man, it lay there beneath the moon, remote from human influence, on the frontier of another world, an alien world, a world tenanted by willows only and the souls of willows. And we, in our rashness, had dared to invade it, even to make use of it! Something more than the power of its mystery stirred in me as I lay on the sand, feet to fire, and peered up through the leaves at the stars. For the last time I rose to get firewood.

"When this has burnt up," I said firmly, "I shall turn in," and my companion watched me lazily as I moved off into the surrounding shadows.

For an unimaginative man I thought he seemed unusually receptive that night, unusually open to suggestion of things other than sensory. He too was touched by the beauty and loneliness of the place. I was not altogether pleased, I remember, to recognize this slight change in him, and instead of immediately collecting sticks, I made my way to the far point of the island where the moonlight on plain and river could be seen to better advantage. The desire to be alone had come suddenly upon me; my former dread returned in force; there was a vague feeling in me I wished to face and probe to the bottom.

When I reached the point of sand jutting out among the waves, the spell of the place descended upon me with a positive shock. No mere "scenery" could have produced such an effect. There was something more here, something to alarm.

I gazed across the waste of wild waters; I watched the whispering willows; I heard the ceaseless beating of the tireless wind; and, one and all, each in its own way, stirred in me this sensation of a strange distress. But the willows especially; for ever they went on chattering and talking among themselves, laughing a little, shrilly crying out, sometimes sighing—but what it was they made so much to-do about belonged to the secret life of the great plain they inhabited. And it was utterly alien to the world I knew, or to that of the wild yet kindly elements. They made me think of a host of beings from another plane of life, another evolution altogether, perhaps, all discussing a mystery known only to themselves. I watched them moving busily together, oddly shaking their big bushy heads, twirling their myriad leaves even when there was no wind. They moved of their own will as though alive, and they touched, by some incalculable method, my own keen sense of the horrible.

There they stood in the moonlight, like a vast army surrounding our camp, shaking their innumerable silver spears defiantly, formed all ready for an attack.

The psychology of places, for some imaginations at least, is very vivid; for the wanderer, especially, camps have their "note" either of welcome or rejection. At first it may not always be apparent, because the busy preparations of tent and cooking prevent, but with the first pause—after supper usually—it comes and announces itself. And the note of this willow-camp now became unmistakably plain to me; we were interlopers, trespassers; we were not welcomed. The sense of unfamiliarity grew upon me as I stood there watching. We touched the frontier of a region where our presence was resented. For a night's lodging we might perhaps be tolerated; but for a prolonged and inquisitive stay—No! by all the gods of the trees and wilderness, no! We were the first human influences upon this island, and we were not wanted. The willows were against us.

Strange thoughts like these, bizarre fancies, borne I know not whence, found lodgment in my mind as I stood listening. What, I thought, if, after all, these crouching willows proved to be alive; if suddenly they should rise up, like a swarm of living creatures, marshaled by the gods whose territory we had invaded, sweep towards us off the vast swamps, booming overhead in the night—and then settle down! As I looked it was so easy to imagine they actually moved, crept nearer, retreated a little, huddled together in masses, hostile, waiting for the great wind that should finally start them a-running. I could have sworn their aspect changed a little, and their ranks deepened and pressed more closely together.

The melancholy shrill cry of a night-bird sounded overhead, and suddenly I nearly lost my balance as the piece of bank I stood upon fell with a great splash into the river, undermined by the flood. I stepped back just in time, and went on hunting for firewood again, half laughing at the odd fancies that crowded so thickly into my mind and cast their spell upon me. I recalled the Swede's remark about moving on next day, and I was just thinking that I fully agreed with him, when I turned with a start and saw the subject of my thoughts standing immediately in front of me. He was quite close. The roar of the elements had covered his approach.

II

"You've been gone so long," he shouted above the wind, "I thought something must have happened to you."

But there was that in his tone, and a certain look in his face as well, that conveyed to me more than his usual words, and in a flash I understood the real reason for his coming. It was because the spell of the place had entered his soul too, and he did not like being alone.

"River still rising," he cried, pointing to the flood in the moonlight, "and the wind's simply awful."

He always said the same things, but it was the cry for companionship that gave the real importance to his words.

"Lucky," I cried back, "our tent's in the hollow. I think it'll hold all right." I added something about the difficulty of finding wood, in order to explain my absence, but the wind caught my words and flung them across the river, so that he did not hear, but just looked at me through the branches, nodding his head.

"Lucky if we get away without disaster!" he shouted, or words to that effect; and I remember feeling half angry with him for putting the thought into words, for it was exactly what I felt myself. There was disaster impending somewhere, and the sense of presentiment lay unpleasantly upon me.

We went back to the fire and made a final blaze, poking it up with our feet. We took a last look round. But for the wind the heat would have been unpleasant. I put this thought into words, and I remember my friend's reply struck me oddly: that he would rather have the heat, the ordinary July weather, than this "diabolical wind."

Everything was snug for the night; the canoe lying turned over beside the tent, with both yellow paddles beneath her; the provision sack hanging from a willow-stem, and the washed-up dishes removed to a safe distance from the fire, all ready for the morning meal.

We smothered the embers of the fire with sand, and then turned in. The flap of the tent door was up, and I saw the branches and the stars and the white moonlight. The shaking willows and the heavy buffetings of the wind against our taut little house were the last things I remembered as sleep came down and covered all with its soft and delicious forgetfulness.

Suddenly I found myself lying awake, peering from my sandy mattress through the door of the tent. I looked at my watch pinned against the canvas, and saw by the bright moonlight that it was past twelve o'clock—the threshold of a new day—and I had therefore slept a couple of hours. The Swede was asleep still beside me; the wind howled as before; something plucked at my heart and made me feel afraid. There was a sense of disturbance in my immediate neighborhood.

I sat up quickly and looked out. The trees were swaying violently to and fro as the gusts smote them, but our little bit of green canvas lay snugly safe in the hollow, for the wind passed over it without meeting enough resistance to make it vicious. The feeling of disquietude did not pass, however, and I crawled quietly out of the tent to see if our belongings were safe. I moved carefully so as not to waken my companion. A curious excitement was on me.

I was half-way out, kneeling on all fours, when my eye first took in that the tops of the bushes opposite, with their moving tracery of leaves, made shapes against the sky. I sat back on my haunches and stared. It was incredible, surely, but there, opposite and slightly above me, were shapes of some indeterminate sort among the willows, and as the branches swayed in the wind they seemed to group themselves about these shapes, forming a series of monstrous outlines that shifted rapidly beneath the moon. Close, about fifty feet in front of me, I saw these things.

My first instinct was to waken my companion, that he too might see them, but something made me hesitate—the sudden realization, probably, that I should not welcome corroboration; and meanwhile I crouched there staring in amazement with smarting eyes. I was wide awake. I remember saying to myself that I was not dreaming.

They first became properly visible, these huge figures, just within the tops of the bushes—immense, bronze-colored, moving, and wholly independent of the swaying of the branches. I saw them plainly and noted, now I came to examine them more calmly, that they were very much larger than human, and indeed that something in their appearance proclaimed them to be not human at all. Certainly they were not merely the moving tracery of the branches against the moonlight. They shifted independently. They rose upwards in a continuous stream from earth to sky, vanishing utterly as soon as they reached the dark of the sky. They were interlaced one with another, making a great column, and I saw their limbs and huge bodies melting in and out of each other, forming this serpentine line that bent and swayed and twisted spirally with the contortions of the wind-tossed trees. They were nude, fluid shapes, passing up the bushes, within the leaves almost—rising up in a living column into the heavens. Their faces I never could see. Unceasingly they poured upwards, swaying in great bending curves, with a hue of dull bronze upon their skins.

I stared, trying to force every atom of vision from my eyes. For a long time I thought they must every moment disappear and resolve themselves into the movements of the branches and prove to be an optical illusion. I searched everywhere for a proof of reality, when all the while I understood quite well that the standard of reality had changed. For the longer I looked the more certain I became that these figures were real and living, though perhaps not according to the standards that the camera and the biologist would insist upon.

Far from feeling fear, I was possessed with a sense of awe and wonder such as I have never known. I seemed to be gazing at the personified elemental forces of this haunted and primeval region. Our intrusion had stirred the powers of the place into activity. It was we who were the cause of the disturbance, and my brain filled to bursting with stories and legends of the spirits and deities of places that have been acknowledged and worshipped by men in all ages of the world's history. But, before I could arrive at any possible explanation, something impelled me to go farther out, and I crept forward on the sand and stood upright. I felt the ground still warm under my bare feet; the wind tore at my hair and face; and the sound of the river burst upon my ears with a sudden roar. These things, I knew, were real, and proved that my senses were acting normally. Yet the figures still rose from earth to heaven, silent, majestically, in a great spiral of grace and strength that overwhelmed me at length with a genuine deep emotion of worship. I felt that I must fall down and worship—absolutely worship.

Perhaps in another minute I might have done so, when a gust of wind swept against me with such force that it blew me sideways, and I nearly stumbled and fell. It seemed to shake the dream violently out of me. At least it gave me another point of view somehow. The figures still remained, still ascended into heaven from the heart of the night, but my reason at last began to assert itself. It must be a subjective experience, I argued—none the less real for that, but still subjective. The moonlight and the branches combined to work out these pictures upon the mirror of my imagination, and for some reason I projected them outwards and made them appear objective. I knew this must be the case, of course. I took courage, and began to move forward across the open patches of sand. By Jove, though, was it all hallucination? Was it merely subjective? Did not my reason argue in the old futile way from the little standard of the known?

I only know that great column of figures ascended darkly into the sky for what seemed a very long period of time, and with a very complete measure of reality as most men are accustomed to gauge reality. Then suddenly they were gone!

And, once they were gone and the immediate wonder of their great presence had passed, fear came down upon me with a cold rush. The esoteric meaning of this lonely and haunted region suddenly flamed up within me, and I began to tremble dreadfully. I took a quick look round—a look of horror that came near to panic—calculating vainly ways of escape; and then, realizing how helpless I was to achieve anything really effective, I crept back silently into the tent and lay down again upon my sandy mattress, first lowering the door-curtain to shut out the sight of the willows in the moonlight, and then burying my head as deeply as possible beneath the blankets to deaden the sound of the terrifying wind.

As though further to convince me that I had not been dreaming, I remember that it was a long time before I fell again into a troubled and restless sleep; and even then only the upper crust of me slept, and underneath there was something that never quite lost consciousness, but lay alert and on the watch.

But this second time I jumped up with a genuine start of terror. It was neither the wind nor the river that woke me, but the slow approach of something that caused the sleeping portion of me to grow smaller and smaller till at last it vanished altogether, and I found myself sitting bolt upright—listening.

Outside there was a sound of multitudinous little patterings. They had been coming, I was aware, for a long time, and in my sleep they had first become audible. I sat there nervously wide awake as though I had not slept at all. It seemed to me that my breathing came with difficulty, and that there was a great weight upon the surface of my body. In spite of the hot night, I felt clammy with cold and shivered. Something surely was pressing steadily against the sides of the tent and weighing down upon it from above. Was it the body of the wind? Was this the pattering rain, the dripping of the leaves? The spray blown from the river by the wind and gathering in big drops? I thought quickly of a dozen things.

Then suddenly the explanation leaped into my mind: a bough from the poplar, the only large tree on the island, had fallen with the wind. Still half caught by the other branches, it would fall with the next gust and crush us, and meanwhile its leaves brushed and tapped upon the tight canvas surface of the tent. I raised a loose flap and rushed out, calling to the Swede to follow.

But when I got out and stood upright I saw that the tent was free. There was no hanging bough; there was no rain or spray; nothing approached.

A cold, grey light filtered down through the bushes and lay on the faintly gleaming sand. Stars still crowded the sky directly overhead, and the wind howled magnificently, but the fire no longer gave out any glow, and I saw the east reddening in streaks through the trees. Several hours must have passed since I stood there before watching the ascending figures, and the memory of it now came back to me horribly, like an evil dream. Oh, how tired it made me feel, that ceaseless raging wind! Yet, though the deep lassitude of a sleepless night was on me, my nerves were tingling with the activity of an equally tireless apprehension, and all idea of repose was out of the question. The river I saw had risen further. Its thunder filled the air, and a fine spray made itself felt through my thin sleeping shirt.

Yet nowhere did I discover the slightest evidence of anything to cause alarm. This deep, prolonged disturbance in my heart remained wholly unaccounted for.

My companion had not stirred when I called him, and there was no need to waken him now. I looked about me carefully, noting everything; the turned-over canoe; the yellow paddles—two of them, I'm certain; the provision sack and the extra lantern hanging together from the tree; and, crowding everywhere about me, enveloping all, the willows, those endless, shaking willows. A bird uttered its morning cry, and a string of duck passed with whirring flight overhead in the twilight. The sand whirled, dry and stinging, about my bare feet in the wind.

I walked round the tent and then went out a little way into the bush, so that I could see across the river to the farther landscape, and the same profound yet indefinable emotion of distress seized upon me again as I saw the interminable sea of bushes stretching to the horizon, looking ghostly and unreal in the wan light of dawn. I walked softly here and there, still puzzling over that odd sound of infinite pattering, and of that pressure upon the tent that had wakened me. It must have been the wind, I reflected—the wind bearing upon the loose, hot sand, driving the dry particles smartly against the taut canvas—the wind dropping heavily upon our fragile roof.

Yet all the time my nervousness and malaise increased appreciably.

I crossed over to the farther shore and noted how the coast-line had altered in the night, and what masses of sand the river had torn away. I dipped my hands and feet into the cool current, and bathed my forehead. Already there was a glow of sunrise in the sky and the exquisite freshness of coming day. On my way back I passed purposely beneath the very bushes where I had seen the column of figures rising into the air, and midway among the clumps I suddenly found myself overtaken by a sense of vast terror. From the shadows a large figure went swiftly by. Someone passed me, as sure as ever man did....

It was a great staggering blow from the wind that helped me forward again, and once out in the more open space, the sense of terror diminished strangely. The winds were about and walking, I remember saying to myself, for the winds often move like great presences under the trees. And altogether the fear that hovered about me was such an unknown and immense kind of fear, so unlike anything I had ever felt before, that it woke a sense of awe and wonder in me that did much to counteract its worst effects; and when I reached a high point in the middle of the island from which I could see the wide stretch of river, crimson in the sunrise, the whole magical beauty of it all was so overpowering that a sort of wild yearning woke in me and almost brought a cry up into the throat.

But this cry found no expression, for as my eyes wandered from the plain beyond to the island round me and noted our little tent half hidden among the willows, a dreadful discovery leaped out at me, compared to which my terror of the walking winds seemed as nothing at all.

For a change, I thought, had somehow come about in the arrangement of the landscape. It was not that my point of vantage gave me a different view, but that an alteration had apparently been effected in the relation of the tent to the willows, and of the willows to the tent. Surely the bushes now crowded much closer—unnecessarily, unpleasantly close. They had moved nearer.

Creeping with silent feet over the shifting sands, drawing imperceptibly nearer by soft, unhurried movements, the willows had come closer during the night. But had the wind moved them, or had they moved of themselves? I recalled the sound of infinite small patterings and the pressure upon the tent and upon my own heart that caused me to wake in terror. I swayed for a moment in the wind like a tree, finding it hard to keep my upright position on the sandy hillock. There was a suggestion here of personal agency, of deliberate intention, of aggressive hostility, and it terrified me into a sort of rigidity.

Then the reaction followed quickly. The idea was so bizarre, so absurd, that I felt inclined to laugh. But the laughter came no more readily than the cry, for the knowledge that my mind was so receptive to such dangerous imaginings brought the additional terror that it was through our minds and not through our physical bodies that the attack would come, and was coming.

The wind buffeted me about, and, very quickly it seemed, the sun came up over the horizon, for it was after four o'clock, and I must have stood on that little pinnacle of sand longer than I knew, afraid to come down to close quarters with the willows. I returned quietly, creepily, to the tent, first taking another exhaustive look round and—yes, I confess it—making a few measurements. I paced out on the warm sand the distances between the willows and the tent, making a note of the shortest distance particularly.

I crawled stealthily into my blankets. My companion, to all appearances, still slept soundly, and I was glad that this was so. Provided my experiences were not corroborated, I could find strength somehow to deny them, perhaps. With the daylight I could persuade myself that it was all a subjective hallucination, a fantasy of the night, a projection of the excited imagination.

Nothing further came in to disturb me, and I fell asleep almost at once, utterly exhausted, yet still in dread of hearing again that weird sound of multitudinous pattering, or of feeling the pressure upon my heart that had made it difficult to breathe.

The sun was high in the heavens when my companion woke me from a heavy sleep and announced that the porridge was cooked and there was just time to bathe. The grateful smell of frizzling bacon entered the tent door.

"River still rising," he said, "and several islands out in mid-stream have disappeared altogether. Our own island's much smaller."

"Any wood left?" I asked sleepily.

"The wood and the island will finish tomorrow in a dead heat," he laughed, "but there's enough to last us till then."

I plunged in from the point of the island, which had indeed altered a lot in size and shape during the night, and was swept down in a moment to the landing-place opposite the tent. The water was icy, and the banks flew by like the country from an express train. Bathing under such conditions was an exhilarating operation, and the terror of the night seemed cleansed out of me by a process of evaporation in the brain. The sun was blazing hot; not a cloud showed itself anywhere; the wind, however, had not abated one little jot.

Quite suddenly then the implied meaning of the Swede's words flashed across me, showing that he no longer wished to leave post-haste, and had changed his mind. "Enough to last till tomorrow"—he assumed we should stay on the island another night. It struck me as odd. The night before he was so positive the other way. How had the change come about?

Great crumblings of the banks occurred at breakfast, with heavy splashings and clouds of spray which the wind brought into our frying-pan, and my fellow-traveler talked incessantly about the difficulty the Vienna-Pesth steamers must have to find the channel in flood. But the state of his mind interested and impressed me far more than the state of the river or the difficulties of the steamers. He had changed somehow since the evening before. His manner was different—a trifle excited, a trifle shy, with a sort of suspicion about his voice and gestures. I hardly know how to describe it now in cold blood, but at the time I remember being quite certain of one thing—that he had become frightened?

He ate very little breakfast, and for once omitted to smoke his pipe. He had the map spread open beside him, and kept studying its markings.

"We'd better get off sharp in an hour," I said presently, feeling for an opening that must bring him indirectly to a partial confession at any rate. And his answer puzzled me uncomfortably: "Rather! If they'll let us."

"Who'll let us? The elements?" I asked quickly, with affected indifference.

"The powers of this awful place, whoever they are," he replied, keeping his eyes on the map. "The gods are here, if they are anywhere at all in the world."

"The elements are always the true immortals," I replied, laughing as naturally as I could manage, yet knowing quite well that my face reflected my true feelings when he looked up gravely at me and spoke across the smoke:

"We shall be fortunate if we get away without further disaster."

This was exactly what I had dreaded, and I screwed myself up to the point of the direct question. It was like agreeing to allow the dentist to extract the tooth; it had to come anyhow in the long run, and the rest was all pretense.

"Further disaster! Why, what's happened?"

"For one thing—the steering paddle's gone," he said quietly.

"The steering paddle gone!" I repeated, greatly excited, for this was our rudder, and the Danube in flood without a rudder was suicide. "But what—"

"And there's a tear in the bottom of the canoe," he added, with a genuine little tremor in his voice.

I continued staring at him, able only to repeat the words in his face somewhat foolishly. There, in the heat of the sun, and on this burning sand, I was aware of a freezing atmosphere descending round us. I got up to follow him, for he merely nodded his head gravely and led the way towards the tent a few yards on the other side of the fireplace. The canoe still lay there as I had last seen her in the night, ribs uppermost, the paddles, or rather, the paddle, on the sand beside her.

"There's only one," he said, stooping to pick it up. "And here's the rent in the base-board."

It was on the tip of my tongue to tell him that I had clearly noticed two paddles a few hours before, but a second impulse made me think better of it, and I said nothing. I approached to see.

There was a long, finely made tear in the bottom of the canoe where a little slither of wood had been neatly taken clean out; it looked as if the tooth of a sharp rock or snag had eaten down her length, and investigation showed that the hole went through. Had we launched out in her without observing it we must inevitably have foundered. At first the water would have made the wood swell so as to close the hole, but once out in mid-stream the water must have poured in, and the canoe, never more than two inches above the surface, would have filled and sunk very rapidly.

"There, you see an attempt to prepare a victim for the sacrifice," I heard him saying, more to himself than to me, "two victims rather," he added as he bent over and ran his fingers along the slit.

I began to whistle—a thing I always do unconsciously when utterly nonplussed—and purposely paid no attention to his words. I was determined to consider them foolish.

"It wasn't there last night," he said presently, straightening up from his examination and looking anywhere but at me.

"We must have scratched her in landing, of course," I stopped whistling to say. "The stones are very sharp."

I stopped abruptly, for at that moment he turned round and met my eye squarely. I knew just as well as he did how impossible my explanation was. There were no stones, to begin with.

"And then there's this to explain too," he added quietly, handing me the paddle and pointing to the blade.

A new and curious emotion spread freezingly over me as I took and examined it. The blade was scraped down all over, beautifully scraped, as though someone had sand-papered it with care, making it so thin that the first vigorous stroke must have snapped it off at the elbow.

"One of us walked in his sleep and did this thing," I said feebly, "or—or it has been filed by the constant stream of sand particles blown against it by the wind, perhaps."

"Ah," said the Swede, turning away, laughing a little, "you can explain everything."

"The same wind that caught the steering paddle and flung it so near the bank that it fell in with the next lump that crumbled," I called out after him, absolutely determined to find an explanation for everything he showed me.

"I see," he shouted back, turning his head to look at me before disappearing among the willow bushes.

Once alone with these perplexing evidences of personal agency, I think my first thoughts took the form of "One of us must have done this thing, and it certainly was not I." But my second thought decided how impossible it was to suppose, under all the circumstances, that either of us had done it. That my companion, the trusted friend of a dozen similar expeditions, could have knowingly had a hand in it, was a suggestion not to be entertained for a moment. Equally absurd seemed the explanation that this imperturbable and densely practical nature had suddenly become insane and was busied with insane purposes.

Yet the fact remained that what disturbed me most, and kept my fear actively alive even in this blaze of sunshine and wild beauty, was the clear certainty that some curious alteration had come about in his mind—that he was nervous, timid, suspicious, aware of goings on he did not speak about, watching a series of secret and hitherto unmentionable events—waiting, in a word, for a climax that he expected, and, I thought, expected very soon. This grew up in my mind intuitively—I hardly knew how.

I made a hurried examination of the tent and its surroundings, but the measurements of the night remained the same. There were deep hollows formed in the sand I now noticed for the first time, basin-shaped and of various depths and sizes, varying from that of a tea-cup to a large bowl. The wind, no doubt, was responsible for these miniature craters, just as it was for lifting the paddle and tossing it towards the water. The rent in the canoe was the only thing that seemed quite inexplicable; and, after all, it was conceivable that a sharp point had caught it when we landed. The examination I made of the shore did not assist this theory, but all the same I clung to it with that diminishing portion of my intelligence which I called my "reason." An explanation of some kind was an absolute necessity, just as some working explanation of the universe is necessary—however absurd—to the happiness of every individual who seeks to do his duty in the world and face the problems of life. The simile seemed to me at the time an exact parallel.

I at once set the pitch melting, and presently the Swede joined me at the work, though under the best conditions in the world the canoe could not be safe for traveling till the following day. I drew his attention casually to the hollows in the sand.

"Yes," he said, "I know. They're all over the island. But you can explain them, no doubt!"

"Wind, of course," I answered without hesitation. "Have you never watched those little whirlwinds in the street that twist and twirl everything into a circle? This sand's loose enough to yield, that's all."

He made no reply, and we worked on in silence for a bit. I watched him surreptitiously all the time, and I had an idea he was watching me. He seemed, too, to be always listening attentively to something I could not hear, or perhaps for something that he expected to hear, for he kept turning about and staring into the bushes, and up into the sky, and out across the water where it was visible through the openings among the willows. Sometimes he even put his hand to his ear and held it there for several minutes. He said nothing to me, however, about it, and I asked no questions. And meanwhile, as he mended that torn canoe with the skill and address of a red Indian, I was glad to notice his absorption in the work, for there was a vague dread in my heart that he would speak of the changed aspect of the willows. And, if he had noticed that, my imagination could no longer be held a sufficient explanation of it.

III

At length, after a long pause, he began to talk.

"Queer thing," he added in a hurried sort of voice, as though he wanted to say something and get it over. "Queer thing. I mean, about that otter last night."

I had expected something so totally different that he caught me with surprise, and I looked up sharply.

"Shows how lonely this place is. Otters are awfully shy things—"

"I don't mean that, of course," he interrupted. "I mean—do you think—did you think it really was an otter?"

"What else, in the name of Heaven, what else?"

"You know, I saw it before you did, and at first it seemed—so much bigger than an otter."

"The sunset as you looked up-stream magnified it, or something," I replied.

He looked at me absently a moment, as though his mind were busy with other thoughts.

"It had such extraordinary yellow eyes," he went on half to himself.

"That was the sun too," I laughed, a trifle boisterously. "I suppose you'll wonder next if that fellow in the boat—"

I suddenly decided not to finish the sentence. He was in the act again of listening, turning his head to the wind, and something in the expression of his face made me halt. The subject dropped, and we went on with our caulking. Apparently he had not noticed my unfinished sentence. Five minutes later, however, he looked at me across the canoe, the smoking pitch in his hand, his face exceedingly grave.

"I did rather wonder, if you want to know," he said slowly, "what that thing in the boat was. I remember thinking at the time it was not a man. The whole business seemed to rise quite suddenly out of the water."

I laughed again boisterously in his face, but this time there was impatience, and a strain of anger too, in my feeling.

"Look here now," I cried, "this place is quite queer enough without going out of our way to imagine things! That boat was an ordinary boat, and the man in it was an ordinary man, and they were both going down-stream as fast as they could lick. And that otter was an otter, so don't let's play the fool about it!"

He looked steadily at me with the same grave expression. He was not in the least annoyed. I took courage from his silence.

"And, for Heaven's sake," I went on, "don't keep pretending you hear things, because it only gives me the jumps, and there's nothing to hear but the river and this cursed old thundering wind."

"You fool!" he answered in a low, shocked voice, "you utter fool. That's just the way all victims talk. As if you didn't understand just as well as I do!" he sneered with scorn in his voice, and a sort of resignation. "The best thing you can do is to keep quiet and try to hold your mind as firm as possible. This feeble attempt at self-deception only makes the truth harder when you're forced to meet it."

My little effort was over, and I found nothing more to say, for I knew quite well his words were true, and that I was the fool, not he. Up to a certain stage in the adventure he kept ahead of me easily, and I think I felt annoyed to be out of it, to be thus proved less psychic, less sensitive than himself to these extraordinary happenings, and half ignorant all the time of what was going on under my very nose. He knew from the very beginning, apparently. But at the moment I wholly missed the point of his words about the necessity of there being a victim, and that we ourselves were destined to satisfy the want. I dropped all pretense thenceforward, but thenceforward likewise my fear increased steadily to the climax.

"But you're quite right about one thing," he added, before the subject passed, "and that is that we're wiser not to talk about it, or even to think about it, because what one thinks finds expression in words, and what one says, happens."

That afternoon, while the canoe dried and hardened, we spent trying to fish, testing the leak, collecting wood, and watching the enormous flood of rising water. Masses of driftwood swept near our shores sometimes, and we fished for them with long willow branches. The island grew perceptibly smaller as the banks were torn away with great gulps and splashes. The weather kept brilliantly fine till about four o'clock, and then for the first time for three days the wind showed signs of abating. Clouds began to gather in the south-west, spreading thence slowly over the sky.

This lessening of the wind came as a great relief, for the incessant roaring, banging, and thundering had irritated our nerves. Yet the silence that came about five o'clock with its sudden cessation was in a manner quite as oppressive. The booming of the river had everything in its own way then; it filled the air with deep murmurs, more musical than the wind noises, but infinitely more monotonous. The wind held many notes, rising, falling always beating out some sort of great elemental tune; whereas the river's song lay between three notes at most—dull pedal notes, that held a lugubrious quality foreign to the wind, and somehow seemed to me, in my then nervous state, to sound wonderfully well the music of doom.

It was extraordinary, too, how the withdrawal suddenly of bright sunlight took everything out of the landscape that made for cheerfulness; and since this particular landscape had already managed to convey the suggestion of something sinister, the change of course was all the more unwelcome and noticeable. For me, I know, the darkening outlook became distinctly more alarming, and I found myself more than once calculating how soon after sunset the full moon would get up in the east, and whether the gathering clouds would greatly interfere with her lighting of the little island.

With this general hush of the wind—though it still indulged in occasional brief gusts—the river seemed to me to grow blacker, the willows to stand more densely together. The latter, too, kept up a sort of independent movement of their own, rustling among themselves when no wind stirred, and shaking oddly from the roots upwards. When common objects in this way be come charged with the suggestion of horror, they stimulate the imagination far more than things of unusual appearance; and these bushes, crowding huddled about us, assumed for me in the darkness a bizarre grotesquerie of appearance that lent to them somehow the aspect of purposeful and living creatures. Their very ordinariness, I felt, masked what was malignant and hostile to us. The forces of the region drew nearer with the coming of night. They were focusing upon our island, and more particularly upon ourselves. For thus, somehow, in the terms of the imagination, did my really indescribable sensations in this extraordinary place present themselves.

I had slept a good deal in the early afternoon, and had thus recovered somewhat from the exhaustion of a disturbed night, but this only served apparently to render me more susceptible than before to the obsessing spell of the haunting. I fought against it, laughing at my feelings as absurd and childish, with very obvious physiological explanations, yet, in spite of every effort, they gained in strength upon me so that I dreaded the night as a child lost in a forest must dread the approach of darkness.

The canoe we had carefully covered with a waterproof sheet during the day, and the one remaining paddle had been securely tied by the Swede to the base of a tree, lest the wind should rob us of that too. From five o'clock onwards I busied myself with the stew-pot and preparations for dinner, it being my turn to cook that night. We had potatoes, onions, bits of bacon fat to add flavor, and a general thick residue from former stews at the bottom of the pot; with black bread broken up into it the result was most excellent, and it was followed by a stew of plums with sugar and a brew of strong tea with dried milk. A good pile of wood lay close at hand, and the absence of wind made my duties easy. My companion sat lazily watching me, dividing his attentions between cleaning his pipe and giving useless advice—an admitted privilege of the off-duty man. He had been very quiet all the afternoon, engaged in re-caulking the canoe, strengthening the tent ropes, and fishing for driftwood while I slept. No more talk about undesirable things had passed between us, and I think his only remarks had to do with the gradual destruction of the island, which he declared was not fully a third smaller than when we first landed.

The pot had just begun to bubble when I heard his voice calling to me from the bank, where he had wandered away without my noticing. I ran up.

"Come and listen," he said, "and see what you make of it." He held his hand cupwise to his ear, as so often before.

"Now do you hear anything?" he asked, watching me curiously.

We stood there, listening attentively together. At first I heard only the deep note of the water and the hissings rising from its turbulent surface. The willows, for once, were motionless and silent. Then a sound began to reach my ears faintly, a peculiar sound—something like the humming of a distant gong. It seemed to come across to us in the darkness from the waste of swamps and willows opposite. It was repeated at regular intervals, but it was certainly neither the sound of a bell nor the hooting of a distant steamer. I can liken it to nothing so much as to the sound of an immense gong, suspended far up in the sky, repeating incessantly its muffled metallic note, soft and musical, as it was repeatedly struck. My heart quickened as I listened.

"I've heard it all day," said my companion. "While you slept this afternoon it came all round the island. I hunted it down, but could never get near enough to see—to localize it correctly. Sometimes it was overhead, and sometimes it seemed under the water. Once or twice, too, I could have sworn it was not outside at all, but within myself—you know—the way a sound in the fourth dimension is supposed to come."

I was too much puzzled to pay much attention to his words. I listened carefully, striving to associate it with any known familiar sound I could think of, but without success. It changed in the direction, too, coming nearer, and then sinking utterly away into remote distance. I cannot say that it was ominous in quality, because to me it seemed distinctly musical, yet I must admit it set going a distressing feeling that made me wish I had never heard it.

"The wind blowing in those sand-funnels," I said determined to find an explanation, "or the bushes rubbing together after the storm perhaps."

"It comes off the whole swamp," my friend answered. "It comes from everywhere at once." He ignored my explanations. "It comes from the willow bushes somehow—"

"But now the wind has dropped," I objected. "The willows can hardly make a noise by themselves, can they?"

His answer frightened me, first because I had dreaded it, and secondly, because I knew intuitively it was true.

"It is because the wind has dropped we now hear it. It was drowned before. It is the cry, I believe, of the—"

I dashed back to my fire, warned by the sound of bubbling that the stew was in danger, but determined at the same time to escape further conversation. I was resolute, if possible, to avoid the exchanging of views. I dreaded, too, that he would begin about the gods, or the elemental forces, or something else disquieting, and I wanted to keep myself well in hand for what might happen later. There was another night to be faced before we escaped from this distressing place, and there was no knowing yet what it might bring forth.

"Come and cut up bread for the pot," I called to him, vigorously stirring the appetizing mixture. That stew-pot held sanity for us both, and the thought made me laugh.

He came over slowly and took the provision sack from the tree, fumbling in its mysterious depths, and then emptying the entire contents upon the ground-sheet at his feet.

"Hurry up!" I cried; "it's boiling."

The Swede burst out into a roar of laughter that startled me. It was forced laughter, not artificial exactly, but mirthless.

"There's nothing here!" he shouted, holding his sides.

"Bread, I mean."

"It's gone. There is no bread. They've taken it!"

I dropped the long spoon and ran up. Everything the sack had contained lay upon the ground-sheet, but there was no loaf.

The whole dead weight of my growing fear fell upon me and shook me. Then I burst out laughing too. It was the only thing to do: and the sound of my laughter also made me understand his. The stain of psychical pressure caused it—this explosion of unnatural laughter in both of us; it was an effort of repressed forces to seek relief; it was a temporary safety-valve. And with both of us it ceased quite suddenly.

"How criminally stupid of me!" I cried, still determined to be consistent and find an explanation. "I clean forgot to buy a loaf at Pressburg. That chattering woman put everything out of my head, and I must have left it lying on the counter or—"

"The oatmeal, too, is much less than it was this morning," the Swede interrupted.

Why in the world need he draw attention to it? I thought angrily.

"There's enough for tomorrow," I said, stirring vigorously, "and we can get lots more at Komorn or Gran. In twenty-four hours we shall be miles from here."

"I hope so—to God," he muttered, putting the things back into the sack, "unless we're claimed first as victims for the sacrifice," he added with a foolish laugh. He dragged the sack into the tent, for safety's sake, I suppose, and I heard him mumbling to himself, but so indistinctly that it seemed quite natural for me to ignore his words.

Our meal was beyond question a gloomy one, and we ate it almost in silence, avoiding one another's eyes, and keeping the fire bright. Then we washed up and prepared for the night, and, once smoking, our minds unoccupied with any definite duties, the apprehension I had felt all day long became more and more acute. It was not then active fear, I think, but the very vagueness of its origin distressed me far more that if I had been able to ticket and face it squarely. The curious sound I have likened to the note of a gong became now almost incessant, and filled the stillness of the night with a faint, continuous ringing rather than a series of distinct notes. At one time it was behind and at another time in front of us. Sometimes I fancied it came from the bushes on our left, and then again from the clumps on our right. More often it hovered directly overhead like the whirring of wings. It was really everywhere at once, behind, in front, at our sides and over our heads, completely surrounding us. The sound really defies description. But nothing within my knowledge is like that ceaseless muffled humming rising off the deserted world of swamps and willows.

We sat smoking in comparative silence, the strain growing every minute greater. The worst feature of the situation seemed to me that we did not know what to expect, and could therefore make no sort of preparation by way of defense. We could anticipate nothing. My explanations made in the sunshine, moreover, now came to haunt me with their foolish and wholly unsatisfactory nature, and it was more and more clear to us that some kind of plain talk with my companion was inevitable, whether I liked it or not. After all, we had to spend the night together, and to sleep in the same tent side by side. I saw that I could not get along much longer without the support of his mind, and for that, of course, plain talk was imperative. As long as possible, however, I postponed this little climax, and tried to ignore or laugh at the occasional sentences he flung into the emptiness.

Some of these sentences, moreover, were confoundedly disquieting to me, coming as they did to corroborate much that I felt myself; corroboration, too—which made it so much more convincing—from a totally different point of view. He composed such curious sentences, and hurled them at me in such an inconsequential sort of way, as though his main line of thought was secret to himself, and these fragments were mere bits he found it impossible to digest. He got rid of them by uttering them. Speech relieved him. It was like being sick.

"There are things about us, I'm sure, that make for disorder, disintegration, destruction, our destruction," he said once, while the fire blazed between us. "We've strayed out of a safe line somewhere."

And, another time, when the gong sounds had come nearer, ringing much louder than before, and directly over our heads, he said as though talking to himself:

"I don't think a gramophone would show any record of that. The sound doesn't come to me by the ears at all. The vibrations reach me in another manner altogether, and seem to be within me, which is precisely how a fourth dimensional sound might be supposed to make itself heard."

I purposely made no reply to this, but I sat up a little closer to the fire and peered about me into the darkness. The clouds were massed all over the sky, and no trace of moonlight came through. Very still, too, everything was, so that the river and the frogs had things all their own way.

"It has that about it," he went on, "which is utterly out of common experience. It is unknown. Only one thing describes it really; it is a non-human sound; I mean a sound outside humanity."

Having rid himself of this indigestible morsel, he lay quiet for a time, but he had so admirably expressed my own feeling that it was a relief to have the thought out, and to have confined it by the limitation of words from dangerous wandering to and fro in the mind.

The solitude of that Danube camping-place, can I ever forget it? The feeling of being utterly alone on an empty planet! My thoughts ran incessantly upon cities and the haunts of men. I would have given my soul, as the saying is, for the "feel" of those Bavarian villages we had passed through by the score; for the normal, human commonplaces; peasants drinking beer, tables beneath the trees, hot sunshine, and a ruined castle on the rocks behind the red-roofed church. Even the tourists would have been welcome.

Yet what I felt of dread was no ordinary ghostly fear. It was infinitely greater, stranger, and seemed to arise from some dim ancestral sense of terror more profoundly disturbing than anything I had known or dreamed of. We had "strayed," as the Swede put it, into some region or some set of conditions where the risks were great, yet unintelligible to us; where the frontiers of some unknown world lay close about us. It was a spot held by the dwellers in some outer space, a sort of peep-hole whence they could spy upon the earth, themselves unseen, a point where the veil between had worn a little thin. As the final result of too long a sojourn here, we should be carried over the border and deprived of what we called "our lives," yet by mental, not physical, processes. In that sense, as he said, we should be the victims of our adventure—a sacrifice.

It took us in different fashion, each according to the measure of his sensitiveness and powers of resistance. I translated it vaguely into a personification of the mightily disturbed elements, investing them with the horror of a deliberate and malefic purpose, resentful of our audacious intrusion into their breeding-place; whereas my friend threw it into the unoriginal form at first of a trespass on some ancient shrine, some place where the old gods still held sway, where the emotional forces of former worshippers still clung, and the ancestral portion of him yielded to the old pagan spell.

At any rate, here was a place unpolluted by men, kept clean by the winds from coarsening human influences, a place where spiritual agencies were within reach and aggressive. Never, before or since, have I been so attacked by indescribable suggestions of a "beyond region," of another scheme of life, another revolution not parallel to the human. And in the end our minds would succumb under the weight of the awful spell, and we should be drawn across the frontier into their world.

Small things testified to the amazing influence of the place, and now in the silence round the fire they allowed themselves to be noted by the mind. The very atmosphere had proved itself a magnifying medium to distort every indication: the otter rolling in the current, the hurrying boatman making signs, the shifting willows, one and all had been robbed of its natural character, and revealed in something of its other aspect—as it existed across the border to that other region. And this changed aspect I felt was now not merely to me, but to the race. The whole experience whose verge we touched was unknown to humanity at all. It was a new order of experience, and in the true sense of the word unearthly.

"It's the deliberate, calculating purpose that reduces one's courage to zero," the Swede said suddenly, as if he had been actually following my thoughts.

"Otherwise imagination might count for much. But the paddle, the canoe, the lessening food—"

"Haven't I explained all that once?" I interrupted viciously.

"You have," he answered dryly; "you have indeed."

He made other remarks too, as usual, about what he called the "plain determination to provide a victim"; but, having now arranged my thoughts better, I recognized that this was simply the cry of his frightened soul against the knowledge that he was being attacked in a vital part, and that he would be somehow taken or destroyed. The situation called for a courage and calmness of reasoning that neither of us could compass, and I have never before been so clearly conscious of two persons in me—the one that explained everything, and the other that laughed at such foolish explanations, yet was horribly afraid.

Meanwhile, in the pitchy night the fire died down and the wood pile grew small. Neither of us moved to replenish the stock, and the darkness consequently came up very close to our faces. A few feet beyond the circle of firelight it was inky black. Occasionally a stray puff of wind set the willows shivering about us, but apart from this not very welcome sound a deep and depressing silence reigned, broken only by the gurgling of the river and the humming in the air overhead.

We both missed, I think, the shouting company of the winds.

At length, at a moment when a stray puff prolonged itself as though the wind were about to rise again, I reached the point for me of saturation, the point where it was absolutely necessary to find relief in plain speech, or else to betray myself by some hysterical extravagance that must have been far worse in its effect upon both of us. I kicked the fire into a blaze, and turned to my companion abruptly. He looked up with a start.

"I can't disguise it any longer," I said; "I don't like this place, and the darkness, and the noises, and the awful feelings I get. There's something here that beats me utterly. I'm in a blue funk, and that's the plain truth. If the other shore was—different, I swear I'd be inclined to swim for it!"

The Swede's face turned very white beneath the deep tan of sun and wind. He stared straight at me and answered quietly, but his voice betrayed his huge excitement by its unnatural calmness. For the moment, at any rate, he was the strong man of the two. He was more phlegmatic, for one thing.

"It's not a physical condition we can escape from by running away," he replied, in the tone of a doctor diagnosing some grave disease; "we must sit tight and wait. There are forces close here that could kill a herd of elephants in a second as easily as you or I could squash a fly. Our only chance is to keep perfectly still. Our insignificance perhaps may save us."

I put a dozen questions into my expression of face, but found no words. It was precisely like listening to an accurate description of a disease whose symptoms had puzzled me.

"I mean that so far, although aware of our disturbing presence, they have not found us—not 'located' us, as the Americans say," he went on. "They're blundering about like men hunting for a leak of gas. The paddle and canoe and provisions prove that. I think they feel us, but cannot actually see us. We must keep our minds quiet—it's our minds they feel. We must control our thoughts, or it's all up with us."

"Death, you mean?" I stammered, icy with the horror of his suggestion.

"Worse—by far," he said. "Death, according to one's belief, means either annihilation or release from the limitations of the senses, but it involves no change of character. You don't suddenly alter just because the body's gone. But this means a radical alteration, a complete change, a horrible loss of oneself by substitution—far worse than death, and not even annihilation. We happen to have camped in a spot where their region touches ours, where the veil between has worn thin"—horrors! he was using my very own phrase, my actual words—"so that they are aware of our being in their neighborhood."

"But who are aware?" I asked.

I forgot the shaking of the willows in the windless calm, the humming overhead, everything except that I was waiting for an answer that I dreaded more than I can possibly explain.

He lowered his voice at once to reply, leaning forward a little over the fire, an indefinable change in his face that made me avoid his eyes and look down upon the ground.

"All my life," he said, "I have been strangely, vividly conscious of another region—not far removed from our own world in one sense, yet wholly different in kind—where great things go on unceasingly, where immense and terrible personalities hurry by, intent on vast purposes compared to which earthly affairs, the rise and fall of nations, the destinies of empires, the fate of armies and continents, are all as dust in the balance; vast purposes, I mean, that deal directly with the soul, and not indirectly with more expressions of the soul—"

"I suggest just now—" I began, seeking to stop him, feeling as though I was face to face with a madman. But he instantly overbore me with his torrent that had to come.

"You think," he said, "it is the spirit of the elements, and I thought perhaps it was the old gods. But I tell you now it is—neither. These would be comprehensible entities, for they have relations with men, depending upon them for worship or sacrifice, whereas these beings who are now about us have absolutely nothing to do with mankind, and it is mere chance that their space happens just at this spot to touch our own."

The mere conception, which his words somehow made so convincing, as I listened to them there in the dark stillness of that lonely island, set me shaking a little all over. I found it impossible to control my movements.

"And what do you propose?" I began again.

"A sacrifice, a victim, might save us by distracting them until we could get away," he went on, "just as the wolves stop to devour the dogs and give the sleigh another start. But—I see no chance of any other victim now."

I stared blankly at him. The gleam in his eye was dreadful. Presently he continued.

"It's the willows, of course. The willows mask the others, but the others are feeling about for us. If we let our minds betray our fear, we're lost, lost utterly." He looked at me with an expression so calm, so determined, so sincere, that I no longer had any doubts as to his sanity. He was as sane as any man ever was. "If we can hold out through the night," he added, "we may get off in the daylight unnoticed, or rather, undiscovered."

"But you really think a sacrifice would—"

That gong-like humming came down very close over our heads as I spoke, but it was my friend's scared face that really stopped my mouth.

"Hush!" he whispered, holding up his hand. "Do not mention them more than you can help. Do not refer to them by name. To name is to reveal; it is the inevitable clue, and our only hope lies in ignoring them, in order that they may ignore us."

"Even in thought?" He was extraordinarily agitated.

"Especially in thought. Our thoughts make spirals in their world. We must keep them out of our minds at all costs if possible."

I raked the fire together to prevent the darkness having everything its own way. I never longed for the sun as I longed for it then in the awful blackness of that summer night.

"Were you awake all last night?" he went on suddenly.

"I slept badly a little after dawn," I replied evasively, trying to follow his instructions, which I knew instinctively were true, "but the wind, of course—"

"I know. But the wind won't account for all the noises."

"Then you heard it too?"

"The multiplying countless little footsteps I heard," he said, adding, after a moment's hesitation, "and that other sound—"

"You mean above the tent, and the pressing down upon us of something tremendous, gigantic?"

He nodded significantly.

"It was like the beginning of a sort of inner suffocation?" I said.

"Partly, yes. It seemed to me that the weight of the atmosphere had been altered—had increased enormously, so that we should have been crushed."

"And that," I went on, determined to have it all out, pointing upwards where the gong-like note hummed ceaselessly, rising and falling like wind. "What do you make of that?"

"It's their sound," he whispered gravely. "It's the sound of their world, the humming in their region. The division here is so thin that it leaks through somehow. But, if you listen carefully, you'll find it's not above so much as around us. It's in the willows. It's the willows themselves humming, because here the willows have been made symbols of the forces that are against us."

I could not follow exactly what he meant by this, yet the thought and idea in my mind were beyond question the thought and idea in his. I realized what he realized, only with less power of analysis than his. It was on the tip of my tongue to tell him at last about my hallucination of the ascending figures and the moving bushes, when he suddenly thrust his face again close into mine across the firelight and began to speak in a very earnest whisper. He amazed me by his calmness and pluck, his apparent control of the situation. This man I had for years deemed unimaginative, stolid!

"Now listen," he said. "The only thing for us to do is to go on as though nothing had happened, follow our usual habits, go to bed, and so forth; pretend we feel nothing and notice nothing. It is a question wholly of the mind, and the less we think about them the better our chance of escape. Above all, don't think, for what you think happens!"

"All right," I managed to reply, simply breathless with his words and the strangeness of it all; "all right, I'll try, but tell me one more thing first. Tell me what you make of those hollows in the ground all about us, those sand-funnels?"

"No!" he cried, forgetting to whisper in his excitement. "I dare not, simply dare not, put the thought into words. If you have not guessed I am glad. Don't try to. They have put it into my mind; try your hardest to prevent their putting it into yours."

He sank his voice again to a whisper before he finished, and I did not press him to explain. There was already just about as much horror in me as I could hold. The conversation came to an end, and we smoked our pipes busily in silence.

Then something happened, something unimportant apparently, as the way is when the nerves are in a very great state of tension, and this small thing for a brief space gave me an entirely different point of view. I chanced to look down at my sand-shoe—the sort we used for the canoe—and something to do with the hole at the toe suddenly recalled to me the London shop where I had bought them, the difficulty the man had in fitting me, and other details of the uninteresting but practical operation. At once, in its train, followed a wholesome view of the modern skeptical world I was accustomed to move in at home. I thought of roast beef, and ale, motor-cars, policemen, brass bands, and a dozen other things that proclaimed the soul of ordinariness or utility. The effect was immediate and astonishing even to myself. Psychologically, I suppose, it was simply a sudden and violent reaction after the strain of living in an atmosphere of things that to the normal consciousness must seem impossible and incredible. But, whatever the cause, it momentarily lifted the spell from my heart, and left me for the short space of a minute feeling free and utterly unafraid. I looked up at my friend opposite.

"You damned old pagan!" I cried, laughing aloud in his face. "You imaginative idiot! You superstitious idolater! You—"

I stopped in the middle, seized anew by the old horror. I tried to smother the sound of my voice as something sacrilegious. The Swede, of course, heard it too—the strange cry overhead in the darkness—and that sudden drop in the air as though something had come nearer.

He had turned ashen white under the tan. He stood bolt upright in front of the fire, stiff as a rod, staring at me.

"After that," he said in a sort of helpless, frantic way, "we must go! We can't stay now; we must strike camp this very instant and go on—down the river."

He was talking, I saw, quite wildly, his words dictated by abject terror—the terror he had resisted so long, but which had caught him at last.

"In the dark?" I exclaimed, shaking with fear after my hysterical outburst, but still realizing our position better than he did. "Sheer madness! The river's in flood, and we've only got a single paddle. Besides, we only go deeper into their country! There's nothing ahead for fifty miles but willows, willows, willows!"

He sat down again in a state of semi-collapse. The positions, by one of those kaleidoscopic changes nature loves, were suddenly reversed, and the control of our forces passed over into my hands. His mind at last had reached the point where it was beginning to weaken.

"What on earth possessed you to do such a thing?" he whispered with the awe of genuine terror in his voice and face.

I crossed round to his side of the fire. I took both his hands in mine, kneeling down beside him and looking straight into his frightened eyes.

"We'll make one more blaze," I said firmly, "and then turn in for the night. At sunrise we'll be off full speed for Komorn. Now, pull yourself together a bit, and remember your own advice about not thinking fear!"

He said no more, and I saw that he would agree and obey. In some measure, too, it was a sort of relief to get up and make an excursion into the darkness for more wood. We kept close together, almost touching, groping among the bushes and along the bank. The humming overhead never ceased, but seemed to me to grow louder as we increased our distance from the fire. It was shivery work!

We were grubbing away in the middle of a thickish clump of willows where some driftwood from a former flood had caught high among the branches, when my body was seized in a grip that made me half drop upon the sand. It was the Swede. He had fallen against me, and was clutching me for support. I heard his breath coming and going in short gasps.

"Look! By my soul!" he whispered, and for the first time in my experience I knew what it was to hear tears of terror in a human voice. He was pointing to the fire, some fifty feet away. I followed the direction of his finger, and I swear my heart missed a beat.

There, in front of the dim glow, something was moving.

I saw it through a veil that hung before my eyes like the gauze drop-curtain used at the back of a theater—hazily a little. It was neither a human figure nor an animal. To me it gave the strange impression of being as large as several animals grouped together, like horses, two or three, moving slowly. The Swede, too, got a similar result, though expressing it differently, for he thought it was shaped and sized like a clump of willow bushes, rounded at the top, and moving all over upon its surface—"coiling upon itself like smoke," he said afterwards.

"I watched it settle downwards through the bushes," he sobbed at me. "Look, by God! It's coming this way! Oh, oh!"—he gave a kind of whistling cry. "They've found us."

I gave one terrified glance, which just enabled me to see that the shadowy form was swinging towards us through the bushes, and then I collapsed backwards with a crash into the branches. These failed, of course, to support my weight, so that with the Swede on top of me we fell in a struggling heap upon the sand. I really hardly knew what was happening. I was conscious only of a sort of enveloping sensation of icy fear that plucked the nerves out of their fleshly covering, twisted them this way and that, and replaced them quivering. My eyes were tightly shut; something in my throat choked me; a feeling that my consciousness was expanding, extending out into space, swiftly gave way to another feeling that I was losing it altogether, and about to die.

An acute spasm of pain passed through me, and I was aware that the Swede had hold of me in such a way that he hurt me abominably. It was the way he caught at me in falling.

But it was the pain, he declared afterwards, that saved me; it caused me to forget them and think of something else at the very instant when they were about to find me. It concealed my mind from them at the moment of discovery, yet just in time to evade their terrible seizing of me. He himself, he says, actually swooned at the same moment, and that was what saved him.

I only know that at a later date, how long or short is impossible to say, I found myself scrambling up out of the slippery network of willow branches, and saw my companion standing in front of me holding out a hand to assist me. I stared at him in a dazed way, rubbing the arm he had twisted for me. Nothing came to me to say, somehow.

"I lost consciousness for a moment or two," I heard him say. "That's what saved me. It made me stop thinking about them."

"You nearly broke my arm in two," I said, uttering my only connected thought at the moment. A numbness came over me.

"That's what saved you!" he replied. "Between us, we've managed to set them off on a false tack somewhere. The humming has ceased. It's gone—for the moment at any rate!"

A wave of hysterical laughter seized me again, and this time spread to my friend too—great healing gusts of shaking laughter that brought a tremendous sense of relief in their train. We made our way back to the fire and put the wood on so that it blazed at once. Then we saw that the tent had fallen over and lay in a tangled heap upon the ground.

We picked it up, and during the process tripped more than once and caught our feet in sand.

"It's those sand-funnels," exclaimed the Swede, when the tent was up again and the firelight lit up the ground for several yards about us. "And look at the size of them!"

All round the tent and about the fireplace where we had seen the moving shadows there were deep funnel-shaped hollows in the sand, exactly similar to the ones we had already found over the island, only far bigger and deeper, beautifully formed, and wide enough in some instances to admit the whole of my foot and leg.

Neither of us said a word. We both knew that sleep was the safest thing we could do, and to bed we went accordingly without further delay, having first thrown sand on the fire and taken the provision sack and the paddle inside the tent with us. The canoe, too, we propped in such a way at the end of the tent that our feet touched it, and the least motion would disturb and wake us.

In case of emergency, too, we again went to bed in our clothes, ready for a sudden start.

It was my firm intention to lie awake all night and watch, but the exhaustion of nerves and body decreed otherwise, and sleep after a while came over me with a welcome blanket of oblivion. The fact that my companion also slept quickened its approach. At first he fidgeted and constantly sat up, asking me if I "heard this" or "heard that." He tossed about on his cork mattress, and said the tent was moving and the river had risen over the point of the island, but each time I went out to look I returned with the report that all was well, and finally he grew calmer and lay still. Then at length his breathing became regular and I heard unmistakable sounds of snoring—the first and only time in my life when snoring has been a welcome and calming influence.

This, I remember, was the last thought in my mind before dozing off.

A difficulty in breathing woke me, and I found the blanket over my face. But something else besides the blanket was pressing upon me, and my first thought was that my companion had rolled off his mattress on to my own in his sleep. I called to him and sat up, and at the same moment it came to me that the tent was surrounded. That sound of multitudinous soft pattering was again audible outside, filling the night with horror.

I called again to him, louder than before. He did not answer, but I missed the sound of his snoring, and also noticed that the flap of the tent was down. This was the unpardonable sin. I crawled out in the darkness to hook it back securely, and it was then for the first time I realized positively that the Swede was not here. He had gone.

I dashed out in a mad run, seized by a dreadful agitation, and the moment I was out I plunged into a sort of torrent of humming that surrounded me completely and came out of every quarter of the heavens at once. It was that same familiar humming—gone mad! A swarm of great invisible bees might have been about me in the air. The sound seemed to thicken the very atmosphere, and I felt that my lungs worked with difficulty.

But my friend was in danger, and I could not hesitate.

The dawn was just about to break, and a faint whitish light spread upwards over the clouds from a thin strip of clear horizon. No wind stirred. I could just make out the bushes and river beyond, and the pale sandy patches. In my excitement I ran frantically to and fro about the island, calling him by name, shouting at the top of my voice the first words that came into my head. But the willows smothered my voice, and the humming muffled it, so that the sound only traveled a few feet round me. I plunged among the bushes, tripping headlong, tumbling over roots, and scraping my face as I tore this way and that among the preventing branches.

Then, quite unexpectedly, I came out upon the island's point and saw a dark figure outlined between the water and the sky. It was the Swede. And already he had one foot in the river! A moment more and he would have taken the plunge.

I threw myself upon him, flinging my arms about his waist and dragging him shorewards with all my strength. Of course he struggled furiously, making a noise all the time just like that cursed humming, and using the most outlandish phrases in his anger about "going inside to Them," and "taking the way of the water and the wind," and God only knows what more besides, that I tried in vain to recall afterwards, but which turned me sick with horror and amazement as I listened. But in the end I managed to get him into the comparative safety of the tent, and flung him breathless and cursing upon the mattress where I held him until the fit had passed.

I think the suddenness with which it all went and he grew calm, coinciding as it did with the equally abrupt cessation of the humming and pattering outside —I think this was almost the strangest part of the whole business perhaps. For he had just opened his eyes and turned his tired face up to me so that the dawn threw a pale light upon it through the doorway, and said, for all the world just like a frightened child:

"My life, old man—it's my life I owe you. But it's all over now anyhow. They've found a victim in our place!"

Then he dropped back upon his blankets and went to sleep literally under my eyes. He simply collapsed, and began to snore again as healthily as though nothing had happened and he had never tried to offer his own life as a sacrifice by drowning. And when the sunlight woke him three hours later—hours of ceaseless vigil for me—it became so clear to me that he remembered absolutely nothing of what he had attempted to do, that I deemed it wise to hold my peace and ask no dangerous questions.

He woke naturally and easily, as I have said, when the sun was already high in a windless hot sky, and he at once got up and set about the preparation of the fire for breakfast. I followed him anxiously at bathing, but he did not attempt to plunge in, merely dipping his head and making some remark about the extra coldness of the water.

"River's falling at last," he said, "and I'm glad of it."

"The humming has stopped too," I said.

He looked up at me quietly with his normal expression. Evidently he remembered everything except his own attempt at suicide.

"Everything has stopped," he said, "because—"

He hesitated. But I knew some reference to that remark he had made just before he fainted was in his mind, and I was determined to know it.

"Because 'They've found another victim'?" I said, forcing a little laugh.

"Exactly," he answered, "exactly! I feel as positive of it as though—as though —I feel quite safe again, I mean," he finished.

He began to look curiously about him. The sunlight lay in hot patches on the sand. There was no wind. The willows were motionless. He slowly rose to feet.

"Come," he said; "I think if we look, we shall find it."

He started off on a run, and I followed him. He kept to the banks, poking with a stick among the sandy bays and caves and little back-waters, myself always close on his heels.

"Ah!" he exclaimed presently, "ah!"

The tone of his voice somehow brought back to me a vivid sense of the horror of the last twenty-four hours, and I hurried up to join him. He was pointing with his stick at a large black object that lay half in the water and half on the sand. It appeared to be caught by some twisted willow roots so that the river could not sweep it away. A few hours before the spot must have been under water.

"See," he said quietly, "the victim that made our escape possible!"

And when I peered across his shoulder I saw that his stick rested on the body of a man. He turned it over. It was the corpse of a peasant, and the face was hidden in the sand. Clearly the man had been drowned, but a few hours before, and his body must have been swept down upon our island somewhere about the hour of the dawn—at the very time the fit had passed.

"We must give it a decent burial, you know."

"I suppose so," I replied. I shuddered a little in spite of myself, for there was something about the appearance of that poor drowned man that turned me cold.

The Swede glanced up sharply at me, an undecipherable expression on his face, and began clambering down the bank. I followed him more leisurely. The current, I noticed, had torn away much of the clothing from the body, so that the neck and part of the chest lay bare.

Halfway down the bank my companion suddenly stopped and held up his hand in warning; but either my foot slipped, or I had gained too much momentum to bring myself quickly to a halt, for I bumped into him and sent him forward with a sort of leap to save himself. We tumbled together on to the hard sand so that our feet splashed into the water. And, before anything could be done, we had collided a little heavily against the corpse.

The Swede uttered a sharp cry. And I sprang back as if I had been shot.

At the moment we touched the body there rose from its surface the loud sound of humming—the sound of several hummings—which passed with a vast commotion as of winged things in the air about us and disappeared upwards into the sky, growing fainter and fainter till they finally ceased in the distance. It was exactly as though we had disturbed some living yet invisible creatures at work.

My companion clutched me, and I think I clutched him, but before either of us had time properly to recover from the unexpected shock, we saw that a movement of the current was turning the corpse round so that it became released from the grip of the willow roots. A moment later it had turned completely over, the dead face uppermost, staring at the sky. It lay on the edge of the main stream. In another moment it would be swept away.

The Swede started to save it, shouting again something I did not catch about a "proper burial"—and then abruptly dropped upon his knees on the sand and covered his eyes with his hands. I was beside him in an instant.

I saw what he had seen.

For just as the body swung round to the current the face and the exposed chest turned full towards us, and showed plainly how the skin and flesh were indented with small hollows, beautifully formed, and exactly similar in shape and kind to the sand-funnels that we had found all over the island.

"Their mark!" I heard my companion mutter under his breath. "Their awful mark!"

And when I turned my eyes again from his ghastly face to the river, the current had done its work, and the body had been swept away into mid-stream and was already beyond our reach and almost out of sight, turning over and over on the waves like an otter.

The Bottle Imp

Robert Louis Stevenson

Note.—Any student of that very unliterary product, the English drama of the early part of the century, will here recognize the name and the root idea of a piece once rendered popular by the redoubtable O. Smith. The root idea is there and identical, and yet I hope I have made it a new thing. And the fact that the tale has been designed and written for a Polynesian audience may lend it some extraneous interest nearer home.— R. L. S.

There was a man of the Island of Hawaii, whom I shall call Keawe; for the truth is, he still lives, and his name must be kept secret; but the place of his birth was not far from Honaunau, where the bones of Keawe the Great lie hidden in a cave. This man was poor, brave, and active; he could read and write like a schoolmaster; he was a first-rate mariner besides, sailed for some time in the island steamers, and steered a whaleboat on the Hamakua coast. At length it came in Keawe's mind to have a sight of the great world and foreign cities, and he shipped on a vessel bound to San Francisco.

This is a fine town, with a fine harbor, and rich people uncountable; and, in particular, there is one hill which is covered with palaces. Upon this hill Keawe was one day taking a walk with his pocket full of money, viewing the great houses upon either hand with pleasure, "What fine houses these are!" he was thinking, "and how happy must those people be who dwell in them, and take no care for the morrow!" The thought was in his mind when he came abreast of a house that was smaller than some others, but all finished and beautified like a toy; the steps of that house shone like silver, and the borders of the garden bloomed like garlands, and the windows were bright like diamond; and Keawe stopped and wondered at the excellence of all he saw. So stopping, he was aware of a man that looked forth upon him through a window so clear that Keawe could see him as you see a fish in a pool upon the reef. The man was elderly, with a bald head and a black beard; and his face was heavy with sorrow, and he bitterly sighed. And the truth of it is, that as Keawe looked in upon the man, and the man looked out upon Keawe, each envied the other.

All of a sudden, the man smiled and nodded, and beckoned Keawe to enter, and met him at the door of the house.

"This is a fine house of mine," said the man, and bitterly sighed. "Would you not care to view the chambers?"

So he led Keawe all over it, from the cellar to the roof, and there was nothing there that was not perfect of its kind, and Keawe was astonished.

"Truly," said Keawe, "this is a beautiful house; if I lived in the like of it, I should be laughing all day long. How comes it, then, that you should be sighing?"

"There is no reason," said the man, "why you should not have a house in all points similar to this, and finer, if you wish. You have some money, I suppose?"

"I have fifty dollars," said Keawe; "but a house like this will cost more than fifty dollars."

The man made a computation. "I am sorry you have no more," said he, "for it may raise you trouble in the future; but it shall be yours at fifty dollars."

"The house?" asked Keawe.

"No, not the house," replied the man; "but the bottle. For, I must tell you, although I appear to you so rich and fortunate, all my fortune, and this house itself and its garden, came out of a bottle not much bigger than a pint. This is it."

And he opened a lockfast place, and took out a round-bellied bottle with a long neck; the glass of it was white like milk, with changing rainbow colors in the grain. Withinsides something obscurely moved, like a shadow and a fire.

"This is the bottle," said the man; and, when Keawe laughed, "You do not believe me?" he added. "Try, then, for yourself. See if you can break it."

So Keawe took the bottle up and dashed it on the floor till he was weary; but it jumped on the floor like a child's ball, and was not injured.

"This is a strange thing," said Keawe. "For by the touch of it, as well as by the look, the bottle should be of glass."

"Of glass it is," replied the man, sighing more heavily than ever; "but the glass of it was tempered in the flames of hell. An imp lives in it, and that is the shadow we behold there moving: or so I suppose. If any man buy this bottle the imp is at his command; all that he desires—love, fame, money, houses like this house, ay, or a city like this city—all are his at the word uttered. Napoleon had this bottle, and by it he grew to be the king of the world; but he sold it at the last, and fell. Captain Cook had this bottle, and by it he found his way to so many islands; but he, too, sold it, and was slain upon Hawaii. For, once it is sold, the power goes and the protection; and unless a man remain content with what he has, ill will befall him."

"And yet you talk of selling it yourself?" Keawe said.

"I have all I wish, and I am growing elderly," replied the man. "There is one thing the imp cannot do—he cannot prolong life; and, it would not be fair to conceal from you, there is a drawback to the bottle; for if a man die before he sells it, he must burn in hell forever."

"To be sure, that is a drawback and no mistake," cried Keawe. "I would not meddle with the thing. I can do without a house, thank God; but there is one thing I could not be doing with one particle, and that is to be damned."

"Dear me, you must not run away with things," returned the man. "All you have to do is to use the power of the imp in moderation, and then sell it to someone else, as I do to you, and finish your life in comfort."

"Well, I observe two things," said Keawe. "All the time you keep sighing like a maid in love, that is one; and, for the other, you sell this bottle very cheap."

"I have told you already why I sigh," said the man. "It is because I fear my health is breaking up; and, as you said yourself, to die and go to the devil is a pity for anyone. As for why I sell so cheap, I must explain to you there is a peculiarity about the bottle. Long ago, when the devil brought it first upon earth, it was extremely expensive, and was sold first of all to Prester John for many millions of dollars; but it cannot be sold at all, unless sold at a loss. If you sell it for as much as you paid for it, back it comes to you again like a homing pigeon. It follows that the price has kept falling in these centuries, and the bottle is now remarkably cheap. I bought it myself from one of my great neighbors on this hill, and the price I paid was only ninety dollars. I could sell it for as high as eighty-nine dollars and ninety-nine cents, but not a penny dearer, or back the thing must come to me. Now, about this there are two bothers. First, when you offer a bottle so singular for eighty odd dollars, people suppose you to be jesting. And second—but there is no hurry about that—and I need not go into it. Only remember it must be coined money that you sell it for."

"How am I to know that this is all true?" asked Keawe.

"Some of it you can try at once," replied the man. "Give me your fifty dollars, take the bottle, and wish your fifty dollars back into your pocket. If that does not happen, I pledge you my honor I will cry off the bargain and restore your money."

"You are not deceiving me?" said Keawe.

The man bound himself with a great oath.

"Well, I will risk that much," said Keawe, "for that can do no harm." And he paid over his money to the man, and the man handed him the bottle.

"Imp of the bottle," said Keawe, "I want my fifty dollars back." And sure enough he had scarce said the word before his pocket was as heavy as ever.

"To be sure this is a wonderful bottle," said Keawe.

"And now good-morning to you, my fine fellow, and the devil go with you for me!" said the man.

"Hold on," said Keawe, "I don't want any more of this fun. Here, take your bottle back."

"You have bought it for less than I paid for it," replied the man, rubbing his hands. "It is yours now; and, for my part, I am only concerned to see the back of you." And with that he rang for his Chinese servant, and had Keawe shown out of the house.

Now, when Keawe was in the street, with the bottle under his arm, he began to think. "If all is true about this bottle, I may have made a losing bargain," thinks he. "But perhaps the man was only fooling me." The first thing he did was to count his money; the sum was exact—forty-nine dollars American money, and one Chili piece. "That looks like the truth," said Keawe. "Now I will try another part."

The streets in that part of the city were as clean as a ship's decks, and though it was noon, there were no passengers. Keawe set the bottle in the gutter and walked away. Twice he looked back, and there was the milky, round-bellied bottle where he left it. A third time he looked back, and turned a corner; but he had scarce done so, when something knocked upon his elbow, and behold! it was the long neck sticking up; and as for the round belly, it was jammed into the pocket of his pilot-coat.

"And that looks like the truth," said Keawe.

The next thing he did was to buy a cork-screw in a shop, and go apart into a secret place in the fields. And there he tried to draw the cork, but as often as he put the screw in, out it came again, and the cork as whole as ever.

"This is some new sort of cork," said Keawe, and all at once he began to shake and sweat, for he was afraid of that bottle.

On his way back to the port-side, he saw a shop where a man sold shells and clubs from the wild islands, old heathen deities, old coined money, pictures from China and Japan, and all manner of things that sailors bring in their sea-chests. And here he had an idea. So he went in and offered the bottle for a hundred dollars. The man of the shop laughed at him at the first, and offered him five; but, indeed, it was a curious bottle—such glass was never blown in any human glassworks, so prettily the colors shone under the milky white, and so strangely the shadow hovered in the midst; so, after he had disputed awhile after the manner of his kind, the shop-man gave Keawe sixty silver dollars for the thing, and set it on a shelf in the midst of his window.

"Now," said Keawe, "I have sold that for sixty which I bought for fifty—or, to say truth, a little less, because one of my dollars was from Chili. Now I shall know the truth upon another point."

So he went back on board his ship, and, when he opened his chest, there was the bottle, and had come more quickly than himself. Now Keawe had a mate on board whose name was Lopaka.

"What ails you?" said Lopaka, "that you stare in your chest?"

They were alone in the ship's forecastle, and Keawe bound him to secrecy, and told all.

"This is a very strange affair," said Lopaka; "and I fear you will be in trouble about this bottle. But there is one point very clear—that you are sure of the trouble, and you had better have the profit in the bargain. Make up your mind what you want with it; give the order, and if it is done as you desire, I will buy the bottle myself; for I have an idea of my own to get a schooner, and go trading through the islands."

"That is not my idea," said Keawe; "but to have a beautiful house and garden on the Kona Coast, where I was born, the sun shining in at the door, flowers in the garden, glass in the windows, pictures on the walls, and toys and fine carpets on the tables, for all the world like the house I was in this day—only a story higher, and with balconies all about like the King's palace; and to live there without care and make merry with my friends and relatives."

"Well," said Lopaka, "let us carry it back with us to Hawaii; and if all comes true, as you suppose, I will buy the bottle, as I said, and ask a schooner."

Upon that they were agreed, and it was not long before the ship returned to Honolulu, carrying Keawe and Lopaka, and the bottle. They were scarce come ashore when they met a friend upon the beach, who began at once to condole with Keawe.

"I do not know what I am to be condoled about," said Keawe.

"Is it possible you have not heard," said the friend, "your uncle—that good old man—is dead, and your cousin—that beautiful boy—was drowned at sea?"

Keawe was filled with sorrow, and, beginning to weep and to lament, he forgot about the bottle. But Lopaka was thinking to himself, and presently, when Keawe's grief was a little abated, "I have been thinking," said Lopaka. "Had not your uncle lands in Hawaii, in the district of Kau?"

"No," said Keawe, "not in Kau; they are on the mountain-side—a little way south of Hookena."

"These lands will now be yours?" asked Lopaka.

"And so they will," says Keawe, and began again to lament for his relatives.

"No," said Lopaka, "do not lament at present. I have a thought in my mind. How if this should be the doing of the bottle? For here is the place ready for your house."

"If this be so," cried Keawe, "it is a very ill way to serve me by killing my relatives. But it may be, indeed; for it was in just such a station that I saw the house with my mind's eye."

"The house, however, is not yet built," said Lopaka.

"No, nor like to be!" said Keawe; "for though my uncle has some coffee and ava and bananas, it will not be more than will keep me in comfort; and the rest of that land is the black lava."

"Let us go to the lawyer," said Lopaka; "I have still this idea in my mind."

Now, when they came to the lawyer's, it appeared Keawe's uncle had grown monstrous rich in the last days, and there was a fund of money.

"And here is the money for the house!" cried Lopaka.

"If you are thinking of a new house," said the lawyer, "here is the card of a new architect, of whom they tell me great things."

"Better and better!" cried Lopaka. "Here is all made plain for us. Let us continue to obey orders."

So they went to the architect, and he had drawings of houses on his table.

"You want something out of the way," said the architect. "How do you like this?" and he handed a drawing to Keawe.

Now, when Keawe set eyes on the drawing, he cried out aloud, for it was the picture of his thought exactly drawn.

"I am in for this house," thought he. "Little as I like the way it comes to me, I am in for it now, and I may as well take the good along with the evil."

So he told the architect all that he wished, and how he would have that house furnished, and about the pictures on the wall and the knick-knacks on the tables; and he asked the man plainly for how much he would undertake the whole affair.

The architect put many questions, and took his pen and made a computation; and when he had done he named the very sum that Keawe had inherited.

Lopaka and Keawe looked at one another and nodded.

"It is quite clear," thought Keawe, "that I am to have this house, whether or no. It comes from the devil, and I fear I will get little good by that; and of one thing I am sure, I will make no more wishes as long as I have this bottle. But with the house I am saddled, and I may as well take the good along with the evil."

So he made his terms with the architect, and they signed a paper; and Keawe and Lopaka took ship again and sailed to Australia; for it was concluded between them they should not interfere at all, but leave the architect and the bottle imp to build and to adorn that house at their own pleasure.

The voyage was a good voyage, only all the time Keawe was holding in his breath, for he had sworn he would utter no more wishes, and take no more favors from the devil. The time was up when they got back. The architect told them that the house was ready, and Keawe and Lopaka took a passage in the *Hall*, and went down Kona way to view the house, and see if all had been done fitly according to the thought that was in Keawe's mind.

Now the house stood on the mountain side, visible to ships. Above, the forest ran up into the clouds of rain; below, the black lava fell in cliffs, where the kings of old lay buried. A garden bloomed about that house with every hue of flowers; and there was an orchard of papaya on the one hand and an orchard of breadfruit on the other, and right in front, toward the sea, a ship's mast had been rigged up and bore a flag. As for the house, it was three stories high, with great chambers and broad balconies on each. The windows were of glass, so excellent that it was as clear as water and as bright as day. All manner of furniture adorned the chambers. Pictures hung upon the wall in golden frames: pictures of ships, and men fighting, and of the most beautiful women, and of singular places; nowhere in the world are there pictures of so bright a color as those Keawe found hanging in his house. As for the knick-knacks, they were extraordinary fine; chiming clocks and musical boxes, little men with nodding heads, books filled with pictures, weapons of price from all quarters of the world, and the most elegant puzzles to entertain the leisure of a solitary man. And as no one would care to live in such chambers, only to walk through and view them, the balconies were made so broad that a whole town might have lived upon them in delight; and Keawe knew not which to prefer, whether the back porch, where you got the land breeze, and looked upon the orchards and the flowers, or the front balcony, where you could drink the wind of the sea, and look down the steep wall of the mountain and see the *Hall* going by once a week or so between Hookena and the hills of Pele, or the schooners plying up the coast for wood and ava and bananas.

When they had viewed all, Keawe and Lopaka sat on the porch.

"Well," asked Lopaka, "is it all as you designed?"

"Words cannot utter it," said Keawe. "It is better than I dreamed, and I am sick with satisfaction."

"There is but one thing to consider," said Lopaka; "all this may be quite natural, and the bottle imp have nothing whatever to say to it. If I were to buy the bottle, and got no schooner after all, I should have put my hand in the fire for nothing. I gave you my word, I know; but yet I think you would not grudge me one more proof."

"I have sworn I would take no more favors," said Keawe. "I have gone already deep enough."

"This is no favor I am thinking of," replied Lopaka. "It is only to see the imp himself. There is nothing to be gained by that, and so nothing to be ashamed of; and yet, if I once saw him, I should be sure of the whole matter. So indulge me so far, and let me see the imp; and, after that, here is the money in my hand, and I will buy it."

"There is only one thing I am afraid of," said Keawe. "The imp may be very ugly to view; and if you once set eyes upon him you might be very undesirous of the bottle."

"I am a man of my word," said Lopaka. "And here is the money betwixt us."

"Very well," replied Keawe. "I have a curiosity myself. So come, let us have one look at you, Mr. Imp."

Now as soon as that was said, the imp looked out of the bottle, and in again, swift as a lizard; and there sat Keawe and Lopaka turned to stone. The night had quite come, before either found a thought to say or voice to say it with; and then Lopaka pushed the money over and took the bottle.

"I am a man of my word," said he, "and had need to be so, or I would not touch this bottle with my foot. Well, I shall get my schooner and a dollar or two for my pocket; and then I will be rid of this devil as fast as I can. For to tell you the plain truth, the look of him has cast me down."

"Lopaka," said Keawe, "do not you think any worse of me than you can help; I know it is night, and the roads bad, and the pass by the tombs an ill place to go by so late, but I declare since I have seen that little face, I cannot eat or sleep or pray till it is gone from me. I will give you a lantern and a basket to put the bottle in, and any picture or fine thing in all my house that takes your fancy;—and be gone at once, and go sleep at Hookena with Nahinu."

"Keawe," said Lopaka, "many a man would take this ill; above all, when I am doing you a turn so friendly, as to keep my word and buy the bottle; and for that matter, the night and the dark, and the way by the tombs, must be all tenfold more dangerous to a man with such a sin upon his conscience, and such a bottle under his arm. But for my part, I am so extremely terrified myself, I have not the heart to blame you. Here I go then; and I pray God you may be happy in your house, and I fortunate with my schooner, and both get to heaven in the end in spite of the devil and his bottle."

So Lopaka went down the mountain; and Keawe stood in his front balcony, and listened to the clink of the horse's shoes, and watched the lantern go shining down the path, and along the cliff of caves where the old dead are buried; and all the time he trembled and clasped his hands, and prayed for his friend, and gave glory to God that he himself was escaped out of that trouble.

But the next day came very brightly, and that new house of his was so delightful to behold that he forgot his terrors. One day followed another, and Keawe dwelt there in perpetual joy. He had his place on the back porch; it was there he ate and lived, and read the stories in the Honolulu newspapers; but when anyone came by they would go in and view the chambers and the pictures. And the fame of the house went far and wide; it was called *Ka-Hale Nui*—the Great House—in all Kona; and sometimes the Bright House, for Keawe kept a Chinaman, who was all day dusting and furbishing; and the glass, and the gilt, and the fine stuffs, and the pictures, shone as bright as the morning. As for Keawe himself, he could not walk in the chambers without singing, his heart was so enlarged; and when ships sailed by upon the sea, he would fly his colors on the mast.

So time went by, until one day Keawe went upon a visit as far as Kailua to certain of his friends. There he was well feasted; and left as soon as he could the next morning, and rode hard, for he was impatient to behold his beautiful house; and, besides, the night then coming on was the night in which the dead of old days go abroad in the sides of Kona; and having already meddled with the devil, he was the more chary of meeting with the dead. A little beyond Honaunau, looking far ahead, he was aware of a woman bathing in the edge of the sea; and she seemed a well-grown girl, but he thought no more of it. Then he saw her white shift flutter as she put it on, and then her red holoku; and by the time he came abreast of her she was done with her toilet, and had come up from the sea, and stood by the track-side in her red holoku, and she was all freshened with the bath, and her eyes shone and were kind. Now Keawe no sooner beheld her than he drew rein.

"I thought I knew everyone in this country," said he. "How comes it that I do not know you?"

"I am Kokua, daughter of Kiano," said the girl, "and I have just returned from Oahu. Who are you?"

"I will tell you who I am in a little," said Keawe, dismounting from his horse, "but not now. For I have a thought in my mind, and if you knew who I was, you might have heard of me, and would not give me a true answer. But tell me, first of all, one thing: Are you married?"

At this Kokua laughed out aloud. "It is you who ask questions," she said. "Are you married yourself?"

"Indeed, Kokua, I am not," replied Keawe, "and never thought to be until this hour. But here is the plain truth. I have met you here at the roadside, and I saw your eyes, which are like the stars, and my heart went to you as swift as a bird. And so now, if you want none of me, say so, and I will go on to my own place; but if you think me no worse than any other young man, say so, too, and I will turn aside to your father's for the night, and to-morrow I will talk with the good man."

Kokua said never a word, but she looked at the sea and laughed.

"Kokua," said Keawe, "if you say nothing, I will take that for the good answer; so let us be stepping to your father's door."

She went on ahead of him, still without speech; only sometimes she glanced back and glanced away again, and she kept the strings of her hat in her mouth.

Now, when they had come to the door, Kiano came out on his verandah, and cried out and welcomed Keawe by name. At that the girl looked over, for the fame of the great house had come to her ears; and, to be sure, it was a great temptation. All that evening they were very merry together; and the girl was as bold as brass under the eyes of her parents, and made a mock of Keawe, for she had a quick wit. The next day he had a word with Kiano, and found the girl alone.

"Kokua," said he, "you made a mock of me all the evening; and it is still time to bid me go. I would not tell you who I was, because I have so fine a house, and I feared you would think too much of that house and too little of the man that loves you. Now you know all, and if you wish to have seen the last of me, say so at once."

"No," said Kokua; but this time she did not laugh, nor did Keawe ask for more.

This was the wooing of Keawe; things had gone quickly; but so an arrow goes, and the ball of a rifle swifter still, and yet both may strike the target. Things had gone fast, but they had gone far also, and the thought of Keawe rang in the maiden's head; she heard his voice in the breach of the surf upon the lava, and for this young man that she had seen but twice she would have left father and mother and her native islands. As for Keawe himself, his horse flew up the path of the mountain under the cliff of tombs, and the sound of the hoofs, and the sound of Keawe singing to himself for pleasure, echoed in the caverns of the dead. He came to the Bright House, and still he was singing. He sat and ate in the broad balcony, and the Chinaman wondered at his master, to hear how he sang between the mouthfuls. The sun went down into the sea, and the night came; and Keawe walked the balconies by lamplight, high on the mountains, and the voice of his singing startled men on ships.

"Here am I now upon my high place," he said to himself. "Life may be no better; this is the mountain top; and all shelves about me toward the worse. For the first time I will light up the chambers, and bathe in my fine bath with the hot water and the cold, and sleep alone in the bed of my bridal chamber."

So the Chinaman had word, and he must rise from sleep and light the furnaces; and as he wrought below, beside the boilers, he heard his master singing and rejoicing above him in the lighted chambers. When the water began to be hot the Chinaman cried to his master; and Keawe went into the bathroom; and the Chinaman heard him sing as he filled the marble basin; and heard him sing, and the singing broken, as he undressed; until of a sudden, the song ceased. The Chinaman listened, and listened; he called up the house to Keawe to ask if all were well, and Keawe answered him "Yes," and bade him go to bed; but there was no more singing in the Bright House; and all night long, the Chinaman heard his master's feet go round and round the balconies without repose.

Now the truth of it was this: as Keawe undressed for his bath, he spied upon his flesh a patch like a patch of lichen on a rock, and it was then that he stopped singing. For he knew the likeness of that patch, and knew that he was taken with leprosy.

Now, it is a sad thing for any man to fall into this sickness. And it would be a sad thing for anyone to leave a house so beautiful and so commodious, and depart from all his friends to the north coast of Molokai between the mighty cliff and the sea-breakers. But what was that to the case of the man Keawe, he who had met his love but yesterday, and won her but that morning, and now saw all his hopes break, in a moment, like a piece of glass?

Awhile he sat upon the edge of the bath; then sprang, with a cry, and ran outside; and to and fro, to and fro, along the balcony, like one despairing.

"Very willingly could I leave Hawaii, the home of my fathers," Keawe was thinking. "Very lightly could I leave my house, the high-placed, the many-windowed, here upon the mountains. Very bravely could I go to Molokai, to Kalaupapa by the cliffs, to live with the smitten and to sleep there, far from my fathers. But what wrong have I done, what sin lies upon my soul, that I should have encountered Kokua coming cool from the sea-water in the evening? Kokua, the soul ensnarer! Kokua, the light of my life! Her may I never wed, her may I look upon no longer, her may I no more handle with my loving hand; and it is for this, it is for you, O Kokua! that I pour my lamentations!"

Now you are to observe what sort of a man Keawe was, for he might have dwelt there in the Bright House for years, and no one been the wiser of his sickness; but he reckoned nothing of that, if he must lose Kokua. And again, he might have wed Kokua even as he was; and so many would have done, because they have the souls of pigs; but Keawe loved the maid manfully, and he would do her no hurt and bring her in no danger.

A little beyond the midst of the night, there came in his mind the recollection of that bottle. He went round to the back porch, and called to memory the day when the devil had looked forth; and at the thought ice ran in his veins.

"A dreadful thing is the bottle," thought Keawe, "and dreadful is the imp, and it is a dreadful thing to risk the flames of hell. But what other hope have I to cure my sickness or to wed Kokua? What!" he thought, "would I beard the devil once, only to get me a house, and not face him again to win Kokua?"

Thereupon he called to mind it was the next day the *Hall* went by on her return to Honolulu. "There must I go first," he thought, "and see Lopaka. For the best hope that I have now is to find that same bottle I was so pleased to be rid of."

Never a wink could he sleep; the food stuck in his throat; but he sent a letter to Kiano, and about the time when the steamer would be coming, rode down beside the cliff of the tombs. It rained; his horse went heavily; he looked up at the black mouths of the caves, and he envied the dead that slept there and were done with trouble; and called to mind how he had galloped by the day before, and was astonished. So he came down to Hookena, and there was all the country gathered for the steamer as usual. In the shed before the store they sat and jested and passed the news; but there was no matter of speech in Keawe's bosom, and he sat in their midst and looked without on the rain falling on the houses, and the surf beating among the rocks, and the sighs arose in his throat.

"Keawe of the Bright House is out of spirits," said one to another. Indeed, and so he was, and little wonder.

Then the *Hall* came, and the whaleboat carried him on board. The after-part of the ship was full of Haoles who had been to visit the volcano, as their custom is; and the midst was crowded with Kanakas, and the forepart with wild bulls from Hilo and horses from Kau; but Keawe sat apart from all in his sorrow, and watched for the house of Kiano. There it sat, low upon the shore in the black rocks, and shaded by the cocoa palms, and there by the door was a red holoku, no greater than a fly, and going to and fro with a fly's busyness. "Ah, queen of my heart," he cried, "I'll venture my dear soul to win you!"

Soon after, darkness fell, and the cabins were lit up, and the Haoles sat and played at the cards and drank whiskey as their custom is; but Keawe walked the deck all night; and all the next day, as they steamed under the lee of Maui or of Molokai, he was still pacing to and fro like a wild animal in a menagerie.

Towards evening they passed Diamond Head, and came to the pier of Honolulu. Keawe stepped out among the crowd and began to ask for Lopaka. It seemed he had become the owner of a schooner—none better in the islands—and was gone upon an adventure as far as Pola-Pola or Kahiki; so there was no help to be looked for from Lopaka. Keawe called to mind a friend of his, a lawyer in the town (I must not tell his name), and inquired of him. They said he was grown suddenly rich, and had a fine new house upon Waikiki shore; and this put a thought in Keawe's head, and he called a hack and drove to the lawyer's house.

The house was all brand new, and the trees in the garden no greater than walking-sticks, and the lawyer, when he came, had the air of a man well pleased.

"What can I do to serve you?" said the lawyer.

"You are a friend of Lopaka's," replied Keawe, "and Lopaka purchased from me a certain piece of goods that I thought you might enable me to trace."

The lawyer's face became very dark. "I do not profess to misunderstand you, Mr. Keawe," said he, "though this is an ugly business to be stirring in. You may be sure I know nothing, but yet I have a guess, and if you would apply in a certain quarter I think you might have news."

And he named the name of a man, which, again, I had better not repeat. So it was for days, and Keawe went from one to another, finding everywhere new clothes and carriages, and fine new houses and men everywhere in great contentment, although, to be sure, when he hinted at his business their faces would cloud over.

"No doubt I am upon the track," thought Keawe. "These new clothes and carriages are all the gifts of the little imp, and these glad faces are the faces of men who have taken their profit and got rid of the accursed thing in safety. When I see pale cheeks and hear sighing, I shall know that I am near the bottle."

So it befell at last that he was recommended to a Haole in Beritania Street. When he came to the door, about the hour of the evening meal, there were the usual marks of the new house, and the young garden, and the electric light shining in the windows; but when the owner came, a shock of hope and fear ran through Keawe; for here was a young man, white as a corpse, and black about the eyes, the hair shedding from his head, and such a look in his countenance as a man may have when he is waiting for the gallows.

"Here it is, to be sure," thought Keawe, and so with this man he noways veiled his errand. "I am come to buy the bottle," said he.

At the word, the young Haole of Beritania Street reeled against the wall. "The bottle!" he gasped. "To buy the bottle!" Then he seemed to choke, and seizing Keawe by the arm carried him into a room and poured out wine in two glasses.

"Here is my respects," said Keawe, who had been much about with Haoles in his time. "Yes," he added, "I am come to buy the bottle. What is the price by now?"

At that word the young man let his glass slip through his fingers, and looked upon Keawe like a ghost.

"The price," says he; "the price! You do not know the price?"

"It is for that I am asking you," returned Keawe. "But why are you so much concerned? Is there anything wrong about the price?"

"It has dropped a great deal in value since your time, Mr. Keawe," said the young man stammering.

"Well, well, I shall have the less to pay for it," says Keawe. "How much did it cost you?"

The young man was as white as a sheet. "Two cents," said he.

"What?" cried Keawe, "two cents? Why, then, you can only sell it for one. And he who buys it—" The words died upon Keawe's tongue; he who bought it could never sell it again, the bottle and the bottle imp must abide with him until he died, and when he died must carry him to the red end of hell.

The young man of Beritania Street fell upon his knees. "For God's sake buy it!" he cried. "You can have all my fortune in the bargain. I was mad when I bought it at that price. I had embezzled money at my store; I was lost else; I must have gone to jail."

"Poor creature," said Keawe, "you would risk your soul upon so desperate an adventure, and to avoid the proper punishment of your own disgrace; and you think I could hesitate with love in front of me. Give me the bottle, and the change which I make sure you have all ready. Here is a five-cent piece."

It was as Keawe supposed; the young man had the change ready in a drawer; the bottle changed hands, and Keawe's fingers were no sooner clasped upon the stalk than he had breathed his wish to be a clean man. And, sure enough, when he got home to his room, and stripped himself before a glass, his flesh was whole like an infant's. And here was the strange thing: he had no sooner seen this miracle, than his mind was changed within him, and he cared naught for the leprosy, and little enough for Kokua; and had but the one thought, that here he was bound to the bottle imp for time and for eternity, and had no better hope but to be a cinder for ever in the flames of hell. Away ahead of him he saw them blaze with his mind's eye, and his soul shrank, and darkness fell upon the light.

When Keawe came to himself a little, he was aware it was the night when the band played at the hotel. Thither he went, because he feared to be alone; and there, among happy faces, walked to and fro, and heard the tunes go up and down, and saw Berger beat the measure, and all the while he heard the flames crackle, and saw the red fire burning in the bottomless pit. Of a sudden the band played *Hiki-ao-ao*; that was a song that he had sung with Kokua, and at the strain courage returned to him.

"It is done now," he thought, "and once more let me take the good along with the evil."

So it befell that he returned to Hawaii by the first steamer, and as soon as it could be managed he was wedded to Kokua, and carried her up the mountain side to the Bright House.

Now it was so with these two, that when they were together, Keawe's heart was stilled; but so soon as he was alone he fell into a brooding horror, and heard the flames crackle, and saw the red fire burn in the bottomless pit. The girl, indeed, had come to him wholly; her heart leapt in her side at sight of him, her hand clung to his; and she was so fashioned from the hair upon her head to the nails upon her toes that none could see her without joy. She was pleasant in her nature. She had the good word always. Full of song she was, and went to and fro in the Bright House, the brightest thing in its three stories, caroling like the birds. And Keawe beheld and heard her with delight, and then must shrink upon one side, and weep and groan to think upon the price that he had paid for her; and then he must dry his eyes, and wash his face, and go and sit with her on the broad balconies, joining in her songs, and, with a sick spirit, answering her smiles.

There came a day when her feet began to be heavy and her songs more rare; and now it was not Keawe only that would weep apart, but each would sunder from the other and sit in opposite balconies with the whole width of the Bright House betwixt. Keawe was so sunk in his despair, he scarce observed the change, and was only glad he had more hours to sit alone and brood upon his destiny, and was not so frequently condemned to pull a smiling face on a sick heart. But one day, coming softly through the house, he heard the sound of a child sobbing, and there was Kokua rolling her face upon the balcony floor, and weeping like the lost.

"You do well to weep in this house, Kokua," he said. "And yet I would give the head off my body that you (at least) might have been happy."

"Happy!" she cried. "Keawe, when you lived alone in your Bright House, you were the word of the island for a happy man; laughter and song were in your mouth, and your face was as bright as the sunrise. Then you wedded poor Kokua; and the good God knows what is amiss in her—but from that day you have not smiled. Oh!" she cried, "what ails me? I thought I was pretty, and I knew I loved him. What ails me that I throw this cloud upon my husband?"

"Poor Kokua," said Keawe. He sat down by her side, and sought to take her hand; but that she plucked away. "Poor Kokua," he said, again. "My poor child—my pretty. And I had thought all this while to spare you! Well, you shall know all. Then, at least, you will pity poor Keawe; then you will understand how much he loved you in the past—that he dared hell for your possession—and how much he loves you still (the poor condemned one), that he can yet call up a smile when he beholds you."

With that, he told her all, even from the beginning.

"You have done this for me?" she cried "Ah, well, then what do I care!"—and she clasped and wept upon him.

"Ah, child!" said Keawe, "and yet, when I consider of the fire of hell, I care a good deal!"

"Never tell me," said she; "no man can be lost because he loved Kokua, and no other fault. I tell you, Keawe, I shall save you with these hands, or perish in your company. What! you loved me, and gave your soul, and you think I will not die to save you in return?"

"Ah, my dear! you might die a hundred times, and what difference would that make?" he cried, "except to leave me lonely till the time comes of my damnation?"

"You know nothing," said she. "I was educated in a school in Honolulu; I am no common girl. And I tell you, I shall save my lover. What is this you say about a cent? But all the world is not American. In England they have a piece they call a farthing, which is about half a cent. Ah! sorrow!" she cried, "that makes it scarcely better, for the buyer must be lost, and we shall find none so brave as my Keawe! But, then, there is France; they have a small coin there which they call a centime, and these go five to the cent or there-about. We could not do better. Come, Keawe, let us go to the French islands; let us go to Tahiti, as fast as ships can bear us. There we have four centimes, three centimes, two centimes, one centime; four possible sales to come and go on; and two of us to push the bargain. Come, my Keawe! kiss me, and banish care. Kokua will defend you."

"Gift of God!" he cried. "I cannot think that God will punish me for desiring aught so good! Be it as you will, then; take me where you please: I put my life and my salvation in your hands."

Early the next day Kokua was about her preparations. She took Keawe's chest that he went with sailoring; and first she put the bottle in a corner; and then packed it with the richest of their clothes and the bravest of the knick-knacks in the house. "For," said she, "we must seem to be rich folks, or who will believe in the bottle?" All the time of her preparation she was as gay as a bird; only when she looked upon Keawe, the tears would spring in her eye, and she must run and kiss him. As for Keawe, a weight was off his soul; now that he had his secret shared, and some hope in front of him, he seemed like a new man, his feet went lightly on the earth, and his breath was good to him again. Yet was terror still at his elbow; and ever and again, as the wind blows out a taper, hope died in him, and he saw the flames toss and the red fire burn in hell.

It was given out in the country they were gone pleasuring to the States, which was thought a strange thing, and yet not so strange as the truth, if any could have guessed it. So they went to Honolulu in the *Hall*, and thence in the *Umatilla* to San Francisco with a crowd of Haoles, and at San Francisco took their passage by the mail brigantine, the *Tropic Bird*, for Papeete, the chief place of the French in the south islands. Thither they came, after a pleasant voyage, on a fair day of the Trade Wind, and saw the reef with the surf breaking, and Motuiti with its palms, and the schooner riding within-side, and the white houses of the town low down along the shore among green trees, and overhead the mountains and the clouds of Tahiti, the wise island.

It was judged the most wise to hire a house, which they did accordingly, opposite the British Consul's, to make a great parade of money, and themselves conspicuous with carriages and horses. This it was very easy to do, so long as they had the bottle in their possession; for Kokua was more bold than Keawe, and, whenever she had a mind, called on the imp for twenty or a hundred dollars. At this rate they soon grew to be remarked in the town; and the strangers from Hawaii, their riding and their driving, the fine holokus and the rich lace of Kokua, became the matter of much talk.

They got on well after the first with the Tahitian language, which is indeed like to the Hawaiian, with a change of certain letters; and as soon as they had any freedom of speech, began to push the bottle. You are to consider it was not an easy subject to introduce; it was not easy to persuade people you were in earnest, when you offered to sell them for four centimes the spring of health and riches inexhaustible. It was necessary besides to explain the dangers of the bottle; and either people disbelieved the whole thing and laughed, or they thought the more of the darker part, became overcast with gravity, and drew away from Keawe and Kokua, as from persons who had dealings with the devil. So far from gaining ground, these two began to find they were avoided in the town; the children ran away from them screaming, a thing intolerable to Kokua; Catholics crossed themselves as they went by; and all persons began with one accord to disengage themselves from their advances.

Depression fell upon their spirits. They would sit at night in their new house, after a day's weariness, and not exchange one word, or the silence would be broken by Kokua bursting suddenly into sobs. Sometimes they would pray together; sometimes they would have the bottle out upon the floor, and sit all evening watching how the shadow hovered in the midst. At such times they would be afraid to go to rest. It was long ere slumber came to them, and, if either dozed off, it would be to wake and find the other silently weeping in the dark, or, perhaps, to wake alone, the other having fled from the house and the neighborhood of that bottle, to pace under the bananas in the little garden, or to wander on the beach by moonlight.

One night it was so when Kokua awoke. Keawe was gone. She felt in the bed and his place was cold. Then fear fell upon her, and she sat up in bed. A little moonshine filtered through the shutters. The room was bright, and she could spy the bottle on the floor. Outside it blew high, the great trees of the avenue cried aloud, and the fallen leaves rattled in the verandah. In the midst of this Kokua was aware of another sound; whether of a beast or of a man she could scarce tell, but it was as sad as death, and cut her to the soul. Softly she arose, set the door ajar, and looked forth into the moonlit yard. There, under the bananas, lay Keawe, his mouth in the dust, and as he lay he moaned.

It was Kokua's first thought to run forward and console him; her second potently withheld her. Keawe had borne himself before his wife like a brave man; it became her little in the hour of weakness to intrude upon his shame. With the thought she drew back into the house.

"Heaven!" she thought, "how careless have I been—how weak! It is he, not I, that stands in this eternal peril; it was he, not I, that took the curse upon his soul. It is for my sake, and for the love of a creature of so little worth and such poor help, that he now beholds so close to him the flames of hell—ay, and smells the smoke of it, lying without there in the wind and moonlight. Am I so dull of spirit that never till now I have surmised my duty, or have I seen it before and turned aside? But now, at least, I take up my soul in both the hands of my affection; now I say farewell to the white steps of heaven and the waiting faces of my friends. A love for a love, and let mine be equalled with Keawe's! A soul for a soul, and be it mine to perish!"

She was a deft woman with her hands, and was soon appareled. She took in her hands the change—the precious centimes they kept ever at their side; for this coin is little used, and they had made provision at a Government office. When she was forth in the avenue clouds came on the wind, and the moon was blackened. The town slept, and she knew not whither to turn till she heard one coughing in the shadow of the trees.

"Old man," said Kokua, "what do you here abroad in the cold night?"

The old man could scarce express himself for coughing, but she made out that he was old and poor, and a stranger in the island.

"Will you do me a service?" said Kokua. "As one stranger to another, and as an old man to a young woman, will you help a daughter of Hawaii?"

"Ah," said the old man. "So you are the witch from the eight islands, and even my old soul you seek to entangle. But I have heard of you, and defy your wickedness."

"Sit down here," said Kokua, "and let me tell you a tale." And she told him the story of Keawe from the beginning to the end.

"And now," said she, "I am his wife, whom he bought with his soul's welfare. And what should I do? If I went to him myself and offered to buy it, he would refuse. But if you go, he will sell it eagerly; I will await you here; you will buy it for four centimes, and I will buy it again for three. And the Lord strengthen a poor girl!"

"If you meant falsely," said the old man, "I think God would strike you dead."

"He would!" cried Kokua. "Be sure he would. I could not be so treacherous —God would not suffer it."

"Give me the four centimes and await me here," said the old man.

Now, when Kokua stood alone in the street, her spirit died. The wind roared in the trees, and it seemed to her the rushing of the flames of hell; the shadows tossed in the light of the street lamp, and they seemed to her the snatching hands of evil ones. If she had had the strength, she must have run away, and if she had had the breath she must have screamed aloud; but, in truth, she could do neither, and stood and trembled in the avenue, like an affrighted child.

Then she saw the old man returning, and he had the bottle in his hand.

"I have done your bidding," said he. "I left your husband weeping like a child; to-night he will sleep easy." And he held the bottle forth.

"Before you give it me," Kokua panted, "take the good with the evil—ask to be delivered from your cough."

"I am an old man," replied the other, "and too near the gate of the grave to take a favor from the devil. But what is this? Why do you not take the bottle? Do you hesitate?"

"Not hesitate!" cried Kokua. "I am only weak. Give me a moment. It is my hand resists, my flesh shrinks back from the accursed thing. One moment only!"

The old man looked upon Kokua kindly. "Poor child!" said he, "you fear; your soul misgives you. Well, let me keep it. I am old, and can never more be happy in this world, and as for the next—"

"Give it me!" gasped Kokua. "There is your money. Do you think I am so base as that? Give me the bottle."

"God bless you, child," said the old man.

Kokua concealed the bottle under her holoku, said farewell to the old man, and walked off along the avenue, she cared not whither. For all roads were now the same to her, and led equally to hell. Sometimes she walked, and sometimes ran; sometimes she screamed out loud in the night, and sometimes lay by the wayside in the dust and wept. All that she had heard of hell came back to her; she saw the flames blaze, and she smelt the smoke, and her flesh withered on the coals.

Near day she came to her mind again, and returned to the house. It was even as the old man said—Keawe slumbered like a child. Kokua stood and gazed upon his face.

"Now, my husband," said she, "it is your turn to sleep. When you wake it will be your turn to sing and laugh. But for poor Kokua, alas! that meant no evil—for poor Kokua no more sleep, no more singing, no more delight, whether in earth or heaven."

With that she lay down in the bed by his side, and her misery was so extreme that she fell in a deep slumber instantly.

Late in the morning her husband woke her and gave her the good news. It seemed he was silly with delight, for he paid no heed to her distress, ill though she dissembled it. The words stuck in her mouth, it mattered not; Keawe did the speaking. She ate not a bite, but who was to observe it? for Keawe cleared the dish. Kokua saw and heard him, like some strange thing in a dream; there were times when she forgot or doubted, and put her hands to her brow; to know herself doomed and hear her husband babble, seemed so monstrous.

All the while Keawe was eating and talking, and planning the time of their return, and thanking her for saving him, and fondling her, and calling her the true helper after all. He laughed at the old man that was fool enough to buy that bottle.

"A worthy old man he seemed," Keawe said. "But no one can judge by appearances. For why did the old reprobate require the bottle?"

"My husband," said Kokua, humbly, "his purpose may have been good."

Keawe laughed like an angry man.

"Fiddle-de-dee!" cried Keawe. "An old rogue, I tell you; and an old ass to boot. For the bottle was hard enough to sell at four centimes; and at three it will be quite impossible. The margin is not broad enough, the thing begins to smell of scorching—brrr!" said he, and shuddered. "It is true I bought it myself at a cent, when I knew not there were smaller coins. I was a fool for my pains; there will never be found another: and whoever has that bottle now will carry it to the pit."

"O my husband!" said Kokua. "Is it not a terrible thing to save oneself by the eternal ruin of another? It seems to me I could not laugh. I would be humbled. I would be filled with melancholy. I would pray for the poor holder."

Then Keawe, because he felt the truth of what she said, grew the more angry. "Heighty-teighty!" cried he. "You may be filled with melancholy if you please. It is not the mind of a good wife. If you thought at all of me, you would sit shamed."

Thereupon he went out, and Kokua was alone.

What chance had she to sell that bottle at two centimes? None, she perceived. And if she had any, here was her husband hurrying her away to a country where there was nothing lower than a cent. And here—on the morrow of her sacrifice—was her husband leaving her and blaming her.

She would not even try to profit by what time she had, but sat in the house, and now had the bottle out and viewed it with unutterable fear, and now, with loathing, hid it out of sight.

By-and-by, Keawe came back, and would have her take a drive.

"My husband, I am ill," she said. "I am out of heart. Excuse me, I can take no pleasure."

Then was Keawe more wroth than ever. With her, because he thought she was brooding over the case of the old man; and with himself, because he thought she was right, and was ashamed to be so happy.

"This is your truth," cried he, "and this your affection! Your husband is just saved from eternal ruin, which he encountered for the love of you—and you can take no pleasure! Kokua, you have a disloyal heart."

He went forth again furious, and wandered in the town all day. He met friends, and drank with them; they hired a carriage and drove into the country, and there drank again. All the time Keawe was ill at ease, because he was taking this pastime while his wife was sad, and because he knew in his heart that she was more right than he; and the knowledge made him drink the deeper.

Now there was an old brutal Haole drinking with him, one that had been a boatswain of a whaler, a runaway, a digger in gold mines, a convict in prisons. He had a low mind and a foul mouth; he loved to drink and to see others drunken; and he pressed the glass upon Keawe. Soon there was no more money in the company.

"Here, you!" says the boatswain, "you are rich, you have been always saying. You have a bottle or some foolishness."

"Yes," says Keawe, "I am rich; I will go back and get some money from my wife, who keeps it."

"That's a bad idea, mate," said the boatswain. "Never you trust a petticoat with dollars. They're all as false as water; you keep an eye on her."

Now, this word struck in Keawe's mind; for he was muddled with what he had been drinking.

"I should not wonder but she was false, indeed," thought he. "Why else should she be so cast down at my release? But I will show her I am not the man to be fooled. I will catch her in the act."

Accordingly, when they were back in town, Keawe bade the boatswain wait for him at the corner, by the old calaboose, and went forward up the avenue alone to the door of his house. The night had come again; there was a light within, but never a sound; and Keawe crept about the corner, opened the back door softly, and looked in.

There was Kokua on the floor, the lamp at her side; before her was a milk-white bottle, with a round belly and a long neck; and as she viewed it, Kokua wrung her hands.

A long time Keawe stood and looked in the doorway. At first he was struck stupid; and then fear fell upon him that the bargain had been made amiss, and the bottle had come back to him as it came at San Francisco; and at that his knees were loosened, and the fumes of the wine departed from his head like mists off a river in the morning. And then he had another thought; and it was a strange one, that made his cheeks to burn.

"I must make sure of this," thought he.

So he closed the door, and went softly round the corner again, and then came noisily in, as though he were but now returned. And, lo! by the time he opened the front door no bottle was to be seen; and Kokua sat in a chair and started up like one awakened out of sleep.

"I have been drinking all day and making merry," said Keawe. "I have been with good companions, and now I only come back for money, and return to drink and carouse with them again."

Both his face and voice were as stern as judgment, but Kokua was too troubled to observe.

"You do well to use your own, my husband," said she, and her words trembled.

"O, I do well in all things," said Keawe, and he went straight to the chest and took out money. But he looked besides in the corner where they kept the bottle, and there was no bottle there.

At that the chest heaved upon the floor like a sea-billow, and the house span about him like a wreath of smoke, for he saw he was lost now, and there was no escape. "It is what I feared," he thought. "It is she who has bought it."

And then he came to himself a little and rose up; but the sweat streamed on his face as thick as the rain and as cold as the well-water.

"Kokua," said he, "I said to you to-day what ill became me. Now I return to carouse with my jolly companions," and at that he laughed a little quietly. "I will take more pleasure in the cup if you forgive me."

She clasped his knees in a moment; she kissed his knees with flowing tears.

"O," she cried, "I asked but a kind word!"

"Let us never one think hardly of the other," said Keawe, and was gone out of the house.

Now, the money that Keawe had taken was only some of that store of centime pieces they had laid in at their arrival. It was very sure he had no mind to be drinking. His wife had given her soul for him, now he must give his for hers; no other thought was in the world with him.

At the corner, by the old calaboose, there was the boatswain waiting.

"My wife has the bottle," said Keawe, "and, unless you help me to recover it, there can be no more money and no more liquor to-night."

"You do not mean to say you are serious about that bottle?" cried the boatswain.

"There is the lamp," said Keawe. "Do I look as if I was jesting?"

"That is so," said the boatswain. "You look as serious as a ghost."

"Well, then," said Keawe, "here are two centimes; you must go to my wife in the house, and offer her these for the bottle, which (if I am not much mistaken) she will give you instantly. Bring it to me here, and I will buy it back from you for one; for that is the law with this bottle, that it still must be sold for a less sum. But whatever you do, never breathe a word to her that you have come from me."

"Mate, I wonder are you making a fool of me?" asked the boatswain.

"It will do you no harm if I am," returned Keawe.

"That is so, mate," said the boatswain.

"And if you doubt me," added Keawe, "you can try. As soon as you are clear of the house, wish to have your pocket full of money, or a bottle of the best rum, or what you please, and you will see the virtue of the thing."

"Very well, Kanaka," says the boatswain. "I will try; but if you are having your fun out of me, I will take my fun out of you with a belaying pin."

So the whaler-man went off up the avenue; and Keawe stood and waited. It was near the same spot where Kokua had waited the night before; but Keawe was more resolved, and never faltered in his purpose; only his soul was bitter with despair.

It seemed a long time he had to wait before he heard a voice singing in the darkness of the avenue. He knew the voice to be the boatswain's; but it was strange how drunken it appeared upon a sudden.

Next, the man himself came stumbling into the light of the lamp. He had the devil's bottle buttoned in his coat; another bottle was in his hand; and even as he came in view he raised it to his mouth and drank.

"You have it," said Keawe. "I see that."

"Hands off!" cried the boatswain, jumping back. "Take a step near me, and I'll smash your mouth. You thought you could make a cat's-paw of me, did you?"

"What do you mean?" cried Keawe.

"Mean?" cried the boatswain. "This is a pretty good bottle, this is; that's what I mean. How I got it for two centimes I can't make out; but I'm sure you shan't have it for one."

"You mean you won't sell?" gasped Keawe.

"No, *sir*!" cried the boatswain. "But I'll give you a drink of the rum, if you like."

"I tell you," said Keawe, "the man who has that bottle goes to hell."

"I reckon I'm going anyway," returned the sailor; "and this bottle's the best thing to go with I've struck yet. No, sir!" he cried again, "this is my bottle now, and you can go and fish for another."

"Can this be true?" Keawe cried. "For your own sake, I beseech you, sell it me!"

"I don't value any of your talk," replied the boatswain. "You thought I was a flat; now you see I'm not; and there's an end. If you won't have a swallow of the rum, I'll have one myself. Here's your health, and good-night to you!"

So off he went down the avenue towards town, and there goes the bottle out of the story.

But Keawe ran to Kokua light as the wind; and great was their joy that night; and great, since then, has been the peace of all their days in the Bright House.

The End

Notes on Authors and Stories

"The Legend of Sleepy Hollow" (1820)

Washington Irving (1783–1859) was the son of European immigrants who settled in Manhattan at the end of the Revolutionary War. Named after the first President of the United States, Irving began writing professionally from the age of nineteen, steadily growing in fame and acclaim over the course of his concurrent life and career. One of the first American writers to gain regard in England, he advocated for stranger copyright laws in the states to protect writers from plagiarism. His last completed work was a five-volume biography of his namesake, published just months before his death from a heart attack. "The Legend of Sleepy Hollow" was originally included *The Sketch Book of Geoffrey Crayon, Gent.*, which included another of Irving's best known stories, *Rip Van Winkle.*

"The Voice in the Night" (1907)

William Hope Hodgson (1877–1918) ran away from his English boarding school to become a sailor at the age of thirteen. Bullied by his fellow seamen, he took up bodybuilding and became a seasonal physical trainer. He began his writing career with articles on fitness and exercise before turning to fiction, with stories of supernatural horror and mystery rooted in his nautical background. He died in gunfire while serving in the British Army during World War I. Some of Hodgson's other works include *The House on the Borderland* (1908) and *The Night Land* (1912), and the "Sargasso Sea Stories" series (1906–1920).

"The Monkey's Paw" (1902)

William Wymark Jacobs (1863–1943) began working as a civil service clerk in as a teenager, writing and publishing his short stories on the side. Though best known for "The Monkey's Paw," the majority of his output was decidedly less macabre. After releasing many critically and commercially popular comedic stories and novels, he adapted some of his prose into scripts for the stage before passing away at the age of 79. Some of Jacobs's other works include *Many Cargoes* (1896), "Jerry Bundler" (1901), and "The Toll House" (1909).

"THE FALL OF THE HOUSE OF USHER" (1839)

EDGAR ALLAN POE (1809–1849) was raised by a merchant and his wife from an early age after his father abandoned his family less than a year after Poe's birth and the passing of his mother from consumption a year later. After serving an enlistment in the United States Army, then as a cadet in then United States Military Academy, Poe began a full-time writing career. Achieving national fame with the release of his 1845 poem "The Raven," Poe's personal life became just as storied as the poetic and prose works he was known for, culminating with this death at 40 from unknown circumstances after a short period of delirium. Some of Poe's other works include "The Pit and the Pendulum" (1842), "The Tell-Tale Heart" (1843), and "The Cask of Amontillado" (1846).

"THE WILLOWS" (1907)

ALGERNON HENRY BLACKWOOD (1869–1951) was a member of both the paranormal ghost-hunting organization The Ghost Club and the Hermetic Order of the Golden Dawn, a secret society steeped in the study and practices of metaphysics, the occult, and paranormal activities. With a varied career that included stints as a bartender, model, essayist, journalist, newspaper reporter, hotel operator, and dairy farmer; Blackwood recounted these journeys in his early life autobiography *Episodes Before Thirty* (1923). With the onset of his thirties, he began his successful career writing supernatural novels, stories, and plays. His other published stories include *The Education of Uncle Paul* (1909), "The Wendigo" (1910), and *The Doll and One Other* (1946).

"THE BOTTLE IMP" (1851)

ROBERT LOUIS STEVENSON (1850–1894) was born in Scotland and spent much of his youth in ill-health that continued into his adulthood. Traveling with his engineer father, he incorporated many of the inspirations he encountered in new territories into his written works. Despite his works being considered only for children or fans of horror, his novels gave him worldwide acclaim. He spent his later years living in the Pacific, dying at his home in the Samoan islands at the age of 44. His other published stories include *Treasure Island* (1883), *Kidnapped* (1886), and *Strange Case of Dr Jekyll and Mr Hyde* (1886).

www.ingramcontent.com/pod-product-compliance
Lightning Source LLC
Chambersburg PA
CBHW011115100726
47898CB00011B/3101
* 9 7 8 1 7 3 5 8 9 6 7 8 6 *

THE TURN OF THE SCREW

The DOUBLE BOOKED® Collection

Desiderio
The Veil and the Shade

Shadows Against the Dark: Collected Tales of Horror
The Turn of the Screw

Cane
The Conjure Woman: Uncle Julius and His Stories

Man Cub: The Complete Mowgli Stories
Rikki-Tikki-Tavi and Other Tales from The Jungle Book

A Christmas Carol
Marie and the Nutcracker

Peter Pan
The Never Boy

Alice's Adventures in Wonderland
Through the Looking Glass

THE TURN OF THE SCREW

Henry James

edited by C.S.R. Calloway

The Turn of the Screw & Shadows Against the Dark: Collected Tales of Horror

Published by CSRC Storytelling
Los Angeles, CA 99503

ISBN: 978-1-7358967-8-6 (Paperback)
ISBN: 978-1-7358967-9-3 (Ebook)

Jacket illustrations by Mateus Roberts
Jacket designed by Ahmed Khalid
First Edition: June 2021

CONTENTS

"The story had held us, round the fire..."

The story had held us, round the fire, sufficiently breathless, but except the obvious remark that it was gruesome, as, on Christmas Eve in an old house, a strange tale should essentially be, I remember no comment uttered till somebody happened to say that it was the only case he had met in which such a visitation had fallen on a child. The case, I may mention, was that of an apparition in just such an old house as had gathered us for the occasion—an appearance, of a dreadful kind, to a little boy sleeping in the room with his mother and waking her up in the terror of it; waking her not to dissipate his dread and soothe him to sleep again, but to encounter also, herself, before she had succeeded in doing so, the same sight that had shaken him. It was this observation that drew from Douglas—not immediately, but later in the evening—a reply that had the interesting consequence to which I call attention. Someone else told a story not particularly effective, which I saw he was not following. This I took for a sign that he had himself something to produce and that we should only have to wait. We waited in fact till two nights later; but that same evening, before we scattered, he brought out what was in his mind.

"I quite agree—in regard to Griffin's ghost, or whatever it was—that its appearing first to the little boy, at so tender an age, adds a particular touch. But it's not the first occurrence of its charming kind that I know to have involved a child. If the child gives the effect another turn of the screw, what do you say to *two* children—?"

"We say, of course," somebody exclaimed, "that they give two turns! Also that we want to hear about them."

I can see Douglas there before the fire, to which he had got up to present his back, looking down at his interlocutor with his hands in his pockets. "Nobody but me, till now, has ever heard. It's quite too horrible." This, naturally, was declared by several voices to give the thing the utmost price, and our friend, with quiet art, prepared his triumph by turning his eyes over the rest of us and going on: "It's beyond everything. Nothing at all that I know touches it."

"For sheer terror?" I remember asking.

He seemed to say it was not so simple as that; to be really at a loss how to qualify it. He passed his hand over his eyes, made a little wincing grimace. "For dreadful—dreadfulness!"

"Oh, how delicious!" cried one of the women.

He took no notice of her; he looked at me, but as if, instead of me, he saw what he spoke of. "For general uncanny ugliness and horror and pain."

"Well then," I said, "just sit right down and begin."

He turned round to the fire, gave a kick to a log, watched it an instant. Then as he faced us again: "I can't begin. I shall have to send to town." There was a unanimous groan at this, and much reproach; after which, in his preoccupied way, he explained. "The story's written. It's in a locked drawer—it has not been out for years. I could write to my man and enclose the key; he could send down the packet as he finds it." It was to me in particular that he appeared to propound this—appeared almost to appeal for aid not to hesitate. He had broken a thickness of ice, the formation of many a winter; had had his reasons for a long silence. The others resented postponement, but it was just his scruples that charmed me. I adjured him to write by the first post and to agree with us for an early hearing; then I asked him if the experience in question had been his own. To this his answer was prompt. "Oh, thank God, no!"

"And is the record yours? You took the thing down?"

"Nothing but the impression. I took that *here*"—he tapped his heart. "I've never lost it."

"Then your manuscript—?"

"Is in old, faded ink, and in the most beautiful hand." He hung fire again. "A woman's. She has been dead these twenty years. She sent me the pages in question before she died." They were all listening now, and of course there was somebody to be arch, or at any rate to draw the inference. But if he put the inference by without a smile it was also

without irritation. "She was a most charming person, but she was ten years older than I. She was my sister's governess," he quietly said. "She was the most agreeable woman I've ever known in her position; she would have been worthy of any whatever. It was long ago, and this episode was long before. I was at Trinity, and I found her at home on my coming down the second summer. I was much there that year—it was a beautiful one; and we had, in her off-hours, some strolls and talks in the garden—talks in which she struck me as awfully clever and nice. Oh yes; don't grin: I liked her extremely and am glad to this day to think she liked me, too. If she hadn't she wouldn't have told me. She had never told anyone. It wasn't simply that she said so, but that I knew she hadn't. I was sure; I could see. You'll easily judge why when you hear."

"Because the thing had been such a scare?"

He continued to fix me. "You'll easily judge," he repeated: "*you* will."

I fixed him, too. "I see. She was in love."

He laughed for the first time. "You *are* acute. Yes, she was in love. That is, she had been. That came out—she couldn't tell her story without its coming out. I saw it, and she saw I saw it; but neither of us spoke of it. I remember the time and the place—the corner of the lawn, the shade of the great beeches and the long, hot summer afternoon. It wasn't a scene for a shudder; but oh—!" He quitted the fire and dropped back into his chair.

"You'll receive the packet Thursday morning?" I inquired.

"Probably not till the second post."

"Well then; after dinner—"

"You'll all meet me here?" He looked us round again. "Isn't anybody going?" It was almost the tone of hope.

"Everybody will stay!"

"*I* will"—and "*I* will!" cried the ladies whose departure had been fixed. Mrs. Griffin, however, expressed the need for a little more light. "Who was it she was in love with?"

"The story will tell," I took upon myself to reply.

"Oh, I can't wait for the story!"

"The story *won't* tell," said Douglas; "not in any literal, vulgar way."

"More's the pity, then. That's the only way I ever understand."

"Won't *you* tell, Douglas?" somebody else inquired.

He sprang to his feet again. "Yes—tomorrow. Now I must go to bed. Good night." And quickly catching up a candlestick, he left us slightly

bewildered. From our end of the great brown hall we heard his step on the stair; whereupon Mrs. Griffin spoke. "Well, if I don't know who she was in love with, I know who *he* was."

"She was ten years older," said her husband.

"*Raison de plus*—at that age! But it's rather nice, his long reticence."

"Forty years!" Griffin put in.

"With this outbreak at last."

"The outbreak," I returned, "will make a tremendous occasion of Thursday night;" and everyone so agreed with me that, in the light of it, we lost all attention for everything else. The last story, however incomplete and like the mere opening of a serial, had been told; we handshook and "candlestuck," as somebody said, and went to bed.

I knew the next day that a letter containing the key had, by the first post, gone off to his London apartments; but in spite of—or perhaps just on account of—the eventual diffusion of this knowledge we quite let him alone till after dinner, till such an hour of the evening, in fact, as might best accord with the kind of emotion on which our hopes were fixed. Then he became as communicative as we could desire and indeed gave us his best reason for being so. We had it from him again before the fire in the hall, as we had had our mild wonders of the previous night. It appeared that the narrative he had promised to read us really required for a proper intelligence a few words of prologue. Let me say here distinctly, to have done with it, that this narrative, from an exact transcript of my own made much later, is what I shall presently give. Poor Douglas, before his death—when it was in sight—committed to me the manuscript that reached him on the third of these days and that, on the same spot, with immense effect, he began to read to our hushed little circle on the night of the fourth. The departing ladies who had said they would stay didn't, of course, thank heaven, stay: they departed, in consequence of arrangements made, in a rage of curiosity, as they professed, produced by the touches with which he had already worked us up. But that only made his little final auditory more compact and select, kept it, round the hearth, subject to a common thrill.

The first of these touches conveyed that the written statement took up the tale at a point after it had, in a manner, begun. The fact to be in possession of was therefore that his old friend, the youngest of several daughters of a poor country parson, had, at the age of twenty, on taking service for the first time in the schoolroom, come up to London, in

trepidation, to answer in person an advertisement that had already placed her in brief correspondence with the advertiser. This person proved, on her presenting herself, for judgment, at a house in Harley Street, that impressed her as vast and imposing—this prospective patron proved a gentleman, a bachelor in the prime of life, such a figure as had never risen, save in a dream or an old novel, before a fluttered, anxious girl out of a Hampshire vicarage. One could easily fix his type; it never, happily, dies out. He was handsome and bold and pleasant, off-hand and gay and kind. He struck her, inevitably, as gallant and splendid, but what took her most of all and gave her the courage she afterward showed was that he put the whole thing to her as a kind of favor, an obligation he should gratefully incur. She conceived him as rich, but as fearfully extravagant—saw him all in a glow of high fashion, of good looks, of expensive habits, of charming ways with women. He had for his own town residence a big house filled with the spoils of travel and the trophies of the chase; but it was to his country home, an old family place in Essex, that he wished her immediately to proceed.

He had been left, by the death of their parents in India, guardian to a small nephew and a small niece, children of a younger, a military brother, whom he had lost two years before. These children were, by the strangest of chances for a man in his position—a lone man without the right sort of experience or a grain of patience—very heavily on his hands. It had all been a great worry and, on his own part doubtless, a series of blunders, but he immensely pitied the poor chicks and had done all he could; had in particular sent them down to his other house, the proper place for them being of course the country, and kept them there, from the first, with the best people he could find to look after them, parting even with his own servants to wait on them and going down himself, whenever he might, to see how they were doing. The awkward thing was that they had practically no other relations and that his own affairs took up all his time. He had put them in possession of Bly, which was healthy and secure, and had placed at the head of their little establishment—but below stairs only—an excellent woman, Mrs. Grose, whom he was sure his visitor would like and who had formerly been maid to his mother. She was now housekeeper and was also acting for the time as superintendent to the little girl, of whom, without children of her own, she was, by good luck, extremely fond. There were plenty of people to help, but of course the young lady who should go down as governess

would be in supreme authority. She would also have, in holidays, to look after the small boy, who had been for a term at school—young as he was to be sent, but what else could be done?—and who, as the holidays were about to begin, would be back from one day to the other. There had been for the two children at first a young lady whom they had had the misfortune to lose. She had done for them quite beautifully—she was a most respectable person—till her death, the great awkwardness of which had, precisely, left no alternative but the school for little Miles. Mrs. Grose, since then, in the way of manners and things, had done as she could for Flora; and there were, further, a cook, a housemaid, a dairywoman, an old pony, an old groom, and an old gardener, all likewise thoroughly respectable.

So far had Douglas presented his picture when someone put a question. "And what did the former governess die of?—of so much respectability?"

Our friend's answer was prompt. "That will come out. I don't anticipate."

"Excuse me—I thought that was just what you *are* doing."

"In her successor's place," I suggested, "I should have wished to learn if the office brought with it—"

"Necessary danger to life?" Douglas completed my thought. "She did wish to learn, and she did learn. You shall hear tomorrow what she learned. Meanwhile, of course, the prospect struck her as slightly grim. She was young, untried, nervous: it was a vision of serious duties and little company, of really great loneliness. She hesitated—took a couple of days to consult and consider. But the salary offered much exceeded her modest measure, and on a second interview she faced the music, she engaged." And Douglas, with this, made a pause that, for the benefit of the company, moved me to throw in—

"The moral of which was of course the seduction exercised by the splendid young man. She succumbed to it."

He got up and, as he had done the night before, went to the fire, gave a stir to a log with his foot, then stood a moment with his back to us. "She saw him only twice."

"Yes, but that's just the beauty of her passion."

A little to my surprise, on this, Douglas turned round to me. "It *was* the beauty of it. There were others," he went on, "who hadn't succumbed. He told her frankly all his difficulty—that for several

applicants the conditions had been prohibitive. They were, somehow, simply afraid. It sounded dull—it sounded strange; and all the more so because of his main condition."

"Which was—?"

"That she should never trouble him—but never, never: neither appeal nor complain nor write about anything; only meet all questions herself, receive all moneys from his solicitor, take the whole thing over and let him alone. She promised to do this, and she mentioned to me that when, for a moment, disburdened, delighted, he held her hand, thanking her for the sacrifice, she already felt rewarded."

"But was that all her reward?" one of the ladies asked.

"She never saw him again."

"Oh!" said the lady; which, as our friend immediately left us again, was the only other word of importance contributed to the subject till, the next night, by the corner of the hearth, in the best chair, he opened the faded red cover of a thin old-fashioned gilt-edged album. The whole thing took indeed more nights than one, but on the first occasion the same lady put another question. "What is your title?"

"I haven't one."

"Oh, *I* have!" I said. But Douglas, without heeding me, had begun to read with a fine clearness that was like a rendering to the ear of the beauty of his author's hand.

I

I remember the whole beginning as a succession of flights and drops, a little seesaw of the right throbs and the wrong. After rising, in town, to meet his appeal, I had at all events a couple of very bad days—found myself doubtful again, felt indeed sure I had made a mistake. In this state of mind I spent the long hours of bumping, swinging coach that carried me to the stopping place at which I was to be met by a vehicle from the house. This convenience, I was told, had been ordered, and I found, toward the close of the June afternoon, a commodious fly in waiting for me. Driving at that hour, on a lovely day, through a country to which the summer sweetness seemed to offer me a friendly welcome, my fortitude mounted afresh and, as we turned into the avenue, encountered a reprieve that was probably but a proof of the point to which it had sunk. I suppose I had expected, or had dreaded, something so melancholy that what greeted me was a good surprise. I remember as a most pleasant impression the broad, clear front, its open windows and fresh curtains and the pair of maids looking out; I remember the lawn and the bright flowers and the crunch of my wheels on the gravel and the clustered treetops over which the rooks circled and cawed in the golden sky. The scene had a greatness that made it a different affair from my own scant home, and there immediately appeared at the door, with a little girl in her hand, a civil person who dropped me as decent a curtsy as if I had been the mistress or a distinguished visitor. I had received in Harley Street a narrower notion of the place, and that, as I recalled it, made me think the proprietor still more of a gentleman, suggested that what I was to enjoy might be something beyond his promise.

I had no drop again till the next day, for I was carried triumphantly through the following hours by my introduction to the younger of my pupils. The little girl who accompanied Mrs. Grose appeared to me on

the spot a creature so charming as to make it a great fortune to have to do with her. She was the most beautiful child I had ever seen, and I afterward wondered that my employer had not told me more of her. I slept little that night—I was too much excited; and this astonished me, too, I recollect, remained with me, adding to my sense of the liberality with which I was treated. The large, impressive room, one of the best in the house, the great state bed, as I almost felt it, the full, figured draperies, the long glasses in which, for the first time, I could see myself from head to foot, all struck me—like the extraordinary charm of my small charge—as so many things thrown in. It was thrown in as well, from the first moment, that I should get on with Mrs. Grose in a relation over which, on my way, in the coach, I fear I had rather brooded. The only thing indeed that in this early outlook might have made me shrink again was the clear circumstance of her being so glad to see me. I perceived within half an hour that she was so glad—stout, simple, plain, clean, wholesome woman—as to be positively on her guard against showing it too much. I wondered even then a little why she should wish not to show it, and that, with reflection, with suspicion, might of course have made me uneasy.

But it was a comfort that there could be no uneasiness in a connection with anything so beatific as the radiant image of my little girl, the vision of whose angelic beauty had probably more than anything else to do with the restlessness that, before morning, made me several times rise and wander about my room to take in the whole picture and prospect; to watch, from my open window, the faint summer dawn, to look at such portions of the rest of the house as I could catch, and to listen, while, in the fading dusk, the first birds began to twitter, for the possible recurrence of a sound or two, less natural and not without, but within, that I had fancied I heard. There had been a moment when I believed I recognized, faint and far, the cry of a child; there had been another when I found myself just consciously starting as at the passage, before my door, of a light footstep. But these fancies were not marked enough not to be thrown off, and it is only in the light, or the gloom, I should rather say, of other and subsequent matters that they now come back to me. To watch, teach, "form" little Flora would too evidently be the making of a happy and useful life. It had been agreed between us downstairs that after this first occasion I should have her as a matter of course at night, her small white bed being already arranged, to that end,

in my room. What I had undertaken was the whole care of her, and she had remained, just this last time, with Mrs. Grose only as an effect of our consideration for my inevitable strangeness and her natural timidity. In spite of this timidity—which the child herself, in the oddest way in the world, had been perfectly frank and brave about, allowing it, without a sign of uncomfortable consciousness, with the deep, sweet serenity indeed of one of Raphael's holy infants, to be discussed, to be imputed to her, and to determine us—I feel quite sure she would presently like me. It was part of what I already liked Mrs. Grose herself for, the pleasure I could see her feel in my admiration and wonder as I sat at supper with four tall candles and with my pupil, in a high chair and a bib, brightly facing me, between them, over bread and milk. There were naturally things that in Flora's presence could pass between us only as prodigious and gratified looks, obscure and roundabout allusions.

"And the little boy—does he look like her? Is he too so very remarkable?"

One wouldn't flatter a child. "Oh, miss, *most* remarkable. If you think well of this one!"—and she stood there with a plate in her hand, beaming at our companion, who looked from one of us to the other with placid heavenly eyes that contained nothing to check us.

"Yes; if I do—?"

"You *will* be carried away by the little gentleman!"

"Well, that, I think, is what I came for—to be carried away. I'm afraid, however," I remember feeling the impulse to add, "I'm rather easily carried away. I was carried away in London!"

I can still see Mrs. Grose's broad face as she took this in. "In Harley Street?"

"In Harley Street."

"Well, miss, you're not the first—and you won't be the last."

"Oh, I've no pretension," I could laugh, "to being the only one. My other pupil, at any rate, as I understand, comes back tomorrow?"

"Not tomorrow—Friday, miss. He arrives, as you did, by the coach, under care of the guard, and is to be met by the same carriage."

I forthwith expressed that the proper as well as the pleasant and friendly thing would be therefore that on the arrival of the public conveyance I should be in waiting for him with his little sister; an idea in which Mrs. Grose concurred so heartily that I somehow took her manner

as a kind of comforting pledge—never falsified, thank heaven!—that we should on every question be quite at one. Oh, she was glad I was there!

What I felt the next day was, I suppose, nothing that could be fairly called a reaction from the cheer of my arrival; it was probably at the most only a slight oppression produced by a fuller measure of the scale, as I walked round them, gazed up at them, took them in, of my new circumstances. They had, as it were, an extent and mass for which I had not been prepared and in the presence of which I found myself, freshly, a little scared as well as a little proud. Lessons, in this agitation, certainly suffered some delay; I reflected that my first duty was, by the gentlest arts I could contrive, to win the child into the sense of knowing me. I spent the day with her out-of-doors; I arranged with her, to her great satisfaction, that it should be she, she only, who might show me the place. She showed it step by step and room by room and secret by secret, with droll, delightful, childish talk about it and with the result, in half an hour, of our becoming immense friends. Young as she was, I was struck, throughout our little tour, with her confidence and courage with the way, in empty chambers and dull corridors, on crooked staircases that made me pause and even on the summit of an old machicolated square tower that made me dizzy, her morning music, her disposition to tell me so many more things than she asked, rang out and led me on. I have not seen Bly since the day I left it, and I daresay that to my older and more informed eyes it would now appear sufficiently contracted. But as my little conductress, with her hair of gold and her frock of blue, danced before me round corners and pattered down passages, I had the view of a castle of romance inhabited by a rosy sprite, such a place as would somehow, for diversion of the young idea, take all color out of storybooks and fairytales. Wasn't it just a storybook over which I had fallen adoze and adream? No; it was a big, ugly, antique, but convenient house, embodying a few features of a building still older, half-replaced and half-utilized, in which I had the fancy of our being almost as lost as a handful of passengers in a great drifting ship. Well, I was, strangely, at the helm!

II

This came home to me when, two days later, I drove over with Flora to meet, as Mrs. Grose said, the little gentleman; and all the more for an incident that, presenting itself the second evening, had deeply disconcerted me. The first day had been, on the whole, as I have expressed, reassuring; but I was to see it wind up in keen apprehension. The postbag, that evening—it came late—contained a letter for me, which, however, in the hand of my employer, I found to be composed but of a few words enclosing another, addressed to himself, with a seal still unbroken. "This, I recognize, is from the headmaster, and the headmaster's an awful bore. Read him, please; deal with him; but mind you don't report. Not a word. I'm off!" I broke the seal with a great effort—so great a one that I was a long time coming to it; took the unopened missive at last up to my room and only attacked it just before going to bed. I had better have let it wait till morning, for it gave me a second sleepless night. With no counsel to take, the next day, I was full of distress; and it finally got so the better of me that I determined to open myself at least to Mrs. Grose.

"What does it mean? The child's dismissed his school."

She gave me a look that I remarked at the moment; then, visibly, with a quick blankness, seemed to try to take it back. "But aren't they all—?"

"Sent home—yes. But only for the holidays. Miles may never go back at all."

Consciously, under my attention, she reddened. "They won't take him?"

"They absolutely decline."

At this she raised her eyes, which she had turned from me; I saw them fill with good tears. "What has he done?"

I hesitated; then I judged best simply to hand her my letter—which, however, had the effect of making her, without taking it, simply put her hands behind her. She shook her head sadly. "Such things are not for me, miss."

My counselor couldn't read! I winced at my mistake, which I attenuated as I could, and opened my letter again to repeat it to her; then, faltering in the act and folding it up once more, I put it back in my pocket. "Is he really *bad*?"

The tears were still in her eyes. "Do the gentlemen say so?"

"They go into no particulars. They simply express their regret that it should be impossible to keep him. That can have only one meaning." Mrs. Grose listened with dumb emotion; she forbore to ask me what this meaning might be; so that, presently, to put the thing with some coherence and with the mere aid of her presence to my own mind, I went on: "That he's an injury to the others."

At this, with one of the quick turns of simple folk, she suddenly flamed up. "Master Miles! *him* an injury?"

There was such a flood of good faith in it that, though I had not yet seen the child, my very fears made me jump to the absurdity of the idea. I found myself, to meet my friend the better, offering it, on the spot, sarcastically. "To his poor little innocent mates!"

"It's too dreadful," cried Mrs. Grose, "to say such cruel things! Why, he's scarce ten years old."

"Yes, yes; it would be incredible."

She was evidently grateful for such a profession. "See him, miss, first. *Then* believe it!" I felt forthwith a new impatience to see him; it was the beginning of a curiosity that, for all the next hours, was to deepen almost to pain. Mrs. Grose was aware, I could judge, of what she had produced in me, and she followed it up with assurance. "You might as well believe it of the little lady. Bless her," she added the next moment—"*look* at her!"

I turned and saw that Flora, whom, ten minutes before, I had established in the schoolroom with a sheet of white paper, a pencil, and a copy of nice "round O's," now presented herself to view at the open door. She expressed in her little way an extraordinary detachment from disagreeable duties, looking to me, however, with a great childish light that seemed to offer it as a mere result of the affection she had conceived for my person, which had rendered necessary that she should follow me. I needed nothing more than this to feel the full force of Mrs. Grose's

comparison, and, catching my pupil in my arms, covered her with kisses in which there was a sob of atonement.

Nonetheless, the rest of the day I watched for further occasion to approach my colleague, especially as, toward evening, I began to fancy she rather sought to avoid me. I overtook her, I remember, on the staircase; we went down together, and at the bottom I detained her, holding her there with a hand on her arm. "I take what you said to me at noon as a declaration that *you've* never known him to be bad."

She threw back her head; she had clearly, by this time, and very honestly, adopted an attitude. "Oh, never known him—I don't pretend *that!*"

I was upset again. "Then you *have* known him—?"

"Yes indeed, miss, thank God!"

On reflection I accepted this. "You mean that a boy who never is—?"

"Is no boy for *me!*"

I held her tighter. "You like them with the spirit to be naughty?" Then, keeping pace with her answer, "So do I!" I eagerly brought out. "But not to the degree to contaminate—"

"To contaminate?"—my big word left her at a loss. I explained it. "To corrupt."

She stared, taking my meaning in; but it produced in her an odd laugh. "Are you afraid he'll corrupt *you?*" She put the question with such a fine bold humor that, with a laugh, a little silly doubtless, to match her own, I gave way for the time to the apprehension of ridicule.

But the next day, as the hour for my drive approached, I cropped up in another place. "What was the lady who was here before?"

"The last governess? She was also young and pretty—almost as young and almost as pretty, miss, even as you."

"Ah, then, I hope her youth and her beauty helped her!" I recollect throwing off. "He seems to like us young and pretty!"

"Oh, he *did,*" Mrs. Grose assented: "it was the way he liked everyone!" She had no sooner spoken indeed than she caught herself up. "I mean that's *his* way—the master's."

I was struck. "But of whom did you speak first?"

She looked blank, but she colored. "Why, of *him.*"

"Of the master?"

"Of who else?"

There was so obviously no one else that the next moment I had lost my impression of her having accidentally said more than she meant; and I merely asked what I wanted to know.

"Did *she* see anything in the boy—?"

"That wasn't right? She never told me."

I had a scruple, but I overcame it. "Was she careful—particular?"

Mrs. Grose appeared to try to be conscientious. "About some things—yes."

"But not about all?"

Again she considered. "Well, miss—she's gone. I won't tell tales."

"I quite understand your feeling," I hastened to reply; but I thought it, after an instant, not opposed to this concession to pursue: "Did she die here?"

"No—she went off."

I don't know what there was in this brevity of Mrs. Grose's that struck me as ambiguous. "Went off to die?" Mrs. Grose looked straight out of the window, but I felt that, hypothetically, I had a right to know what young persons engaged for Bly were expected to do. "She was taken ill, you mean, and went home?"

"She was not taken ill, so far as appeared, in this house. She left it, at the end of the year, to go home, as she said, for a short holiday, to which the time she had put in had certainly given her a right. We had then a young woman—a nursemaid who had stayed on and who was a good girl and clever; and *she* took the children altogether for the interval. But our young lady never came back, and at the very moment I was expecting her I heard from the master that she was dead."

I turned this over. "But of what?"

"He never told me! But please, miss," said Mrs. Grose, "I must get to my work."

III

Her thus turning her back on me was fortunately not, for my just preoccupations, a snub that could check the growth of our mutual esteem. We met, after I had brought home little Miles, more intimately than ever on the ground of my stupefaction, my general emotion: so monstrous was I then ready to pronounce it that such a child as had now been revealed to me should be under an interdict. I was a little late on the scene, and I felt, as he stood wistfully looking out for me before the door of the inn at which the coach had put him down, that I had seen him, on the instant, without and within, in the great glow of freshness, the same positive fragrance of purity, in which I had, from the first moment, seen his little sister. He was incredibly beautiful, and Mrs. Grose had put her finger on it: everything but a sort of passion of tenderness for him was swept away by his presence. What I then and there took him to my heart for was something divine that I have never found to the same degree in any child—his indescribable little air of knowing nothing in the world but love. It would have been impossible to carry a bad name with a greater sweetness of innocence, and by the time I had got back to Bly with him I remained merely bewildered—so far, that is, as I was not outraged—by the sense of the horrible letter locked up in my room, in a drawer. As soon as I could compass a private word with Mrs. Grose I declared to her that it was grotesque.

She promptly understood me. "You mean the cruel charge—?"

"It doesn't live an instant. My dear woman, *look* at him!"

She smiled at my pretention to have discovered his charm. "I assure you, miss, I do nothing else! What will you say, then?" she immediately added.

"In answer to the letter?" I had made up my mind. "Nothing."

"And to his uncle?"

I was incisive. "Nothing."

"And to the boy himself?"

I was wonderful. "Nothing."

She gave with her apron a great wipe to her mouth. "Then I'll stand by you. We'll see it out."

"We'll see it out!" I ardently echoed, giving her my hand to make it a vow.

She held me there a moment, then whisked up her apron again with her detached hand. "Would you mind, miss, if I used the freedom—"

"To kiss me? No!" I took the good creature in my arms and, after we had embraced like sisters, felt still more fortified and indignant.

This, at all events, was for the time: a time so full that, as I recall the way it went, it reminds me of all the art I now need to make it a little distinct. What I look back at with amazement is the situation I accepted. I had undertaken, with my companion, to see it out, and I was under a charm, apparently, that could smooth away the extent and the far and difficult connections of such an effort. I was lifted aloft on a great wave of infatuation and pity. I found it simple, in my ignorance, my confusion, and perhaps my conceit, to assume that I could deal with a boy whose education for the world was all on the point of beginning. I am unable even to remember at this day what proposal I framed for the end of his holidays and the resumption of his studies. Lessons with me, indeed, that charming summer, we all had a theory that he was to have; but I now feel that, for weeks, the lessons must have been rather my own. I learned something—at first, certainly—that had not been one of the teachings of my small, smothered life; learned to be amused, and even amusing, and not to think for the morrow. It was the first time, in a manner, that I had known space and air and freedom, all the music of summer and all the mystery of nature. And then there was consideration—and consideration was sweet. Oh, it was a trap—not designed, but deep—to my imagination, to my delicacy, perhaps to my vanity; to whatever, in me, was most excitable. The best way to picture it all is to say that I was off my guard. They gave me so little trouble—they were of a gentleness so extraordinary. I used to speculate—but even this with a dim disconnectedness—as to how the rough future (for all futures are rough!) would handle them and might bruise them. They had the bloom of health and happiness; and yet, as if I had been in charge of a pair of little grandees, of princes of the blood, for whom everything, to be right,

would have to be enclosed and protected, the only form that, in my fancy, the afteryears could take for them was that of a romantic, a really royal extension of the garden and the park. It may be, of course, above all, that what suddenly broke into this gives the previous time a charm of stillness—that hush in which something gathers or crouches. The change was actually like the spring of a beast.

In the first weeks the days were long; they often, at their finest, gave me what I used to call my own hour, the hour when, for my pupils, teatime and bedtime having come and gone, I had, before my final retirement, a small interval alone. Much as I liked my companions, this hour was the thing in the day I liked most; and I liked it best of all when, as the light faded—or rather, I should say, the day lingered and the last calls of the last birds sounded, in a flushed sky, from the old trees—I could take a turn into the grounds and enjoy, almost with a sense of property that amused and flattered me, the beauty and dignity of the place. It was a pleasure at these moments to feel myself tranquil and justified; doubtless, perhaps, also to reflect that by my discretion, my quiet good sense and general high propriety, I was giving pleasure—if he ever thought of it!—to the person to whose pressure I had responded. What I was doing was what he had earnestly hoped and directly asked of me, and that I *could*, after all, do it proved even a greater joy than I had expected. I daresay I fancied myself, in short, a remarkable young woman and took comfort in the faith that this would more publicly appear. Well, I needed to be remarkable to offer a front to the remarkable things that presently gave their first sign.

It was plump, one afternoon, in the middle of my very hour: the children were tucked away, and I had come out for my stroll. One of the thoughts that, as I don't in the least shrink now from noting, used to be with me in these wanderings was that it would be as charming as a charming story suddenly to meet someone. Someone would appear there at the turn of a path and would stand before me and smile and approve. I didn't ask more than that—I only asked that he should *know;* and the only way to be sure he knew would be to see it, and the kind light of it, in his handsome face. That was exactly present to me—by which I mean the face was—when, on the first of these occasions, at the end of a long June day, I stopped short on emerging from one of the plantations and coming into view of the house. What arrested me on the spot—and with a shock much greater than any vision had allowed for—was the sense that my

imagination had, in a flash, turned real. He did stand there!—but high up, beyond the lawn and at the very top of the tower to which, on that first morning, little Flora had conducted me. This tower was one of a pair—square, incongruous, crenelated structures—that were distinguished, for some reason, though I could see little difference, as the new and the old. They flanked opposite ends of the house and were probably architectural absurdities, redeemed in a measure indeed by not being wholly disengaged nor of a height too pretentious, dating, in their gingerbread antiquity, from a romantic revival that was already a respectable past. I admired them, had fancies about them, for we could all profit in a degree, especially when they loomed through the dusk, by the grandeur of their actual battlements; yet it was not at such an elevation that the figure I had so often invoked seemed most in place.

It produced in me, this figure, in the clear twilight, I remember, two distinct gasps of emotion, which were, sharply, the shock of my first and that of my second surprise. My second was a violent perception of the mistake of my first: the man who met my eyes was not the person I had precipitately supposed. There came to me thus a bewilderment of vision of which, after these years, there is no living view that I can hope to give. An unknown man in a lonely place is a permitted object of fear to a young woman privately bred; and the figure that faced me was—a few more seconds assured me—as little anyone else I knew as it was the image that had been in my mind. I had not seen it in Harley Street—I had not seen it anywhere. The place, moreover, in the strangest way in the world, had, on the instant, and by the very fact of its appearance, become a solitude. To me at least, making my statement here with a deliberation with which I have never made it, the whole feeling of the moment returns. It was as if, while I took in—what I did take in—all the rest of the scene had been stricken with death. I can hear again, as I write, the intense hush in which the sounds of evening dropped. The rooks stopped cawing in the golden sky, and the friendly hour lost, for the minute, all its voice. But there was no other change in nature, unless indeed it were a change that I saw with a stranger sharpness. The gold was still in the sky, the clearness in the air, and the man who looked at me over the battlements was as definite as a picture in a frame. That's how I thought, with extraordinary quickness, of each person that he might have been and that he was not. We were confronted across our distance quite long enough for me to ask myself with intensity who then he was and to

feel, as an effect of my inability to say, a wonder that in a few instants more became intense.

The great question, or one of them, is, afterward, I know, with regard to certain matters, the question of how long they have lasted. Well, this matter of mine, think what you will of it, lasted while I caught at a dozen possibilities, none of which made a difference for the better, that I could see, in there having been in the house—and for how long, above all?—a person of whom I was in ignorance. It lasted while I just bridled a little with the sense that my office demanded that there should be no such ignorance and no such person. It lasted while this visitant, at all events—and there was a touch of the strange freedom, as I remember, in the sign of familiarity of his wearing no hat—seemed to fix me, from his position, with just the question, just the scrutiny through the fading light, that his own presence provoked. We were too far apart to call to each other, but there was a moment at which, at shorter range, some challenge between us, breaking the hush, would have been the right result of our straight mutual stare. He was in one of the angles, the one away from the house, very erect, as it struck me, and with both hands on the ledge. So I saw him as I see the letters I form on this page; then, exactly, after a minute, as if to add to the spectacle, he slowly changed his place—passed, looking at me hard all the while, to the opposite corner of the platform. Yes, I had the sharpest sense that during this transit he never took his eyes from me, and I can see at this moment the way his hand, as he went, passed from one of the crenellations to the next. He stopped at the other corner, but less long, and even as he turned away still markedly fixed me. He turned away; that was all I knew.

IV

It was not that I didn't wait, on this occasion, for more, for I was rooted as deeply as I was shaken. Was there a "secret" at Bly—a mystery of Udolpho or an insane, an unmentionable relative kept in unsuspected confinement? I can't say how long I turned it over, or how long, in a confusion of curiosity and dread, I remained where I had had my collision; I only recall that when I re-entered the house darkness had quite closed in. Agitation, in the interval, certainly had held me and driven me, for I must, in circling about the place, have walked three miles; but I was to be, later on, so much more overwhelmed that this mere dawn of alarm was a comparatively human chill. The most singular part of it, in fact—singular as the rest had been—was the part I became, in the hall, aware of in meeting Mrs. Grose. This picture comes back to me in the general train—the impression, as I received it on my return, of the wide white panelled space, bright in the lamplight and with its portraits and red carpet, and of the good surprised look of my friend, which immediately told me she had missed me. It came to me straightway, under her contact, that, with plain heartiness, mere relieved anxiety at my appearance, she knew nothing whatever that could bear upon the incident I had there ready for her. I had not suspected in advance that her comfortable face would pull me up, and I somehow measured the importance of what I had seen by my thus finding myself hesitate to mention it. Scarce anything in the whole history seems to me so odd as this fact that my real beginning of fear was one, as I may say, with the instinct of sparing my companion. On the spot, accordingly, in the pleasant hall and with her eyes on me, I, for a reason that I couldn't then have phrased, achieved an inward resolution—offered a vague pretext for my lateness and, with the plea of the beauty of the night and of the heavy dew and wet feet, went as soon as possible to my room.

Here it was another affair; here, for many days after, it was a queer affair enough. There were hours, from day to day—or at least there were moments, snatched even from clear duties—when I had to shut myself up to think. It was not so much yet that I was more nervous than I could bear to be as that I was remarkably afraid of becoming so; for the truth I had now to turn over was, simply and clearly, the truth that I could arrive at no account whatever of the visitor with whom I had been so inexplicably and yet, as it seemed to me, so intimately concerned. It took little time to see that I could sound without forms of inquiry and without exciting remark any domestic complications. The shock I had suffered must have sharpened all my senses; I felt sure, at the end of three days and as the result of mere closer attention, that I had not been practiced upon by the servants nor made the object of any "game." Of whatever it was that I knew, nothing was known around me. There was but one sane inference: someone had taken a liberty rather gross. That was what, repeatedly, I dipped into my room and locked the door to say to myself. We had been, collectively, subject to an intrusion; some unscrupulous traveler, curious in old houses, had made his way in unobserved, enjoyed the prospect from the best point of view, and then stolen out as he came. If he had given me such a bold hard stare, that was but a part of his indiscretion. The good thing, after all, was that we should surely see no more of him.

This was not so good a thing, I admit, as not to leave me to judge that what, essentially, made nothing else much signify was simply my charming work. My charming work was just my life with Miles and Flora, and through nothing could I so like it as through feeling that I could throw myself into it in trouble. The attraction of my small charges was a constant joy, leading me to wonder afresh at the vanity of my original fears, the distaste I had begun by entertaining for the probable gray prose of my office. There was to be no gray prose, it appeared, and no long grind; so how could work not be charming that presented itself as daily beauty? It was all the romance of the nursery and the poetry of the schoolroom. I don't mean by this, of course, that we studied only fiction and verse; I mean I can express no otherwise the sort of interest my companions inspired. How can I describe that except by saying that instead of growing used to them—and it's a marvel for a governess: I call the sisterhood to witness!—I made constant fresh discoveries. There was one direction, assuredly, in which these discoveries stopped: deep

obscurity continued to cover the region of the boy's conduct at school. It had been promptly given me, I have noted, to face that mystery without a pang. Perhaps even it would be nearer the truth to say that—without a word—he himself had cleared it up. He had made the whole charge absurd. My conclusion bloomed there with the real rose flush of his innocence: he was only too fine and fair for the little horrid, unclean school-world, and he had paid a price for it. I reflected acutely that the sense of such differences, such superiorities of quality, always, on the part of the majority—which could include even stupid, sordid headmasters—turn infallibly to the vindictive.

Both the children had a gentleness (it was their only fault, and it never made Miles a muff) that kept them—how shall I express it?—almost impersonal and certainly quite unpunishable. They were like the cherubs of the anecdote, who had—morally, at any rate—nothing to whack! I remember feeling with Miles in especial as if he had had, as it were, no history. We expect of a small child a scant one, but there was in this beautiful little boy something extraordinarily sensitive, yet extraordinarily happy, that, more than in any creature of his age I have seen, struck me as beginning anew each day. He had never for a second suffered. I took this as a direct disproof of his having really been chastised. If he had been wicked he would have "caught" it, and I should have caught it by the rebound—I should have found the trace. I found nothing at all, and he was therefore an angel. He never spoke of his school, never mentioned a comrade or a master; and I, for my part, was quite too much disgusted to allude to them. Of course I was under the spell, and the wonderful part is that, even at the time, I perfectly knew I was. But I gave myself up to it; it was an antidote to any pain, and I had more pains than one. I was in receipt in these days of disturbing letters from home, where things were not going well. But with my children, what things in the world mattered? That was the question I used to put to my scrappy retirements. I was dazzled by their loveliness.

There was a Sunday—to get on—when it rained with such force and for so many hours that there could be no procession to church; in consequence of which, as the day declined, I had arranged with Mrs. Grose that, should the evening show improvement, we would attend together the late service. The rain happily stopped, and I prepared for our walk, which, through the park and by the good road to the village, would be a matter of twenty minutes. Coming downstairs to meet my

colleague in the hall, I remembered a pair of gloves that had required three stitches and that had received them—with a publicity perhaps not edifying—while I sat with the children at their tea, served on Sundays, by exception, in that cold, clean temple of mahogany and brass, the "grown-up" dining room. The gloves had been dropped there, and I turned in to recover them. The day was gray enough, but the afternoon light still lingered, and it enabled me, on crossing the threshold, not only to recognize, on a chair near the wide window, then closed, the articles I wanted, but to become aware of a person on the other side of the window and looking straight in. One step into the room had sufficed; my vision was instantaneous; it was all there. The person looking straight in was the person who had already appeared to me. He appeared thus again with I won't say greater distinctness, for that was impossible, but with a nearness that represented a forward stride in our intercourse and made me, as I met him, catch my breath and turn cold. He was the same—he was the same, and seen, this time, as he had been seen before, from the waist up, the window, though the dining room was on the ground floor, not going down to the terrace on which he stood. His face was close to the glass, yet the effect of this better view was, strangely, only to show me how intense the former had been. He remained but a few seconds—long enough to convince me he also saw and recognized; but it was as if I had been looking at him for years and had known him always. Something, however, happened this time that had not happened before; his stare into my face, through the glass and across the room, was as deep and hard as then, but it quitted me for a moment during which I could still watch it, see it fix successively several other things. On the spot there came to me the added shock of a certitude that it was not for me he had come there. He had come for someone else.

The flash of this knowledge—for it was knowledge in the midst of dread—produced in me the most extraordinary effect, started as I stood there, a sudden vibration of duty and courage. I say courage because I was beyond all doubt already far gone. I bounded straight out of the door again, reached that of the house, got, in an instant, upon the drive, and, passing along the terrace as fast as I could rush, turned a corner and came full in sight. But it was in sight of nothing now—my visitor had vanished. I stopped, I almost dropped, with the real relief of this; but I took in the whole scene—I gave him time to reappear. I call it time, but how long was it? I can't speak to the purpose today of the duration of

these things. That kind of measure must have left me: they couldn't have lasted as they actually appeared to me to last. The terrace and the whole place, the lawn and the garden beyond it, all I could see of the park, were empty with a great emptiness. There were shrubberies and big trees, but I remember the clear assurance I felt that none of them concealed him. He was there or was not there: not there if I didn't see him. I got hold of this; then, instinctively, instead of returning as I had come, went to the window. It was confusedly present to me that I ought to place myself where he had stood. I did so; I applied my face to the pane and looked, as he had looked, into the room. As if, at this moment, to show me exactly what his range had been, Mrs. Grose, as I had done for himself just before, came in from the hall. With this I had the full image of a repetition of what had already occurred. She saw me as I had seen my own visitant; she pulled up short as I had done; I gave her something of the shock that I had received. She turned white, and this made me ask myself if I had blanched as much. She stared, in short, and retreated on just *my* lines, and I knew she had then passed out and come round to me and that I should presently meet her. I remained where I was, and while I waited I thought of more things than one. But there's only one I take space to mention. I wondered why *she* should be scared.

these things. That kind of meaning must have left me: they couldn't have lasted as they actually appeared to me to last. The terrace and the whole place, the lawn and the garden beyond it, all I could see of the park, were empty with a great emptiness. There were shrubberies and big trees, but I remember the clear assurance I felt that none of them concealed him. He was there or was not there: not there if I didn't see him. I got hold of this; then, instinctively, instead of returning as I had come, went to the window. It was confusedly present to me that I ought to place myself where he had stood. I did so; I applied my face to the pane and looked, as he had looked, into the room. As if, at this moment, to show me exactly what his range had been, Mrs. Grose, as I had done for himself just before, came in from the hall. With this I had the full image of a repetition of what had already occurred. She saw me as I had seen my own visitant; she pulled up short as I had done; I gave her something of the shock that I had received. She turned white, and this made me ask myself if I had blanched as much. She stared, in short, and retreated on just my lines, and I knew she had then passed out and come round to me and that I should presently meet her. I remained where I was, and while I waited I thought of more things than one. But there's only one I take space to mention. I wondered why she should be scared.

V

Oh, she let me know as soon as, round the corner of the house, she loomed again into view. "What in the name of goodness is the matter —?" She was now flushed and out of breath.

I said nothing till she came quite near. "With me?" I must have made a wonderful face. "Do I show it?"

"You're as white as a sheet. You look awful."

I considered; I could meet on this, without scruple, any innocence. My need to respect the bloom of Mrs. Grose's had dropped, without a rustle, from my shoulders, and if I wavered for the instant it was not with what I kept back. I put out my hand to her and she took it; I held her hard a little, liking to feel her close to me. There was a kind of support in the shy heave of her surprise. "You came for me for church, of course, but I can't go."

"Has anything happened?"

"Yes. You must know now. Did I look very queer?"

"Through this window? Dreadful!"

"Well," I said, "I've been frightened." Mrs. Grose's eyes expressed plainly that *she* had no wish to be, yet also that she knew too well her place not to be ready to share with me any marked inconvenience. Oh, it was quite settled that she *must* share! "Just what you saw from the dining room a minute ago was the effect of that. What *I* saw—just before—was much worse."

Her hand tightened. "What was it?"

"An extraordinary man. Looking in."

"What extraordinary man?"

"I haven't the least idea."

Mrs. Grose gazed round us in vain. "Then where is he gone?"

"I know still less."

"Have you seen him before?"

"Yes—once. On the old tower."

She could only look at me harder. "Do you mean he's a stranger?"

"Oh, very much!"

"Yet you didn't tell me?"

"No—for reasons. But now that you've guessed—"

Mrs. Grose's round eyes encountered this charge. "Ah, I haven't guessed!" she said very simply. "How can I if *you* don't imagine?"

"I don't in the very least."

"You've seen him nowhere but on the tower?"

"And on this spot just now."

Mrs. Grose looked round again. "What was he doing on the tower?"

"Only standing there and looking down at me."

She thought a minute. "Was he a gentleman?"

I found I had no need to think. "No." She gazed in deeper wonder. "No."

"Then nobody about the place? Nobody from the village?"

"Nobody—nobody. I didn't tell you, but I made sure."

She breathed a vague relief: this was, oddly, so much to the good. It only went indeed a little way. "But if he isn't a gentleman—"

"What *is* he? He's a horror."

"A horror?"

"He's—God help me if I know *what* he is!"

Mrs. Grose looked round once more; she fixed her eyes on the duskier distance, then, pulling herself together, turned to me with abrupt inconsequence. "It's time we should be at church."

"Oh, I'm not fit for church!"

"Won't it do you good?"

"It won't do *them*—!" I nodded at the house.

"The children?"

"I can't leave them now."

"You're afraid—?"

I spoke boldly. "I'm afraid of *him.*"

Mrs. Grose's large face showed me, at this, for the first time, the faraway faint glimmer of a consciousness more acute: I somehow made out in it the delayed dawn of an idea I myself had not given her and that was as yet quite obscure to me. It comes back to me that I thought instantly of this as something I could get from her; and I felt it to be

connected with the desire she presently showed to know more. "When was it—on the tower?"

"About the middle of the month. At this same hour."

"Almost at dark," said Mrs. Grose.

"Oh, no, not nearly. I saw him as I see you."

"Then how did he get in?"

"And how did he get out?" I laughed. "I had no opportunity to ask him! This evening, you see," I pursued, "he has not been able to get in."

"He only peeps?"

"I hope it will be confined to that!" She had now let go my hand; she turned away a little. I waited an instant; then I brought out: "Go to church. Goodbye. I must watch."

Slowly she faced me again. "Do you fear for them?"

We met in another long look. "Don't *you?*" Instead of answering she came nearer to the window and, for a minute, applied her face to the glass. "You see how he could see," I meanwhile went on.

She didn't move. "How long was he here?"

"Till I came out. I came to meet him."

Mrs. Grose at last turned round, and there was still more in her face. "*I* couldn't have come out."

"Neither could I!" I laughed again. "But I did come. I have my duty."

"So have I mine," she replied; after which she added: "What is he like?"

"I've been dying to tell you. But he's like nobody."

"Nobody?" she echoed.

"He has no hat." Then seeing in her face that she already, in this, with a deeper dismay, found a touch of picture, I quickly added stroke to stroke. "He has red hair, very red, close-curling, and a pale face, long in shape, with straight, good features and little, rather queer whiskers that are as red as his hair. His eyebrows are, somehow, darker; they look particularly arched and as if they might move a good deal. His eyes are sharp, strange—awfully; but I only know clearly that they're rather small and very fixed. His mouth's wide, and his lips are thin, and except for his little whiskers he's quite clean-shaven. He gives me a sort of sense of looking like an actor."

"An actor!" It was impossible to resemble one less, at least, than Mrs. Grose at that moment.

"I've never seen one, but so I suppose them. He's tall, active, erect," I continued, "but never—no, never!—a gentleman."

My companion's face had blanched as I went on; her round eyes started and her mild mouth gaped. "A gentleman?" she gasped, confounded, stupefied: "a gentleman *he?*"

"You know him then?"

She visibly tried to hold herself. "But he *is* handsome?"

I saw the way to help her. "Remarkably!"

"And dressed—?"

"In somebody's clothes." "They're smart, but they're not his own."

She broke into a breathless affirmative groan: "They're the master's!"

I caught it up. "You *do* know him?"

She faltered but a second. "Quint!" she cried.

"Quint?"

"Peter Quint—his own man, his valet, when he was here!"

"When the master was?"

Gaping still, but meeting me, she pieced it all together. "He never wore his hat, but he did wear—well, there were waistcoats missed. They were both here—last year. Then the master went, and Quint was alone."

I followed, but halting a little. "Alone?"

"Alone with *us*." Then, as from a deeper depth, "In charge," she added.

"And what became of him?"

She hung fire so long that I was still more mystified. "He went, too," she brought out at last.

"Went where?"

Her expression, at this, became extraordinary. "God knows where! He died."

"Died?" I almost shrieked.

She seemed fairly to square herself, plant herself more firmly to utter the wonder of it. "Yes. Mr. Quint is dead."

VI

It took of course more than that particular passage to place us together in presence of what we had now to live with as we could—my dreadful liability to impressions of the order so vividly exemplified, and my companion's knowledge, henceforth—a knowledge half consternation and half compassion—of that liability. There had been, this evening, after the revelation left me, for an hour, so prostrate—there had been, for either of us, no attendance on any service but a little service of tears and vows, of prayers and promises, a climax to the series of mutual challenges and pledges that had straightway ensued on our retreating together to the schoolroom and shutting ourselves up there to have everything out. The result of our having everything out was simply to reduce our situation to the last rigor of its elements. She herself had seen nothing, not the shadow of a shadow, and nobody in the house but the governess was in the governess's plight; yet she accepted without directly impugning my sanity the truth as I gave it to her, and ended by showing me, on this ground, an awestricken tenderness, an expression of the sense of my more than questionable privilege, of which the very breath has remained with me as that of the sweetest of human charities.

What was settled between us, accordingly, that night, was that we thought we might bear things together; and I was not even sure that, in spite of her exemption, it was she who had the best of the burden. I knew at this hour, I think, as well as I knew later, what I was capable of meeting to shelter my pupils; but it took me some time to be wholly sure of what my honest ally was prepared for to keep terms with so compromising a contract. I was queer company enough—quite as queer as the company I received; but as I trace over what we went through I see how much common ground we must have found in the one idea that, by good fortune, *could* steady us. It was the idea, the second movement, that

led me straight out, as I may say, of the inner chamber of my dread. I could take the air in the court, at least, and there Mrs. Grose could join me. Perfectly can I recall now the particular way strength came to me before we separated for the night. We had gone over and over every feature of what I had seen.

"He was looking for someone else, you say—someone who was not you?"

"He was looking for little Miles." A portentous clearness now possessed me. "*That's* whom he was looking for."

"But how do you know?"

"I know, I know, I know!" My exaltation grew. "And *you* know, my dear!"

She didn't deny this, but I required, I felt, not even so much telling as that. She resumed in a moment, at any rate: "What if *he* should see him?"

"Little Miles? That's what he wants!"

She looked immensely scared again. "The child?"

"Heaven forbid! The man. He wants to appear to *them*." That he might was an awful conception, and yet, somehow, I could keep it at bay; which, moreover, as we lingered there, was what I succeeded in practically proving. I had an absolute certainty that I should see again what I had already seen, but something within me said that by offering myself bravely as the sole subject of such experience, by accepting, by inviting, by surmounting it all, I should serve as an expiatory victim and guard the tranquility of my companions. The children, in especial, I should thus fence about and absolutely save. I recall one of the last things I said that night to Mrs. Grose.

"It does strike me that my pupils have never mentioned—"

She looked at me hard as I musingly pulled up. "His having been here and the time they were with him?"

"The time they were with him, and his name, his presence, his history, in any way."

"Oh, the little lady doesn't remember. She never heard or knew."

"The circumstances of his death?" I thought with some intensity. "Perhaps not. But Miles would remember—Miles would know."

"Ah, don't try him!" broke from Mrs. Grose.

I returned her the look she had given me. "Don't be afraid." I continued to think. "It *is* rather odd."

"That he has never spoken of him?"

"Never by the least allusion. And you tell me they were 'great friends'?"

"Oh, it wasn't *him!*" Mrs. Grose with emphasis declared. "It was Quint's own fancy. To play with him, I mean—to spoil him." She paused a moment; then she added: "Quint was much too free."

This gave me, straight from my vision of his face—*such* a face!—a sudden sickness of disgust. "Too free with *my* boy?"

"Too free with everyone!"

I forbore, for the moment, to analyze this description further than by the reflection that a part of it applied to several of the members of the household, of the half-dozen maids and men who were still of our small colony. But there was everything, for our apprehension, in the lucky fact that no discomfortable legend, no perturbation of scullions, had ever, within anyone's memory attached to the kind old place. It had neither bad name nor ill fame, and Mrs. Grose, most apparently, only desired to cling to me and to quake in silence. I even put her, the very last thing of all, to the test. It was when, at midnight, she had her hand on the schoolroom door to take leave. "I have it from you then—for it's of great importance—that he was definitely and admittedly bad?"

"Oh, not admittedly. *I* knew it—but the master didn't."

"And you never told him?"

"Well, he didn't like tale-bearing—he hated complaints. He was terribly short with anything of that kind, and if people were all right to *him*—"

"He wouldn't be bothered with more?" This squared well enough with my impressions of him: he was not a trouble-loving gentleman, nor so very particular perhaps about some of the company *he* kept. All the same, I pressed my interlocutress. "I promise you *I* would have told!"

She felt my discrimination. "I daresay I was wrong. But, really, I was afraid."

"Afraid of what?"

"Of things that man could do. Quint was so clever—he was so deep."

I took this in still more than, probably, I showed. "You weren't afraid of anything else? Not of his effect—?"

"His effect?" she repeated with a face of anguish and waiting while I faltered.

"On innocent little precious lives. They were in your charge."

"No, they were not in mine!" she roundly and distressfully returned. "The master believed in him and placed him here because he was supposed not to be well and the country air so good for him. So he had everything to say. Yes"—she let me have it—"even about *them.*"

"Them—that creature?" I had to smother a kind of howl. "And you could bear it!"

"No. I couldn't—and I can't now!" And the poor woman burst into tears.

A rigid control, from the next day, was, as I have said, to follow them; yet how often and how passionately, for a week, we came back together to the subject! Much as we had discussed it that Sunday night, I was, in the immediate later hours in especial—for it may be imagined whether I slept—still haunted with the shadow of something she had not told me. I myself had kept back nothing, but there was a word Mrs. Grose had kept back. I was sure, moreover, by morning, that this was not from a failure of frankness, but because on every side there were fears. It seems to me indeed, in retrospect, that by the time the morrow's sun was high I had restlessly read into the fact before us almost all the meaning they were to receive from subsequent and more cruel occurrences. What they gave me above all was just the sinister figure of the living man—the dead one would keep awhile!—and of the months he had continuously passed at Bly, which, added up, made a formidable stretch. The limit of this evil time had arrived only when, on the dawn of a winter's morning, Peter Quint was found, by a laborer going to early work, stone dead on the road from the village: a catastrophe explained—superficially at least—by a visible wound to his head; such a wound as might have been produced—and as, on the final evidence, *had* been—by a fatal slip, in the dark and after leaving the public house, on the steepish icy slope, a wrong path altogether, at the bottom of which he lay. The icy slope, the turn mistaken at night and in liquor, accounted for much—practically, in the end and after the inquest and boundless chatter, for everything; but there had been matters in his life—strange passages and perils, secret disorders, vices more than suspected—that would have accounted for a good deal more.

I scarce know how to put my story into words that shall be a credible picture of my state of mind; but I was in these days literally able to find a joy in the extraordinary flight of heroism the occasion demanded of me.

I now saw that I had been asked for a service admirable and difficult; and there would be a greatness in letting it be seen—oh, in the right quarter! —that I could succeed where many another girl might have failed. It was an immense help to me—I confess I rather applaud myself as I look back!—that I saw my service so strongly and so simply. I was there to protect and defend the little creatures in the world the most bereaved and the most lovable, the appeal of whose helplessness had suddenly become only too explicit, a deep, constant ache of one's own committed heart. We were cut off, really, together; we were united in our danger. They had nothing but me, and I—well, I had *them*. It was in short a magnificent chance. This chance presented itself to me in an image richly material. I was a screen—I was to stand before them. The more I saw, the less they would. I began to watch them in a stifled suspense, a disguised excitement that might well, had it continued too long, have turned to something like madness. What saved me, as I now see, was that it turned to something else altogether. It didn't last as suspense—it was superseded by horrible proofs. Proofs, I say, yes—from the moment I really took hold.

This moment dated from an afternoon hour that I happened to spend in the grounds with the younger of my pupils alone. We had left Miles indoors, on the red cushion of a deep window seat; he had wished to finish a book, and I had been glad to encourage a purpose so laudable in a young man whose only defect was an occasional excess of the restless. His sister, on the contrary, had been alert to come out, and I strolled with her half an hour, seeking the shade, for the sun was still high and the day exceptionally warm. I was aware afresh, with her, as we went, of how, like her brother, she contrived—it was the charming thing in both children—to let me alone without appearing to drop me and to accompany me without appearing to surround. They were never importunate and yet never listless. My attention to them all really went to seeing them amuse themselves immensely without me: this was a spectacle they seemed actively to prepare and that engaged me as an active admirer. I walked in a world of their invention—they had no occasion whatever to draw upon mine; so that my time was taken only with being, for them, some remarkable person or thing that the game of the moment required and that was merely, thanks to my superior, my exalted stamp, a happy and highly distinguished sinecure. I forget what I was on the present occasion; I only remember that I was something very important and very quiet and that Flora was playing very hard. We were

on the edge of the lake, and, as we had lately begun geography, the lake was the Sea of Azof.

Suddenly, in these circumstances, I became aware that, on the other side of the Sea of Azof, we had an interested spectator. The way this knowledge gathered in me was the strangest thing in the world—the strangest, that is, except the very much stranger in which it quickly merged itself. I had sat down with a piece of work—for I was something or other that could sit—on the old stone bench which overlooked the pond; and in this position I began to take in with certitude, and yet without direct vision, the presence, at a distance, of a third person. The old trees, the thick shrubbery, made a great and pleasant shade, but it was all suffused with the brightness of the hot, still hour. There was no ambiguity in anything; none whatever, at least, in the conviction I from one moment to another found myself forming as to what I should see straight before me and across the lake as a consequence of raising my eyes. They were attached at this juncture to the stitching in which I was engaged, and I can feel once more the spasm of my effort not to move them till I should so have steadied myself as to be able to make up my mind what to do. There was an alien object in view—a figure whose right of presence I instantly, passionately questioned. I recollect counting over perfectly the possibilities, reminding myself that nothing was more natural, for instance, then the appearance of one of the men about the place, or even of a messenger, a postman, or a tradesman's boy, from the village. That reminder had as little effect on my practical certitude as I was conscious—still even without looking—of its having upon the character and attitude of our visitor. Nothing was more natural than that these things should be the other things that they absolutely were not.

Of the positive identity of the apparition I would assure myself as soon as the small clock of my courage should have ticked out the right second; meanwhile, with an effort that was already sharp enough, I transferred my eyes straight to little Flora, who, at the moment, was about ten yards away. My heart had stood still for an instant with the wonder and terror of the question whether she too would see; and I held my breath while I waited for what a cry from her, what some sudden innocent sign either of interest or of alarm, would tell me. I waited, but nothing came; then, in the first place—and there is something more dire in this, I feel, than in anything I have to relate—I was determined by a sense that, within a minute, all sounds from her had previously dropped;

and, in the second, by the circumstance that, also within the minute, she had, in her play, turned her back to the water. This was her attitude when I at last looked at her—looked with the confirmed conviction that we were still, together, under direct personal notice. She had picked up a small flat piece of wood, which happened to have in it a little hole that had evidently suggested to her the idea of sticking in another fragment that might figure as a mast and make the thing a boat. This second morsel, as I watched her, she was very markedly and intently attempting to tighten in its place. My apprehension of what she was doing sustained me so that after some seconds I felt I was ready for more. Then I again shifted my eyes—I faced what I had to face.

VII

I got hold of Mrs. Grose as soon after this as I could; and I can give no intelligible account of how I fought out the interval. Yet I still hear myself cry as I fairly threw myself into her arms: "They *know*—it's too monstrous: they know, they know!"

"And what on earth—?" I felt her incredulity as she held me.

"Why, all that *we* know—and heaven knows what else besides!" Then, as she released me, I made it out to her, made it out perhaps only now with full coherency even to myself. "Two hours ago, in the garden" —I could scarce articulate—"Flora *saw!*"

Mrs. Grose took it as she might have taken a blow in the stomach. "She has told you?" she panted.

"Not a word—that's the horror. She kept it to herself! The child of eight, *that* child!" Unutterable still, for me, was the stupefaction of it.

Mrs. Grose, of course, could only gape the wider. "Then how do you know?"

"I was there—I saw with my eyes: saw that she was perfectly aware."

"Do you mean aware of *him?*"

"No—of *her*." I was conscious as I spoke that I looked prodigious things, for I got the slow reflection of them in my companion's face. "Another person—this time; but a figure of quite as unmistakable horror and evil: a woman in black, pale and dreadful—with such an air also, and such a face!—on the other side of the lake. I was there with the child—quiet for the hour; and in the midst of it she came."

"Came how—from where?"

"From where they come from! She just appeared and stood there—but not so near."

"And without coming nearer?"

"Oh, for the effect and the feeling, she might have been as close as you!"

My friend, with an odd impulse, fell back a step. "Was she someone you've never seen?"

"Yes. But someone the child has. Someone *you* have." Then, to show how I had thought it all out: "My predecessor—the one who died."

"Miss Jessel?"

"Miss Jessel. You don't believe me?" I pressed.

She turned right and left in her distress. "How can you be sure?"

This drew from me, in the state of my nerves, a flash of impatience. "Then ask Flora—*she's* sure!" But I had no sooner spoken than I caught myself up. "No, for God's sake, *don't!* She'll say she isn't—she'll lie!"

Mrs. Grose was not too bewildered instinctively to protest. "Ah, how *can* you?"

"Because I'm clear. Flora doesn't want me to know."

"It's only then to spare you."

"No, no—there are depths, depths! The more I go over it, the more I see in it, and the more I see in it, the more I fear. I don't know what I *don't* see—what I *don't* fear!"

Mrs. Grose tried to keep up with me. "You mean you're afraid of seeing her again?"

"Oh, no; that's nothing—now!" Then I explained. "It's of *not* seeing her."

But my companion only looked wan. "I don't understand you."

"Why, it's that the child may keep it up—and that the child assuredly *will*—without my knowing it."

At the image of this possibility Mrs. Grose for a moment collapsed, yet presently to pull herself together again, as if from the positive force of the sense of what, should we yield an inch, there would really be to give way to. "Dear, dear—we must keep our heads! And after all, if she doesn't mind it—!" She even tried a grim joke. "Perhaps she likes it!"

"Likes *such* things—a scrap of an infant!"

"Isn't it just a proof of her blessed innocence?" my friend bravely inquired.

She brought me, for the instant, almost round. "Oh, we must clutch at *that*—we must cling to it! If it isn't a proof of what you say, it's a proof of—God knows what! For the woman's a horror of horrors."

Mrs. Grose, at this, fixed her eyes a minute on the ground; then at last raising them, "Tell me how you know," she said.

"Then you admit it's what she was?" I cried.

"Tell me how you know," my friend simply repeated.

"Know? By seeing her! By the way she looked."

"At you, do you mean—so wickedly?"

"Dear me, no—I could have borne that. She gave me never a glance. She only fixed the child."

Mrs. Grose tried to see it. "Fixed her?"

"Ah, with such awful eyes!"

She stared at mine as if they might really have resembled them. "Do you mean of dislike?"

"God help us, no. Of something much worse."

"Worse than dislike?"—this left her indeed at a loss.

"With a determination—indescribable. With a kind of fury of intention."

I made her turn pale. "Intention?"

"To get hold of her." Mrs. Grose—her eyes just lingering on mine—gave a shudder and walked to the window; and while she stood there looking out I completed my statement. "*That's* what Flora knows."

After a little she turned round. "The person was in black, you say?"

"In mourning—rather poor, almost shabby. But—yes—with extraordinary beauty." I now recognized to what I had at last, stroke by stroke, brought the victim of my confidence, for she quite visibly weighed this. "Oh, handsome—very, very," I insisted; "wonderfully handsome. But infamous."

She slowly came back to me. "Miss Jessel—*was* infamous." She once more took my hand in both her own, holding it as tight as if to fortify me against the increase of alarm I might draw from this disclosure. "They were both infamous," she finally said.

So, for a little, we faced it once more together; and I found absolutely a degree of help in seeing it now so straight. "I appreciate," I said, "the great decency of your not having hitherto spoken; but the time has certainly come to give me the whole thing." She appeared to assent to this, but still only in silence; seeing which I went on: "I must have it now. Of what did she die? Come, there was something between them."

"There was everything."

"In spite of the difference—?"

"Oh, of their rank, their condition"—she brought it woefully out. "*She* was a lady."

I turned it over; I again saw. "Yes—she was a lady."

"And he so dreadfully below," said Mrs. Grose.

I felt that I doubtless needn't press too hard, in such company, on the place of a servant in the scale; but there was nothing to prevent an acceptance of my companion's own measure of my predecessor's abasement. There was a way to deal with that, and I dealt; the more readily for my full vision—on the evidence—of our employer's late clever, good-looking "own" man; impudent, assured, spoiled, depraved. "The fellow was a hound."

Mrs. Grose considered as if it were perhaps a little a case for a sense of shades. "I've never seen one like him. He did what he wished."

"With *her?*"

"With them all."

It was as if now in my friend's own eyes Miss Jessel had again appeared. I seemed at any rate, for an instant, to see their evocation of her as distinctly as I had seen her by the pond; and I brought out with decision: "It must have been also what *she* wished!"

Mrs. Grose's face signified that it had been indeed, but she said at the same time: "Poor woman—she paid for it!"

"Then you do know what she died of?" I asked.

"No—I know nothing. I wanted not to know; I was glad enough I didn't; and I thanked heaven she was well out of this!"

"Yet you had, then, your idea—"

"Of her real reason for leaving? Oh, yes—as to that. She couldn't have stayed. Fancy it here—for a governess! And afterward I imagined—and I still imagine. And what I imagine is dreadful."

"Not so dreadful as what *I* do," I replied; on which I must have shown her—as I was indeed but too conscious—a front of miserable defeat. It brought out again all her compassion for me, and at the renewed touch of her kindness my power to resist broke down. I burst, as I had, the other time, made her burst, into tears; she took me to her motherly breast, and my lamentation overflowed. "I don't do it!" I sobbed in despair; "I don't save or shield them! It's far worse than I dreamed—they're lost!"

VIII

What I had said to Mrs. Grose was true enough: there were in the matter I had put before her depths and possibilities that I lacked resolution to sound; so that when we met once more in the wonder of it we were of a common mind about the duty of resistance to extravagant fancies. We were to keep our heads if we should keep nothing else—difficult indeed as that might be in the face of what, in our prodigious experience, was least to be questioned. Late that night, while the house slept, we had another talk in my room, when she went all the way with me as to its being beyond doubt that I had seen exactly what I had seen. To hold her perfectly in the pinch of that, I found I had only to ask her how, if I had "made it up," I came to be able to give, of each of the persons appearing to me, a picture disclosing, to the last detail, their special marks—a portrait on the exhibition of which she had instantly recognized and named them. She wished of course—small blame to her!—to sink the whole subject; and I was quick to assure her that my own interest in it had now violently taken the form of a search for the way to escape from it. I encountered her on the ground of a probability that with recurrence—for recurrence we took for granted—I should get used to my danger, distinctly professing that my personal exposure had suddenly become the least of my discomforts. It was my new suspicion that was intolerable; and yet even to this complication the later hours of the day had brought a little ease.

On leaving her, after my first outbreak, I had of course returned to my pupils, associating the right remedy for my dismay with that sense of their charm which I had already found to be a thing I could positively cultivate and which had never failed me yet. I had simply, in other words, plunged afresh into Flora's special society and there become aware—it was almost a luxury!—that she could put her little conscious hand

straight upon the spot that ached. She had looked at me in sweet speculation and then had accused me to my face of having "cried." I had supposed I had brushed away the ugly signs: but I could literally—for the time, at all events—rejoice, under this fathomless charity, that they had not entirely disappeared. To gaze into the depths of blue of the child's eyes and pronounce their loveliness a trick of premature cunning was to be guilty of a cynicism in preference to which I naturally preferred to abjure my judgment and, so far as might be, my agitation. I couldn't abjure for merely wanting to, but I could repeat to Mrs. Grose—as I did there, over and over, in the small hours—that with their voices in the air, their pressure on one's heart, and their fragrant faces against one's cheek, everything fell to the ground but their incapacity and their beauty. It was a pity that, somehow, to settle this once for all, I had equally to re-enumerate the signs of subtlety that, in the afternoon, by the lake had made a miracle of my show of self-possession. It was a pity to be obliged to reinvestigate the certitude of the moment itself and repeat how it had come to me as a revelation that the inconceivable communion I then surprised was a matter, for either party, of habit. It was a pity that I should have had to quaver out again the reasons for my not having, in my delusion, so much as questioned that the little girl saw our visitant even as I actually saw Mrs. Grose herself, and that she wanted, by just so much as she did thus see, to make me suppose she didn't, and at the same time, without showing anything, arrive at a guess as to whether I myself did! It was a pity that I needed once more to describe the portentous little activity by which she sought to divert my attention—the perceptible increase of movement, the greater intensity of play, the singing, the gabbling of nonsense, and the invitation to romp.

Yet if I had not indulged, to prove there was nothing in it, in this review, I should have missed the two or three dim elements of comfort that still remained to me. I should not for instance have been able to asseverate to my friend that I was certain—which was so much to the good—that *I* at least had not betrayed myself. I should not have been prompted, by stress of need, by desperation of mind—I scarce know what to call it—to invoke such further aid to intelligence as might spring from pushing my colleague fairly to the wall. She had told me, bit by bit, under pressure, a great deal; but a small shifty spot on the wrong side of it all still sometimes brushed my brow like the wing of a bat; and I remember how on this occasion—for the sleeping house and the

concentration alike of our danger and our watch seemed to help—I felt the importance of giving the last jerk to the curtain. "I don't believe anything so horrible," I recollect saying; "no, let us put it definitely, my dear, that I don't. But if I did, you know, there's a thing I should require now, just without sparing you the least bit more—oh, not a scrap, come!—to get out of you. What was it you had in mind when, in our distress, before Miles came back, over the letter from his school, you said, under my insistence, that you didn't pretend for him that he had not literally *ever* been 'bad'? He has *not* literally 'ever,' in these weeks that I myself have lived with him and so closely watched him; he has been an imperturbable little prodigy of delightful, lovable goodness. Therefore you might perfectly have made the claim for him if you had not, as it happened, seen an exception to take. What was your exception, and to what passage in your personal observation of him did you refer?"

It was a dreadfully austere inquiry, but levity was not our note, and, at any rate, before the gray dawn admonished us to separate I had got my answer. What my friend had had in mind proved to be immensely to the purpose. It was neither more nor less than the circumstance that for a period of several months Quint and the boy had been perpetually together. It was in fact the very appropriate truth that she had ventured to criticize the propriety, to hint at the incongruity, of so close an alliance, and even to go so far on the subject as a frank overture to Miss Jessel. Miss Jessel had, with a most strange manner, requested her to mind her business, and the good woman had, on this, directly approached little Miles. What she had said to him, since I pressed, was that *she* liked to see young gentlemen not forget their station.

I pressed again, of course, at this. "You reminded him that Quint was only a base menial?"

"As you might say! And it was his answer, for one thing, that was bad."

"And for another thing?" I waited. "He repeated your words to Quint?"

"No, not that. It's just what he *wouldn't!*" she could still impress upon me. "I was sure, at any rate," she added, "that he didn't. But he denied certain occasions."

"What occasions?"

"When they had been about together quite as if Quint were his tutor —and a very grand one—and Miss Jessel only for the little lady. When he had gone off with the fellow, I mean, and spent hours with him."

"He then prevaricated about it—he said he hadn't?" Her assent was clear enough to cause me to add in a moment: "I see. He lied."

"Oh!" Mrs. Grose mumbled. This was a suggestion that it didn't matter; which indeed she backed up by a further remark. "You see, after all, Miss Jessel didn't mind. She didn't forbid him."

I considered. "Did he put that to you as a justification?"

At this she dropped again. "No, he never spoke of it."

"Never mentioned her in connection with Quint?"

She saw, visibly flushing, where I was coming out. "Well, he didn't show anything. He denied," she repeated; "he denied."

Lord, how I pressed her now! "So that you could see he knew what was between the two wretches?"

"I don't know—I don't know!" the poor woman groaned.

"You do know, you dear thing," I replied; "only you haven't my dreadful boldness of mind, and you keep back, out of timidity and modesty and delicacy, even the impression that, in the past, when you had, without my aid, to flounder about in silence, most of all made you miserable. But I shall get it out of you yet! There was something in the boy that suggested to you," I continued, "that he covered and concealed their relation."

"Oh, he couldn't prevent—"

"Your learning the truth? I daresay! But, heavens," I fell, with vehemence, athinking, "what it shows that they must, to that extent, have succeeded in making of him!"

"Ah, nothing that's not nice *now!*" Mrs. Grose lugubriously pleaded.

"I don't wonder you looked queer," I persisted, "when I mentioned to you the letter from his school!"

"I doubt if I looked as queer as you!" she retorted with homely force. "And if he was so bad then as that comes to, how is he such an angel now?"

"Yes, indeed—and if he was a fiend at school! How, how, how? Well," I said in my torment, "you must put it to me again, but I shall not be able to tell you for some days. Only, put it to me again!" I cried in a way that made my friend stare. "There are directions in which I must not for the present let myself go." Meanwhile I returned to her first example

—the one to which she had just previously referred—of the boy's happy capacity for an occasional slip. "If Quint—on your remonstrance at the time you speak of—was a base menial, one of the things Miles said to you, I find myself guessing, was that you were another." Again her admission was so adequate that I continued: "And you forgave him that?"

"Wouldn't *you?*"

"Oh, yes!" And we exchanged there, in the stillness, a sound of the oddest amusement. Then I went on: "At all events, while he was with the man—"

"Miss Flora was with the woman. It suited them all!"

It suited me, too, I felt, only too well; by which I mean that it suited exactly the particularly deadly view I was in the very act of forbidding myself to entertain. But I so far succeeded in checking the expression of this view that I will throw, just here, no further light on it than may be offered by the mention of my final observation to Mrs. Grose. "His having lied and been impudent are, I confess, less engaging specimens than I had hoped to have from you of the outbreak in him of the little natural man. Still," I mused, "They must do, for they make me feel more than ever that I must watch."

It made me blush, the next minute, to see in my friend's face how much more unreservedly she had forgiven him than her anecdote struck me as presenting to my own tenderness an occasion for doing. This came out when, at the schoolroom door, she quitted me. "Surely you don't accuse *him*—"

"Of carrying on an intercourse that he conceals from me? Ah, remember that, until further evidence, I now accuse nobody." Then, before shutting her out to go, by another passage, to her own place, "I must just wait," I wound up.

IX

I waited and waited, and the days, as they elapsed, took something from my consternation. A very few of them, in fact, passing, in constant sight of my pupils, without a fresh incident, sufficed to give to grievous fancies and even to odious memories a kind of brush of the sponge. I have spoken of the surrender to their extraordinary childish grace as a thing I could actively cultivate, and it may be imagined if I neglected now to address myself to this source for whatever it would yield. Stranger than I can express, certainly, was the effort to struggle against my new lights; it would doubtless have been, however, a greater tension still had it not been so frequently successful. I used to wonder how my little charges could help guessing that I thought strange things about them; and the circumstances that these things only made them more interesting was not by itself a direct aid to keeping them in the dark. I trembled lest they should see that they *were* so immensely more interesting. Putting things at the worst, at all events, as in meditation I so often did, any clouding of their innocence could only be—blameless and foredoomed as they were—a reason the more for taking risks. There were moments when, by an irresistible impulse, I found myself catching them up and pressing them to my heart. As soon as I had done so I used to say to myself: "What will they think of that? Doesn't it betray too much?" It would have been easy to get into a sad, wild tangle about how much I might betray; but the real account, I feel, of the hours of peace that I could still enjoy was that the immediate charm of my companions was a beguilement still effective even under the shadow of the possibility that it was studied. For if it occurred to me that I might occasionally excite suspicion by the little outbreaks of my sharper passion for them, so too I remember wondering if I mightn't see a queerness in the traceable increase of their own demonstrations.

They were at this period extravagantly and preternaturally fond of me; which, after all, I could reflect, was no more than a graceful response in children perpetually bowed over and hugged. The homage of which they were so lavish succeeded, in truth, for my nerves, quite as well as if I never appeared to myself, as I may say, literally to catch them at a purpose in it. They had never, I think, wanted to do so many things for their poor protectress; I mean—though they got their lessons better and better, which was naturally what would please her most—in the way of diverting, entertaining, surprising her; reading her passages, telling her stories, acting her charades, pouncing out at her, in disguises, as animals and historical characters, and above all astonishing her by the "pieces" they had secretly got by heart and could interminably recite. I should never get to the bottom—were I to let myself go even now—of the prodigious private commentary, all under still more private correction, with which, in these days, I overscored their full hours. They had shown me from the first a facility for everything, a general faculty which, taking a fresh start, achieved remarkable flights. They got their little tasks as if they loved them, and indulged, from the mere exuberance of the gift, in the most unimposed little miracles of memory. They not only popped out at me as tigers and as Romans, but as Shakespeareans, astronomers, and navigators. This was so singularly the case that it had presumably much to do with the fact as to which, at the present day, I am at a loss for a different explanation: I allude to my unnatural composure on the subject of another school for Miles. What I remember is that I was content not, for the time, to open the question, and that contentment must have sprung from the sense of his perpetually striking show of cleverness. He was too clever for a bad governess, for a parson's daughter, to spoil; and the strangest if not the brightest thread in the pensive embroidery I just spoke of was the impression I might have got, if I had dared to work it out, that he was under some influence operating in his small intellectual life as a tremendous incitement.

If it was easy to reflect, however, that such a boy could postpone school, it was at least as marked that for such a boy to have been "kicked out" by a schoolmaster was a mystification without end. Let me add that in their company now—and I was careful almost never to be out of it—I could follow no scent very far. We lived in a cloud of music and love and success and private theatricals. The musical sense in each of the children was of the quickest, but the elder in especial had a marvelous knack of

catching and repeating. The schoolroom piano broke into all gruesome fancies; and when that failed there were confabulations in corners, with a sequel of one of them going out in the highest spirits in order to "come in" as something new. I had had brothers myself, and it was no revelation to me that little girls could be slavish idolaters of little boys. What surpassed everything was that there was a little boy in the world who could have for the inferior age, sex, and intelligence so fine a consideration. They were extraordinarily at one, and to say that they never either quarreled or complained is to make the note of praise coarse for their quality of sweetness. Sometimes, indeed, when I dropped into coarseness, I perhaps came across traces of little understandings between them by which one of them should keep me occupied while the other slipped away. There is a *naïf* side, I suppose, in all diplomacy; but if my pupils practiced upon me, it was surely with the minimum of grossness. It was all in the other quarter that, after a lull, the grossness broke out.

I find that I really hang back; but I must take my plunge. In going on with the record of what was hideous at Bly, I not only challenge the most liberal faith—for which I little care; but—and this is another matter—I renew what I myself suffered, I again push my way through it to the end. There came suddenly an hour after which, as I look back, the affair seems to me to have been all pure suffering; but I have at least reached the heart of it, and the straightest road out is doubtless to advance. One evening—with nothing to lead up or to prepare it—I felt the cold touch of the impression that had breathed on me the night of my arrival and which, much lighter then, as I have mentioned, I should probably have made little of in memory had my subsequent sojourn been less agitated. I had not gone to bed; I sat reading by a couple of candles. There was a roomful of old books at Bly—last-century fiction, some of it, which, to the extent of a distinctly deprecated renown, but never to so much as that of a stray specimen, had reached the sequestered home and appealed to the unavowed curiosity of my youth. I remember that the book I had in my hand was Fielding's *Amelia*; also that I was wholly awake. I recall further both a general conviction that it was horribly late and a particular objection to looking at my watch. I figure, finally, that the white curtain draping, in the fashion of those days, the head of Flora's little bed, shrouded, as I had assured myself long before, the perfection of childish rest. I recollect in short that, though I was deeply interested in my author, I found myself, at the turn of a page and with his spell all scattered,

looking straight up from him and hard at the door of my room. There was a moment during which I listened, reminded of the faint sense I had had, the first night, of there being something undefinably astir in the house, and noted the soft breath of the open casement just move the half-drawn blind. Then, with all the marks of a deliberation that must have seemed magnificent had there been anyone to admire it, I laid down my book, rose to my feet, and, taking a candle, went straight out of the room and, from the passage, on which my light made little impression, noiselessly closed and locked the door.

I can say now neither what determined nor what guided me, but I went straight along the lobby, holding my candle high, till I came within sight of the tall window that presided over the great turn of the staircase. At this point I precipitately found myself aware of three things. They were practically simultaneous, yet they had flashes of succession. My candle, under a bold flourish, went out, and I perceived, by the uncovered window, that the yielding dusk of earliest morning rendered it unnecessary. Without it, the next instant, I saw that there was someone on the stair. I speak of sequences, but I required no lapse of seconds to stiffen myself for a third encounter with Quint. The apparition had reached the landing halfway up and was therefore on the spot nearest the window, where at sight of me, it stopped short and fixed me exactly as it had fixed me from the tower and from the garden. He knew me as well as I knew him; and so, in the cold, faint twilight, with a glimmer in the high glass and another on the polish of the oak stair below, we faced each other in our common intensity. He was absolutely, on this occasion, a living, detestable, dangerous presence. But that was not the wonder of wonders; I reserve this distinction for quite another circumstance: the circumstance that dread had unmistakably quitted me and that there was nothing in me there that didn't meet and measure him.

I had plenty of anguish after that extraordinary moment, but I had, thank God, no terror. And he knew I had not—I found myself at the end of an instant magnificently aware of this. I felt, in a fierce rigor of confidence, that if I stood my ground a minute I should cease—for the time, at least—to have him to reckon with; and during the minute, accordingly, the thing was as human and hideous as a real interview: hideous just because it *was* human, as human as to have met alone, in the small hours, in a sleeping house, some enemy, some adventurer, some criminal. It was the dead silence of our long gaze at such close quarters

that gave the whole horror, huge as it was, its only note of the unnatural. If I had met a murderer in such a place and at such an hour, we still at least would have spoken. Something would have passed, in life, between us; if nothing had passed, one of us would have moved. The moment was so prolonged that it would have taken but little more to make me doubt if even *I* were in life. I can't express what followed it save by saying that the silence itself—which was indeed in a manner an attestation of my strength—became the element into which I saw the figure disappear; in which I definitely saw it turn as I might have seen the low wretch to which it had once belonged turn on receipt of an order, and pass, with my eyes on the villainous back that no hunch could have more disfigured, straight down the staircase and into the darkness in which the next bend was lost.

X

I remained awhile at the top of the stair, but with the effect presently of understanding that when my visitor had gone, he had gone: then I returned to my room. The foremost thing I saw there by the light of the candle I had left burning was that Flora's little bed was empty; and on this I caught my breath with all the terror that, five minutes before, I had been able to resist. I dashed at the place in which I had left her lying and over which (for the small silk counterpane and the sheets were disarranged) the white curtains had been deceivingly pulled forward; then my step, to my unutterable relief, produced an answering sound: I perceived an agitation of the window blind, and the child, ducking down, emerged rosily from the other side of it. She stood there in so much of her candor and so little of her nightgown, with her pink bare feet and the golden glow of her curls. She looked intensely grave, and I had never had such a sense of losing an advantage acquired (the thrill of which had just been so prodigious) as on my consciousness that she addressed me with a reproach. "You naughty: where *have* you been?"—instead of challenging her own irregularity I found myself arraigned and explaining. She herself explained, for that matter, with the loveliest, eagerest simplicity. She had known suddenly, as she lay there, that I was out of the room, and had jumped up to see what had become of me. I had dropped, with the joy of her reappearance, back into my chair—feeling then, and then only, a little faint; and she had pattered straight over to me, thrown herself upon my knee, given herself to be held with the flame of the candle full in the wonderful little face that was still flushed with sleep. I remember closing my eyes an instant, yieldingly, consciously, as before the excess of something beautiful that shone out of the blue of her own. "You were looking for me out of the window?" I said. "You thought I might be walking in the grounds?"

"Well, you know, I thought someone was"—she never blanched as she smiled out that at me.

Oh, how I looked at her now! "And did you see anyone?"

"Ah, *no!*" she returned, almost with the full privilege of childish inconsequence, resentfully, though with a long sweetness in her little drawl of the negative.

At that moment, in the state of my nerves, I absolutely believed she lied; and if I once more closed my eyes it was before the dazzle of the three or four possible ways in which I might take this up. One of these, for a moment, tempted me with such singular intensity that, to withstand it, I must have gripped my little girl with a spasm that, wonderfully, she submitted to without a cry or a sign of fright. Why not break out at her on the spot and have it all over?—give it to her straight in her lovely little lighted face? "You see, you see, you *know* that you do and that you already quite suspect I believe it; therefore, why not frankly confess it to me, so that we may at least live with it together and learn perhaps, in the strangeness of our fate, where we are and what it means?" This solicitation dropped, alas, as it came: if I could immediately have succumbed to it I might have spared myself—well, you'll see what. Instead of succumbing I sprang again to my feet, looked at her bed, and took a helpless middle way. "Why did you pull the curtain over the place to make me think you were still there?"

Flora luminously considered; after which, with her little divine smile: "Because I don't like to frighten you!"

"But if I had, by your idea, gone out—?"

She absolutely declined to be puzzled; she turned her eyes to the flame of the candle as if the question were as irrelevant, or at any rate as impersonal, as Mrs. Marcet or nine-times-nine. "Oh, but you know," she quite adequately answered, "that you might come back, you dear, and that you *have!*" And after a little, when she had got into bed, I had, for a long time, by almost sitting on her to hold her hand, to prove that I recognized the pertinence of my return.

You may imagine the general complexion, from that moment, of my nights. I repeatedly sat up till I didn't know when; I selected moments when my roommate unmistakably slept, and, stealing out, took noiseless turns in the passage and even pushed as far as to where I had last met Quint. But I never met him there again; and I may as well say at once that I on no other occasion saw him in the house. I just missed, on the

staircase, on the other hand, a different adventure. Looking down it from the top I once recognized the presence of a woman seated on one of the lower steps with her back presented to me, her body half-bowed and her head, in an attitude of woe, in her hands. I had been there but an instant, however, when she vanished without looking round at me. I knew, nonetheless, exactly what dreadful face she had to show; and I wondered whether, if instead of being above I had been below, I should have had, for going up, the same nerve I had lately shown Quint. Well, there continued to be plenty of chance for nerve. On the eleventh night after my latest encounter with that gentleman—they were all numbered now—I had an alarm that perilously skirted it and that indeed, from the particular quality of its unexpectedness, proved quite my sharpest shock. It was precisely the first night during this series that, weary with watching, I had felt that I might again without laxity lay myself down at my old hour. I slept immediately and, as I afterward knew, till about one o'clock; but when I woke it was to sit straight up, as completely roused as if a hand had shook me. I had left a light burning, but it was now out, and I felt an instant certainty that Flora had extinguished it. This brought me to my feet and straight, in the darkness, to her bed, which I found she had left. A glance at the window enlightened me further, and the striking of a match completed the picture.

The child had again got up—this time blowing out the taper, and had again, for some purpose of observation or response, squeezed in behind the blind and was peering out into the night. That she now saw—as she had not, I had satisfied myself, the previous time—was proved to me by the fact that she was disturbed neither by my reillumination nor by the haste I made to get into slippers and into a wrap. Hidden, protected, absorbed, she evidently rested on the sill—the casement opened forward—and gave herself up. There was a great still moon to help her, and this fact had counted in my quick decision. She was face to face with the apparition we had met at the lake, and could now communicate with it as she had not then been able to do. What I, on my side, had to care for was, without disturbing her, to reach, from the corridor, some other window in the same quarter. I got to the door without her hearing me; I got out of it, closed it, and listened, from the other side, for some sound from her. While I stood in the passage I had my eyes on her brother's door, which was but ten steps off and which, indescribably, produced in me a renewal of the strange impulse that I lately spoke of as my

temptation. What if I should go straight in and march to *his* window?—what if, by risking to his boyish bewilderment a revelation of my motive, I should throw across the rest of the mystery the long halter of my boldness?

This thought held me sufficiently to make me cross to his threshold and pause again. I preternaturally listened; I figured to myself what might portentously be; I wondered if his bed were also empty and he too were secretly at watch. It was a deep, soundless minute, at the end of which my impulse failed. He was quiet; he might be innocent; the risk was hideous; I turned away. There was a figure in the grounds—a figure prowling for a sight, the visitor with whom Flora was engaged; but it was not the visitor most concerned with my boy. I hesitated afresh, but on other grounds and only for a few seconds; then I had made my choice. There were empty rooms at Bly, and it was only a question of choosing the right one. The right one suddenly presented itself to me as the lower one—though high above the gardens—in the solid corner of the house that I have spoken of as the old tower. This was a large, square chamber, arranged with some state as a bedroom, the extravagant size of which made it so inconvenient that it had not for years, though kept by Mrs. Grose in exemplary order, been occupied. I had often admired it and I knew my way about in it; I had only, after just faltering at the first chill gloom of its disuse, to pass across it and unbolt as quietly as I could one of the shutters. Achieving this transit, I uncovered the glass without a sound and, applying my face to the pane, was able, the darkness without being much less than within, to see that I commanded the right direction. Then I saw something more. The moon made the night extraordinarily penetrable and showed me on the lawn a person, diminished by distance, who stood there motionless and as if fascinated, looking up to where I had appeared—looking, that is, not so much straight at me as at something that was apparently above me. There was clearly another person above me—there was a person on the tower; but the presence on the lawn was not in the least what I had conceived and had confidently hurried to meet. The presence on the lawn—I felt sick as I made it out—was poor little Miles himself.

XI

It was not till late next day that I spoke to Mrs. Grose; the rigor with which I kept my pupils in sight making it often difficult to meet her privately, and the more as we each felt the importance of not provoking—on the part of the servants quite as much as on that of the children—any suspicion of a secret flurry or that of a discussion of mysteries. I drew a great security in this particular from her mere smooth aspect. There was nothing in her fresh face to pass on to others my horrible confidences. She believed me, I was sure, absolutely: if she hadn't I don't know what would have become of me, for I couldn't have borne the business alone. But she was a magnificent monument to the blessing of a want of imagination, and if she could see in our little charges nothing but their beauty and amiability, their happiness and cleverness, she had no direct communication with the sources of my trouble. If they had been at all visibly blighted or battered, she would doubtless have grown, on tracing it back, haggard enough to match them; as matters stood, however, I could feel her, when she surveyed them, with her large white arms folded and the habit of serenity in all her look, thank the Lord's mercy that if they were ruined the pieces would still serve. Flights of fancy gave place, in her mind, to a steady fireside glow, and I had already begun to perceive how, with the development of the conviction that—as time went on without a public accident—our young things could, after all, look out for themselves, she addressed her greatest solicitude to the sad case presented by their instructress. That, for myself, was a sound simplification: I could engage that, to the world, my face should tell no tales, but it would have been, in the conditions, an immense added strain to find myself anxious about hers.

At the hour I now speak of she had joined me, under pressure, on the terrace, where, with the lapse of the season, the afternoon sun was now

agreeable; and we sat there together while, before us, at a distance, but within call if we wished, the children strolled to and fro in one of their most manageable moods. They moved slowly, in unison, below us, over the lawn, the boy, as they went, reading aloud from a storybook and passing his arm round his sister to keep her quite in touch. Mrs. Grose watched them with positive placidity; then I caught the suppressed intellectual creak with which she conscientiously turned to take from me a view of the back of the tapestry. I had made her a receptacle of lurid things, but there was an odd recognition of my superiority—my accomplishments and my function—in her patience under my pain. She offered her mind to my disclosures as, had I wished to mix a witch's broth and proposed it with assurance, she would have held out a large clean saucepan. This had become thoroughly her attitude by the time that, in my recital of the events of the night, I reached the point of what Miles had said to me when, after seeing him, at such a monstrous hour, almost on the very spot where he happened now to be, I had gone down to bring him in; choosing then, at the window, with a concentrated need of not alarming the house, rather that method than a signal more resonant. I had left her meanwhile in little doubt of my small hope of representing with success even to her actual sympathy my sense of the real splendor of the little inspiration with which, after I had got him into the house, the boy met my final articulate challenge. As soon as I appeared in the moonlight on the terrace, he had come to me as straight as possible; on which I had taken his hand without a word and led him, through the dark spaces, up the staircase where Quint had so hungrily hovered for him, along the lobby where I had listened and trembled, and so to his forsaken room.

Not a sound, on the way, had passed between us, and I had wondered—oh, *how* I had wondered!—if he were groping about in his little mind for something plausible and not too grotesque. It would tax his invention, certainly, and I felt, this time, over his real embarrassment, a curious thrill of triumph. It was a sharp trap for the inscrutable! He couldn't play any longer at innocence; so how the deuce would he get out of it? There beat in me indeed, with the passionate throb of this question an equal dumb appeal as to how the deuce *I* should. I was confronted at last, as never yet, with all the risk attached even now to sounding my own horrid note. I remember in fact that as we pushed into his little chamber, where the bed had not been slept in at all and the window, uncovered to

the moonlight, made the place so clear that there was no need of striking a match—I remember how I suddenly dropped, sank upon the edge of the bed from the force of the idea that he must know how he really, as they say, "had" me. He could do what he liked, with all his cleverness to help him, so long as I should continue to defer to the old tradition of the criminality of those caretakers of the young who minister to superstitions and fears. He "had" me indeed, and in a cleft stick; for who would ever absolve me, who would consent that I should go unhung, if, by the faintest tremor of an overture, I were the first to introduce into our perfect intercourse an element so dire? No, no: it was useless to attempt to convey to Mrs. Grose, just as it is scarcely less so to attempt to suggest here, how, in our short, stiff brush in the dark, he fairly shook me with admiration. I was of course thoroughly kind and merciful; never, never yet had I placed on his little shoulders hands of such tenderness as those with which, while I rested against the bed, I held him there well under fire. I had no alternative but, in form at least, to put it to him.

"You must tell me now—and all the truth. What did you go out for? What were you doing there?"

I can still see his wonderful smile, the whites of his beautiful eyes, and the uncovering of his little teeth shine to me in the dusk. "If I tell you why, will you understand?" My heart, at this, leaped into my mouth. *Would* he tell me why? I found no sound on my lips to press it, and I was aware of replying only with a vague, repeated, grimacing nod. He was gentleness itself, and while I wagged my head at him he stood there more than ever a little fairy prince. It was his brightness indeed that gave me a respite. Would it be so great if he were really going to tell me? "Well," he said at last, "just exactly in order that you should do this."

"Do what?"

"Think me—for a change—*bad!*" I shall never forget the sweetness and gaiety with which he brought out the word, nor how, on top of it, he bent forward and kissed me. It was practically the end of everything. I met his kiss and I had to make, while I folded him for a minute in my arms, the most stupendous effort not to cry. He had given exactly the account of himself that permitted least of my going behind it, and it was only with the effect of confirming my acceptance of it that, as I presently glanced about the room, I could say—

"Then you didn't undress at all?"

He fairly glittered in the gloom. "Not at all. I sat up and read."

"And when did you go down?"

"At midnight. When I'm bad I *am* bad!"

"I see, I see—it's charming. But how could you be sure I would know it?"

"Oh, I arranged that with Flora." His answers rang out with a readiness! "She was to get up and look out."

"Which is what she did do." It was I who fell into the trap!

"So she disturbed you, and, to see what she was looking at, you also looked—you saw."

"While you," I concurred, "caught your death in the night air!"

He literally bloomed so from this exploit that he could afford radiantly to assent. "How otherwise should I have been bad enough?" he asked. Then, after another embrace, the incident and our interview closed on my recognition of all the reserves of goodness that, for his joke, he had been able to draw upon.

XII

The particular impression I had received proved in the morning light, I repeat, not quite successfully presentable to Mrs. Grose, though I reinforced it with the mention of still another remark that he had made before we separated. "It all lies in half a dozen words," I said to her, "words that really settle the matter. 'Think, you know, what I *might* do!' He threw that off to show me how good he is. He knows down to the ground what he 'might' do. That's what he gave them a taste of at school."

"Lord, you do change!" cried my friend.

"I don't change—I simply make it out. The four, depend upon it, perpetually meet. If on either of these last nights you had been with either child, you would clearly have understood. The more I've watched and waited the more I've felt that if there were nothing else to make it sure it would be made so by the systematic silence of each. *Never*, by a slip of the tongue, have they so much as alluded to either of their old friends, any more than Miles has alluded to his expulsion. Oh, yes, we may sit here and look at them, and they may show off to us there to their fill; but even while they pretend to be lost in their fairytale they're steeped in their vision of the dead restored. He's not reading to her," I declared; "they're talking of *them*—they're talking horrors! I go on, I know, as if I were crazy; and it's a wonder I'm not. What I've seen would have made *you* so; but it has only made me more lucid, made me get hold of still other things."

My lucidity must have seemed awful, but the charming creatures who were victims of it, passing and repassing in their interlocked sweetness, gave my colleague something to hold on by; and I felt how tight she held as, without stirring in the breath of my passion, she covered them still with her eyes. "Of what other things have you got hold?"

"Why, of the very things that have delighted, fascinated, and yet, at bottom, as I now so strangely see, mystified and troubled me. Their more than earthly beauty, their absolutely unnatural goodness. It's a game," I went on; "it's a policy and a fraud!"

"On the part of little darlings—?"

"As yet mere lovely babies? Yes, mad as that seems!" The very act of bringing it out really helped me to trace it—follow it all up and piece it all together. "They haven't been good—they've only been absent. It has been easy to live with them, because they're simply leading a life of their own. They're not mine—they're not ours. They're his and they're hers!"

"Quint's and that woman's?"

"Quint's and that woman's. They want to get to them."

Oh, how, at this, poor Mrs. Grose appeared to study them! "But for what?"

"For the love of all the evil that, in those dreadful days, the pair put into them. And to ply them with that evil still, to keep up the work of demons, is what brings the others back."

"Laws!" said my friend under her breath. The exclamation was homely, but it revealed a real acceptance of my further proof of what, in the bad time—for there had been a worse even than this!—must have occurred. There could have been no such justification for me as the plain assent of her experience to whatever depth of depravity I found credible in our brace of scoundrels. It was in obvious submission of memory that she brought out after a moment: "They *were* rascals! But what can they now do?" she pursued.

"Do?" I echoed so loud that Miles and Flora, as they passed at their distance, paused an instant in their walk and looked at us. "Don't they do enough?" I demanded in a lower tone, while the children, having smiled and nodded and kissed hands to us, resumed their exhibition. We were held by it a minute; then I answered: "They can destroy them!" At this my companion did turn, but the inquiry she launched was a silent one, the effect of which was to make me more explicit. "They don't know, as yet, quite how—but they're trying hard. They're seen only across, as it were, and beyond—in strange places and on high places, the top of towers, the roof of houses, the outside of windows, the further edge of pools; but there's a deep design, on either side, to shorten the distance and overcome the obstacle; and the success of the tempters is only a question of time. They've only to keep to their suggestions of danger."

"For the children to come?"

"And perish in the attempt!" Mrs. Grose slowly got up, and I scrupulously added: "Unless, of course, we can prevent!"

Standing there before me while I kept my seat, she visibly turned things over. "Their uncle must do the preventing. He must take them away."

"And who's to make him?"

She had been scanning the distance, but she now dropped on me a foolish face. "You, miss."

"By writing to him that his house is poisoned and his little nephew and niece mad?"

"But if they *are*, miss?"

"And if I am myself, you mean? That's charming news to be sent him by a governess whose prime undertaking was to give him no worry."

Mrs. Grose considered, following the children again. "Yes, he do hate worry. That was the great reason—"

"Why those fiends took him in so long? No doubt, though his indifference must have been awful. As I'm not a fiend, at any rate, I shouldn't take him in."

My companion, after an instant and for all answer, sat down again and grasped my arm. "Make him at any rate come to you."

I stared. "To *me?*" I had a sudden fear of what she might do. "'Him'?"

"He ought to *be* here—he ought to help."

I quickly rose, and I think I must have shown her a queerer face than ever yet. "You see me asking him for a visit?" No, with her eyes on my face she evidently couldn't. Instead of it even—as a woman reads another—she could see what I myself saw: his derision, his amusement, his contempt for the breakdown of my resignation at being left alone and for the fine machinery I had set in motion to attract his attention to my slighted charms. She didn't know—no one knew—how proud I had been to serve him and to stick to our terms; yet she nonetheless took the measure, I think, of the warning I now gave her. "If you should so lose your head as to appeal to him for me—"

She was really frightened. "Yes, miss?"

"I would leave, on the spot, both him and you."

XIII

It was all very well to join them, but speaking to them proved quite as much as ever an effort beyond my strength—offered, in close quarters, difficulties as insurmountable as before. This situation continued a month, and with new aggravations and particular notes, the note above all, sharper and sharper, of the small ironic consciousness on the part of my pupils. It was not, I am as sure today as I was sure then, my mere infernal imagination: it was absolutely traceable that they were aware of my predicament and that this strange relation made, in a manner, for a long time, the air in which we moved. I don't mean that they had their tongues in their cheeks or did anything vulgar, for that was not one of their dangers: I do mean, on the other hand, that the element of the unnamed and untouched became, between us, greater than any other, and that so much avoidance could not have been so successfully effected without a great deal of tacit arrangement. It was as if, at moments, we were perpetually coming into sight of subjects before which we must stop short, turning suddenly out of alleys that we perceived to be blind, closing with a little bang that made us look at each other—for, like all bangs, it was something louder than we had intended—the doors we had indiscreetly opened. All roads lead to Rome, and there were times when it might have struck us that almost every branch of study or subject of conversation skirted forbidden ground. Forbidden ground was the question of the return of the dead in general and of whatever, in especial, might survive, in memory, of the friends little children had lost. There were days when I could have sworn that one of them had, with a small invisible nudge, said to the other: "She thinks she'll do it this time—but she *won't!*" To "do it" would have been to indulge for instance—and for once in a way—in some direct reference to the lady who had prepared them for my discipline. They had a delightful endless appetite

for passages in my own history, to which I had again and again treated them; they were in possession of everything that had ever happened to me, had had, with every circumstance the story of my smallest adventures and of those of my brothers and sisters and of the cat and the dog at home, as well as many particulars of the eccentric nature of my father, of the furniture and arrangement of our house, and of the conversation of the old women of our village. There were things enough, taking one with another, to chatter about, if one went very fast and knew by instinct when to go round. They pulled with an art of their own the strings of my invention and my memory; and nothing else perhaps, when I thought of such occasions afterward, gave me so the suspicion of being watched from under cover. It was in any case over *my* life, *my* past, and *my* friends alone that we could take anything like our ease—a state of affairs that led them sometimes without the least pertinence to break out into sociable reminders. I was invited—with no visible connection—to repeat afresh Goody Gosling's celebrated *mot* or to confirm the details already supplied as to the cleverness of the vicarage pony.

It was partly at such junctures as these and partly at quite different ones that, with the turn my matters had now taken, my predicament, as I have called it, grew most sensible. The fact that the days passed for me without another encounter ought, it would have appeared, to have done something toward soothing my nerves. Since the light brush, that second night on the upper landing, of the presence of a woman at the foot of the stair, I had seen nothing, whether in or out of the house, that one had better not have seen. There was many a corner round which I expected to come upon Quint, and many a situation that, in a merely sinister way, would have favored the appearance of Miss Jessel. The summer had turned, the summer had gone; the autumn had dropped upon Bly and had blown out half our lights. The place, with its gray sky and withered garlands, its bared spaces and scattered dead leaves, was like a theater after the performance—all strewn with crumpled playbills. There were exactly states of the air, conditions of sound and of stillness, unspeakable impressions of the *kind* of ministering moment, that brought back to me, long enough to catch it, the feeling of the medium in which, that June evening out of doors, I had had my first sight of Quint, and in which, too, at those other instants, I had, after seeing him through the window, looked for him in vain in the circle of shrubbery. I recognized the signs, the portents—I recognized the moment, the spot. But they remained

unaccompanied and empty, and I continued unmolested; if unmolested one could call a young woman whose sensibility had, in the most extraordinary fashion, not declined but deepened. I had said in my talk with Mrs. Grose on that horrid scene of Flora's by the lake—and had perplexed her by so saying—that it would from that moment distress me much more to lose my power than to keep it. I had then expressed what was vividly in my mind: the truth that, whether the children really saw or not—since, that is, it was not yet definitely proved—I greatly preferred, as a safeguard, the fullness of my own exposure. I was ready to know the very worst that was to be known. What I had then had an ugly glimpse of was that my eyes might be sealed just while theirs were most opened. Well, my eyes *were* sealed, it appeared, at present—a consummation for which it seemed blasphemous not to thank God. There was, alas, a difficulty about that: I would have thanked him with all my soul had I not had in a proportionate measure this conviction of the secret of my pupils.

How can I retrace today the strange steps of my obsession? There were times of our being together when I would have been ready to swear that, literally, in my presence, but with my direct sense of it closed, they had visitors who were known and were welcome. Then it was that, had I not been deterred by the very chance that such an injury might prove greater than the injury to be averted, my exultation would have broken out. "They're here, they're here, you little wretches," I would have cried, "and you can't deny it now!" The little wretches denied it with all the added volume of their sociability and their tenderness, in just the crystal depths of which—like the flash of a fish in a stream—the mockery of their advantage peeped up. The shock, in truth, had sunk into me still deeper than I knew on the night when, looking out to see either Quint or Miss Jessel under the stars, I had beheld the boy over whose rest I watched and who had immediately brought in with him—had straightway, there, turned it on me—the lovely upward look with which, from the battlements above me, the hideous apparition of Quint had played. If it was a question of a scare, my discovery on this occasion had scared me more than any other, and it was in the condition of nerves produced by it that I made my actual inductions. They harassed me so that sometimes, at odd moments, I shut myself up audibly to rehearse—it was at once a fantastic relief and a renewed despair—the manner in which I might come to the point. I approached it from one side and the other while, in my room, I flung myself about, but I always broke down

in the monstrous utterance of names. As they died away on my lips, I said to myself that I should indeed help them to represent something infamous, if, by pronouncing them, I should violate as rare a little case of instinctive delicacy as any schoolroom, probably, had ever known. When I said to myself: "*They* have the manners to be silent, and you, trusted as you are, the baseness to speak!" I felt myself crimson and I covered my face with my hands. After these secret scenes I chattered more than ever, going on volubly enough till one of our prodigious, palpable hushes occurred—I can call them nothing else—the strange, dizzy lift or swim (I try for terms!) into a stillness, a pause of all life, that had nothing to do with the more or less noise that at the moment we might be engaged in making and that I could hear through any deepened exhilaration or quickened recitation or louder strum of the piano. Then it was that the others, the outsiders, were there. Though they were not angels, they "passed," as the French say, causing me, while they stayed, to tremble with the fear of their addressing to their younger victims some yet more infernal message or more vivid image than they had thought good enough for myself.

What it was most impossible to get rid of was the cruel idea that, whatever I had seen, Miles and Flora saw *more*—things terrible and unguessable and that sprang from dreadful passages of intercourse in the past. Such things naturally left on the surface, for the time, a chill which we vociferously denied that we felt; and we had, all three, with repetition, got into such splendid training that we went, each time, almost automatically, to mark the close of the incident, through the very same movements. It was striking of the children, at all events, to kiss me inveterately with a kind of wild irrelevance and never to fail—one or the other—of the precious question that had helped us through many a peril. "When do you think he *will* come? Don't you think we *ought* to write?"—there was nothing like that inquiry, we found by experience, for carrying off an awkwardness. "He" of course was their uncle in Harley Street; and we lived in much profusion of theory that he might at any moment arrive to mingle in our circle. It was impossible to have given less encouragement than he had done to such a doctrine, but if we had not had the doctrine to fall back upon we should have deprived each other of some of our finest exhibitions. He never wrote to them—that may have been selfish, but it was a part of the flattery of his trust of me; for the way in which a man pays his highest tribute to a woman is apt to be but

by the more festal celebration of one of the sacred laws of his comfort; and I held that I carried out the spirit of the pledge given not to appeal to him when I let my charges understand that their own letters were but charming literary exercises. They were too beautiful to be posted; I kept them myself; I have them all to this hour. This was a rule indeed which only added to the satiric effect of my being plied with the supposition that he might at any moment be among us. It was exactly as if my charges knew how almost more awkward than anything else that might be for me. There appears to me, moreover, as I look back, no note in all this more extraordinary than the mere fact that, in spite of my tension and of their triumph, I never lost patience with them. Adorable they must in truth have been, I now reflect, that I didn't in these days hate them! Would exasperation, however, if relief had longer been postponed, finally have betrayed me? It little matters, for relief arrived. I call it relief, though it was only the relief that a snap brings to a strain or the burst of a thunderstorm to a day of suffocation. It was at least change, and it came with a rush.

XIV

Walking to church a certain Sunday morning, I had little Miles at my side and his sister, in advance of us and at Mrs. Grose's, well in sight. It was a crisp, clear day, the first of its order for some time; the night had brought a touch of frost, and the autumn air, bright and sharp, made the church bells almost gay. It was an odd accident of thought that I should have happened at such a moment to be particularly and very gratefully struck with the obedience of my little charges. Why did they never resent my inexorable, my perpetual society? Something or other had brought nearer home to me that I had all but pinned the boy to my shawl and that, in the way our companions were marshaled before me, I might have appeared to provide against some danger of rebellion. I was like a gaoler with an eye to possible surprises and escapes. But all this belonged—I mean their magnificent little surrender—just to the special array of the facts that were most abysmal. Turned out for Sunday by his uncle's tailor, who had had a free hand and a notion of pretty waistcoats and of his grand little air, Miles's whole title to independence, the rights of his sex and situation, were so stamped upon him that if he had suddenly struck for freedom I should have had nothing to say. I was by the strangest of chances wondering how I should meet him when the revolution unmistakably occurred. I call it a revolution because I now see how, with the word he spoke, the curtain rose on the last act of my dreadful drama, and the catastrophe was precipitated. "Look here, my dear, you know," he charmingly said, "when in the world, please, am I going back to school?"

Transcribed here the speech sounds harmless enough, particularly as uttered in the sweet, high, casual pipe with which, at all interlocutors, but above all at his eternal governess, he threw off intonations as if he were tossing roses. There was something in them that always made one

"catch," and I caught, at any rate, now so effectually that I stopped as short as if one of the trees of the park had fallen across the road. There was something new, on the spot, between us, and he was perfectly aware that I recognized it, though, to enable me to do so, he had no need to look a whit less candid and charming than usual. I could feel in him how he already, from my at first finding nothing to reply, perceived the advantage he had gained. I was so slow to find anything that he had plenty of time, after a minute, to continue with his suggestive but inconclusive smile: "You know, my dear, that for a fellow to be with a lady *always*—!" His "my dear" was constantly on his lips for me, and nothing could have expressed more the exact shade of the sentiment with which I desired to inspire my pupils than its fond familiarity. It was so respectfully easy.

But, oh, how I felt that at present I must pick my own phrases! I remember that, to gain time, I tried to laugh, and I seemed to see in the beautiful face with which he watched me how ugly and queer I looked. "And always with the same lady?" I returned.

He neither blanched nor winked. The whole thing was virtually out between us. "Ah, of course, she's a jolly, 'perfect' lady; but, after all, I'm a fellow, don't you see? that's—well, getting on."

I lingered there with him an instant ever so kindly. "Yes, you're getting on." Oh, but I felt helpless!

I have kept to this day the heartbreaking little idea of how he seemed to know that and to play with it. "And you can't say I've not been awfully good, can you?"

I laid my hand on his shoulder, for, though I felt how much better it would have been to walk on, I was not yet quite able. "No, I can't say that, Miles."

"Except just that one night, you know—!"

"That one night?" I couldn't look as straight as he.

"Why, when I went down—went out of the house."

"Oh, yes. But I forget what you did it for."

"You forget?"—he spoke with the sweet extravagance of childish reproach. "Why, it was to show you I could!"

"Oh, yes, you could."

"And I can again."

I felt that I might, perhaps, after all, succeed in keeping my wits about me. "Certainly. But you won't."

"No, not *that* again. It was nothing."

"It was nothing," I said. "But we must go on."

He resumed our walk with me, passing his hand into my arm. "Then when *am* I going back?"

I wore, in turning it over, my most responsible air. "Were you very happy at school?"

He just considered. "Oh, I'm happy enough anywhere!"

"Well, then," I quavered, "if you're just as happy here—!"

"Ah, but that isn't everything! Of course *you* know a lot—"

"But you hint that you know almost as much?" I risked as he paused.

"Not half I want to!" Miles honestly professed. "But it isn't so much that."

"What is it, then?"

"Well—I want to see more life."

"I see; I see." We had arrived within sight of the church and of various persons, including several of the household of Bly, on their way to it and clustered about the door to see us go in. I quickened our step; I wanted to get there before the question between us opened up much further; I reflected hungrily that, for more than an hour, he would have to be silent; and I thought with envy of the comparative dusk of the pew and of the almost spiritual help of the hassock on which I might bend my knees. I seemed literally to be running a race with some confusion to which he was about to reduce me, but I felt that he had got in first when, before we had even entered the churchyard, he threw out—

"I want my own sort!"

It literally made me bound forward. "There are not many of your own sort, Miles!" I laughed. "Unless perhaps dear little Flora!"

"You really compare me to a baby girl?"

This found me singularly weak. "Don't you, then, *love* our sweet Flora?"

"If I didn't—and you, too; if I didn't—!" he repeated as if retreating for a jump, yet leaving his thought so unfinished that, after we had come into the gate, another stop, which he imposed on me by the pressure of his arm, had become inevitable. Mrs. Grose and Flora had passed into the church, the other worshippers had followed, and we were, for the minute, alone among the old, thick graves. We had paused, on the path from the gate, by a low, oblong, table-like tomb.

"Yes, if you didn't—?"

He looked, while I waited, at the graves. "Well, you know what!" But he didn't move, and he presently produced something that made me drop straight down on the stone slab, as if suddenly to rest. "Does my uncle think what *you* think?"

I markedly rested. "How do you know what I think?"

"Ah, well, of course I don't; for it strikes me you never tell me. But I mean does *he* know?"

"Know what, Miles?"

"Why, the way I'm going on."

I perceived quickly enough that I could make, to this inquiry, no answer that would not involve something of a sacrifice of my employer. Yet it appeared to me that we were all, at Bly, sufficiently sacrificed to make that venial. "I don't think your uncle much cares."

Miles, on this, stood looking at me. "Then don't you think he can be made to?"

"In what way?"

"Why, by his coming down."

"But who'll get him to come down?"

"*I* will!" the boy said with extraordinary brightness and emphasis. He gave me another look charged with that expression and then marched off alone into church.

XV

The business was practically settled from the moment I never followed him. It was a pitiful surrender to agitation, but my being aware of this had somehow no power to restore me. I only sat there on my tomb and read into what my little friend had said to me the fullness of its meaning; by the time I had grasped the whole of which I had also embraced, for absence, the pretext that I was ashamed to offer my pupils and the rest of the congregation such an example of delay. What I said to myself above all was that Miles had got something out of me and that the proof of it, for him, would be just this awkward collapse. He had got out of me that there was something I was much afraid of and that he should probably be able to make use of my fear to gain, for his own purpose, more freedom. My fear was of having to deal with the intolerable question of the grounds of his dismissal from school, for that was really but the question of the horrors gathered behind. That his uncle should arrive to treat with me of these things was a solution that, strictly speaking, I ought now to have desired to bring on; but I could so little face the ugliness and the pain of it that I simply procrastinated and lived from hand to mouth. The boy, to my deep discomposure, was immensely in the right, was in a position to say to me: "Either you clear up with my guardian the mystery of this interruption of my studies, or you cease to expect me to lead with you a life that's so unnatural for a boy." What was so unnatural for the particular boy I was concerned with was this sudden revelation of a consciousness and a plan.

That was what really overcame me, what prevented my going in. I walked round the church, hesitating, hovering; I reflected that I had already, with him, hurt myself beyond repair. Therefore I could patch up nothing, and it was too extreme an effort to squeeze beside him into the pew: he would be so much more sure than ever to pass his arm into mine

and make me sit there for an hour in close, silent contact with his commentary on our talk. For the first minute since his arrival I wanted to get away from him. As I paused beneath the high east window and listened to the sounds of worship, I was taken with an impulse that might master me, I felt, completely should I give it the least encouragement. I might easily put an end to my predicament by getting away altogether. Here was my chance; there was no one to stop me; I could give the whole thing up—turn my back and retreat. It was only a question of hurrying again, for a few preparations, to the house which the attendance at church of so many of the servants would practically have left unoccupied. No one, in short, could blame me if I should just drive desperately off. What was it to get away if I got away only till dinner? That would be in a couple of hours, at the end of which—I had the acute prevision—my little pupils would play at innocent wonder about my nonappearance in their train.

"What *did* you do, you naughty, bad thing? Why in the world, to worry us so—and take our thoughts off, too, don't you know?—did you desert us at the very door?" I couldn't meet such questions nor, as they asked them, their false little lovely eyes; yet it was all so exactly what I should have to meet that, as the prospect grew sharp to me, I at last let myself go.

I got, so far as the immediate moment was concerned, away; I came straight out of the churchyard and, thinking hard, retraced my steps through the park. It seemed to me that by the time I reached the house I had made up my mind I would fly. The Sunday stillness both of the approaches and of the interior, in which I met no one, fairly excited me with a sense of opportunity. Were I to get off quickly, this way, I should get off without a scene, without a word. My quickness would have to be remarkable, however, and the question of a conveyance was the great one to settle. Tormented, in the hall, with difficulties and obstacles, I remember sinking down at the foot of the staircase—suddenly collapsing there on the lowest step and then, with a revulsion, recalling that it was exactly where more than a month before, in the darkness of night and just so bowed with evil things, I had seen the specter of the most horrible of women. At this I was able to straighten myself; I went the rest of the way up; I made, in my bewilderment, for the schoolroom, where there were objects belonging to me that I should have to take. But I opened the

door to find again, in a flash, my eyes unsealed. In the presence of what I saw I reeled straight back upon my resistance.

Seated at my own table in clear noonday light I saw a person whom, without my previous experience, I should have taken at the first blush for some housemaid who might have stayed at home to look after the place and who, availing herself of rare relief from observation and of the schoolroom table and my pens, ink, and paper, had applied herself to the considerable effort of a letter to her sweetheart. There was an effort in the way that, while her arms rested on the table, her hands with evident weariness supported her head; but at the moment I took this in I had already become aware that, in spite of my entrance, her attitude strangely persisted. Then it was—with the very act of its announcing itself—that her identity flared up in a change of posture. She rose, not as if she had heard me, but with an indescribable grand melancholy of indifference and detachment, and, within a dozen feet of me, stood there as my vile predecessor. Dishonored and tragic, she was all before me; but even as I fixed and, for memory, secured it, the awful image passed away. Dark as midnight in her black dress, her haggard beauty and her unutterable woe, she had looked at me long enough to appear to say that her right to sit at my table was as good as mine to sit at hers. While these instants lasted, indeed, I had the extraordinary chill of feeling that it was I who was the intruder. It was as a wild protest against it that, actually addressing her—"You terrible, miserable woman!"—I heard myself break into a sound that, by the open door, rang through the long passage and the empty house. She looked at me as if she heard me, but I had recovered myself and cleared the air. There was nothing in the room the next minute but the sunshine and a sense that I must stay.

XVI

I had so perfectly expected that the return of my pupils would be marked by a demonstration that I was freshly upset at having to take into account that they were dumb about my absence. Instead of gaily denouncing and caressing me, they made no allusion to my having failed them, and I was left, for the time, on perceiving that she too said nothing, to study Mrs. Grose's odd face. I did this to such purpose that I made sure they had in some way bribed her to silence; a silence that, however, I would engage to break down on the first private opportunity. This opportunity came before tea: I secured five minutes with her in the housekeeper's room, where, in the twilight, amid a smell of lately baked bread, but with the place all swept and garnished, I found her sitting in pained placidity before the fire. So I see her still, so I see her best: facing the flame from her straight chair in the dusky, shining room, a large clean image of the "put away"—of drawers closed and locked and rest without a remedy.

"Oh, yes, they asked me to say nothing; and to please them—so long as they were there—of course I promised. But what had happened to you?"

"I only went with you for the walk," I said. "I had then to come back to meet a friend."

She showed her surprise. "A friend—*you?*"

"Oh, yes, I have a couple!" I laughed. "But did the children give you a reason?"

"For not alluding to your leaving us? Yes; they said you would like it better. Do you like it better?"

My face had made her rueful. "No, I like it worse!" But after an instant I added: "Did they say why I should like it better?"

"No; Master Miles only said, 'We must do nothing but what she likes!'"

"I wish indeed he would. And what did Flora say?"

"Miss Flora was too sweet. She said, 'Oh, of course, of course!'—and I said the same."

I thought a moment. "You were too sweet, too—I can hear you all. But nonetheless, between Miles and me, it's now all out."

"All out?" My companion stared. "But what, miss?"

"Everything. It doesn't matter. I've made up my mind. I came home, my dear," I went on, "for a talk with Miss Jessel."

I had by this time formed the habit of having Mrs. Grose literally well in hand in advance of my sounding that note; so that even now, as she bravely blinked under the signal of my word, I could keep her comparatively firm. "A talk! Do you mean she spoke?"

"It came to that. I found her, on my return, in the schoolroom."

"And what did she say?" I can hear the good woman still, and the candor of her stupefaction.

"That she suffers the torments—!"

It was this, of a truth, that made her, as she filled out my picture, gape. "Do you mean," she faltered, "—of the lost?"

"Of the lost. Of the damned. And that's why, to share them—" I faltered myself with the horror of it.

But my companion, with less imagination, kept me up. "To share them—?"

"She wants Flora." Mrs. Grose might, as I gave it to her, fairly have fallen away from me had I not been prepared. I still held her there, to show I was. "As I've told you, however, it doesn't matter."

"Because you've made up your mind? But to what?"

"To everything."

"And what do you call 'everything'?"

"Why, sending for their uncle."

"Oh, miss, in pity do," my friend broke out. "ah, but I will, I *will!* I see it's the only way. What's 'out,' as I told you, with Miles is that if he thinks I'm afraid to—and has ideas of what he gains by that—he shall see he's mistaken. Yes, yes; his uncle shall have it here from me on the spot (and before the boy himself, if necessary) that if I'm to be reproached with having done nothing again about more school—"

"Yes, miss—" my companion pressed me.

"Well, there's that awful reason."

There were now clearly so many of these for my poor colleague that she was excusable for being vague. "But—a—which?"

"Why, the letter from his old place."

"You'll show it to the master?"

"I ought to have done so on the instant."

"Oh, no!" said Mrs. Grose with decision.

"I'll put it before him," I went on inexorably, "that I can't undertake to work the question on behalf of a child who has been expelled—"

"For we've never in the least known what!" Mrs. Grose declared.

"For wickedness. For what else—when he's so clever and beautiful and perfect? Is he stupid? Is he untidy? Is he infirm? Is he ill-natured? He's exquisite—so it can be only *that*; and that would open up the whole thing. After all," I said, "it's their uncle's fault. If he left here such people —!"

"He didn't really in the least know them. The fault's mine." She had turned quite pale.

"Well, you shan't suffer," I answered.

"The children shan't!" she emphatically returned.

I was silent awhile; we looked at each other. "Then what am I to tell him?"

"You needn't tell him anything. *I'll* tell him."

I measured this. "Do you mean you'll write—?" Remembering she couldn't, I caught myself up. "How do you communicate?"

"I tell the bailiff. *He* writes."

"And should you like him to write our story?"

My question had a sarcastic force that I had not fully intended, and it made her, after a moment, inconsequently break down. The tears were again in her eyes. "Ah, miss, *you* write!"

"Well—tonight," I at last answered; and on this we separated.

XVII

I went so far, in the evening, as to make a beginning. The weather had changed back, a great wind was abroad, and beneath the lamp, in my room, with Flora at peace beside me, I sat for a long time before a blank sheet of paper and listened to the lash of the rain and the batter of the gusts. Finally I went out, taking a candle; I crossed the passage and listened a minute at Miles's door. What, under my endless obsession, I had been impelled to listen for was some betrayal of his not being at rest, and I presently caught one, but not in the form I had expected. His voice tinkled out. "I say, you there—come in." It was a gaiety in the gloom!

I went in with my light and found him, in bed, very wide awake, but very much at his ease. "Well, what are *you* up to?" he asked with a grace of sociability in which it occurred to me that Mrs. Grose, had she been present, might have looked in vain for proof that anything was "out."

I stood over him with my candle. "How did you know I was there?"

"Why, of course I heard you. Did you fancy you made no noise? You're like a troop of cavalry!" he beautifully laughed.

"Then you weren't asleep?"

"Not much! I lie awake and think."

I had put my candle, designedly, a short way off, and then, as he held out his friendly old hand to me, had sat down on the edge of his bed. "What is it," I asked, "that you think of?"

"What in the world, my dear, but *you?*"

"Ah, the pride I take in your appreciation doesn't insist on that! I had so far rather you slept."

"Well, I think also, you know, of this queer business of ours."

I marked the coolness of his firm little hand. "Of what queer business, Miles?"

"Why, the way you bring me up. And all the rest!"

I fairly held my breath a minute, and even from my glimmering taper there was light enough to show how he smiled up at me from his pillow. "What do you mean by all the rest?"

"Oh, you know, you know!"

I could say nothing for a minute, though I felt, as I held his hand and our eyes continued to meet, that my silence had all the air of admitting his charge and that nothing in the whole world of reality was perhaps at that moment so fabulous as our actual relation. "Certainly you shall go back to school," I said, "if it be that that troubles you. But not to the old place—we must find another, a better. How could I know it did trouble you, this question, when you never told me so, never spoke of it at all?" His clear, listening face, framed in its smooth whiteness, made him for the minute as appealing as some wistful patient in a children's hospital; and I would have given, as the resemblance came to me, all I possessed on earth really to be the nurse or the sister of charity who might have helped to cure him. Well, even as it was, I perhaps might help! "Do you know you've never said a word to me about your school—I mean the old one; never mentioned it in any way?"

He seemed to wonder; he smiled with the same loveliness. But he clearly gained time; he waited, he called for guidance. "Haven't I?" It wasn't for *me* to help him—it was for the thing I had met!

Something in his tone and the expression of his face, as I got this from him, set my heart aching with such a pang as it had never yet known; so unutterably touching was it to see his little brain puzzled and his little resources taxed to play, under the spell laid on him, a part of innocence and consistency. "No, never—from the hour you came back. You've never mentioned to me one of your masters, one of your comrades, nor the least little thing that ever happened to you at school. Never, little Miles—no, never—have you given me an inkling of anything that *may* have happened there. Therefore you can fancy how much I'm in the dark. Until you came out, that way, this morning, you had, since the first hour I saw you, scarce even made a reference to anything in your previous life. You seemed so perfectly to accept the present." It was extraordinary how my absolute conviction of his secret precocity (or whatever I might call the poison of an influence that I dared but half to phrase) made him, in spite of the faint breath of his inward trouble, appear as accessible as an older person—imposed him almost as an intellectual equal. "I thought you wanted to go on as you are."

It struck me that at this he just faintly colored. He gave, at any rate, like a convalescent slightly fatigued, a languid shake of his head. "I don't—I don't. I want to get away."

"You're tired of Bly?"

"Oh, no, I like Bly."

"Well, then—?"

"Oh, *you* know what a boy wants!"

I felt that I didn't know so well as Miles, and I took temporary refuge. "You want to go to your uncle?"

Again, at this, with his sweet ironic face, he made a movement on the pillow. "Ah, you can't get off with that!"

I was silent a little, and it was I, now, I think, who changed color. "My dear, I don't want to get off!"

"You can't, even if you do. You can't, you can't!"—he lay beautifully staring. "My uncle must come down, and you must completely settle things."

"If we do," I returned with some spirit, "you may be sure it will be to take you quite away."

"Well, don't you understand that that's exactly what I'm working for? You'll have to tell him—about the way you've let it all drop: you'll have to tell him a tremendous lot!"

The exultation with which he uttered this helped me somehow, for the instant, to meet him rather more. "And how much will *you*, Miles, have to tell him? There are things he'll ask you!"

He turned it over. "Very likely. But what things?"

"The things you've never told me. To make up his mind what to do with you. He can't send you back—"

"Oh, I don't want to go back!" he broke in. "I want a new field."

He said it with admirable serenity, with positive unimpeachable gaiety; and doubtless it was that very note that most evoked for me the poignancy, the unnatural childish tragedy, of his probable reappearance at the end of three months with all this bravado and still more dishonor. It overwhelmed me now that I should never be able to bear that, and it made me let myself go. I threw myself upon him and in the tenderness of my pity I embraced him. "Dear little Miles, dear little Miles—!"

My face was close to his, and he let me kiss him, simply taking it with indulgent good humor. "Well, old lady?"

"Is there nothing—nothing at all that you want to tell me?"

He turned off a little, facing round toward the wall and holding up his hand to look at as one had seen sick children look. "I've told you—I told you this morning."

Oh, I was sorry for him! "That you just want me not to worry you?"

He looked round at me now, as if in recognition of my understanding him; then ever so gently, "To let me alone," he replied.

There was even a singular little dignity in it, something that made me release him, yet, when I had slowly risen, linger beside him. God knows I never wished to harass him, but I felt that merely, at this, to turn my back on him was to abandon or, to put it more truly, to lose him. "I've just begun a letter to your uncle," I said.

"Well, then, finish it!"

I waited a minute. "What happened before?"

He gazed up at me again. "Before what?"

"Before you came back. And before you went away."

For some time he was silent, but he continued to meet my eyes. "What happened?"

It made me, the sound of the words, in which it seemed to me that I caught for the very first time a small faint quaver of consenting consciousness—it made me drop on my knees beside the bed and seize once more the chance of possessing him. "Dear little Miles, dear little Miles, if you *knew* how I want to help you! It's only that, it's nothing but that, and I'd rather die than give you a pain or do you a wrong—I'd rather die than hurt a hair of you. Dear little Miles"—oh, I brought it out now even if I *should* go too far—"I just want you to help me to save you!" But I knew in a moment after this that I had gone too far. The answer to my appeal was instantaneous, but it came in the form of an extraordinary blast and chill, a gust of frozen air, and a shake of the room as great as if, in the wild wind, the casement had crashed in. The boy gave a loud, high shriek, which, lost in the rest of the shock of sound, might have seemed, indistinctly, though I was so close to him, a note either of jubilation or of terror. I jumped to my feet again and was conscious of darkness. So for a moment we remained, while I stared about me and saw that the drawn curtains were unstirred and the window tight. "Why, the candle's out!" I then cried.

"It was I who blew it, dear!" said Miles.

XVIII

The next day, after lessons, Mrs. Grose found a moment to say to me quietly: "Have you written, miss?"

"Yes—I've written." But I didn't add—for the hour—that my letter, sealed and directed, was still in my pocket. There would be time enough to send it before the messenger should go to the village. Meanwhile there had been, on the part of my pupils, no more brilliant, more exemplary morning. It was exactly as if they had both had at heart to gloss over any recent little friction. They performed the dizziest feats of arithmetic, soaring quite out of *my* feeble range, and perpetrated, in higher spirits than ever, geographical and historical jokes. It was conspicuous of course in Miles in particular that he appeared to wish to show how easily he could let me down. This child, to my memory, really lives in a setting of beauty and misery that no words can translate; there was a distinction all his own in every impulse he revealed; never was a small natural creature, to the uninitiated eye all frankness and freedom, a more ingenious, a more extraordinary little gentleman. I had perpetually to guard against the wonder of contemplation into which my initiated view betrayed me; to check the irrelevant gaze and discouraged sigh in which I constantly both attacked and renounced the enigma of what such a little gentleman could have done that deserved a penalty. Say that, by the dark prodigy I knew, the imagination of all evil *had* been opened up to him: all the justice within me ached for the proof that it could ever have flowered into an act.

He had never, at any rate, been such a little gentleman as when, after our early dinner on this dreadful day, he came round to me and asked if I shouldn't like him, for half an hour, to play to me. David playing to Saul could never have shown a finer sense of the occasion. It was literally a charming exhibition of tact, of magnanimity, and quite tantamount to

his saying outright: "The true knights we love to read about never push an advantage too far. I know what you mean now: you mean that—to be let alone yourself and not followed up—you'll cease to worry and spy upon me, won't keep me so close to you, will let me go and come. Well, I 'come,' you see—but I don't go! There'll be plenty of time for that. I do really delight in your society, and I only want to show you that I contended for a principle." It may be imagined whether I resisted this appeal or failed to accompany him again, hand in hand, to the schoolroom. He sat down at the old piano and played as he had never played; and if there are those who think he had better have been kicking a football I can only say that I wholly agree with them. For at the end of a time that under his influence I had quite ceased to measure, I started up with a strange sense of having literally slept at my post. It was after luncheon, and by the schoolroom fire, and yet I hadn't really, in the least, slept: I had only done something much worse—I had forgotten. Where, all this time, was Flora? When I put the question to Miles, he played on a minute before answering and then could only say: "Why, my dear, how do *I* know?"—breaking moreover into a happy laugh which, immediately after, as if it were a vocal accompaniment, he prolonged into incoherent, extravagant song.

I went straight to my room, but his sister was not there; then, before going downstairs, I looked into several others. As she was nowhere about she would surely be with Mrs. Grose, whom, in the comfort of that theory, I accordingly proceeded in quest of. I found her where I had found her the evening before, but she met my quick challenge with blank, scared ignorance. She had only supposed that, after the repast, I had carried off both the children; as to which she was quite in her right, for it was the very first time I had allowed the little girl out of my sight without some special provision. Of course now indeed she might be with the maids, so that the immediate thing was to look for her without an air of alarm. This we promptly arranged between us; but when, ten minutes later and in pursuance of our arrangement, we met in the hall, it was only to report on either side that after guarded inquiries we had altogether failed to trace her. For a minute there, apart from observation, we exchanged mute alarms, and I could feel with what high interest my friend returned me all those I had from the first given her.

"She'll be above," she presently said—"in one of the rooms you haven't searched."

"No; she's at a distance." I had made up my mind. "She has gone out."

Mrs. Grose stared. "Without a hat?"

I naturally also looked volumes. "Isn't that woman always without one?"

"She's with *her?*"

"She's with *her!*" I declared. "We must find them."

My hand was on my friend's arm, but she failed for the moment, confronted with such an account of the matter, to respond to my pressure. She communed, on the contrary, on the spot, with her uneasiness. "And where's Master Miles?"

"Oh, *he's* with Quint. They're in the schoolroom."

"Lord, miss!" My view, I was myself aware—and therefore I suppose my tone—had never yet reached so calm an assurance.

"The trick's played," I went on; "they've successfully worked their plan. He found the most divine little way to keep me quiet while she went off."

"'Divine'?" Mrs. Grose bewilderedly echoed.

"Infernal, then!" I almost cheerfully rejoined. "He has provided for himself as well. But come!"

She had helplessly gloomed at the upper regions. "You leave him—?"

"So long with Quint? Yes—I don't mind that now."

She always ended, at these moments, by getting possession of my hand, and in this manner she could at present still stay me. But after gasping an instant at my sudden resignation, "Because of your letter?" she eagerly brought out.

I quickly, by way of answer, felt for my letter, drew it forth, held it up, and then, freeing myself, went and laid it on the great hall table. "Luke will take it," I said as I came back. I reached the house door and opened it; I was already on the steps.

My companion still demurred: the storm of the night and the early morning had dropped, but the afternoon was damp and gray. I came down to the drive while she stood in the doorway. "You go with nothing on?"

"What do I care when the child has nothing? I can't wait to dress," I cried, "and if you must do so, I leave you. Try meanwhile, yourself, upstairs."

"With *them?*" Oh, on this, the poor woman promptly joined me!

XIX

We went straight to the lake, as it was called at Bly, and I daresay rightly called, though I reflect that it may in fact have been a sheet of water less remarkable than it appeared to my untraveled eyes. My acquaintance with sheets of water was small, and the pool of Bly, at all events on the few occasions of my consenting, under the protection of my pupils, to affront its surface in the old flat-bottomed boat moored there for our use, had impressed me both with its extent and its agitation. The usual place of embarkation was half a mile from the house, but I had an intimate conviction that, wherever Flora might be, she was not near home. She had not given me the slip for any small adventure, and, since the day of the very great one that I had shared with her by the pond, I had been aware, in our walks, of the quarter to which she most inclined. This was why I had now given to Mrs. Grose's steps so marked a direction—a direction that made her, when she perceived it, oppose a resistance that showed me she was freshly mystified. "You're going to the water, Miss?—you think she's *in*—?"

"She may be, though the depth is, I believe, nowhere very great. But what I judge most likely is that she's on the spot from which, the other day, we saw together what I told you."

"When she pretended not to see—?"

"With that astounding self-possession? I've always been sure she wanted to go back alone. And now her brother has managed it for her."

Mrs. Grose still stood where she had stopped. "You suppose they really *talk* of them?"

"I could meet this with a confidence! They say things that, if we heard them, would simply appall us."

"And if she *is* there—"

"Yes?"

"Then Miss Jessel is?"

"Beyond a doubt. You shall see."

"Oh, thank you!" my friend cried, planted so firm that, taking it in, I went straight on without her. By the time I reached the pool, however, she was close behind me, and I knew that, whatever, to her apprehension, might befall me, the exposure of my society struck her as her least danger. She exhaled a moan of relief as we at last came in sight of the greater part of the water without a sight of the child. There was no trace of Flora on that nearer side of the bank where my observation of her had been most startling, and none on the opposite edge, where, save for a margin of some twenty yards, a thick copse came down to the water. The pond, oblong in shape, had a width so scant compared to its length that, with its ends out of view, it might have been taken for a scant river. We looked at the empty expanse, and then I felt the suggestion of my friend's eyes. I knew what she meant and I replied with a negative headshake.

"No, no; wait! She has taken the boat."

My companion stared at the vacant mooring place and then again across the lake. "Then where is it?"

"Our not seeing it is the strongest of proofs. She has used it to go over, and then has managed to hide it."

"All alone—that child?"

"She's not alone, and at such times she's not a child: she's an old, old woman." I scanned all the visible shore while Mrs. Grose took again, into the queer element I offered her, one of her plunges of submission; then I pointed out that the boat might perfectly be in a small refuge formed by one of the recesses of the pool, an indentation masked, for the hither side, by a projection of the bank and by a clump of trees growing close to the water.

"But if the boat's there, where on earth's *she?*" my colleague anxiously asked.

"That's exactly what we must learn." And I started to walk further.

"By going all the way round?"

"Certainly, far as it is. It will take us but ten minutes, but it's far enough to have made the child prefer not to walk. She went straight over."

"Laws!" cried my friend again; the chain of my logic was ever too much for her. It dragged her at my heels even now, and when we had got halfway round—a devious, tiresome process, on ground much broken

and by a path choked with overgrowth—I paused to give her breath. I sustained her with a grateful arm, assuring her that she might hugely help me; and this started us afresh, so that in the course of but few minutes more we reached a point from which we found the boat to be where I had supposed it. It had been intentionally left as much as possible out of sight and was tied to one of the stakes of a fence that came, just there, down to the brink and that had been an assistance to disembarking. I recognized, as I looked at the pair of short, thick oars, quite safely drawn up, the prodigious character of the feat for a little girl; but I had lived, by this time, too long among wonders and had panted to too many livelier measures. There was a gate in the fence, through which we passed, and that brought us, after a trifling interval, more into the open. Then, "There she is!" we both exclaimed at once.

Flora, a short way off, stood before us on the grass and smiled as if her performance was now complete. The next thing she did, however, was to stoop straight down and pluck—quite as if it were all she was there for—a big, ugly spray of withered fern. I instantly became sure she had just come out of the copse. She waited for us, not herself taking a step, and I was conscious of the rare solemnity with which we presently approached her. She smiled and smiled, and we met; but it was all done in a silence by this time flagrantly ominous. Mrs. Grose was the first to break the spell: she threw herself on her knees and, drawing the child to her breast, clasped in a long embrace the little tender, yielding body. While this dumb convulsion lasted I could only watch it—which I did the more intently when I saw Flora's face peep at me over our companion's shoulder. It was serious now—the flicker had left it; but it strengthened the pang with which I at that moment envied Mrs. Grose the simplicity of *her* relation. Still, all this while, nothing more passed between us save that Flora had let her foolish fern again drop to the ground. What she and I had virtually said to each other was that pretexts were useless now. When Mrs. Grose finally got up she kept the child's hand, so that the two were still before me; and the singular reticence of our communion was even more marked in the frank look she launched me. "I'll be hanged," it said, "if *I'll* speak!"

It was Flora who, gazing all over me in candid wonder, was the first. She was struck with our bareheaded aspect. "Why, where are your things?"

"Where yours are, my dear!" I promptly returned.

She had already got back her gaiety, and appeared to take this as an answer quite sufficient. "And where's Miles?" she went on.

There was something in the small valor of it that quite finished me: these three words from her were, in a flash like the glitter of a drawn blade, the jostle of the cup that my hand, for weeks and weeks, had held high and full to the brim that now, even before speaking, I felt overflow in a deluge. "I'll tell you if you'll tell *me*—" I heard myself say, then heard the tremor in which it broke.

"Well, what?"

Mrs. Grose's suspense blazed at me, but it was too late now, and I brought the thing out handsomely. "Where, my pet, is Miss Jessel?"

XX

Just as in the churchyard with Miles, the whole thing was upon us. Much as I had made of the fact that this name had never once, between us, been sounded, the quick, smitten glare with which the child's face now received it fairly likened my breach of the silence to the smash of a pane of glass. It added to the interposing cry, as if to stay the blow, that Mrs. Grose, at the same instant, uttered over my violence—the shriek of a creature scared, or rather wounded, which, in turn, within a few seconds, was completed by a gasp of my own. I seized my colleague's arm. "She's there, she's there!"

Miss Jessel stood before us on the opposite bank exactly as she had stood the other time, and I remember, strangely, as the first feeling now produced in me, my thrill of joy at having brought on a proof. She was there, and I was justified; she was there, and I was neither cruel nor mad. She was there for poor scared Mrs. Grose, but she was there most for Flora; and no moment of my monstrous time was perhaps so extraordinary as that in which I consciously threw out to her—with the sense that, pale and ravenous demon as she was, she would catch and understand it—an inarticulate message of gratitude. She rose erect on the spot my friend and I had lately quitted, and there was not, in all the long reach of her desire, an inch of her evil that fell short. This first vividness of vision and emotion were things of a few seconds, during which Mrs. Grose's dazed blink across to where I pointed struck me as a sovereign sign that she too at last saw, just as it carried my own eyes precipitately to the child. The revelation then of the manner in which Flora was affected startled me, in truth, far more than it would have done to find her also merely agitated, for direct dismay was of course not what I had expected. Prepared and on her guard as our pursuit had actually made her, she would repress every betrayal; and I was therefore shaken,

on the spot, by my first glimpse of the particular one for which I had not allowed. To see her, without a convulsion of her small pink face, not even feign to glance in the direction of the prodigy I announced, but only, instead of that, turn at *me* an expression of hard, still gravity, an expression absolutely new and unprecedented and that appeared to read and accuse and judge me—this was a stroke that somehow converted the little girl herself into the very presence that could make me quail. I quailed even though my certitude that she thoroughly saw was never greater than at that instant, and in the immediate need to defend myself I called it passionately to witness. "She's there, you little unhappy thing—there, there, *there*, and you see her as well as you see me!" I had said shortly before to Mrs. Grose that she was not at these times a child, but an old, old woman, and that description of her could not have been more strikingly confirmed than in the way in which, for all answer to this, she simply showed me, without a concession, an admission, of her eyes, a countenance of deeper and deeper, of indeed suddenly quite fixed, reprobation. I was by this time—if I can put the whole thing at all together—more appalled at what I may properly call her manner than at anything else, though it was simultaneously with this that I became aware of having Mrs. Grose also, and very formidably, to reckon with. My elder companion, the next moment, at any rate, blotted out everything but her own flushed face and her loud, shocked protest, a burst of high disapproval. "What a dreadful turn, to be sure, miss! Where on earth do you see anything?"

I could only grasp her more quickly yet, for even while she spoke the hideous plain presence stood undimmed and undaunted. It had already lasted a minute, and it lasted while I continued, seizing my colleague, quite thrusting her at it and presenting her to it, to insist with my pointing hand. "You don't see her exactly as *we* see?—you mean to say you don't now—*now?* She's as big as a blazing fire! Only look, dearest woman, *look*—!" She looked, even as I did, and gave me, with her deep groan of negation, repulsion, compassion—the mixture with her pity of her relief at her exemption—a sense, touching to me even then, that she would have backed me up if she could. I might well have needed that, for with this hard blow of the proof that her eyes were hopelessly sealed I felt my own situation horribly crumble, I felt—I saw—my livid predecessor press, from her position, on my defeat, and I was conscious, more than all, of what I should have from this instant to deal with in the astounding little

attitude of Flora. Into this attitude Mrs. Grose immediately and violently entered, breaking, even while there pierced through my sense of ruin a prodigious private triumph, into breathless reassurance.

"She isn't there, little lady, and nobody's there—and you never see nothing, my sweet! How can poor Miss Jessel—when poor Miss Jessel's dead and buried? *We* know, don't we, love?"—and she appealed, blundering in, to the child. "It's all a mere mistake and a worry and a joke—and we'll go home as fast as we can!"

Our companion, on this, had responded with a strange, quick primness of propriety, and they were again, with Mrs. Grose on her feet, united, as it were, in pained opposition to me. Flora continued to fix me with her small mask of reprobation, and even at that minute I prayed God to forgive me for seeming to see that, as she stood there holding tight to our friend's dress, her incomparable childish beauty had suddenly failed, had quite vanished. I've said it already—she was literally, she was hideously, hard; she had turned common and almost ugly. "I don't know what you mean. I see nobody. I see nothing. I never *have*. I think you're cruel. I don't like you!" Then, after this deliverance, which might have been that of a vulgarly pert little girl in the street, she hugged Mrs. Grose more closely and buried in her skirts the dreadful little face. In this position she produced an almost furious wail. "Take me away, take me away—oh, take me away from *her!*"

"From *me?*" I panted.

"From you—from you!" she cried.

Even Mrs. Grose looked across at me dismayed, while I had nothing to do but communicate again with the figure that, on the opposite bank, without a movement, as rigidly still as if catching, beyond the interval, our voices, was as vividly there for my disaster as it was not there for my service. The wretched child had spoken exactly as if she had got from some outside source each of her stabbing little words, and I could therefore, in the full despair of all I had to accept, but sadly shake my head at her. "If I had ever doubted, all my doubt would at present have gone. I've been living with the miserable truth, and now it has only too much closed round me. Of course I've lost you: I've interfered, and you've seen—under *her* dictation"—with which I faced, over the pool again, our infernal witness—"the easy and perfect way to meet it. I've done my best, but I've lost you. Goodbye." For Mrs. Grose I had an imperative, an almost frantic "Go, go!" before which, in infinite distress,

but mutely possessed of the little girl and clearly convinced, in spite of her blindness, that something awful had occurred and some collapse engulfed us, she retreated, by the way we had come, as fast as she could move.

Of what first happened when I was left alone I had no subsequent memory. I only knew that at the end of, I suppose, a quarter of an hour, an odorous dampness and roughness, chilling and piercing my trouble, had made me understand that I must have thrown myself, on my face, on the ground and given way to a wildness of grief. I must have lain there long and cried and sobbed, for when I raised my head the day was almost done. I got up and looked a moment, through the twilight, at the gray pool and its blank, haunted edge, and then I took, back to the house, my dreary and difficult course. When I reached the gate in the fence the boat, to my surprise, was gone, so that I had a fresh reflection to make on Flora's extraordinary command of the situation. She passed that night, by the most tacit, and I should add, were not the word so grotesque a false note, the happiest of arrangements, with Mrs. Grose. I saw neither of them on my return, but, on the other hand, as by an ambiguous compensation, I saw a great deal of Miles. I saw—I can use no other phrase—so much of him that it was as if it were more than it had ever been. No evening I had passed at Bly had the portentous quality of this one; in spite of which—and in spite also of the deeper depths of consternation that had opened beneath my feet—there was literally, in the ebbing actual, an extraordinarily sweet sadness. On reaching the house I had never so much as looked for the boy; I had simply gone straight to my room to change what I was wearing and to take in, at a glance, much material testimony to Flora's rupture. Her little belongings had all been removed. When later, by the schoolroom fire, I was served with tea by the usual maid, I indulged, on the article of my other pupil, in no inquiry whatever. He had his freedom now—he might have it to the end! Well, he did have it; and it consisted—in part at least—of his coming in at about eight o'clock and sitting down with me in silence. On the removal of the tea things I had blown out the candles and drawn my chair closer: I was conscious of a mortal coldness and felt as if I should never again be warm. So, when he appeared, I was sitting in the glow with my thoughts. He paused a moment by the door as if to look at me; then—as if to share them—came to the other side of the hearth and

sank into a chair. We sat there in absolute stillness; yet he wanted, I felt, to be with me.

XXI

Before a new day, in my room, had fully broken, my eyes opened to Mrs. Grose, who had come to my bedside with worse news. Flora was so markedly feverish that an illness was perhaps at hand; she had passed a night of extreme unrest, a night agitated above all by fears that had for their subject not in the least her former, but wholly her present, governess. It was not against the possible re-entrance of Miss Jessel on the scene that she protested—it was conspicuously and passionately against mine. I was promptly on my feet of course, and with an immense deal to ask; the more that my friend had discernibly now girded her loins to meet me once more. This I felt as soon as I had put to her the question of her sense of the child's sincerity as against my own. "She persists in denying to you that she saw, or has ever seen, anything?"

My visitor's trouble, truly, was great. "Ah, miss, it isn't a matter on which I can push her! Yet it isn't either, I must say, as if I much needed to. It has made her, every inch of her, quite old."

"Oh, I see her perfectly from here. She resents, for all the world like some high little personage, the imputation on her truthfulness and, as it were, her respectability. 'Miss Jessel indeed—*she?*' Ah, she's 'respectable,' the chit! The impression she gave me there yesterday was, I assure you, the very strangest of all; it was quite beyond any of the others. I *did* put my foot in it! She'll never speak to me again."

Hideous and obscure as it all was, it held Mrs. Grose briefly silent; then she granted my point with a frankness which, I made sure, had more behind it. "I think indeed, miss, she never will. She do have a grand manner about it!"

"And that manner"—I summed it up—"is practically what's the matter with her now!"

Oh, that manner, I could see in my visitor's face, and not a little else besides! "She asks me every three minutes if I think you're coming in."

"I see—I see." I, too, on my side, had so much more than worked it out. "Has she said to you since yesterday—except to repudiate her familiarity with anything so dreadful—a single other word about Miss Jessel?"

"Not one, miss. And of course you know," my friend added, "I took it from her, by the lake, that, just then and there at least, there *was* nobody."

"Rather! and, naturally, you take it from her still."

"I don't contradict her. What else can I do?"

"Nothing in the world! You've the cleverest little person to deal with. They've made them—their two friends, I mean—still cleverer even than nature did; for it was wondrous material to play on! Flora has now her grievance, and she'll work it to the end."

"Yes, miss; but to *what* end?"

"Why, that of dealing with me to her uncle. She'll make me out to him the lowest creature—!"

I winced at the fair show of the scene in Mrs. Grose's face; she looked for a minute as if she sharply saw them together. "And him who thinks so well of you!"

"He has an odd way—it comes over me now," I laughed, "—of proving it! But that doesn't matter. What Flora wants, of course, is to get rid of me."

My companion bravely concurred. "Never again to so much as look at you."

"So that what you've come to me now for," I asked, "is to speed me on my way?" Before she had time to reply, however, I had her in check. "I've a better idea—the result of my reflections. My going *would* seem the right thing, and on Sunday I was terribly near it. Yet that won't do. It's *you* who must go. You must take Flora."

My visitor, at this, did speculate. "But where in the world—?"

"Away from here. Away from *them*. Away, even most of all, now, from me. Straight to her uncle."

"Only to tell on you—?"

"No, not 'only'! To leave me, in addition, with my remedy."

She was still vague. "And what *is* your remedy?"

"Your loyalty, to begin with. And then Miles's."

She looked at me hard. "Do you think he—?"

"Won't, if he has the chance, turn on me? Yes, I venture still to think it. At all events, I want to try. Get off with his sister as soon as possible and leave me with him alone." I was amazed, myself, at the spirit I had still in reserve, and therefore perhaps a trifle the more disconcerted at the way in which, in spite of this fine example of it, she hesitated. "There's one thing, of course," I went on: "they mustn't, before she goes, see each other for three seconds." Then it came over me that, in spite of Flora's presumable sequestration from the instant of her return from the pool, it might already be too late. "Do you mean," I anxiously asked, "that they *have* met?"

At this she quite flushed. "Ah, miss, I'm not such a fool as that! If I've been obliged to leave her three or four times, it has been each time with one of the maids, and at present, though she's alone, she's locked in safe. And yet—and yet!" There were too many things.

"And yet what?"

"Well, are you so sure of the little gentleman?"

"I'm not sure of anything but *you*. But I have, since last evening, a new hope. I think he wants to give me an opening. I do believe that—poor little exquisite wretch!—he wants to speak. Last evening, in the firelight and the silence, he sat with me for two hours as if it were just coming."

Mrs. Grose looked hard, through the window, at the gray, gathering day. "And did it come?"

"No, though I waited and waited, I confess it didn't, and it was without a breach of the silence or so much as a faint allusion to his sister's condition and absence that we at last kissed for good night. All the same," I continued, "I can't, if her uncle sees her, consent to his seeing her brother without my having given the boy—and most of all because things have got so bad—a little more time."

My friend appeared on this ground more reluctant than I could quite understand. "What do you mean by more time?"

"Well, a day or two—really to bring it out. He'll then be on *my* side—of which you see the importance. If nothing comes, I shall only fail, and you will, at the worst, have helped me by doing, on your arrival in town, whatever you may have found possible." So I put it before her, but she continued for a little so inscrutably embarrassed that I came again to her aid. "Unless, indeed," I wound up, "you really want *not* to go."

I could see it, in her face, at last clear itself; she put out her hand to me as a pledge. "I'll go—I'll go. I'll go this morning."

I wanted to be very just. "If you *should* wish still to wait, I would engage she shouldn't see me."

"No, no: it's the place itself. She must leave it." She held me a moment with heavy eyes, then brought out the rest. "Your idea's the right one. I myself, miss—"

"Well?"

"I can't stay."

The look she gave me with it made me jump at possibilities. "You mean that, since yesterday, you *have* seen—?"

She shook her head with dignity. "I've *heard*—!"

"Heard?"

"From that child—horrors! There!" she sighed with tragic relief. "On my honor, miss, she says things—!" But at this evocation she broke down; she dropped, with a sudden sob, upon my sofa and, as I had seen her do before, gave way to all the grief of it.

It was quite in another manner that I, for my part, let myself go. "Oh, thank God!"

She sprang up again at this, drying her eyes with a groan. "'Thank God'?"

"It so justifies me!"

"It does that, miss!"

I couldn't have desired more emphasis, but I just hesitated. "She's so horrible?"

I saw my colleague scarce knew how to put it. "Really shocking."

"And about me?"

"About you, miss—since you must have it. It's beyond everything, for a young lady; and I can't think wherever she must have picked up—"

"The appalling language she applied to me? I can, then!" I broke in with a laugh that was doubtless significant enough.

It only, in truth, left my friend still more grave. "Well, perhaps I ought to also—since I've heard some of it before! Yet I can't bear it," the poor woman went on while, with the same movement, she glanced, on my dressing table, at the face of my watch. "But I must go back."

I kept her, however. "Ah, if you can't bear it—!"

"How can I stop with her, you mean? Why, just *for* that: to get her away. Far from this," she pursued, "far from *them*—"

"She may be different? She may be free?" I seized her almost with joy. "Then, in spite of yesterday, you *believe*—"

"In such doings?" Her simple description of them required, in the light of her expression, to be carried no further, and she gave me the whole thing as she had never done. "I believe."

Yes, it was a joy, and we were still shoulder to shoulder: if I might continue sure of that I should care but little what else happened. My support in the presence of disaster would be the same as it had been in my early need of confidence, and if my friend would answer for my honesty, I would answer for all the rest. On the point of taking leave of her, nonetheless, I was to some extent embarrassed. "There's one thing, of course—it occurs to me—to remember. My letter, giving the alarm, will have reached town before you."

I now perceived still more how she had been beating about the bush and how weary at last it had made her. "Your letter won't have got there. Your letter never went."

"What then became of it?"

"Goodness knows! Master Miles—"

"Do you mean *he* took it?" I gasped.

She hung fire, but she overcame her reluctance. "I mean that I saw yesterday, when I came back with Miss Flora, that it wasn't where you had put it. Later in the evening I had the chance to question Luke, and he declared that he had neither noticed nor touched it." We could only exchange, on this, one of our deeper mutual soundings, and it was Mrs. Grose who first brought up the plumb with an almost elated "You see!"

"Yes, I see that if Miles took it instead he probably will have read it and destroyed it."

"And don't you see anything else?"

I faced her a moment with a sad smile. "It strikes me that by this time your eyes are open even wider than mine."

They proved to be so indeed, but she could still blush, almost, to show it. "I make out now what he must have done at school." And she gave, in her simple sharpness, an almost droll disillusioned nod. "He stole!"

I turned it over—I tried to be more judicial. "Well—perhaps."

She looked as if she found me unexpectedly calm. "He stole *letters!*"

She couldn't know my reasons for a calmness after all pretty shallow; so I showed them off as I might. "I hope then it was to more purpose

than in this case! The note, at any rate, that I put on the table yesterday," I pursued, "will have given him so scant an advantage—for it contained only the bare demand for an interview—that he is already much ashamed of having gone so far for so little, and that what he had on his mind last evening was precisely the need of confession." I seemed to myself, for the instant, to have mastered it, to see it all. "Leave us, leave us"—I was already, at the door, hurrying her off. "I'll get it out of him. He'll meet me—he'll confess. If he confesses, he's saved. And if he's saved—"

"Then *you* are?" The dear woman kissed me on this, and I took her farewell. "I'll save you without him!" she cried as she went.

XXII

Yet it was when she had got off—and I missed her on the spot—that the great pinch really came. If I had counted on what it would give me to find myself alone with Miles, I speedily perceived, at least, that it would give me a measure. No hour of my stay in fact was so assailed with apprehensions as that of my coming down to learn that the carriage containing Mrs. Grose and my younger pupil had already rolled out of the gates. Now I *was*, I said to myself, face to face with the elements, and for much of the rest of the day, while I fought my weakness, I could consider that I had been supremely rash. It was a tighter place still than I had yet turned round in; all the more that, for the first time, I could see in the aspect of others a confused reflection of the crisis. What had happened naturally caused them all to stare; there was too little of the explained, throw out whatever we might, in the suddenness of my colleague's act. The maids and the men looked blank; the effect of which on my nerves was an aggravation until I saw the necessity of making it a positive aid. It was precisely, in short, by just clutching the helm that I avoided total wreck; and I dare say that, to bear up at all, I became, that morning, very grand and very dry. I welcomed the consciousness that I was charged with much to do, and I caused it to be known as well that, left thus to myself, I was quite remarkably firm. I wandered with that manner, for the next hour or two, all over the place and looked, I have no doubt, as if I were ready for any onset. So, for the benefit of whom it might concern, I paraded with a sick heart.

The person it appeared least to concern proved to be, till dinner, little Miles himself. My perambulations had given me, meanwhile, no glimpse of him, but they had tended to make more public the change taking place in our relation as a consequence of his having at the piano, the day before, kept me, in Flora's interest, so beguiled and befooled. The stamp

of publicity had of course been fully given by her confinement and departure, and the change itself was now ushered in by our nonobservance of the regular custom of the schoolroom. He had already disappeared when, on my way down, I pushed open his door, and I learned below that he had breakfasted—in the presence of a couple of the maids—with Mrs. Grose and his sister. He had then gone out, as he said, for a stroll; than which nothing, I reflected, could better have expressed his frank view of the abrupt transformation of my office. What he would not permit this office to consist of was yet to be settled: there was a queer relief, at all events—I mean for myself in especial—in the renouncement of one pretension. If so much had sprung to the surface, I scarce put it too strongly in saying that what had perhaps sprung highest was the absurdity of our prolonging the fiction that I had anything more to teach him. It sufficiently stuck out that, by tacit little tricks in which even more than myself he carried out the care for my dignity, I had had to appeal to him to let me off straining to meet him on the ground of his true capacity. He had at any rate his freedom now; I was never to touch it again; as I had amply shown, moreover, when, on his joining me in the schoolroom the previous night, I had uttered, on the subject of the interval just concluded, neither challenge nor hint. I had too much, from this moment, my other ideas. Yet when he at last arrived, the difficulty of applying them, the accumulations of my problem, were brought straight home to me by the beautiful little presence on which what had occurred had as yet, for the eye, dropped neither stain nor shadow.

To mark, for the house, the high state I cultivated I decreed that my meals with the boy should be served, as we called it, downstairs; so that I had been awaiting him in the ponderous pomp of the room outside of the window of which I had had from Mrs. Grose, that first scared Sunday, my flash of something it would scarce have done to call light. Here at present I felt afresh—for I had felt it again and again—how my equilibrium depended on the success of my rigid will, the will to shut my eyes as tight as possible to the truth that what I had to deal with was, revoltingly, against nature. I could only get on at all by taking "nature" into my confidence and my account, by treating my monstrous ordeal as a push in a direction unusual, of course, and unpleasant, but demanding, after all, for a fair front, only another turn of the screw of ordinary human virtue. No attempt, nonetheless, could well require more tact than just this attempt to supply, one's self, *all* the nature. How could I put even

a little of that article into a suppression of reference to what had occurred? How, on the other hand, could I make reference without a new plunge into the hideous obscure? Well, a sort of answer, after a time, had come to me, and it was so far confirmed as that I was met, incontestably, by the quickened vision of what was rare in my little companion. It was indeed as if he had found even now—as he had so often found at lessons—still some other delicate way to ease me off. Wasn't there light in the fact which, as we shared our solitude, broke out with a specious glitter it had never yet quite worn?—the fact that (opportunity aiding, precious opportunity which had now come) it would be preposterous, with a child so endowed, to forego the help one might wrest from absolute intelligence? What had his intelligence been given him for but to save him? Mightn't one, to reach his mind, risk the stretch of an angular arm over his character? It was as if, when we were face to face in the dining room, he had literally shown me the way. The roast mutton was on the table, and I had dispensed with attendance. Miles, before he sat down, stood a moment with his hands in his pockets and looked at the joint, on which he seemed on the point of passing some humorous judgment. But what he presently produced was: "I say, my dear, is she really very awfully ill?"

"Little Flora? Not so bad but that she'll presently be better. London will set her up. Bly had ceased to agree with her. Come here and take your mutton."

He alertly obeyed me, carried the plate carefully to his seat, and, when he was established, went on. "Did Bly disagree with her so terribly suddenly?"

"Not so suddenly as you might think. One had seen it coming on."

"Then why didn't you get her off before?"

"Before what?"

"Before she became too ill to travel."

I found myself prompt. "She's *not* too ill to travel: she only might have become so if she had stayed. This was just the moment to seize. The journey will dissipate the influence"—oh, I was grand!—"and carry it off."

"I see, I see"—Miles, for that matter, was grand, too. He settled to his repast with the charming little "table manner" that, from the day of his arrival, had relieved me of all grossness of admonition. Whatever he had been driven from school for, it was not for ugly feeding. He was

irreproachable, as always, today; but he was unmistakably more conscious. He was discernibly trying to take for granted more things than he found, without assistance, quite easy; and he dropped into peaceful silence while he felt his situation. Our meal was of the briefest—mine a vain pretense, and I had the things immediately removed. While this was done Miles stood again with his hands in his little pockets and his back to me—stood and looked out of the wide window through which, that other day, I had seen what pulled me up. We continued silent while the maid was with us—as silent, it whimsically occurred to me, as some young couple who, on their wedding journey, at the inn, feel shy in the presence of the waiter. He turned round only when the waiter had left us. "Well—so we're alone!"

XXIII

"Oh, more or less." I fancy my smile was pale. "Not absolutely. We shouldn't like that!" I went on.

"No—I suppose we shouldn't. Of course we have the others."

"We have the others—we have indeed the others," I concurred.

"Yet even though we have them," he returned, still with his hands in his pockets and planted there in front of me, "they don't much count, do they?"

I made the best of it, but I felt wan. "It depends on what you call 'much'!"

"Yes"—with all accommodation—"everything depends!" On this, however, he faced to the window again and presently reached it with his vague, restless, cogitating step. He remained there awhile, with his forehead against the glass, in contemplation of the stupid shrubs I knew and the dull things of November. I had always my hypocrisy of "work," behind which, now, I gained the sofa. Steadying myself with it there as I had repeatedly done at those moments of torment that I have described as the moments of my knowing the children to be given to something from which I was barred, I sufficiently obeyed my habit of being prepared for the worst. But an extraordinary impression dropped on me as I extracted a meaning from the boy's embarrassed back—none other than the impression that I was not barred now. This inference grew in a few minutes to sharp intensity and seemed bound up with the direct perception that it was positively *he* who was. The frames and squares of the great window were a kind of image, for him, of a kind of failure. I felt that I saw him, at any rate, shut in or shut out. He was admirable, but not comfortable: I took it in with a throb of hope. Wasn't he looking, through the haunted pane, for something he couldn't see?—and wasn't it the first time in the whole business that he had known such a lapse? The

first, the very first: I found it a splendid portent. It made him anxious, though he watched himself; he had been anxious all day and, even while in his usual sweet little manner he sat at table, had needed all his small strange genius to give it a gloss. When he at last turned round to meet me, it was almost as if this genius had succumbed. "Well, I think I'm glad Bly agrees with *me!*"

"You would certainly seem to have seen, these twenty-four hours, a good deal more of it than for some time before. I hope," I went on bravely, "that you've been enjoying yourself."

"Oh, yes, I've been ever so far; all round about—miles and miles away. I've never been so free."

He had really a manner of his own, and I could only try to keep up with him. "Well, do you like it?"

He stood there smiling; then at last he put into two words—"Do *you?*"—more discrimination than I had ever heard two words contain. Before I had time to deal with that, however, he continued as if with the sense that this was an impertinence to be softened. "Nothing could be more charming than the way you take it, for of course if we're alone together now it's you that are alone most. But I hope," he threw in, "you don't particularly mind!"

"Having to do with you?" I asked. "My dear child, how can I help minding? Though I've renounced all claim to your company—you're so beyond me—I at least greatly enjoy it. What else should I stay on for?"

He looked at me more directly, and the expression of his face, graver now, struck me as the most beautiful I had ever found in it. "You stay on just for *that?*"

"Certainly. I stay on as your friend and from the tremendous interest I take in you till something can be done for you that may be more worth your while. That needn't surprise you." My voice trembled so that I felt it impossible to suppress the shake. "Don't you remember how I told you, when I came and sat on your bed the night of the storm, that there was nothing in the world I wouldn't do for you?"

"Yes, yes!" He, on his side, more and more visibly nervous, had a tone to master; but he was so much more successful than I that, laughing out through his gravity, he could pretend we were pleasantly jesting. "Only that, I think, was to get me to do something for *you!*"

"It was partly to get you to do something," I conceded. "But, you know, you didn't do it."

"Oh, yes," he said with the brightest superficial eagerness, "you wanted me to tell you something."

"That's it. Out, straight out. What you have on your mind, you know."

"Ah, then, is *that* what you've stayed over for?"

He spoke with a gaiety through which I could still catch the finest little quiver of resentful passion; but I can't begin to express the effect upon me of an implication of surrender even so faint. It was as if what I had yearned for had come at last only to astonish me. "Well, yes—I may as well make a clean breast of it, it was precisely for that."

He waited so long that I supposed it for the purpose of repudiating the assumption on which my action had been founded; but what he finally said was: "Do you mean now—here?"

"There couldn't be a better place or time." He looked round him uneasily, and I had the rare—oh, the queer!—impression of the very first symptom I had seen in him of the approach of immediate fear. It was as if he were suddenly afraid of me—which struck me indeed as perhaps the best thing to make him. Yet in the very pang of the effort I felt it vain to try sternness, and I heard myself the next instant so gentle as to be almost grotesque. "You want so to go out again?"

"Awfully!" He smiled at me heroically, and the touching little bravery of it was enhanced by his actually flushing with pain. He had picked up his hat, which he had brought in, and stood twirling it in a way that gave me, even as I was just nearly reaching port, a perverse horror of what I was doing. To do it in *any* way was an act of violence, for what did it consist of but the obtrusion of the idea of grossness and guilt on a small helpless creature who had been for me a revelation of the possibilities of beautiful intercourse? Wasn't it base to create for a being so exquisite a mere alien awkwardness? I suppose I now read into our situation a clearness it couldn't have had at the time, for I seem to see our poor eyes already lighted with some spark of a prevision of the anguish that was to come. So we circled about, with terrors and scruples, like fighters not daring to close. But it was for each other we feared! That kept us a little longer suspended and unbruised. "I'll tell you everything," Miles said—"I mean I'll tell you anything you like. You'll stay on with me, and we shall both be all right, and I *will* tell you—I *will*. But not now."

"Why not now?"

My insistence turned him from me and kept him once more at his window in a silence during which, between us, you might have heard a pin drop. Then he was before me again with the air of a person for whom, outside, someone who had frankly to be reckoned with was waiting. "I have to see Luke."

I had not yet reduced him to quite so vulgar a lie, and I felt proportionately ashamed. But, horrible as it was, his lies made up my truth. I achieved thoughtfully a few loops of my knitting. "Well, then, go to Luke, and I'll wait for what you promise. Only, in return for that, satisfy, before you leave me, one very much smaller request."

He looked as if he felt he had succeeded enough to be able still a little to bargain. "Very much smaller—?"

"Yes, a mere fraction of the whole. Tell me"—oh, my work preoccupied me, and I was offhand!—"if, yesterday afternoon, from the table in the hall, you took, you know, my letter."

XXIV

My sense of how he received this suffered for a minute from something that I can describe only as a fierce split of my attention—a stroke that at first, as I sprang straight up, reduced me to the mere blind movement of getting hold of him, drawing him close, and, while I just fell for support against the nearest piece of furniture, instinctively keeping him with his back to the window. The appearance was full upon us that I had already had to deal with here: Peter Quint had come into view like a sentinel before a prison. The next thing I saw was that, from outside, he had reached the window, and then I knew that, close to the glass and glaring in through it, he offered once more to the room his white face of damnation. It represents but grossly what took place within me at the sight to say that on the second my decision was made; yet I believe that no woman so overwhelmed ever in so short a time recovered her grasp of the *act.* It came to me in the very horror of the immediate presence that the act would be, seeing and facing what I saw and faced, to keep the boy himself unaware. The inspiration—I can call it by no other name—was that I felt how voluntarily, how transcendently, I *might.* It was like fighting with a demon for a human soul, and when I had fairly so appraised it I saw how the human soul—held out, in the tremor of my hands, at arm's length—had a perfect dew of sweat on a lovely childish forehead. The face that was close to mine was as white as the face against the glass, and out of it presently came a sound, not low nor weak, but as if from much further away, that I drank like a waft of fragrance.

"Yes—I took it."

At this, with a moan of joy, I enfolded, I drew him close; and while I held him to my breast, where I could feel in the sudden fever of his little body the tremendous pulse of his little heart, I kept my eyes on the thing at the window and saw it move and shift its posture. I have likened it to a

sentinel, but its slow wheel, for a moment, was rather the prowl of a baffled beast. My present quickened courage, however, was such that, not too much to let it through, I had to shade, as it were, my flame. Meanwhile the glare of the face was again at the window, the scoundrel fixed as if to watch and wait. It was the very confidence that I might now defy him, as well as the positive certitude, by this time, of the child's unconsciousness, that made me go on. "What did you take it for?"

"To see what you said about me."

"You opened the letter?"

"I opened it."

My eyes were now, as I held him off a little again, on Miles's own face, in which the collapse of mockery showed me how complete was the ravage of uneasiness. What was prodigious was that at last, by my success, his sense was sealed and his communication stopped: he knew that he was in presence, but knew not of what, and knew still less that I also was and that I did know. And what did this strain of trouble matter when my eyes went back to the window only to see that the air was clear again and—by my personal triumph—the influence quenched? There was nothing there. I felt that the cause was mine and that I should surely get *all*. "And you found nothing!"—I let my elation out.

He gave the most mournful, thoughtful little headshake. "Nothing."

"Nothing, nothing!" I almost shouted in my joy.

"Nothing, nothing," he sadly repeated.

I kissed his forehead; it was drenched. "So what have you done with it?"

"I've burned it."

"Burned it?" It was now or never. "Is that what you did at school?"

Oh, what this brought up! "At school?"

"Did you take letters?—or other things?"

"Other things?" He appeared now to be thinking of something far off and that reached him only through the pressure of his anxiety. Yet it did reach him. "Did I *steal?*"

I felt myself redden to the roots of my hair as well as wonder if it were more strange to put to a gentleman such a question or to see him take it with allowances that gave the very distance of his fall in the world. "Was it for that you mightn't go back?"

The only thing he felt was rather a dreary little surprise. "Did you know I mightn't go back?"

"I know everything."

He gave me at this the longest and strangest look. "Everything?"

"Everything. Therefore *did* you—?" But I couldn't say it again.

Miles could, very simply. "No. I didn't steal."

My face must have shown him I believed him utterly; yet my hands—but it was for pure tenderness—shook him as if to ask him why, if it was all for nothing, he had condemned me to months of torment. "What then did you do?"

He looked in vague pain all round the top of the room and drew his breath, two or three times over, as if with difficulty. He might have been standing at the bottom of the sea and raising his eyes to some faint green twilight. "Well—I said things."

"Only that?"

"They thought it was enough!"

"To turn you out for?"

Never, truly, had a person "turned out" shown so little to explain it as this little person! He appeared to weigh my question, but in a manner quite detached and almost helpless. "Well, I suppose I oughtn't."

"But to whom did you say them?"

He evidently tried to remember, but it dropped—he had lost it. "I don't know!"

He almost smiled at me in the desolation of his surrender, which was indeed practically, by this time, so complete that I ought to have left it there. But I was infatuated—I was blind with victory, though even then the very effect that was to have brought him so much nearer was already that of added separation. "Was it to everyone?" I asked.

"No; it was only to—" But he gave a sick little headshake. "I don't remember their names."

"Were they then so many?"

"No—only a few. Those I liked."

Those he liked? I seemed to float not into clearness, but into a darker obscure, and within a minute there had come to me out of my very pity the appalling alarm of his being perhaps innocent. It was for the instant confounding and bottomless, for if he *were* innocent, what then on earth was *I?* Paralyzed, while it lasted, by the mere brush of the question, I let him go a little, so that, with a deep-drawn sigh, he turned away from me again; which, as he faced toward the clear window, I suffered, feeling that

I had nothing now there to keep him from. "And did they repeat what you said?" I went on after a moment.

He was soon at some distance from me, still breathing hard and again with the air, though now without anger for it, of being confined against his will. Once more, as he had done before, he looked up at the dim day as if, of what had hitherto sustained him, nothing was left but an unspeakable anxiety. "Oh, yes," he nevertheless replied—"they must have repeated them. To those *they* liked," he added.

There was, somehow, less of it than I had expected; but I turned it over. "And these things came round—?"

"To the masters? Oh, yes!" he answered very simply. "But I didn't know they'd tell."

"The masters? They didn't—they've never told. That's why I ask you."

He turned to me again his little beautiful fevered face. "Yes, it was too bad."

"Too bad?"

"What I suppose I sometimes said. To write home."

I can't name the exquisite pathos of the contradiction given to such a speech by such a speaker; I only know that the next instant I heard myself throw off with homely force: "Stuff and nonsense!" But the next after that I must have sounded stern enough. "What *were* these things?"

My sternness was all for his judge, his executioner; yet it made him avert himself again, and that movement made *me*, with a single bound and an irrepressible cry, spring straight upon him. For there again, against the glass, as if to blight his confession and stay his answer, was the hideous author of our woe—the white face of damnation. I felt a sick swim at the drop of my victory and all the return of my battle, so that the wildness of my veritable leap only served as a great betrayal. I saw him, from the midst of my act, meet it with a divination, and on the perception that even now he only guessed, and that the window was still to his own eyes free, I let the impulse flame up to convert the climax of his dismay into the very proof of his liberation. "No more, no more, no more!" I shrieked, as I tried to press him against me, to my visitant.

"Is she *here?*" Miles panted as he caught with his sealed eyes the direction of my words. Then as his strange "she" staggered me and, with a gasp, I echoed it, "Miss Jessel, Miss Jessel!" he with a sudden fury gave me back.

I seized, stupefied, his supposition—some sequel to what we had done to Flora, but this made me only want to show him that it was better still than that. "It's not Miss Jessel! But it's at the window—straight before us. It's *there*—the coward horror, there for the last time!"

At this, after a second in which his head made the movement of a baffled dog's on a scent and then gave a frantic little shake for air and light, he was at me in a white rage, bewildered, glaring vainly over the place and missing wholly, though it now, to my sense, filled the room like the taste of poison, the wide, overwhelming presence. "It's *he?*"

I was so determined to have all my proof that I flashed into ice to challenge him. "Whom do you mean by 'he'?"

"Peter Quint—you devil!" His face gave again, round the room, its convulsed supplication. "*Where?*"

They are in my ears still, his supreme surrender of the name and his tribute to my devotion. "What does he matter now, my own?—what will he *ever* matter? *I* have you," I launched at the beast, "but he has lost you forever!" Then, for the demonstration of my work, "There, *there!*" I said to Miles.

But he had already jerked straight round, stared, glared again, and seen but the quiet day. With the stroke of the loss I was so proud of he uttered the cry of a creature hurled over an abyss, and the grasp with which I recovered him might have been that of catching him in his fall. I caught him, yes, I held him—it may be imagined with what a passion; but at the end of a minute I began to feel what it truly was that I held. We were alone with the quiet day, and his little heart, dispossessed, had stopped.

About the Author

HENRY JAMES OM (1843–1916) was born in New York City, the second oldest of his parents' five children. Traveling with his family between Europe and America, James became fluent in French—interestingly, he had a stutter in his native tongue, but the disorder did not affect his French at all. While attending Harvard Law School he developed an interest in writing, publishing his first novel, *Watch and Ward* in 1871.

A prolific writer of novels, plays and short form narratives, his most celebrated works include *The Portrait of a Lady* (1881), *The Turn of the Screw* (1898), *The Wings of the Dove* (1902), *The Ambassadors* (1903), and *The Golden Bowl* (1904).

A life-long bachelor, James had several well-documented intimate relationships with men, evidenced through his extensive written correspondence with them. He died in London, and his ashes were buried in Massachusetts, according to his wishes.

BOOKED

DOUBLE®

DOUBLE®
BOOKED